HUNTER

The Second Book In The

Hunter Trilogy

DAVID WOOD

ISBN 9781535385169

First American Edition

For information:
Murmaid Publishing
Murmaid@tampabay.rr.com

Author's picture taken at the Seacrest Wolf Preserve, Chipley, Florida

Other books by David Wood
Legend

Cover and Book Design
theMurmaid tm for Sirena Press

Printed in the United States of America

HUNTER

The Second Book In The

Hunter Trilogy

DAVID WOOD

Sirena Press

Madeira Beach, FL

Contents

The Hunter Trilogy

LEGEND

Legend

Hunter

Guardian

Dedication

John Homer, my youngest brother
Shelia Homer, my sister-in-law
Jacqueline and Samantha Homer, my nieces

Thank You

I wish to thank the many people who helped me create this story over a period of decades: the PINAWOR writing group, in particular Diane Marcou, Eleanora Sabin, and Nancy Frederich, my editor. Pat Rukavina and her husband Richard, as well as their son, Mark Aldridge, for editing and formatting my story all the way through. My mother, Elsie Homer, who ran copies at great expense when my novel was in its hand-printed first draft so I could pass it around. My father, Robert Wood, who paid for typing it up when I thought it was ready.

I also want to thank the many readers, including: Charles Jackson, Kati Nakamoto, Clifford Bowling, Theodore Schultz, John Kingham, Denny Brown, Matthew McConnaughy, Gerald Webb, Bruce Morrison, John and Rita Park, Billie Jones, and others I can no longer remember. The suggestions and input I got were very helpful. Special thanks to Russell Cera, author of **Cry, Wolf, Cry**, for suggestions and catching a few errors I made regarding wolf behavior, a few of wicth I kept anyway.

I wish to thank the staff and volunteers of the Seacrest Wolf Preserve in Chipley, Florida, especialy Wayne and Cynthia Watkins, the owners and caretakers, for giving me and my editor, Nancy Frederich, a chance to meet wolves, literally, face to face; a chance to howl with them; and get to learn a few things about them I would never get through books and research papers. God bless all of you who have given so many people the chance to learn about wolves.

Credits of Those who Inspired Me

Some of the events in this novel are based on events from the book, **Of Wolves and Men,** by Barry Holstun Lopez including pivotal events of the cubs growing up and being trained, and the game betwen wolves and ravens he called "raven-tag," a term I borrowed from him. The prologue was based on events surrounding the naturalist Ernest Thompson Seton and his hunt for the Currumpaw Wolf and his mate Blanca.

I tried to be as accurate about wolves as possible, changing a few details to fit the story but sticking mostly to the facts. Any errors or discrepancies are my own and nobody else's.

"A wolf, it is said, can hear a cloud pass overhead."

— *Native American proverb*

All my pretty ones?
Did you say all? O hell-kite! All?
What, all my pretty chickens and their dam
At one fell swoop?
                    —*Macduff*

(On hearing that Macbeth had just murdered his wife and children after he escaped Macbeth's clutches himself.).

["Macbeth", Act IV, Scene 3, Lines 216-219]

Prologue

(Minnesota)
1965

Once, a long time ago, Mother Earth and Father Sky mated, and all life came from them, and trees and ferns grew, and rabbits and deer and elk and mice ran, and when their numbers became too many, Mother Earth decreed that the Hunters would feed on all of them and keep their numbers down, and so the Hunters became the Guardians of all living creatures, and in their hunting and eating, maintained the balance and followed the Way.

We were one pack back then, and followed one leader, Thickfur, but one day we snuck onto Father Sky's back and, in our desire for their meat, killed off all his favorite creatures, the Nameless, and Father Sky was set on killing us, every last one. In fear, we scattered and became many packs with different territories, and Father Sky could not kill us without killing off all life, so he sent a species that could.

Twolegs.

We soon realized that they, Twolegs, were weaker and slower and not as wise in the currents and branches of the Way, but they had fire, and they had their tricks, and many things that could kill endlessly. They sought us out, killing off whole packs, and they knew, and we knew, that a day would come when they would kill us off completely, and the balance and flowing of the Way would come to an end.

Then, one day, one of our kind came forth to challenge Twolegs.

He knew them well. They killed his pack, and they almost killed him, too, but he got away, barely, with his life. He was large, larger than most, his fur white as new snow, his claws and teeth sharp, his mind strong, his sight, hearing, and sense of smell acute. He lost much, he suffered much, but he was stronger for it.

We called him Cloudwalker, Snaretripper, Thundersnarl, Dogslayer, and Winddancer, and he traveled through territories like a soft breeze, unseen, unheard, invisible. He was a Hunter like any other Hunter, a Guardian as well, but he was the Guardian of Guardians, protector against the Twolegs who came to kill our kind and claim our skins, they who would kill without eating, devour without taking meat.

Cloudwalker was the last of his pack, and with nothing left to him but his life, he chose to learn their ways, these Twolegs, so he could fight back, to do everything he could to stop the killings. He looked for the Jaws, the things that bit and held a Hunter's legs, and he broke them, one by one. He found the tainted meat, buried it, hid it, pissed on it, did what he had to so others would not eat it. He snuck through the trees, leading Twolegs away from our packs, protecting us, protecting our cubs, always guarding, always vigilant.

From one Winter to the next, he protected us, his kind, until Twolegs realized that he was following them, watching them, and Twolegs was afraid. One by one, they stopped their killing, sought their dens and caves away from our territories. We all knew the day would come when our kind was no more, that our kind would be gone from the fur of Mother Earth's back, but Cloudwalker was watching, waiting, sneaking in the shadows, undoing what Twolegs did, and in time, Cloudwalker thought, maybe our kind might survive after all.

Maybe we did have a chance.

Then there arose one of them, angry, bitter, mad with rage, twisted of spirit, who killed us, many of us, and when Cloudwalker broke his traps and buried his tainted meat, this one, the Dark Twolegs, became even more determined, redoubled his efforts, knowing Cloudwalker was out there, not afraid but drawn into the fight, determined to kill us all to reach him, just to get him.

Cloudwalker saw him, the Dark Twolegs, and he who feared no death or dying, who would stand and face many of them to protect one of his kind, he, for the first time, was afraid. For the first time he saw the end of his kind, the end of us, and he realized that, after all these years, he had grown old and frail, that his teeth were chipping, that his legs were growing weak, that he was not as fast, and this one, the Dark Twolegs, was strong enough and mean enough to never stop killing. For the first time in a long time he realized that he finally might lose, that everything he did during his lifetime might be for nothing.

For the first time he admitted to himself that he could not do it alone any more, that he needed help, if he were to survive.

If we were to survive.

Isle Royale

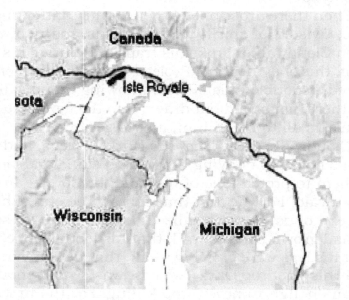

"To step into Isle Royale is to leave behind one's own self and one's world and to begin a new exploration into the nature of life."
—Napier Shelton, Superior Wilderness 1997

Isle Royale is within about 15 miles of the Canadian and Minnesotan shores of Lake Superior.

The island is 45 miles long and 9 miles wide, with an area of 206.73 square miles, making it the largest natural island in the lake.

Volcanic eruptions have caused Isle Royale to shape into a saucer-like island. Thus creating a natural environment for wolves and moose.

According to the National Park Service, the North sides of the ridges tend to be steeper than the South sides.

Coastal areas were once submerged beneath prehistoric lake waters.

In prehistoric times, large quantities of copper were mined on Isle Royale. The region is scarred by ancient mine pits and trenches up to 20 feet deep. Carbon-14 testing of wood remains found in sockets of copper artifacts indicates that they are at least 5700 years old.

The Park Service has allowed this area to be returned to its natural habitat, offering a stable environment for wildlife that inhabits its natural beauty.

The Ecological Study of Wolves on Isle Royale is the longest running large mammal predator-prey study on earth. The park offers outstanding possibilities for research in a remote, relatively simple ecosystem where overt human influences are limited.

Why are wolves so important on Isle Royale?

Scientific evidence is that ecosystems unravel when wolves and other "keystone" predators are removed.

Trophic cascade is an ecological phenomenon triggered by the addition or removal of top predators and involving reciprocal changes in the relative populations of predator and prey through a food chain, which often results in dramatic changes in ecosystem structure and nutrient cycling.

In a three-level food chain, an increase (or decrease) in carnivores causes a decrease (or increase) in herbivores and an increase (or decrease) in primary producers such as plants. In eastern North America the removal of wolves has been associated with an increase in white-tailed deer and a decline in plants eaten by deer.

American zoologist Robert Paine coined the term trophic cascade in 1980 to describe reciprocal changes in food webs caused by experimental manipulations of top predators.

Chapter One

"The Wolf"
(Early Spring, 1965)

"You kill," he growled, just out of the hearing of the ones he watched. "You kill, but you never eat what you kill. You destroy, you ruin, and you never care about what you have left behind, the great loss, the terrible devouring." He scraped the ground with a forepaw, glancing up at the ravens perched in a tree which was branching over the ones he saw in the distance.

Look what they did!

They killed one of us!

They'll kill us all!

The voices in his head were panicked, but he ignored them, staring at the four Twolegs sitting by the fire.

"I never killed your kind before," he snarled, "but you---you have killed many of mine, and this one, he was one of them. He was part of a pack, a gentle Hunter, and you just killed him with no thought. There is no sense in what you do."

He bared his teeth. "I found you. It wasn't easy, but I found you. Kill you, I can, but I will not. Hurt you, I can, but I will not. But there is something I can do. Something..."

"So everybody knew about Mac 'The Hook' Raven, the Lover's Lane Killer," Jared Smith said, tossing another stick into the crackling fire.

"That's just another urban legend." Steve Keillor took a swig from the flask and passed it to Bert Lansing.

"We heard this story before," Kyle Johnson said, tossing a pebble at the front bumper of the old white Ford pickup. "They guy never existed, Jared, and you know it."

Jared opened his eyes wide, mimicking surprise that the others didn't believe him. "Oh c'mon now, you know so much, then do you know how he lost his hand? He was stalking another teenaged couple in a car on Lover's Lane, he had already killed three couples before, but this was a smart kid and his girl, and the kid was careful. He brought his father's shotgun."

"This isn't scary," Bert grumbled, stirring the fire with a stick.

"You want to see scary?" Kyle , pointed, "Look at those three ravens on the branch up there. They're watching us like demons. One even has a twisted beak and is missing an eyeball. Right out of an Edgar Allen Poe story." Kyle was still feeling shaken about how they killed the wolf earlier that day. The mangled body was still tied to the back bumper of the truck, out of sight, but for Kyle, not out of mind. And now there were these ravens watching them, creepy...and for some reason, he believed that they were somehow connected to the dead wolf. He shook his head and grinned at Jared, trying to act like it didn't bother him.

"Anyhoo," Jared went on, "Mac Raven snuck up on them, holding the cleaver he used to kill his victims with, and when he knew the time was right, he yanked open the car door and was about to start chopping when the boy aimed and fired at him, blowing off the hand that held the cleaver. Mac fell to the ground, writhing in pain, his right hand blown clean off, and that was just how the police found him, and off to jail he went. The kids at Lover's Lane were safe."

"You just can't swing a shotgun around in a car that fast," Kyle said.

"The boy heard him and was waiting for him," Jared said.

"The boy was thinking about grabbing some tit," Steve argued. "It was Lover's Lane, for God sake!"

Jared shrugged. "Anyhoo, years passed, and someone said Mac died, and someone said he escaped from prison, got a hook for his missing hand, and started killing again. And then one night a boy and his gal were up at Lover's Lane making out when she heard rustling in the bushes outside. Of course the boy wanted to keep going, but the girl remembered the legend and was scared. Somehow she was panicked enough that the boy, against his better judgment and urges, stopped things mid-stream and cranked up his car. He sped off and drove her home, all the while she's talking about Mac and how she heard he broke out of prison and all, and the boy's frustrated and just thinking about the hard on in his pants but trying real hard to be a gentleman..."

The others laughed.

"And once he gets her home, she's weeping and all, and he knew it wouldn't be a great night no matter what, but being gentlemanly, he got out and came around to open her door. And that's when he saw it. A hook on the door handle, and blood still dripping where it got yanked off Mac's arm when they drove off."

They laughed again. "Hey, Jared," Steve said. "Did you

fart, or is your story that stinky?"

"Gentlemen, this is real," Jared went on, keeping his right hand behind his back. "Mac Raven is still alive and still out there, and he still goes around these woods looking for victims. He got himself a new hook, and he wants to kill again. Do you hear it? The bushes rustling? That could be him. Wait, it IS him!" Jared brought his right hand out, brandishing a hook where his hand used to be. "Hah!"

The other three men glanced at him, then looked at each other and passed the flask around one more time. "Great story, Jared," Steve said.

"But did you really fart?" Kyle grumbled. "Something stinks so bad I'd rather smell a skunk right now."

"I told you, it was Jared's story that stank," Steve said.

"I smell it too," Bert noted. "Like rotten meat mixed with shit."

"Like decay," Jared said. "You think it could be the wolf?"

"The wolf's only been dead a few hours, not enough time to decay," Kyle said, again remembering, with unease and a little shame, what they did.

They had found the wolf that afternoon, a couple days after they set out traps. Its hind leg was held fast in the trap, and it growled fiercely at them. They didn't bring their rifles—it was the first wolf they captured—but Jared had a plan. They hiked the mile to the road where Jared parked his pickup truck and drove through the woods, getting stuck, then unstuck, again and again, as the men pushed the truck on, until they reached the trapped wolf.

Jared backed up, then pulled a bull rope out of the bed and tied one end onto the back bumper. He then lassoed the stake that held the chain of the trap, managing to secure it so the wolf couldn't attack him in the process, and then got everybody crowded back into the truck. He floored it, and they drove out of the woods, bouncing and sliding and dragging the rope and chain and trap and wolf with them. Once they hit the tarmac of the two-lane, Jared gunned the engine and took off down the road. Kyle didn't look back but silently mouthed the Lord's Prayer to himself to block the image of what was behind them. When they finally stopped and walked behind the truck, they found the wolf dead, its body mangled and stripped of fur and skin on one side.

Kyle had to turn away and throw up, but the others prodded the body with sticks until Jared noted there was not much fur left on it to sell. They turned down a dirt road, found a clearing and made a fire, eating the cold fried chicken they brought with them and the warm beer they meant to drink earlier. When the beer was gone they passed around Steve's flask and warmed up to the idea of getting rid of the body and heading home.

"So what about that wolf?" Jared said. "Kyle, why don't you get the rope off it and get us ready to go? Just leave it where it is, we don't need to take it any where. We gotta go. The night's getting cold."

"Why don't you do it?"

"Because I bought the beer."

"The beer's gone," Kyle said. "And besides, my girlfriend made us the fried chicken."

"The fried chicken's gone too," Jared said. "And this flask is almost empty. Oh, hell, Kyle, just do it, please."

"But..."

"Pleeeeease..." Jared mimicked, and the other two added their voices in mock politeness.

"Oh fuck you all," Kyle said, tossing a stick in the fire and standing. "I just don't give a shit." He flipped them off, turned and walked around the truck, hearing his friends begin singing, "Who's afraid of the big bad wolf, the big bad wolf, the big bad wolf..."

He came around to the back, looking for the wolf, knowing it was at least ten feet from the back bumper, but he couldn't see anything. Staring at the damn fire, he thought, it's messing up my night vision... The smell was worse now, and he pulled his pocket knife out, intending to cut the rope at the bumper and never mind untying it from the wolf, he didn't even want to go near the body.

But something was wrong. He couldn't hear anything except his friends at the front of the truck. He couldn't hear the wind or night birds, and now not even the crickets were making any noise. He'd gone camping since he was ten, and the one thing he knew, noises in the woods never stopped. Especially crickets. He shook his head and felt for the rope at the bumper. "Let's get this over with," he mumbled, starting to cut the rope.

A shuffling in the leaves caught his attention, and he looked where he knew the wolf's body lay. In the blackness of the shadows, there was movement, and then the wolf was slowly shuffling to its feet. He dropped the knife. The wolf stood, twice as tall as he knew it could be, twice as tall as he remembered, a large shadow, just ten feet away. He could see its eyes, and as it snarled he saw its teeth, white against the blackness of its silhouette. He could hear it breathing, snorting, and the air stank like rot.

He turned and ran around the truck, shaking violently, stumbling over a root, almost tripping over Jared. "What the fuck, man?"

"It's alive!" Kyle screamed, gasping. He braced himself, both hands on the hood. His friends laughed. "No, I'm not joking, it's alive! I saw it stand! And it's bigger now!"

"C'mon, Kyle," Jared snapped. "Did you use some drugs before I gave you that beer? Hell, you can't even hold your booze, can you?"

"We need to get outta here! Now!"

"Calm down, Kyle," Steve said. "It's your imagination."
They rose and surrounded him. "C'mon, we'll show you."

"No! We can't go that way! I'm telling you!"

"Kyle, did you shit yourself?" Bert asked. "Christ, you stink."

"It's the wolf!"

"Oh, fuck, Kyle, come on!" Jared growled, grabbing the front of his shirt and dragging him to the back of the truck. Kyle was trying to pull away, but the fight had gone out of him. He couldn't speak, he gestured for them to go back, but his friends pushed him on.

Bert opened the driver's side door and pulled out a flashlight. The wolf's mangled body lay where they left it, on the ground tied with ten feet of bull rope to the bumper. "There!" Jared snapped. "You see? Nothing to fear, just a dead wolf." The others laughed, but Kyle stared, seeing claw marks in the dirt next to the body. He already knew.

A burning coal sailed past Jared's shoulder and landed next to the dead wolf. "What the hell," Steve grunted, looking back at the fire. Bert poked the ember with a stick. Then they all looked back at the same time.

They couldn't see the flames in front of the truck, but saw sparks flying into the branches, burning chunks of wood hurling from the fire. They heard snorting, digging, shuffling around. "What is that?" Steve whispered. They walked back around the truck, Jared holding Kyle in front of him like a shield, Kyle feeling too weak to pull free.

As they came around, they saw it, a giant wolf, digging into the fire, snarling and whining, backing off, attacking the fire again, leaping over the flames, enraged, its teeth grasping a burning log and dragging it out, then digging into the flames again. And then it stopped and looked back at them. It had a massive, white, scarred head, blazing eyes and sharp, long teeth. It growled low, watching them, pieces of smouldering embers in its fur, but it didn't notice them, or didn't care. Just looking at the eyes, they could see rage, malice, and a blazing that almost made the fire seem dim.

As one, they turned and ran, not even talking or making a noise other than gasping for breath, tripping over rocks and logs, getting back up and running some more. Branches slapped them in the face, the darkness closed around them, the night air hissed at them, the woods they knew so well were now a threat. They ran, not talking, until they reached the road, then slowed and walked, heading for a gas station they knew was just a mile away.

"What the fuck was that thing?" Jared gasped.

"A monster," Bert said.

"Is it still following us?"

"I don't think so."

"Just shut up. It might still hear us." They glanced at each other but were unable to say anything more. They kept walking, listening for any sound of pursuit from the beast they just saw.

In the morning, they returned with two sheriff deputies. The truck was still there, dusty and still, large scratches on the paint on the doors. The fire pit was dug out, pieces of charcoal scattered everywhere. The dead wolf was gone, and the rope chewed apart near the bumper. They found no paw prints or any sign, other than the scratches and fire pit, of a giant wolf. But the place carried with it a terrible stench, a smell of rotten meat, and they all had that feeling, even the deputies, of being watched.

Chapter Two

"Skins"

(Early Spring, 1965)

"I was ten years old when I saw my first tit," Ben Rose shouted over the wind. "Aunt Rosie always breast-fed her new baby anyplace and anytime it was hungry."

He spit tobacco juice on the ground as he sat on a rock and looked down into the woods. He was on the trail along the ridge, and he could see for miles. "From that time on, I've always been a tit man. Some guys look at legs—remember Marilyn, Betty Page? Those gals had legs, but I was different. Jane Russell, that's for me."

"You like legs too," Jessie George Custer Armstrong said. "I've seen you look before." He was skinning the last wolf, loosening the skin at the backbone with his Bowie knife. "I even caught you looking at Patty Tilton's legs a few times at the Crooked River."

Ben shook his head and smirked. "Talk nice about Patty, Cutter. She's like a daughter to me." He spit again. "Besides, with Patty, you gotta be a leg man, she has so little on top." He took off his sunglasses and wiped them with a handkerchief.

Cutter glanced back at Ben and smiled. They had been friends since they met during the Korean War. Since then,

Ben moved to Caleb after Cutter loaned him the money to start his flying business at the municipal airport, and they were like brothers ever since.

People in Caleb knew how things were, knew that Cutter was a man who was susceptible to anger, and Ben was like his Jiminy Cricket, always talking him down if he were too pissed off or drunk to reason adequately. Cutter knew that Ben somehow calmed him, and had Ben not been around, he might now be on death row somewhere.

Cutter finished skinning the wolf and threw the skin on the pile. That made five skins here and two they left on the other side of the pass, which they could pick up on the walk back. When he got the skins back to the cabin, he planned to stretch them on frames, dry them, scrape them, and sell them. The thirty-five-dollar-per-wolf bounty recently ended, rescinded by the state senate, but there were still people who would pay a good price for a decent pelt. "'Bout ready to head back?" Cutter asked, rolling a cigarette one-handed.

"'Bout ready for a hot lunch and a few cold beers," Ben answered. "This is supposed to be spring, but it feels colder than the winter ever did."

"The weatherman on TV blamed it on arctic air coming down from up north. It brought the blizzard a few weeks ago and kept things cold." He turned his back to the wind, cupped his hands as he lit his cigarette with a wooden match. "Nature has a funny way of playing tricks on you like that," he said, glancing down the mountainside at the leafless forest below.

"Still thinking about that big one?"

"Yeah," Cutter said, turning towards Ben. "Did you see the size of him?" In his mind he could see the wolf far below, running through the trees, out of reach.

Ben chased the wolf along the barren ridge, flying his helicopter low after Cutter, in the passenger seat, had killed off most of the rest of the pack, herding the last wolf to the end of the path. They figured it would either stop at the edge, turn and face them, or leap off and die at the bottom.

"I still can't believe he simply leaped off a two-hundred-foot cliff like that," Ben said.

"I still can't believe he lived," Cutter added, recalling the plume of snow rising from the snowdrift when the wolf hit. He thought for sure it was dead, and then it leaped out of the snow, ran through the trees, stopped, turned around and gazed up at them. "We almost had him, too," he added. "If only my rifle hadn't jammed. If only I'd brought my other one as well."

"Goddam, Cutter," Ben said. "We wouldn't be here right now if you and I weren't visiting Ed." The icy wind blew Ben's red, curly hair as he spit downwind. "We only stopped at Ed Palmer's ranch because he wanted us to look for wolves. And we would have been back at the airport last night had my chopper not broken down. We weren't planning to be overnight house guests until you got drunk and collapsed on the couch."

Cutter looked at Ben and grinned. "I wasn't drunk, just tired. And besides, it was your machine that broke down, not me. Those wolves, they weren't even from around here, and if we had searched yesterday we would never have seen them, so it was dumb luck we got them the way we did. They were heading over the mountains, which means they travelled from another territory."

"Hell, Cutter, you definitely were drunk. But whatever you were," Ben said, spitting, "I couldn't chance flying off with you and having you toppling out of my chopper."

Cutter finished tying the skins together with bull rope and hefted them over a shoulder.

"Need some help with that?" Ben asked, standing.

"Nah," Cutter said. His face and hands were spotted

with blood, and his long-sleeved flannel shirt was stained with sweat. Grinning at Ben, he started walking back to the pass and to the other side.

Earlier that morning, after they killed the wolves, Ben had to land on the ranch side of the mountains because there was no other place to land. Cutter complained all along the hike up to the pass, though the mountains at their highest were no more than 2,500 feet.

Years ago Ben hiked the Cascades in Oregon and Washington, peaks that rose ten to fifteen thousand feet, making these ones look like hills. At the pass, they skinned a female, and a yearling (the cub Cutter killed was mangled by the kill shot and useless), leaving the two skins for their return.

Coming down the other side, they skinned five more wolves. They spotted one wolf that had slipped over the edge of the ridge during its attempted escape and landed on a ledge fifty feet down, breaking its forelegs. It was beyond reach, a hundred feet above the ground and fifty feet down, and would probably die of starvation or dehydration. That one was another giant wolf, almost as big as the one that got away. Three times, Cutter looked over the edge, seeing it stare back at him from its perch on the ledge, and he wondered if it knew how hopeless things were.

Cutter would have rappelled down just to get it if they had enough rope, but they didn't, and though he wouldn't admit it to Ben, he didn't have the energy to climb back up after that hike.

As they reached the pass, Ben glanced at Cutter. "You still thinking about the one that got away?"

"Yeah," Cutter said. "The one that got away. It really sounds like a fish story, doesn't it?" He laughed, holding his hands apart. "It was thissss.....big!"

"It was pretty damn big, though," Ben said. When

they saw the two large wolves from the air, they were both awed by the striking difference of size. The wolves were humongous, almost seeming like a trick of the eye. Two giant wolves, he thought as he walked. He then had a funny feeling, and he stopped and turned around. Cutter had stopped and was looking longingly back the way they had come.

"He's long gone, "Ben said.

"I'm not thinking of him," Cutter said as Ben stepped closer. "I'm thinking of the Shadow Wolf. I'm thinking, maybe we found two of his offspring by accident."

"It's a loner," Ben said. "The Shadow Wolf is a loner. Otherwise it couldn't be traveling from one county to the next. Loners don't have offspring."

Cutter set the skins and bag on the ground and rolled another cigarette, thinking of the night a year and a half ago when he talked with the other men at the Crooked River tavern about the large wolf. Since then the "Shadow Wolf" became a household word around Caleb, a name Ben gave the giant wolf nobody could catch, and Cutter's ongoing search for the wolf became common knowledge.

At first other men would rib him about searching for something as elusive as the Loch Ness Monster or Bigfoot — "Bigpaw," they would jokingly refer to it — but a few men would talk to him one-on-one, telling him in a low voice of the giant paw prints they had seen, of the broken leghold traps they had retrieved, and though they never admitted it, he knew the men were afraid of something.

In time, hunters from other parts of the state would stop in Caleb on their way through, having heard of Cutter, just to tell him their story. The words "Shadow Wolf" became a name for something dark and ominous hidden deep in the woods, maybe deep in the imagination, and though the creature hadn't killed anybody, more than a few of them hinted they believed it would.

"Are you going to light that cigarette or just stand there and suck on it?" Ben asked.

Cutter glanced at Ben, grinning, then turned his back to the wind as he struck a match and cupped his hands over it, taking a few puffs before tossing the match. "I was thinking about the wolf that leaped off the cliff. He fell two hundred feet and didn't break a bone."

"He would've never lived if he hadn't hit that snow-drift. Sometimes luck is everything."

"I know," Cutter said. "But I also know I hit him, wounded him somewhere, and still he leaped out of that snowdrift like he could run forever. Only he didn't. He stopped and turned around and looked at us, at me, mocking me, like he knew the damn rifle was jammed and I couldn't shoot at him. If I had my other rifle...." He let out a blast of smoke, "Hell, even if I had my bow and arrows...."

"You'd never kill him with an arrow," Ben said. "Not that far. And, Christ, the way you cursed when I turned around! You were looking bug-eyed crazy when you couldn't shoot the wolf. You were about to leap off the side and land on its back."

"If I had my bow and arrows, I could've made that shot."

"C'mon, Cutter, no point in chasing that thing when it's long gone."

Cutter glanced at Ben, and then re-shouldered his load. "Yeah, you're right. Let's get back to the chopper." He turned and started walking with Ben beside him. "We'll stop at Ed's ranch and tell him what we did. He'll be pleased we got most of them, though he was sure pissed at finding three of his cows killed and eaten."

"That last blizzard killed about a hundred," Ben said, spitting tobacco juice. "I can't see where three more would break him."

"Yeah, but that big one...."

"It's not the Shadow Wolf."

'Maybe not," Cutter said. "But it gave me ideas, and maybe I know how to get the Shadow Wolf now." Cutter smiled at Ben, then walked on over the trampled snow as Ben spit against a rock and followed.

For a brief moment, Ben wondered what would happen to the wolf that leaped off the cliff, and he wondered, knowing what it faced, how much longer it would live without a pack.

Chapter Three

"Dreams"
(Spring, 1965)

The snow on Bearback, the butte at the center of the Pawsore Pack Territory, was melting, trickling down the slopes in small rivulets or soaking into the ground. The spring on the south slope gurgled as it flowed lustily, almost dancing from the earth. Even so, most of the butte was still blanketed in deep snow from the last blizzard; it would take a week of warm weather to melt it all.

Rabbitrunner returned to the dens on three paws, his right foreleg swollen and held carefully off the ground. As he limped slowly uphill, his three paw pads raw and sore, he glanced nervously back and forth, watching out for something dangerous to leap at him from behind a tree or from the sky. When he reached the dens, he collapsed on his side and rested.

The distance he originally covered in one day took him several to return because he had to change direction several times to avoid the Hunters of the Tailless Pack as he passed through their territory. Now he was in his own territory, but still far from comfortable. The wound in his right foreleg was oozing blood. The area around the wound was raw from all the times he stopped and bit or scratched at it with his hind paw. The pain and itching were maddening.

As he rested on his side, panting and occasionally coughing, his mind moved in a slow turn, his thoughts a blur between the present and the past, and he could hear thunderous explosions in the air, still see blood on the snow, and with his eyes closed he saw, over and over again, his pack members falling to the snow, dying, one by one. And every time he opened his eyes, he kept thinking that it would only be a matter of time, a night and a day perhaps, before they would all be back at the dens, dragging in wounded and tired as he did.

He slept where he collapsed, too weary to dream, or even care about his surroundings. Had Bigbird come right then, he would have been killed, too tired to move, too tired to care. When he finally woke, it was night, he was shivering and his right foreleg was throbbing.

The stars sparkled in the black sky, surrounding a moon that was not as large as it was a few days ago. He lay still, watching the moon make its slow circuit across the sky, watching the stars turn in a vast, slow circle above the silhouettes of the trees, numerous lights glaring down at him. He felt comfort, smelling the familiar odors of Bearback, and he thought about the Twolegs den he saw days ago, that they saw, the dark shape in the distance with glowing lights coming from it as though Twolegs had captured the starlight and put it to use, like the dogs and the cows, and as he watched the stars, he saw a beam of light moving from the sky, searching the ground until it stopped on him, a bright, glaring light that blinded him, and then he heard the loud, explosive, killing crack....

"No!" Rabbitrunner whined.

Rabbitrunner!

He shuffled to his feet, his wounded leg still held off the ground as he stared at the sky, but all he could see were stars. He must have dreamed the beam of light, there was nothing now, but still his heart pounded as he gasped for breath.

Then he glanced around. It seemed that someone called his name. "Newmoon?" he puled. "Ravenplay? Is that you?"

A wind blew gently through the budding branches as he listened futilely for a reply. He felt abandoned and scared as his eyes searched the trees for some movement to indicate that they were back, but he knew he was alone. He let out a soft whine, knowing there would be no reply.

Turning, he took a few shaky steps, keeping his wounded foreleg off the ground. The stiffness and weariness of his body weighed him down as though he carried another Hunter on his back. He limped a little further, stumbled, fell, and pulled himself back up. He didn't feel right at all.

Squatting carefully, he glanced around as he let out a steaming stream of urine that melted a hole in the dirty snow. Maybe they were at the clearing at the top of Bearback. Maybe they were waiting for him. Feeling empty, he turned and limped uphill into the shadow of the trees.

The ascent was tiring, and he stopped frequently to rest, gasping for breath as though he were again ascending the mountain. If only he could use his right foreleg, he could move easier, he wouldn't be so tired.

Suddenly a tearing of branches and limbs sounded from above as a strong wind bellowed down from above, blowing hard against his back. He fell to the ground, cowering as he glanced up; a great shadow blocked the starlight as something hovered over his head just above the trees. As he watched, two massive, black talons reached down through the branches, the claws just above his head, grasping. He closed his eyes, waiting to die, too scared to run, and then he heard a loud crack.

He opened his eyes and saw an old, dead branch hit the ground just in front of him. An owl flew off, beating its wings rhythmically, but there was nothing else. He gazed at the stars, still feeling adrenaline race through his body.

Rabbitrunner! We're here!

"Newmoon!" he whuffed. This time there was no mistaking her voice. He rose from the snow and hobbled up the hill as fast as he could go.

When he finally reached the clearing at the top of Bearback, he wandered around the area, indulging himself in familiar smells, the dead grasses protruding through clumps of snow, the muddy patches, the trees with their damp bark, the cool breeze bringing the scent of a distant herd of deer.

The clearing was surrounded by trees, and the last of the snow glowed light gray from the moonlight. Rabbitrunner glanced around, wondering where Newmoon and the others were, listening for their voices. He licked his lips and cocked his ears; nothing but the blowing wind.

Frustrated, he raised his head and howled. "This, this is our Life!" He paused, waiting for another voice to continue the Litany, but nothing happened. "This, this is our Life!" he howled again, and still no answer came. His tail slowly lowered as disappointment set in. Glancing off into the distance, he could barely see the woods beyond Bearback. If they are not yet here, he thought to himself, they are out there somewhere, finding their way back. I'll see them in the morning.

He convulsed in a frenzied fit of shivering. "Newmoon!" he whined. "Treepisser, Mousehunter, Ravenplay, where are you?" He glanced around at the trees surrounding the clearing. "Scentcatcher, Watersplasher, Sleepfarter, anybody." No answer but the wind.

Shaking out his fur, he glanced at his right foreleg. It was still contracted, folded, swollen. He tried moving it, lowering it to the ground, but it hurt too much. The pain, the ache—what did Twolegs do to him?

The wind changed direction, coming from the east, where the sky was turning gray. Dawn was coming. He turned and started down Bearback, stumbling several times until he reached the dens. By then the stars were no longer visible, and the sky was mostly gray. He limped over to a den and crawled inside, dirt crumbling from the roof of the tunnel as he made his way to the chamber. He curled up in the darkness and was soon asleep.

For the next several days he slept, coming out of the den only at night and just long enough to urinate and eat dirty snow to quench his thirst. It wasn't until the night that he heard the distant howls from the Blackpaw Pack that he crawled out and remained for awhile.

It was the Litany he was listening to, bringing back memories and reminding him how alone he was. He longed to join in, adding his howls to theirs, but couldn't bring himself to do so. The pull of their voices was painful, and he went through his routine of urinating and drinking, this time from a mud puddle, before he crawled back into the den to escape their sounds.

He was hungry. But he just didn't care.

The den was like a womb, he realized, warm and comforting and enclosing, protecting him from the unknown things that could hurt him. Sometimes he would dream, and he'd be a cub again, playing with his sisters, stealing meat from Ravenplay or Sleepfarter and drawing them into a chase. And what started as a dream of play became a dream of horror with him and the others of the pack running for their lives from some massive, dark, noisy thing blowing wind at them—Rabbitrunner knew it was Bigbird but he couldn't see it.

He would wake with a jerk, calm himself down, then, if he could tell it was still dark outside, crawl out through the tunnel, enlarging it by his passage, and repeat the routine. Sometimes he would wake and hear voices calling him, alternately scaring him or comforting him, and he'd occasionally call out, hoping to coax one of them closer.

But it was the hunger that was the worst, not because it was so annoying but because he could ignore it so easily now, just as he could ignore the dull throb in his contracted foreleg. The urge to hunt was all but gone, and he couldn't understand why. He could say his leg hadn't healed, but that wasn't really it. Instead, he continued the pattern of his existence as he had before, trying not to think too much of how everything now was.

One night he dreamed he was again with the pack as they ran from Bigbird. The wind blew against his pelage like a storm as his paws pounded the dirt and ice. The snow around him was blinding in the morning sunlight as he and the others ran from the claws and beating wings just above them. Rabbitrunner kept thinking: All of us—this time, all of us!

Then something changed; he ran into a different world. The noise of Bigbird vanished, and he stopped running. He was standing on ice, and it was like nothing he'd ever seen before. The ice was flat, grayish, and extended in all directions to the horizon as though he was in the center of a vast, frozen lake. The air smelled of winter, and the sun was directly overhead in a cloudless sky.

He glanced around looking for the others. He was alone on the ice, and felt deserted and afraid. How could they leave him like that? He stood still, scanning the bare horizon for some sign of distant movement, some chance of hope.

He quickly spun around when he heard splashing behind him. Where once there was nothing but the expanse of flat, gray ice, now there was a circular, shallow puddle, thirty feet wide and a foot deep. In the center of the puddle, gazing intently into the water, Deerchaser seemed out of place in the vast emptiness. The sick Hunter seemed unusually youthful and spritely as he reared up on his hind legs and pounced with his forelegs, splashing water about.

His pelage was thick and shiny instead of mangy, matted and dull as Rabbitrunner remembered it. His body was now muscular and healthy, but it was still Deerchaser, playful and simple-minded. Rabbitrunner felt elated at seeing him. He raised his tail as he turned around and whuffed.

Deerchaser pounced again, his ears bent forward in fascination. Suddenly he looked up and glared at Rabbitrunner, his tail raised high. *It's easy*, Deerchaser said. *I can't do it, but you can.* And then he slowly began sinking into the water.

Joy turned to fear as Rabbitrunner realized Deerchaser was in danger. Get out, he thought, but he couldn't verbalize it, couldn't make the sounds.

Deerchaser didn't move a leg, didn't turn his head, and just stared at him as he slowly sank into the water, as though he were unaware of his predicament. *I can't do it...*

Get out!

The water was up to his neck, and part of his tail was still above water. *I can't do it, but you can!* he yipped, cub-like. *It's easy.* Then his head slipped beneath the water, silently, without a ripple.

Deerchaser!

Suddenly the water became turbulent and turned

black as blood, overflowing onto the ice. Rabbitrunner could smell the coppery scent of it, and he backed away, baring his teeth, terrorized. The quiet breeze became a roaring wind, and Rabbitrunner looked behind him.

He was at the rocky foot of the cliff where he leaped off to escape from Bigbird. The flying beast again hovered over him at the top of the cliff. Fear turned to rage as he remembered the Hunters who were killed. He gazed up, daring Bigbird to attack.

The great creature remained at the top of the cliff, hovering as the cliff became black with oozing blood running over the edge, running down the rock walls, droplets of blood blowing off the cliff, splattering around Rabbitrunner like rain. Blood.

And then it stopped. He glanced around, but everything was dark. So this is death, he thought, but he was wrong. In the distance he could see the gray of the sunrise, and as he looked down, he saw, just at his paws, the bird, a sparrow in a circle dug into the grass. It was dead, on its back, its neck snapped and head to one side, its wings spread out, as though in flight had it not been on its back. He knew what it was, and he knew what it meant.

Something happened.

He looked up, saw Pawsore standing in front of him. The old wolf was once their Alpha Male, their One, for many seasons, before he was beaten in a fight by Treepisser, his Second, and driven off Bearback. Rabbitrunner remembered how it happened, how he and the others left Bearback to go to the grasslands to meet him, again and again, until the day he wandered off and most likely died. *Something happened,* Pawsore said again.

His fur was matted, one eye was shut and oozed pus. He held his right, swollen forepaw off the ground just as Rabbitrunner did, and he stank of gangrene, but he looked as alive as any Hunter could. *So tell me.*

"Tell you what?"

What happened to my pack?

Rabbitrunner looked down. "After you were gone, after you—died—Treepisser became the One of the pack. We were hit by a terrible blizzard, and there was no food, so Treepisser led us through the Tailless Pack Territory to the mountains and we crossed over."

Twolegs are there. I saw them.

"Yes, Twolegs," Rabbitrunner went on. "We tried to kill a couple cows and escape, but Bigbird came after us. Now they're all gone."

Pawsore nodded. *That son of a dog. I would never have led you all there. I would have found a way, even if there was no way to be found.*

"They're all dead."

But you're still alive. Pawsore nodded and glanced at the dead bird on the ground. *You aren't dead yet, are you?*

Rabbitrunner glanced at the bird. "You left this for me."

I knew you would jump off a cliff. I knew you would live.

"Then you knew the others would die, didn't you?"

Pawsore nodded.

"Why didn't you stop us?"

Pawsore glanced away. *Deerchaser was trying to warn us for years. He couldn't convince me, and I couldn't convince anybody else, especially in my last days when I was broken and almost dead. Some things you cannot stop.*

"But you knew I would live. You knew I would be the only one to see the dead bird. You knew I would leap off the cliff."

Yes, Pawsore said, raising his tail. *You leaped off the cliff, you fell all that way and you lived. But that was easy. It gets worse after this.*

"How could it get worse?" Rabbitrunner puled. "I'm alone. I'm hungry. Who knows if I'll live or die. Or when."

But That's just it, Pawsore snarled, his eyes blazing with life. *That's just it. You're not dead yet.*

Rabbitrunner felt a jolt run through his body. He glanced down at the dead bird, but it was gone. Instead he saw a giant pawprint, a Hunter's pawprint, and a second one, smaller, fitting completely inside the pad of the first. The smaller one, he knew, was his.

He woke with an uncomfortable fit of shaking, then raised his head. The dream was very strong in his memory, too real to ignore. He shook his head and sniffed the air, smelling the earthy scent of the den and his own body odors. A very small amount of moonlight made it into the tunnel past the bend, so he could make out his own shape in the darkness.

He felt a sudden urge to see everything outside, and he began crawling up the tunnel towards the light. As he pulled himself into the open air, his fur filthy and unkempt, he gazed at the moon.

It was no more than a sliver in the sky. A new moon, Father Sky's bad eye only partially open, a sleepy eye staring down at him.

He realized that he hadn't eaten in many days; it had been a full moon when he last filled his stomach. The hunger pains he'd been ignoring for so long now grumbled inside him for attention. He glanced over his body, surprised at his own emaciated condition. And yet it seemed as though only a few days ago he had been with them all.

He looked back up at the sky and thought about Newmoon, his mate. He wondered if she had given birth to her cubs yet, and then he wondered when she would be back, with the cubs, of course. And the others, when would they be back? He was growing tired of waiting.

Then the dream returned to him in all its cold reality, and he remembered the thing he left out of the dream, the thing he left out of all his dreams—the others had all died. Only he returned to Bearback.

"They're all dead." Rabbitrunner snarled at the moon. "They're all dead. I saw them fall, all of them. I saw them die, and you did, too."

I can't do it, but you can.

He jerked his head around at the voice, then decided it was his imagination, the last fragments of his dream. He glanced around, feeling a deep sadness inside, remembering them before the last hunt. He lifted his head and howled: "This, this is our Death!" He held the last note until his lungs could no longer sustain it, then he arched his back and howled again: "This, this is our Death!" He howled again. And again.

Loneliness flooded over him, cold and heavy as a snowdrift, overwhelming him as he remembered the dream, the blood, their blood, trying to comprehend what was so difficult to believe, that he was the last of his pack, and he would be alone for the rest of his life.

Then he remembered Deerchaser in the dream, splashing in the water....Only it wasn't just in the dream, he'd seen it before, Deerchaser splashing in a creek, pouncing in the shallows at the reflection of the full moon, trying to catch Father Sky's bad eye, and then he turned and said, "*I can't do it, but you can.*"

Do what? He wondered. Catch Father Sky's bad eye—the way Thickfur, in the Story of Beginnings, caught His good eye? By climbing a mountain? Rabbitrunner snarled at the thought—he'd climbed enough mountains for a lifetime.

He glanced at his right foreleg, still contracted. He'd pampered it for many days now, and now it seemed permanently stuck that way.

If I'm going to survive, he thought, I'm going to have to eat, and to eat I have to hunt. If I'm going to survive, I'm going to survive alone, because they're gone, they're all gone, and they aren't coming back. Even right then, knowing the reality, he couldn't help but believe they would be coming back, and he realized it was a trick of his memory, a need to have them back that was affecting how he thought. He would have to focus hard to keep the craziness away, even if he didn't want to.

If I'm going to survive, I'm going to need four paws, not three. He tried lowering his right forepaw towards the ground. The pain shot up his shoulder, and he winced and snarled. White light exploded in his head from so much pain. He tried again, and this time his paw touched the muddy soil. The contact between his paw pad and Mother Earth felt good.

He closed his eyes and inhaled, his black nostrils flaring as he picked up the odors of water, mud, wet mildewing leaves on the ground, and other creatures—a rabbit, a raccoon, deer. He inhaled again, thinking that the scent would change ever so slightly when the sun rose.

Somewhere uphill a seed dropped from a maple tree and spun in the air in its slow descent to the ground, catching Rabbitrunner's eye as it landed next to his right forepaw. A maple seedling was sprouting next to it, the two small maple leaves glistening in the moonlight, bright and healthy-looking. Rabbitrunner remembered Deerchaser saying something about a seed, a sprout, and a blossom, but he never figured out what the old Hunter meant.

Shrugging it off, he put his weight on his right foreleg and looked up at the moon as if to show Father Sky that he was still a strong Hunter. Then he looked down at the woods beyond Bearback. He was hungry, and he needed to hunt. Father Sky's bad eye likewise looked down indifferently at the lone Hunter, not caring if he survived.

Rabbitrunner glanced up at the moon, knowing the thought, feeling the uncaring. But then again, a Hunter would expect no more and no less from Father Sky. He began limping downhill.

Chapter Four

"A Seed on the Wind"
(Spring, 1965)

"...and that was how Mac 'The Hook' Raven lost his hook, caught on the door handle of a nineteen-sixty Ford Galaxie Five Hundred when two lovebirds quickly drove off at Lover's Lane."

The fire crackled in the center of the four friends. Theodore Gallagher tossed a few more pieces of rotten wood into the flames, then poked the fire with a stick. "I thought you said it was a ghost story, Billy," he grumbled.

Billy Masters laughed. "Well, not quite. Nobody died yet, but someone might have, given enough time."

"I thought you said I never heard this story before," Andy Graham added. "I heard this one when I was a kid."

Billy shrugged. "Well, I didn't know you heard it."

"I heard it too," Theo said.

"Ditto," Frank Samuels added. He tossed his toothpick in the fire.

"Well, it's a very popular story," Billy said, holding his hands behind his back. "I just didn't know how popular."

"Everybody knows this story," Theo grumbled. "And

this is the point when you reach behind your back and bring out a hook in one last ditch effort to scare the shit out of us. Isn't that right?"

Billy quickly held up his hands. "Look, no hooks. All right, all right already, I get it, the story sucked, but you didn't have to pop my balloon like that!"

Frank laughed. "There's no balloons to be popped, Billy, the story sucked real bad. Was that the best you could do?"

Billy shrugged and glanced at his nails, as though contemplating how they looked, "Not much else," he said. "Just this." Looking up, he quickly reached behind and pulled out a full sized rubber head, holding it up by the hair. It was almost realistic, with red plastic tentacles reaching down from the severed neck like torn arteries and muscles, but they could still tell it was fake.

Theo, sitting across from him at the fire, was about to tell him to toss the head into the flames when he saw the shadow coming up behind Billy. He could hear the crunching of footfalls on the ground, saw the figure stumble closer. At first he thought it was another of Billy's tricks, then he realized Billy had no idea what was behind him. Theo leaped to his feet and pointed. "Jee-zus!"

Andy and Frank saw it too, leaping up and backing away. "Shit, Billy, drop that thing and run!"

Billy laughed, shaking the head back and forth. "I knew I'd get you guys with this one! Don't worry, it's fake..." The shadow reached his back, and the stranger walking up behind him tripped over him, falling into the fire. Billy dropped the rubber head and rolled out from under the legs, screaming like a girl.

The man in the fire, wearing a thick coat with a dirty backpack on his back, seemed to be pulling the coals to his chest using his arms. It was as though he were trying to pull the heat into his body. Theo was the first to react, leaping forward and yanking the man out buy his collar. The stranger was filthy, muddy, with long, blond hair and beard, tattered blue jeans, and barefoot. Theo dragged him away from the fire and onto his back. "Guys, help me!" The other three, as though charged by his voice, quickly surrounded him, knocking burning embers off his chest.

Billy took off his coat and made a pillow for the man's head. "Christ, this guy smells like a goddam corpse!" he grumbled. Frank brought a canteen and gave him a drink. The man drank lustily, taking the canteen and gulping the water down. "Where did he come from?"

"Christ, I don't know," Theo said. "We gotta get him to a hospital. Check and see if the fire burnt him through his coat."

Andy unbuttoned his coat. "No, it was thick enough, thank God. But he stinks like hell." He gazed at the man's eyes. The stranger seemed to be looking at the stars. "Hey mister, where'd you come from? What happened to you? What's your name?"

The man looked at him, noticing him for the first time. His voice was gravelly, he had been sick recently. "My name is Dean." He blinked. "Dean Hoover."

Before anybody could move, he grabbed Andy by the shoulders and pulled him close. Andy tried to pull free, but the guy's grip was powerful. "Listen," he went on. "Listen... I found the cave."

"You know what he did," Sarah said, her long, blond hair tangled with burrs, leaves and sticks, as though she had been running and rolling on the ground in the autumn forest. Dean nodded, watching her, missing her, profoundly sad. "You know what he did." She pulled a burr from her hair and angrily tossed it onto the ground.

Dean opened his eyes, not sure if it was a memory or

a dream.

For the first time, there was no pain, no fear, no dread, and no depression. Dean Hoover felt normal, or what he believed might be normal. He was hooked up to a tube draining liquid from a glass bottle on a pole that led down to a needle that poked into his arm, sterile saline water, the nurses told him, for dehydration. He got shots every few hours, antibiotics, among other things, and a bedpan and urinal were kept on a table beside the bed. He let the nurse shave his beard off, then give him a sponge bath.

He insisted he could take a shower on his own, but the first time he rose up to go to the bathroom, his equilibrium went haywire and he flopped back in bed, and he opted instead to use the stainless steel urinal they left for him. It was the first time he saw his feet, wrapped up in gauze and surgical tape to the ankles, smelling of betadyne and rotten meat. They told him that he was found barefoot, sick and confused, and his feet would have to heal.

There were scratches and puncture wounds around his right leg, mostly on the calf, something they told him he did when he was running through the woods. He wondered why his feet didn't hurt, but the nurses wouldn't tell him.

Earlier that day, he was visited by Dr. Bowler, the Dean of Education, and Dr. Coneurs, the Dean of Zoology Studies, bringing him a large bouquet of flowers and a box of candy as a get well gift from the university. They reassured him that his classes were being taught by Dr. Stemmons, an elderly gentleman they claimed to drag out of retirement kicking and screaming. "But you'll have your classes back next semester when you're better," Coneurs said.

"Jesus, Dr. Stemmons, that old walking mummy? How long was I away?" Dean asked.

"Awhile," Bowler told him. "You really should never have gone hiking into a blizzard like that. You almost got yourself killed, and you really had us worried, but we're glad you're back."

When they left, he looked at the burns on his hands and arms. The men who found him said he leaped into their campfire, wanting its warmth, but it was a warm night, he could remember that much, and he was wearing a coat, so it didn't make sense. When the nurse brought him a bowl of broth, he insisted this time he wanted solid food. She brought him spaghetti from the kitchen on a hospital tray, which he ate in seconds, and five minutes later threw back up.

After the nurses cleaned him up, he asked for a mirror, and he looked at his face. There were black splotches on his cheeks, and he wondered if the fire caused that. But it didn't look like a burn, not quite anyway. He noticed black spots on his fingers too, and he began thinking that something else happened to him, not just the fire.

The last thing he remembered was wandering through the blizzard, lost, unable to find his tent and sleeping bag. He remembered being cold, shivering with hypothermia. The weather man said there would be a little early spring snow, but he did not predict the massive blizzard that hit, not so soon after the last blizzard. He was caught totally off guard.

All things considered, he was lucky to be alive, and he had been a fool to go out camping when he did. He was lucky those campers found him, lucky they knew to give him water when they did, take him to the hospital. And above all else, lucky he found the cave.

He remembered sitting down on what he thought was a hill, but falling through into the cave. It was the cave of the giant wolf they all now called the Shadow Wolf.

He had been looking for it a long time, in a way on the

trail since he first knew about the wolf five years before, when he wandered into the very same cave by accident. On that occasion, he actually saw the wolf, He saw it, and in the end it let him live. It took him five years to find the cave again, and once again he found it when he was dying, and once again, he lived any way. But he couldn't remember how long he was there, or what happened, or how he stayed warm, anything. And it haunted him.

"Hey, Krazy Kat! You look like shit in a blender!"

Dean looked up and saw his friend, Fribitz Grinner, standing in the doorway, leaning against the door jamb, his arms crossed. He was bald again, had shaved his head and eyebrows, and wore a black suit, black shirt and black tie. Dark sunglasses in round frames hid his eyes. "You don't look so hot yourself," Dean said, smiling.

"All the other rooms in this hospital smell like piss and rubbing alcohol and betadyne. This room smells of piss and vinegar. I wonder why. And I wonder why you're keeping that vase of flowers next to your bedpan. Not even flowers can make your shit smell any sweeter." He stepped forward. "How're you doing? You had a harrowing ordeal there, Dr. Hoover, and everybody agrees you're lucky to be alive."

"Yeah, I'm alive, and glad of it, just surprised I'm not in pain."

"Demerol," Fribitz said. "They tried giving you morphine but you refused, you said it would make you dopey and confused."

Dean nodded. "They gave me morphine when I was in the mental institution, that and Thorazine, and lithium. That stuff turns you into a drooling fool. But the Demerol---I just don't remember saying anything about that to the nurses." He paused, staring out the window. "I don't remember much of anything."

"But you found the cave, didn't you?" Fribitz said. "You

told the guys who brought you here. You told the nurses and doctors. You told just about everybody."

"Yeah, why did I do all that? I'm making myself look like a nut case all over again."

"Well, considering that you found the cave in the middle of a blizzard, and you found the guys who ended up rescuing you by wandering through the woods, do you think you can find the cave one more time again after all that?"

Dean nodded. "I have a pretty good idea." He sighed.

Fribitz shook his head. "You don't seem so enthused, Krazy Kat."

"It's the Demerol," Dean said. "That, and my patchwork memory. I found the cave just about when I was on the verge of dying from hypothermia. Hell, I hiked a lot, I knew the signs. And apparently I got the flu in the process, so I was in the cave sick as a dog. Came all that way to see it and I ended up practically comatose. How long was I gone, by the way? A few days, a week?"

"You don't know? They didn't tell you?"

"They aren't telling me shit."

Fribitz uncrossed his arms, removed his glasses and shook his head. "A month, Krazy Kat. You've been missing a month."

Dean looked up. "That can't be right. The flu, hell any cold, doesn't last more than a week, maybe two."

"A month," Fribitz said. "You don't remember?"

"A month? What did I eat? How did I stay alive?"

"Eat? Hell, you could survive a month without eating, but a month without water... Hell, you'd die after five days without anything to drink."

"Maybe I ate the snow."

"After the blizzard, the snow was gone in a week. Christ, Krazy Kat, what the hell happened in that cave of yours?"

Dean looked at his hands. "And look at me, I'm messed up. My skin's messed up. And my feet are bandaged."

"Frostbite."

Dean glanced at him. "What?"

"You got frostbite. Your right foot was okay, and they managed to save two toes on your left foot."

Dean stared at him, his jaw dropping. Before Fribitz could speak again, he leaped up and started tearing the bandages off his feet. "Shit! Shit! Shit!" Both his feet were splotched with black and reddish flesh, infections, and when he removed the bandages on his left foot, he saw the wounds where his toes used to be. He still had his big toe and the one next to it, but the rest were gone. "Oh shit!" Dean was shouting now, and gazing at Fribitz. "A month, a month, and look what I did to myself! Oh shit!"

Two nurses came into the room, one holding a needle. Fribitz stood, blocking their way. "He'll be okay, he's just in shock."

"He needs those bandages on his feet!"

"Just give us a minute, please."

He looked at Dean as the nurses were leaving. Dean was weeping, gripping his blackened feet at the ankles, staring at where his toes should have been. "Jesus, Fribitz," he whispered. "Look what I'm doing to myself! My damn toes for God sake! When will my life be normal? When will my goddam life be normal?"

"Calm down, Dean, my man, I know it's hard to take, but after everything you went through, you're stronger for it, and you've already gone through the worst."

Dean closed his eyes. "Fribitz just shut up." He leaned against his pillow, opened his eyes, looked at his feet. "That mental place—where I first met you, remember?"

"Yes."

"I'm beginning to think, maybe I shouldn't have left." He pointed to his toes. "If I can't kill myself completely,

I'll do it piece by piece."

"Krazy Kat, you ain't thinking suicide again, are you?"

"I was in that cave a month, you said so. Yeah, I believe you, somehow. But I was in there a month. And do you know what I remember? I remember falling into the cave when I was lost in the snow. That, and falling onto a fire where those guys found me. Everything in between... I remember nothing else except my father, and my family, all of them, before he killed them all and then himself."

"I can dig it," Fribitz said, rubbing his head. "I really can, Krazy Kat. And I promise, I'll be there for you as best as I can, help you get on your feet, no matter how many toes you have left, and in time get you in better shape so you can go back to the cave again."

"No!" he snapped. "I'm not going back."

Fribitz leaned back, stung. "Oh, Dean, you don't mean that. You wanted to go back all along. What, you don't believe in the wolf any more?"

"Yeah, I believe in the goddamn fucking wolf. I saw him with my own eyes. You think I'm crazy? I'm just not going back. Chasing this thing, believing in it, hell even when I didn't believe in it, it caused me nothing but heartache. I need to get back to my job, get myself a life, save money, buy a house, hell, a new car instead of the jalopies I get at fifty bucks a shot."

"But the wolf..."

"No more wolf," Dean said. "Let's not talk about it. Call the nurse. Have her bandage my foot up. It stinks, and I want it healed before it all rots off."

Fribitz nodded. "Listen, Krazy Kat..."

"Go." Fribitz glanced at him one more time, then walked out the door. Dean felt tears running down his cheeks. Frostbite. He needed a stiff drink. A joint. Anything.

Chapter Five

"Bow and Arrow"
(Spring, 1965)

The cabin squatted wearily in the grassy clearing, shadowed by tall pines, looking like a moss-covered ogre nursing a hangover. Built of logs and relatively square with a door in front and two windows at each side, the single-story edifice, frozen in perpetual sag, was still sturdy despite its age, and would probably stand for many more years.

The large, wooden door still hung from the original metal hinges, rusty and heavily greased, and had nothing more than a wooden latch to keep animals out. There were two weathered window boxes, one at each front window, with dried grass instead of flowers growing out of them.

The cabin, with moss two inches thick on its ancient cedar shingles, might have looked like a quaint illustration from a dusty book of fairy tales had it not been for the three rusted, old Ford pickups—one still usable, the other two in various stages of being cannibalized to keep the first one running—parked in a row to the left. There were also three engine blocks leaning against the cabin's right wall, an old, rusted-out tractor, a useless gasoline generator missing spark plugs and wires, a pump for a well that was never drilled, and a massive pile of beer cans, food cans, and broken kitchen crockery piled between two spruce trees to the right of the cabin.

The clearing was sloped, and downhill of the front of the cabin, and at the other end of the clearing was a sturdy, old wooden outhouse, built on heavy wooden runners, so it could be pulled over a new pit when the old one was full. Off to the side, there were several large, wooden frames, some made of two-by-fours, some made of young spruce tree trunks, on which wolf skins were stretched, their sides pierced and tied to the wood by string so they could properly dry before they were scraped.

As Jessie "Cutter" Armstrong drove into the clearing from the old road, parking the jeep in front of the cabin, a pheasant broke from the tall grass, flapping frantically as it called out its panic. Cutter watched it disappear from sight, thinking that, if only he had his rifle...

He glanced at his cabin, built over sixty years ago by a great uncle who grew tired of town life. Cutter inherited the cabin and surrounding land from his father, Jake. It required few repairs, which was about the number of repairs Cutter usually did, sometimes plugging chinks between logs with old rags or replacing a broken window pane with a piece of shingle or cardboard until he could remember, while still in town, to pick up a new glass pane.

Cutter was very much alone here; the only access to the cabin was ten miles of a deep-rutted, meandering road that touched Highway 79 the way an eagle would touch the water of a lake and pull up with a fish in its talons.

The only person who visited Cutter on a regular basis was Ben Rose. Nobody else ever spent more than half an hour there, as though they had stumbled on the home of a family with smallpox and bubonic plague, and they were determined to leave without being too rude. The cabin made most people uneasy, though they could never understand why, but, unlike the rest of them, Ben had been a friend for a long time, and the cabin was more of a comfort to him.

The cabin was conveniently secluded, and though Cutter found himself snowed in a few times every winter, he was never lacking comfort. He always stocked enough beans, potatoes, and dried meat to keep him fed until he was ready to dig out.

As he stepped from the jeep, he looked over his home. He'd been thinking of installing plumbing for the last ten years, but water pipelines led to a hot water tank, a porcelain toilet and sink, septic tank, an electric wire hookup to the power company, and his land taxes going up. Too much trouble. Besides, he didn't feel much need for anything the cabin didn't actually have.

There were few expenses beyond food, taxes, beer and tobacco, and there were times he considered brewing his own beer and raising his own tobacco to cut back even more. If ever he felt like a real bath, he would shell out a few bucks and stay at the motel down the road. A real dinner meant going to the Crooked River or the local McDonalds. Otherwise, beans and rice and potatoes worked just as well.

He pulled out his leather pouch and tapped some tobacco onto a rolling paper. As he did so, he glanced at the skin frames. The wolf skins were just about ready to be scraped. What a waste, he thought, looking at them and remembering how the state bounty on wolves had been discontinued. But in the long run, that was not why he hunted.

He rolled his cigarette one-handed and put it between his lips. He pulled out a wooden match and lit it with a thumbnail, touching the flame to the tip and puffing calmly.

"That boy of yours, Jake, is something else. What do you call him? Little General Custer? Custer is really his middle name? You ought to call him Cutter; you see how fast he skinned that rabbit, like peeling a banana. He don't care about getting blood on his hands, do you, boy? Look, he even has blood on his cheeks, he looks like he took a bite out of that damn animal. Give him a sip of moonshine from that jar, what do you say, Jake? Hey, General, your daddy says you can do a trick, roll a cigarette one-handed!"

Cutter took a slow drag, stepping over to the cabin door. The sky was blue and cloudless, the sun hanging over the western horizon, already turning orange.

He held his cigarette between his fingers and spit out the peach pit he'd been sucking on the last ten minutes into the window box under the front left window of the cabin.

There used to be window boxes for all eight windows, back when Annie had lived with him, back when she came up with the idea of making the cabin look nicer. Annie was tough as nails, but one black eye too many and she decided to leave. Since then, all but the two front window boxes had dropped off, and if he needed a good fuck, he'd just go into the city for a whore or two, just something to tide him over.

As Cutter thought about Annie, he noticed a plant growing from the box full of gray, weathered peach pits. Surrounded in the box by stalks of grass and weeds, there was what looked like the start of a peach tree. Cutter smirked and nodded; Annie would approve of something growing in her window box besides all that mess, though the tree would probably be dead by winter. He sucked on his cigarette as he turned away and reached in the passenger side of his jeep.

Hours ago, back at the Crooked River, he was drinking a pitcher of beer alone, thinking of going back to work at the lodge with the Indians, getting paid to be a guide for weekend fishermen and hunters, though he really didn't need the money, when Jack Fipps at the bar hollered back to him, asking if he was retiring now that the state bounty was dead. Cutter smiled and shrugged noncommittally, then Jack turned and began talking to Flint about the latest story of the Shadow Wolf he'd heard.

Cutter listened as three other patrons got into the conversation, adding stories of their own. He glanced at the shelf behind the bar, where three plaster casts, made in three different counties, showed the giant paw print of the unseen wolf.

"One thing about the Shadow Wolf," Jack said to Flint. "Nobody'll catch that sonovabitch. If it dies, it'll be of old age." Jack, the skeptic who last year didn't believe the wolf even existed, was now the expert, as though he'd been keeping track of the wolf's progress since the beginning.

"I can get it," Cutter said.

"Bullshit, "Jack said. "You've been trying for three years."

"I can find the Shadow Wolf," he said, "and I can kill it."

Flint ran his hand over his bald head, then reached over and grabbed Jack's arm before he could answer. "I don't think you'll ever find it," Flint said, pulling out a twenty dollar bill. "Let alone kill it."

"I may not even need a rifle to kill it," Cutter said, pulling two tens from his pocket and holding them up. "Once I do find it, that is."

The patrons glanced from Flint to Cutter back to Flint. "You've been at it for three years," Flint said, smiling. "Think you'll need three more?"

"Nah," Cutter said. "It'll be dead by winter."

He stared at the tiny peach tree in the window box. "It'll be dead by winter," he repeated. He pushed the door open with a boot and stepped into his cabin, carrying two unstrung bows, two quivers with arrows and a large cardboard box.

The room he now stood in was a combination living room/dining room/kitchen and sometimes bathhouse when he got the urge to pull the large steel tub off the nail on the wall. It was one of four rooms, each twenty by fifteen feet, separated by plywood partitions and old skins over the doorways. As Cutter set everything on the table, he remembered the bet. Now he was committed to finding the giant wolf. That was fine by him; he was sure he would find it.

"There's a big wolf out there," Luke Spencer told Jessie Armstrong. "There's a big wolf out there called the Mangler of Caleb County. My Pa told me so. The ranchers are complaining and they're all talking at the Crooked River. My Pa keeps the hound dogs inside now, because Cuthbert down the road, well, that wolf killed three of his dogs. They been laying traps but they ain't got it yet." And Jessie, all of thirteen, like Luke, turned to him and smiled and said. "But we can get it. I bet we can."

The floor of the cabin was solid oak carpeted by accumulated dust and dry mud. After Cutter set everything aside he reached down and pulled on an iron ring, opening a trap door in the floor. Old, wooden steps led into the cellar, a small dirt room his father dug out years ago. He stomped down the steps and shuffled about in the dark, then came back up with a case of beer in his arms. Kicking the trap door shut, he sat the case down, picked up a bottle of beer, and opened it with a churchkey he kept hanging on a string from the wall.

He took one last drag on his cigarette, sipped his beer and gazed around. The room had one window on the front and one window at the side, both oily and thick with grime. In the corner between the two windows was a bulky, black cast iron wood stove with four burner plates on top. Its sides were rusty and discolored, but the top was shiny and black, seasoned with animal fat and food drippings.

On the shelf over the wood stove, just above the flue, were two empty mason jars with flecks of soil still stuck on them. Cutter stared at the jars; thinking about what he still needed to do.

"What're you buryin' in back there, Pa?" Jessie asked, scraping a muskrat skin. "You'd think you was hidin' a body, piece by piece, all the little holes you're leavin' back there."

Jessie's old man, Jake, turned to him from the rifle he was oiling and smirked. "You never mind what the fuck's back there, boy. If'n I catch you pokin' around there, I'll smack you clear into Georgia. You'll see someday what it's buried there; you'll see when you need to see and not before." And Jessie nodded, working the scraping knife over the skin, scraping dried fat and muscle tissue onto the floor.

Cutter finished off the beer and set the bottle in a crate near the door, then stepped outside and went around back where a lean-to jutted out from the cabin between the two back windows. There were two stacks of wood beneath it, the left one cut and stacked the last few months and still smelling of tree sap, the right one a couple cords of seasoned wood, gray and dry and ready to burn. A dozen feet out from the lean-to was a large chopping block with an axe embedded in the edge and a steel wedge and sledge hammer nearby. The grass had been trampled around it years ago, and the ground was carpeted in woodchips.

Cutter picked up an armload of seasoned wood, stomped back around to the front and went inside, dropping the wood into an old barrel by the door. "Damn wood gets heavier every year," he muttered as he opened the wood stove door and began making layers from the bottom up of old newspapers, twigs, woodchips, sticks, and four pieces of stove length from the barrel.

He struck a match, lit the newspaper in several spots and shut the door, knowing the rest would catch on its own. He widened the vent on the cast iron stove door and opened the valve half way up on the flue to increase the draft, then checked the coffeepot on the stove, still half-full of yesterday's coffee. Just by listening, he could tell the fire was blazing properly. He readjusted the flue valve, slowing the draft, then tossed in two more chunks of wood.

Picking up a heavy stainless steel bucket, the kind used by dairy farmers, he stepped outside to get water. He glanced at the skins drying on the frames and thought about the wolf bounty again. He felt a slow rage rise inside, then checked himself. "I don't need your money," he said. "I don't need your fucking money."

Jake was snoring like a diesel in the bedroom when Jessie in the front room crawled off his cot, wearing only his longjohns. He grabbed the shovel, freezing in panic as it clanked against the door, but Jake was still snoring. He'd already taken a beating with the strap for accidentally shooting and wounding one of the hounds while horsing around with his .22, and those bruises were still fresh.

He quietly slipped out the door, gritting his teeth as he shut it behind him. There was already frost on the ground as he padded barefoot around the side of the cabin and followed the moonbeam-lit trail into the woods. It must've been a good mile. When he reached the area, his feet were numb. He located the freshest mounds where his father had buried something just yesterday, and began digging, using his bare foot to push the shovel down.

He shoveled out the dirt slowly, thinking he would find mason jars full of moonshine. A foot and a half down something clinked, and he tossed the shovel away and removed dirt with his hands. When he pulled out one of the jars and held it in the moonlight, his heart leaped. The jar was full from top to bottom with money, bills thickly wrapped around each other, tight and neat. Pressing against the glass was the likeness of Benjamin Franklin.

As Cutter walked around the cabin he glanced across the clearing at the outhouse, noticing a raccoon dash around its corner. Then he walked uphill. The spring was up the trail a quarter mile, and he headed that way. He built the wood slew so he could set the bucket at the end and catch the water. It was always cold and tasted of minerals. He whistled a tune from "Oklahoma" as it filled, then scooped it up and headed back. By the time he reached the cabin, it was dusk.

The coffee was hot and steaming when he returned. Cutter set the bucket down, covered it with a lid and poured himself a cup. In between sips he half-filled an iron pot with spring water and set it on the stove, adding dried pinto beans and salt pork, plus a little salt and pepper he kept in mason jars.

He settled into a dusty, stuffed easy chair that had no business being in a log cabin and drank his coffee, lit the oil lamp on the table, then rolled a cigarette and lit that from the lamp. He gazed at the cobwebs on the front window, thinking about the peach pit tree growing in the window box outside. Then he glanced at the bleached wolf skull just inside over the door. He thought about the large female wolf he saw on the ledge in Buford County on that mountain, wished he had her skull up there instead, and he wondered how much bigger the Shadow Wolf would be.

Jessie woke in the hospital. Jake and Deputy Tanner stood over his bed, a doctor and two nurses by their side. The room was too bright and stunk of rubbing alcohol. Jake was shaved, now that was different. Jessie raised his fingers to his neck, feeling the gauze bandages, feeling the wetness he knew was his blood soaking through. He looked at their faces, but he already knew about Luke. How could he not know?

When his cigarette was out and his coffee cup empty, Cutter stood and checked on the beans. The water was boiling and it smelled enticing, but it would probably take another hour or two.

He walked through a bearskin that passed for a door into the other front room, the storage room, where he lit a candle and opened a dusty chest resting on crates. He dug through old pelts and rusty traps and removed a large hunting knife with a cracked leather sheath and a deer horn handle. He examined it in the candlelight, then glanced around. Traps of all sizes dangled from the roof boards. Boxes and crates were everywhere, and to one side was a large, red steel box with automobile tools.

Several bales of old clothes covered one corner, and a stack of old boots was in another. Cobwebs and dust covered everything.

Cutter stepped through another skin-covered door to the tanning room in back. There was a workbench, two stools, two empty barrel vats, scraping tools, poisons, more traps and knives, several pelts hanging from the wall and a folded bearskin he had made into leather. Cutter felt though the clutter on the table then picked out his best whetstone. He stepped back into the storage room and examined it in the candlelight. When he looked up, he spotted his father's razor strop, a long, cracking section of leather dangling from the wall collecting dust.

"Goddam you, boy!" Jake yelled, brandishing the razor strop. "I told you not to go poking around where I was diggin'!" He swung, catching Jessie on the bare buttocks. Jessie winced. "What the fuck, did that goddam friend of yours, Luke, put you up to it? If I catch him coming around again I'll kill him. He's a thief and twice the devil his dad is! If I were you, boy, I'd stay away from him! That child is evil, the spawn of the devil!" Another slap, leather to skin. Jessie's pants and underpants were wrapped around his ankles, and he was naked from there on up. He gripped the trunk of the tree with both hands, the way his father demanded, holding back the tears as the strop came down again, this time across his back.

Welts rose over welts with each slap of leather against his skin, but Jessie held firm, bit down every scream that threatened to come out, and despite the pain he grinned, knowing that Jake was burying the money for him, for his inheritance. Another slap against his back, another welt stinging and red, and Jessie held on.

Cutter looked away and blew out the candle. He took the knife and whetstone through the tanning room and into the other back room, his bedroom. He lit an oil lamp that dangled from a rafter, adjusting the flame, then looked around. A wooden platform and mattress made up his bed, with several army blankets and a bearskin covering it. There was an old table in the corner, and another oil lamp on that. There was a warped dresser under one of the windows and seven rifles—three with scopes—on the rack over his bed, all of them cleaned and oiled.

Cutter lifted his mattress, pulled loose bills from his pocket, and jammed them under the mattress with other bills. All told, he figured he had a thousand dollars and then some stashed under there. Ben constantly worried about him being robbed, but he always laughed it off, noting that nobody would come out so far to rob him. He pulled out the last few dollars and loose change, tossed them under his mattress and let it drop, making sure the bearskin on top was smooth.

"Jessie knows the woods in these parts like I know the back of my hand," Jake often used to say.

Jessie wandered through the dark, wearing a black sweatshirt and pants, black boots, and a black knit cap. At thirteen, he was long and quick like a deer, lean, light, limber. His night vision was as good as a hawk's, and he knew how to walk silent. He followed his father through the woods, never losing sight of the lamp Jake carried, until he got in the rowboat at the lake's edge and began rowing across the dark waters.

This time he was ready, pulling the canoe out of its hiding place behind the bushes and into the water. He paddled slowly, not making any noise as he followed the distant lamplight across the lake and among the islands.

When he finally reached the empty rowboat, he pulled the canoe ashore and wandered through the trees on the island until he could see the light of a fire. He stopped behind some bushes where he could watch his father and the Ojibway men who worked for him walking among the five massive stills where Jake made his product. Cases of empty mason jars sat at one end of the clearing while filled ones were at the other. It was a factory without a roof.

Jessie was satisfied, confirming what he'd suspected so long. He ducked back into the shadows and moved swiftly back to his canoe, but his night vision was hampered after seeing the campfire, and he got lost. Suddenly the ground went out from beneath him, and he fell into a pit.

"Unh!" he grunted, feeling something giving beneath him. He reached out, felt a face, cold with death. His other hand felt the badge on the shirt, remembered talk in town the day before about the revenuer who got lost in the woods. "God!" Jessie shouted, and was about to scream when he was lifted by the collar out of the hole, gripped by a strong arm while a hand smelling of fresh soil covered his mouth.

"Don't scream," a calm voice said. One of the Ojibway men, "You Jake's boy?" Jessie nodded. "Don't scream. Get the hell home and keep your mouth shut. You tell Big Jake you been here he'll kill you like he killed that man you just found. Understand?" Jessie nodded, his body shaking. "Go." The man released him, and, for once in his life terrorized and trembling, he ran back to the canoe.

Cutter jerked open a drawer on the dresser and poked through old clothes until he found the framed photograph. He blew out the lamp, closed the dresser drawer, and took the photograph, knife, and whetstone back into the main room. He set the things on the table and sat on one of the four chairs around it. Setting the photo on the table, he dunked the whetstone in the water bucket and began sharpening the blade on the stone.

He stared at the photograph as he drew the blade slowly back and forth. It was a black-and-white photo of him at twelve, with the bear he killed, his first bear. He stood by the body, grinning, gripping the bear's ear and lifting the head, his rifle in his other hand, his father standing behind him, a weathered, unsmiling face that made him look twenty years older than he was.

Cutter drew the blade across the stone slowly, remembering talks with his father, arguments about him finishing high school and going to college, but he ended that argument by joining the army when World War II began.

Jessie George Custer "Cutter" Armstrong stood over the pit, dressed in his Sergeant's uniform, looking down at the Mason jar lids, holding the shovel with both hands as though it were his rifle. He had just seen his father's grave, now that he was stateside, and now he looked at the Mason jars, all full of money, and remembering that Jake still refused to go to a doctor about his heart, all that money. Mason jars, Jake's Swiss bank, and there were other places in the woods like this, and Jake died of a bad heart in a dilapidated cabin when he could have owned a mansion. The pain gripped Cutter's chest. He raised the shovel, brought it down, and heard the sound of breaking glass.

The blade slid against the whetstone, its edge growing sharper at each stroke. Cutter looked up at the two bows he bought by mail from the Grizzly Outdoor Archery Company. They were both three and a half feet long, recurved with eighty pounds of pull, composite fiberglass-horn with carbon fibers for strength, horsehair bowstrings, leather-wood grips made specifically to fit Cutter's left hand.

The box contained four sets of arrows, two sets aluminum shafts, one set each 25 and 30 inches; two sets fiberglass, one sets each 25 and 30 inches. The black, barbed steel arrowheads were four-sided and sharp enough to slice a steak. The arrowheads could be unscrewed and replaced, if damaged, with a box of extra ones that Cutter also bought. Each had the correct feather fletching for hunting with Cutter's requested color pattern, red for the henfeathers, black for the cockfeather. Cutter stared at his new archery equipment and nodded approval as the blade scraped against the stone.

The bandana he wore around his neck was new and blood-red.

When he was thirteen, he knew the woods like the back of his hand. Jessie could walk through the woods to Caleb, fifteen miles, in less than a day, and run the distance and back by sunset. He knew animal trails no other human eye ever saw, and he knew parts of the woods not even the Ojibway knew about.

When he was thirteen, Jessie was just a bullheaded as his father. He knew there was a large wolf out there, named Mangler, and he spent days, weeks, the entire summer, tracking it, figuring out its pattern, recognizing its paw print from those of other wolves. He wasn't going to follow it, only figure out which trail it used.

He had seen his father trap wolves before, but his father no longer kept wolf traps. One night he went out after Jake was asleep, dug up one of the jars by hand and pulled out a handful of bills before replacing it and hiding any trace he'd been there. The next day he bought a dozen wolf traps. They were unlike the small traps he used to catch raccoons and muskrats. They were powerful and mean-looking. Good, Jessie thought, just what I need.

The smell of pork and beans pulled Cutter back to reality. He recalled how hungry he was, set the stone and knife down, and fixed himself a big bowl. He poured the last of the coffee into his cup and set the pot aside, then sat at the table looking at the last items he purchased.

Four army surplus walkie-talkies with chipped camouflage paint, wires and earpieces sat on his table where he left them earlier. He still hadn't purchased batteries for them yet, but there would be time enough to test them.

Jack Fipps had suggested the walkie-talkies the day Cutter found out about the end of the bounty on wolves. Cutter took a bite of beans from his bowl and looked at one, holding it up, turning it back and forth, wondering if it really would come in handy for catching the wolf. He set the bowl down and reached for the side of his neck, feeling an electric shock beneath the bandana. It was a memory deep inside the scar. He already knew.

"We can get it!" Jessie told Luke as they set another trap and staked it to the ground. They worked in tandem, Luke holding the spring down as Jessie set the trigger, though it could have just as easily been set by either one of them.

Jessie carefully covered the leghold trap with leaves and twigs then did the same over the chain. "How do you know the wolf will come this way?" Luke asked.

"I don't know for sure," Jessie said, "But he's been here before, several times, and he's bound to come back. He's bound to pass this way again."

He stepped back to admire his handiwork, then tossed a few handfuls of dirt over it. It appeared level because the trap sat in a slight depression he dug out.

"Just remember, Luke, when we catch it, I kill it."

"Sure, Jessie, sure, it's all yours." Luke said.

Jessie glanced at him, and for a moment saw an unfamiliar smirk, a sign that Luke had different plans, and a blaze in his friend's eyes that made him look as evil and vicious as Jake often said he was. He felt an odd chill, and almost decided to stop the project right there.

He shook his head, erasing the feeling, nodded, and slipped down the trail, and Luke followed; they had a few more traps to set before heading home.

Cutter sipped the last of his coffee, old and bitter with grounds at the bottom, before getting back to sharpening his knife. The framed photograph stared at him, ghosts from a happier past, and ghosts of a twelve-year-old boy, his father, and an old bear whose time had come.

Cutter stopped sharpening. He was staring at his reflection in the glass. He gingerly set the knife and stone on the table and picked up the photo, staring at his image, the whiskered face, the unkempt black hair with encroaching gray, the face of a forty-two-year-old man, wrinkles around the eyes and across the forehead.

He stared at the eyes, almost recognizing something, and then his gaze moved to the bandana, and back to the eyes, comparing them to the eyes of the boy in the photograph, noticing that something was missing in the eyes, something was lost over the years. He looked at the boy's neck, just twelve years old and already he had a football player's neck, like his father's, clean and smooth and unmarked, and as he stared, his hand went to the bandana.

Jessie stared into Mangler's eyes, big, brown, almost-human eyes that stared back at him, angry, pained, raging, and waiting. "Jesus, Jessie," Luke said. "He's so big." Caught in the leghold trap, the wolf was monstrous. Normally, Jessie knew, they wouldn't grow larger than a Collie or a Dalmatian, but this one was half a foot higher at the shoulders and a foot longer from nose to tail. Its thick coat was several shades of gray, with black markings outlining its muzzle, eyes, and ears.

"I told you we'd get it," Jessie said, elated. The afternoon sun barely squeaked through the canopy of leaves above, but in the shadow of the trees, Jessie felt as though he were glowing. He nocked an arrow and raised his hunting bow. "One good shot to the heart," Jessie said, "And he's dead."

The knife cut into his neck like butter, and the pain was like molten lead poured into the wound. He dropped the bow and arrow and staggered back. Luke, his black hair oily and flat, his right hand speckled with Jesse's blood, stepped in front of him, grinning. "I'm sorry, Jessie, but it seems that Mangler broke free and killed you. And when you died, I had to kill the wolf instead. Now ain't that something?"

Jessie gurgled, watched as Luke reached out, took the knife handle and twisted. He moaned and fell to his knees, then collapsed on his side, grasping Luke's wrist, too weak to stop him. "No. Please. Please." He gurgled blood, not sure what the twisting knife had pierced, but blood was gushing from his lips as he tried to make more words. He knew somewhere in all that sliced flesh was the artery, and if it was cut, he would bleed to death in minutes. He knew that much.

Luke stood, grinning. "Don't die yet, I want you to watch." Jessie gazed at him, his vision tunneling. In all the times Jake killed a man, he never was so cruel and brutal as Luke was now.

He watched Luke stand, take the arrow, and aim at the wolf. The arrow hissed through the air and hit Mangler in the chest. The wolf fell to its side, silent, and Luke turned back to him. "You taught me that, remember? But you always wanted to do the killing. Well, today I do the killing." He dropped the bow, fell to his knees and grabbed Jesse's neck in both hands.

Jesse gurgled, grabbing both wrists. The pain was everywhere, and he was afraid of dying. Then, he felt his hands grow stronger, and he squeezed Luke's wrists. Luke started losing his grip.

"Motherfucker," Jessie gasped, "I'm gonna kill you back!" Even as he spoke, though, he could feel his strength waning. He barely heard the sound of snapping metal, was almost out when Luke was knocked from his body. Still weak and dizzy, he realized that he had a brief window to make his move.

Luke was on his back, and Jessie crawled up and fell on him, wrapping his hands around Luke's neck. He squeezed, not even feeling his hands, not even thinking clearly any more, and minute after minute passed, and he only knew that he could not let go. Luke would kill him if he didn't kill him first.

Somehow he inhaled, and consciousness returned briefly. He let go of the boy, knowing before he even looked that he was dead. He gasped, trying to remain awake a little longer. He heard the shuffling, looked to his left, and saw Mangler, not ten feet away, that close, the trap still on his paw, the chain broken, the arrow protruding from the side of his chest, right where his heart should have been. He was still alive.

Right then Jessie hated the wolf. He hated the wolf for knocking Luke off him, for saving his life, for not being the wolf he killed. The wolf turned and ran off. He was dying, and would be killed several days later. Jessie watched him leave. If I can't kill you, he thought, I'll kill a hundred of you.

Reaching up, he felt his neck, felt the knife. He grabbed it and pulled it out. It was Luke's bowie knife. He stared at the blade, realizing for the first time that Luke missed the artery, that he just might live after all. He reached up, felt his fingers touch the wound, enter the wound, like a cave dug into his neck. The pain didn't matter any more. He passed out.

They found him like that hours later. Nobody ever talked about it, but somehow they knew, they knew the wolf didn't kill Luke, he did, and they knew why, and somehow they understood.

Cutter set the framed photo on the table, still staring at his reflection. He reached up and removed the bandana, exposing the scar on the side of his neck, a deep pit, still almost looking raw, mottled, tattered, red and white skin covering the depression.

He reached up, slid his fingers into the wound. The skin in the cratered scar was hard in spots and supple in others. He tilted his head to see the reflection better in the glass, his image superimposed over the photograph. The jugular vein had been missed, but just barely.

Cutter remembered that day, remembered how he began hunting wolves regularly from that time on, by bow or by trap, by rifle or revolver, each time thinking of Luke when he killed one, each time putting a notch in the log wall of the cabin, telling his father it was for the bounty, Jake nodding, never looking at him because he knew the real reason. At first he planned to kill ten, to make up for the big one, Mangler, he didn't kill, but after ten wolf skins, he decided on twenty, then fifty, then a hundred, and the notches were made in the wood, using the same knife, Luke's Bowie with the deer horn handle, and still his father wouldn't look at them. Then he decided, if he killed one hundred fifty it would be enough.

His goal was interrupted by a war, his father's death, another war, but still he kept at it, for the one that got away, the one that the scar reminded him of, the one that brought the demon out of Luke, because in his mind Luke was never a real human, but every wolf was smaller, nowhere near as vicious and intelligent and malevolent as the big one.

Then one day, when Ben was there, he realized he'd had enough, the number no longer mattered, and he made the last notch, the one hundred fiftieth, broke the blade of the knife he'd used since he was thirteen, smiled at Ben. He reached his goal, but no number would be good enough. No wolf he'd killed was the same as that one, the Mangler of Caleb County.

Cutter set the photo aside, tying the bandana around his neck as he glanced up at the bleached wolf skull above the door. More now than ever before, more now because of the wolf and his father, he wanted the Shadow Wolf, so big, yet invisible to human eyes. This one, this Shadow Wolf, was a true challenge, but more than that, a redemption, a freedom from the deaths that followed him, unlike the deaths he caused during the war, guiltless deaths.

As he picked up the knife and stone, began sharpening the blade with slow, thoughtful strokes, he gazed at the skull, gazed with a determination that he would sometime soon get what truly belonged to him, the giant wolf in the shadow of the woods, as invisible as the ghosts that haunted him. The blade scraped gently, again and again, as the fire crackled longingly in the hollow of the cabin.

Chapter Six

"The Cave
(1965-1966)

"You know what he did," Sarah said, her long, blond hair tangled with burrs, leaves and sticks, as though she had been running and rolling on the ground in the autumn forest. Dean nodded, watching her, missing her, profoundly sad. "You know what he did." She pulled a burr from her hair and angrily tossed it onto the ground.

He woke with a start inside the cave. It was pitch black, stinking of that deathly odor of the large wolf. He reached for the flashlight, found it, turned it on, pointed the beam at the objects he left behind the last time he was in the cave: his bow and quiver of arrows, the family photograph, his camera, scattered candles, the razor, rusted now, the other things....left untouched by the wolf, now a part of its mausoleum. He'd meant to bring the things back with him, but now that he was here he knew he couldn't. It was like robbing an old church of its icons.

The flashlight beam was dimming. He switched it off

and reclined as he listened to the rain, thinking of the cave paintings on the wall. He had photographs of the cave and plaster casts of the large paw prints, and he thought they could be a jumping board for a research paper, but now he wanted to hide them away, hide the secret of the cave from everybody else. It would be like showing them a scar that went deeper than the ones on his wrists.

As he listened to the rain, he recalled standing outside the cave, seeing the smiling cave mouth again for the first time, and a young pine tree, next to the dead spruce, growing beside the cave, where none had been the last time. Nature had a way of renewing itself, he realized, and as he drifted off to sleep, lulled by the rain and distant thunder, he dreamed of his childhood, alive, with his mother, father, sister, and brother.

The blare of a train horn startled him, and for a moment he wondered what happened, and where the cave went. He was in a bed, the covers scattered, a red light flashing outside the tattered drapes, no vacancy, and the distant rumble of the train. The cave was a dream, as was his sister. And this room, with his clothes piled in the corner, this was his reality. In the dim light of the room, he felt along the bedside table until he grasped the bottle of gin and found the dirty bathroom glass. Not even adding orange juice this time, he poured a little, then took a sip. He winced at the taste, but took another drink, feeling the liquid burning down his throat.

He reached for the baggie, turned on the lamp and held it up. There was nothing left but seeds and stems. "Shit," he mumbled, tossing it on the floor. He poured more gin, almost filling the glass, and took another sip. Glancing around, he looked at his clothes spread across the motel floor. His last landlord, thinking he left for good, threw out all his old clothes when he didn't return after the blizzard, and he had to replace everything he once owned at the Salvation Army. Now, he realized, he had to either make a trip to the Laundromat or buy more clothes.

A sharp stab in his left foot reminded him he needed another pain pill. He grabbed the bottle of Mellaril off the stand, fumbled it open and tossed three down, chasing them with a gulp of gin. Was it supposed to be three pills or two? It really didn't matter now, it was one in the morning, and he should be asleep anyway.

He yawned and stared out the window. The red "No Vacancy" sign dutifully flashed its Morse code through the drapes, and he listened to the distant train whistle sounding one last time. He thought about the dream again, him sleeping in the cave, waking up in the cave, looking at the objects, looking at the plaster casts he made of giant pawprints. Problem was, none of that happened.

He had gone to the cave, found it, that he remembered, but he was sick and had no memory of what he did inside. In his dream he was in a sleeping bag, but he didn't have one when he found the cave. His sleeping bag was lost along with his tent, somewhere in the forest. And the things he left inside the cave from the first time he found it...

He must have been delirious, but then again, he must have done something right in his delirious state, if he stayed alive for a month and could not remember a thing.

He took another drink. The autumn semester was about to begin.

"You really need to go back to that cave," Fribitz told him. "It's just like falling off a horse..."

"Yeah, yeah, yeah, all right already, you have to get back on," Dean mumbled, gulping from his flask. He was in Fribitz's studio, sitting at the table where the rolls of canvas were stacked.

"No, you don't have to get on," Fribitz said, making sweeping brush strokes on a six by six canvas. "You have to land in the horse shit and roll in the grass. You have to experience, and if you fell off the horse, there's a reason."

"The reason is you lost your balance."

"The reason is the fates ordained that you needed to change direction and learn something new."

"Bullshit," Dean snapped, standing and grabbing his crutches. "Maybe you haven't noticed, but sometimes the fates are cruel and evil." He limped around the table, glancing at the high ceiling festooned with dozens of unsold metal mobiles dangling over their heads. "Sometimes the fates drop your ceiling artwork on our heads in an attempt to kill us."

"No chance, I hung them up too well." Fribitz turned and glanced back. "Look, Krazy Kat, you think just because you were dropped in the flames it means someone is against you. Not true. In order to purify gold, you have to put it through the fire. That's all." He returned to his painting.

"All I'm saying is, I've been at this five years, this thing about finding a cave and finding a wolf, and it's nothing more than an obsession on my part. And this obsession is killing me. There's no gold to be had."

"Krazy Kat, that's because you are the gold." Fribitz looked at him and smiled. "Now I'm going to do my special painting. Do you want to stay or leave?"

Dean snorted, snatched his flask, and walked off. Fribitz's special painting involved brushing paint with his genitals, and he was determined not to watch.

"Does this hurt?"

"No... Not yet... No... Yeah, there, stop it! Stop it now!"

"Next leg." Brad, the therapist, wearing blue scrubs and black nursing shoes, took his other ankle and flexed Dean's leg, working the knee to loosen up movement. Dean winced, noting how stiff his legs had gotten lately. He was on his belly with two hospital gowns on, one meant to cover his bare rear, and he squinted as his knee bent just a little more. His skin was healing slowly, but the hospital stay had worn him out. He was on Demerol long enough that he became constipated, and he was in the hospital long enough that they had to re-teach him to walk. Now he came back once a week to get therapy.

"That's enough, Doc."

"One more."

"I said no!" Dean spun around so fast he almost fell off the table. He rocked his legs off, stood and braced himself against the wall as he grabbed his crutches.

"I'm sorry, Dean, if I hurt you," Brad offered.

Dean turned around. "There are much deeper pains than the ones in the legs, Doc. Just let it go. Just let it go."

He pointed, and Brad gathered his clothes off the chair. Dean pulled his shirt on, thinking of his first drink of the day. Damn medications, he thought, pain pills and whiskey and pot. And still there's pain.

The therapist helped him with his pants, and he began weeping silently, wondering if the pain would ever come to an end.

The first day was a disaster.

Dean limped into class using his new cane, wearing his tweed suit, and sporting his fake eyeglasses. It was only ten in the morning, and he was already tipsy, but, he knew, he worked best when drunk.

There were thirty-five first year students in his classroom, fresh out of high school and ready for Zoology 101. After all this time, he was teaching what he wanted to teach.

He quickly glanced at his students—he already had memorized their names—and then turned and wrote his name on the blackboard.

"Ladies and gentlemen," he began, "this class will introduce you to animal anatomy and physiology, animal behavior, family, genus, species, extinction, and pretty much everything you'll need to get started on becoming a veterinarian or scientist."

He turned and faced the students, looking just over their heads. He was always nervous in front of a crowd, and it helped to not look into their eyes. He limped around the desk, knowing they were scribbling down every word they heard—first year's were like that. "You will be graded on your participation in class, a midterm and final, as well as a twenty page paper with footnotes and..."

He suddenly stumbled against his desk. A few students in the back snickered, and he gazed in their direction. "A recent injury," he explained.

"He must have injured himself opening the bottle," someone whispered. He heard a few titters.

"Among other things," he went on, focusing on his balance and steadying himself with his cane, "we will dissect a baby pig and a cat, study several animal skeletons, and view films of animals in the wild. You will be expected to know all the organs and their locations, the reproductive habits of different animals, and...."

He blinked. His mind was blank, and the room was rocking. He gripped his cane with both hands in front of him, trying to think what to say next. The students were silent for a moment, waiting, but it didn't last long.

"Look, he's really toasted."

"I can smell him from here."

"His glasses are fake. No lenses. See?"

"Fuck, he's not even looking at us. I think he's watching the clock on the back wall."

"You guys aren't nice. You think he's having a stroke?"

"Now he's really swaying."

Dean listened, embarrassed, unable to move, he felt so sick. Wanting to do something, he swung his cane and smacked the top of his desk. "Listen, you assholes, if you want to learn something..." He couldn't go on. He threw up before he passed out.

Hours later, Dean lay in a fetal position on the cot in the studio. Fribitz brought two mugs of hot cocoa and handed him one. He glanced at Fribitz, then at the dozens, hundreds, of painted and unpainted canvasses in the studio, the metal sculptures made of car parts, the stone statues, the plaster casts, the wooden carvings, the mobiles, paints, drop cloths, paintbrushes, easels, tables, all of it in the name of Fribitz's art. He carefully eased himself up to a sitting position and took a mug. "What else could possibly go wrong?"

"Well, it could be raining," Fribitz said. His bald head was splattered with oils, pastels and acrylics because of an off-site project involving a ceiling in a bar. "So how did all this happen?"

"I'm suspended with pay and under investigation for drunkenness, drug use and unprofessional behavior."

"So are you guilty?"

"Sure I am. What do you think?" He sipped some cocoa. "I also have a possible battery charge for hitting another professor with my cane."

"Guilty?"

"I don't remember, but it sounds about right. And add to that, three complaints from female students who said

I attempted to seduce them for better grades. And yes, I did do that. Who could forget that one?" He gazed at the small marshmallows floating in his cocoa. "Fribitz, I haven't been right since I got back. I lost half my foot, possibly lost my job, I feel deeply depressed, and I just really don't care about much of anything."

Fribitz nodded, stirring his cocoa with his pinky. "And it's not half a foot, Krazy Kat, it's three little toes."

"My goddam foot hurts like hell," Dean added. "Every time I go back to have it rewrapped, I see how bad it looks, and I don't think I'm healing. And it stinks too, I think I have gangrene, but the nurse says it's looking just terrific. On top of that, I lost my hotel room and half my new clothes."

Fribitz nodded. "You can stay here," he said. "There's a good diner just down the street, and I can bring in a bed if you want."

"I got money," he said. "I can go to another hotel." He pulled out his wallet to emphasize his comment, wiggling it like a toy. "That's not the point. I just can't seem to focus or get back on track." He set his wallet down. "And I have a recurring dream about the cave."

"A good dream?"

Dean shook his head. "I left things inside the cave, my mother's Bible, my brother's toy plane, my sister's records... they belonged to my family, and the first time I went to the cave, I left them inside."

"I remember you telling me," Fribitz said. "You were making an altar inside the cave to honor your family. You said your father killed them all and then shot himself. And then you were going to kill yourself and maybe join them or whatever."

Dean glared at him. "You make it sound so lackadaisical, like you're telling me the plot of a movie or play."

"Sorry." Fribitz smiled and shrugged.

"This was my family. This was a catastrophic event in my life. My sister was fourteen, and my brother was eight. They were murdered. Jesus, Fribitz, don't you get the horror of it all?"

"I'm sorry, but tell me about the dream."

"I'm sleeping with this stuff, and I'm in the cave in a sleeping bag. I have the candles lit again. I know I left candles behind six years ago, and I probably saw them when I found the cave again. But it's a very peaceful dream. And it was not real, except that I really was there under different circumstances."

"What does it mean?"

"It means I'm losing my mind. And there was something else. That dream came after another dream, where I saw my sister, but she was ten instead of fourteen, and talking as though she were fourteen. And God I missed her every time I had that dream. She would be twenty right now. Twenty. If she lived."

He reached into his briefcase and pulled out his flask. Fribitz grabbed his wrist. "C'mon, Krazy Kat, just rest up. You had enough booze and pot and other good stuff, and yeah I like it too, but you need to stop. And I promise, if you stop, I'll stop with you. You can stay here. I promise."

Dean glared at him, then pulled his wrist free and poured whiskey into his cocoa.

"Dean, C'mon, that doesn't even look good! Stop it!" He snatched the flask, spilling whiskey.

Dean leaped up and pushed him, knocking him backwards off his chair. As Fribitz tried to stand, Dean toppled and fell onto the cement floor, then climbed back up, using the cot and table for support, and snatched his cane. Fribitz stumbled up and grabbed his arm. Dean shook him off and headed for the door. "Where're you going?"

"I don't know," he said.

"You can stay here, you know."

Dean stopped and glared back at him. "No. I can't."
He charged out the front door.

Fribitz had a brief jolt of fear. He was not sure, for
once, if he would ever see his friend again.

On that day, Dean began his longest binge.

Walking down the street, he counted his money. When
he was sure he was far enough away that Fribitz couldn't
find him, he stepped into a bar and ordered a Manhat-
tan, followed by another. His dinner was peanuts and
pickled eggs. When the bar closed, he stumbled into the
rain, wandered until he found a deserted doorway, and
brought out his flask. Eventually the flask was empty
and he slept standing up in the doorway.

The next morning he found a flophouse for two dollars
a night. No bath, no toilet, but he relieved himself in the
alley before he went to his bed. He bought sacks of weed
and rolled joints. He wandered from bar to bar, bought
sandwiches at automats, occasionally spent a night in a
motel so he could shower after a week. He stayed away
from the University because he knew Fribitz lived near
there and often had art projects on campus. Nonetheless,
once a week he had to go there to pick up his check. It
was usually gone in three days.

One day the checks stopped coming. He figured he did
not do well in the investigation the university conducted.

He could have gone back to the university and dis-
puted the decision, but it was too much trouble. Instead
he panhandled. He slept behind buildings.

One day – Weeks? Months? – he saw Fribitz walking
by. His old friend once again had a full head of hair, dark
blue suit, and fedora. He didn't want to be seen, but he
didn't have a chance to blend into the crowd or turn
away, so he was determined that, if Fribitz tried to stop

him, he would shove him away and keep walking. They passed on the sidewalk, and Fribitz never acknowledged him. He didn't recognize him. Dean was shocked, and for the first time realized how much he had changed in that little time.

On that day he stopped near a mirror and looked at the homeless man he could not recognize. He smiled, and the homeless man in the mirror smiled back. "Doctor Hoover, I presume," he chortled, and walked on his way.

He continued to walk the streets, putting his hand out for money, aware of how bad he looked but not caring. Sometimes he would stand still, watching the traffic, suddenly feeling scared that he had fallen so low, realizing that he might not get back up. He fantasized about someone finding his body in the alleyway, dead of exposure, or dead from being beaten to death, or dead of just plain drunkenness, but dead nonetheless.

And then the feeling would ease, and he would walk on, begging more money, buying cheap wine, because he seldom went to bars any more, they cost too much, and he sometimes was thrown out for being so dirty. All I have to do is get a job, he told himself, and I can get back on my feet again. But he wondered if he was lying to himself, and he wondered if he even wanted to get back into that rat race.

He walked through snowy streets, wondering what month it was, wondering what happened to summer, but by now he had acquired four coats to keep warm and gloves missing the fingers. He lost his wallet somewhere, but it didn't matter as there was no money in it any way. Then one day he looked up at the falling snow through haloes of streetlamps, wondering why he felt so lonely.

That night it was snowing hard, and he found a warm place over a sewer grate spewing out steam. He lay down, a garbage bag for a pillow, newspapers for a blanket.

He was a pro at survival skills at this point, covering the newspapers with an old tarp he found at a deserted storefront. He dreamed of the cave again, wrapped in his sleeping bag, listening to the rain outside, only this time he was not sure what was real and what was not. And then he remembered his sister.

"You know what he did," Sarah said, her long, blond hair tangled with burrs, leaves and sticks, as though she had been running and rolling on the ground in the autumn forest. Dean nodded, watching her, missing her, profoundly sad. "You know what he did." She pulled a burr from her hair and angrily tossed it onto the ground.

This time he wanted to reach out and touch her, bring her back from the dead, talk to her, because all she did was repeat herself, and it was just not real. Not any more. He felt tears streaming down his cheeks.

Warm water splashing against his face woke him up. He leaped to a sitting position, surprising the bum who was urinating on him. "Oh, sorry, guy, I didn't know anybody was there. You were covered in snow. I didn't know."

The man zipped up and quickly moved on, and Dean, disgusted and angry, wiped his face with a dirty rag he found next to his foot. He pulled the tarp off his legs, then pulled off his boots and socks to examine his feet. Feeling weak, he rubbed his arches and heels, examining the wounds where three toes used to be. Despite some dark spots, the flesh was mostly pinkish and bright. His feet were at least no worse than before, and for once, except for being so dirty, his feet looked halfway healed. How long had it been? It seemed like yesterday.

He glanced at the bum walking down the street, and he longed for a drink, but remembered he was broke. "You need a job, Doctor Dean Hoover," he mumbled, his fingers rubbing the beard covering his chin. "And you need to get rid of this thing to get one."

He thought about the Salvation Army where he once bought clothes. They could help him get back on his feet, he was sure of it. "Just don't tell them you need the job for drinking money," he mumbled, "and maybe they'll help you out."

After pulling on his shoes and pulling himself together, he stood and began limping down the road, leaning into his cane, thinking of cave paintings, remembering Sarah, and wondering if he would ever get her back again. She said that once, you know what he did, but what did he do? Bitter and cold and smelling like urine, he was determined to crawl out of this hole he dug for himself, one way or the other.

Chapter Seven

"White Death"
(1965-1966)

You can do it!

He ran quickly through the trees, kicking up dust, closing in on the rabbit, the starlight making it just bright enough for him to see it dodge left, then right in its effort to lose him. He came closer, the dew flying off the ferns as he brushed past them, the air rich in smells of damp soil and decaying logs, bracket fungi and plants. And Rabbitrunner heard the voices.

Keep at it!

Don't let it get away!

You need the meat!

Rabbitrunner closed in, his legs pumping so hard he couldn't remember which one was wounded last spring, and in one swift motion he tripped the rabbit and grabbed it in his teeth, then, still running, he shook it back and forth, breaking its neck. He slowed, then stopped, dropping the carcass at his forepaws. Panting, he lifted his tail as he sniffed his new acquisition, then glanced off into the distance.

He could see them through the trees, silhouetted by the starlight, the outlines of the distant mountains where the other Hunters of his pack were killed. It was late summer, the air was turning cooler, but his body was thick with muscle from good hunting. He had recovered well from the wound in his leg, and he was as strong and fast now as he ever was. But the air was turning cooler already, and he knew that winter was waiting in the distance, White Death.

You can make it!

You can survive!

You have to survive!

Rabbitrunner turned from those thoughts and concentrated on his catch, holding the body down with a forepaw as he ripped a hind leg off with his teeth. He voraciously chewed muscle, bone, sinew, and fur, just about swallowing it whole to appease his hunger, then took another bite. In no time the rabbit was gone, and he looked up, chewing the last of it, just as the sky was turning light gray over the eastern horizon.

He had to return to Bearback.

He set off at once, not even stopping to groom the blood off his fur.

As was his habit lately, he only hunted at night, returning by daybreak to his enlarged den to sleep through the day until the next sunset, when he would hunt again. He made it a point to travel to different parts of the territory, often marking the scent markers to maintain the boundaries, though there was now nobody but him in the territory. It kept him hopeful, though, his extra efforts, for the day that he would discover a pack member who survived, a Hunter who came back after all.

As Bearback came into view, he thought about how ominous the butte had become now that he was alone. He sometimes dreamed that Bearback itself woke up, rose from the ground and lumbered off, searching for food. Bearback—a large beast with a large head and many, many teeth, and Rabbitrunner, who was enlarging his den, was no more than a mite under Bearback's skin, waiting for the day when the great beast would feel an itch, scratch, and kill him.

Rabbitrunner reached the dens as the sun rose above the horizon. Only one den appeared used, with fresh dirt spilling from its entrance and running downhill like a waterfall. He crawled a few feet into the cool darkness, made a right turn and crawled a little farther, then turned left where a chamber for a dam and her cubs used to be. He continued down into the dark until he entered a chamber large enough for six adult Hunters. A tunnel extended beyond that, going deeper still, part of Rabbitrunner's labors. Should the voices in his head ever materialize, he would have room for them all.

The den was a place of darkness, where he moved by touch and memory. The chamber had the smell of fresh dirt, hair and sweat from his body, and the few bones left over from a meal or two. It was his home, his hiding place, his womb. It was all he had left of his pack, that, and the voices.

Each day led into the next, and the air turned cold, and the leaves trickled from the branches in the trees. Rabbitrunner went out hunting during cold, rainy nights when the air was strong with the scent of wet leaves, but animal scents were harder to find these days. The nights grew colder, the wind stronger, but he still went each night to a different part of the territory, relying more on field mice and ground squirrels than on rabbits, woodchucks, and beavers.

Whenever he did catch something, he would sometimes

play a game by himself, tossing the body into the air and catching it again in his teeth, then tossing it again, trying to create some sense of fun. Then he'd stop, look around, feeling like a fool, and eat as the rain fell around him.

One night the air turned extremely cold, and by the time he returned to the den, there was frost on the grass and ground. Several nights later, snowflakes began falling from a dark, cloudy sky, the clouds so thick the moonlight couldn't even break through. That night he caught several mice and a groundhog, the night after that, a rabbit, and the next night nothing.

Then the snow fell harder.

You've got to survive.

Survive.

For all of us.

Every night, as he left the den, he listened to the voices in his head, his only companions. Every night, as he crawled from the den, feeling hungry and cold despite his thick fur, he'd look through the bare trees down the white slope of Bearback, moonlight reflecting bright off the snow when the sky was clear, or if cloudy, the snowy landscape looked like a dark dream of desolation. Every night, he would sniff the air for smells of food and find none. His tail would lower as he proceeded downhill, and some nights, he might catch something, and most nights, he wouldn't.

His fur grew sticky from lack of grooming after each kill, making it less protective from the cold, but he was too worried about finding food to think about grooming. He grew thinner, his ribs were making outlines around his chest, his belly was growing concave, and his legs, losing their mass, seemed to always be shaking.

On nights when he had traveled too far to get back to

the den before daylight, he would curl up beneath a low-hanging pine bough with his thick-haired tail curling over his nose and paw pads as he slept. It was nowhere near as warm as it was inside the den, but at least he could sleep until nightfall, out of sight from the sky.

One night passed when he caught nothing. There had been other nights of hunting like that, but this time he knew there would be no more small animals to be hunted for the rest of the winter. He was coming to the end of the time when he could find any meat at all. Night after night he desperately wandered the territory, searching for something to ease his hunger, but there was nothing to be hunted. Once in awhile he caught the scent of a moose, but he had no pack to help him bring it down, and he could not bring it down himself.

He was getting used to the hunger pangs, sometimes easing them by eating snow or bark off the side of a tree, but the weakness was something else, the feeling that he was always on the verge of collapsing, the partial blurring of his eyesight, the occasional dizziness and tunnel vision.

One night he spotted a lone deer. He began running after it, chasing it through a field of thick snow. They went on for a while, but the deer was getting too far ahead, and Rabbitrunner, his body weary, his lungs bellowing to get enough air, came to a stop and watched the deer run from sight. The night was still young, but he turned and headed for Bearback, knowing that he didn't have the energy to go much further.

The next night he was at the edge of his territory when, fighting his own anxiety, he crossed over the boundary, barely smelling the scent posts but knowing the invisible line he was breaching.

He hadn't traveled far when he spotted a pack of Hunters, charging at him over a hill, Solohunter and his pack. Rabbitrunner turned and ran back the way he came, the

Hunters close on his tail until he crossed back over onto his side. Solohunter's pack stopped at the scent markers as though coming to the edge of a cliff. They watched him until he was out of sight, then returned to their trek along their own territory, re-marking the scent-posts as they went.

I can't survive on my own, Rabbitrunner thought, as he watched their blurry shapes from a distance. He wandered south, keeping the border to his left, thinking, I have to join another pack, because I can't survive on my own.

Several nights later, he crossed into Blackpaw's territory, with the same results. Blackpaw's pack happened to be near the border when they spotted him. Again, he was driven back over the boundary into his territory.

He no longer felt the hunger now, only the extreme weariness. Every time he went to sleep under a log or pine bough, he wondered if he would wake up, because he felt so tired, he thought he would be dead soon.

Several nights later he approached Dirtscratcher's territory, cautiously crossing over the boundary. He spotted several Hunters from the Dirtscratcher Pack, but no sooner had they picked up his scent than they charged at him, snarling and snapping. Rabbitrunner turned and ran, bitter disappointment raging inside as he raced back to his boundary. Then he noticed they were closing in, and he tried to go faster, but he was already tired and gasping for breath. He collapsed on the snow, rolled onto his back with his neck and belly exposed in a plea for mercy.

The first Hunter who reached him bit his flank, teeth penetrating right down to the bone. Rabbitrunner ki-yii-ed and twisted around, just as a second Hunter tried to sink his teeth into his throat. Another grabbed the other hind leg, and the next sank his teeth into Rabbitrunner's gut.

The pain was excruciating, pulling his consciousness up through the fog as he twisted and turned and kicked, realizing that the Hunters were going to kill him soon.

Finally he just stopped moving, feeling pain each time teeth sank into him, as the Hunters got better grips on his limbs and body, and he listened lethargically to the snarls as he felt his body being dragged through the snow like a piece of meat. He wondered how much longer it would be before he died. By the light of the stars and the moon, he looked up and saw his own blood, black and wet, on their faces. I don't want to die, he thought.

Then he heard a familiar voice next to his ear, *You fool! Get yourself out of there! Survive!* It was Newmoon.

With the last of his energy, Rabbitrunner rose up and bit hard into a Hunter's head, the one tearing at his belly. The Hunter howled and leaped away, whining in pain, his left eye punctured beyond healing. Rabbitrunner twisted back and forth, snarling and kicking and baring his teeth, spurred on by the pain, and spurred on by his one successful bite. The remaining Hunters, surprised by the burst of energy, backed away. Rabbitrunner rolled onto his paws and stood, facing them, his teeth bared.

They eased back further, not expecting such aggressiveness from a Hunter they were in the middle of killing. Before they could renew their attack, he turned and ran again for the border. He heard them running behind him, all but the one whose eye he ripped out, and he could hear Newmoon's voice. *Survive! Survive!*

There was no way he could outrun them, but he kept on running. They were right behind him now, snarling, and one snapped at his bloody rump, missing and trying again. Rabbitrunner's head was spinning, the tunnel vision was starting, and he knew that they were right behind him, knew that they would soon have him down again.

And then the Hunters suddenly stopped as though coming to a great river. Rabbitrunner, his tail pulled up between his legs, his ears held flat against his head, looked back as he slowed down. The other Hunters stood still, watching him, not moving any further. He was back in his own territory. They had stopped at his scent markers.

Rabbitrunner continued on, limping until he could no longer see them when he looked back. He collapsed in the snow, his consciousness fading, and he drifted off into a dreamless sleep.

He woke once, finding himself in the open in the daylight of morning, but he was too weak to move. He stayed there, lying in the snow, until he dozed off again. When he woke a second time, shivering and feverish, he saw the full moon in a cloudless sky.

He rose stiffly, feeling pain everywhere. He finally caught his balance, stood on his paws, looked down, saw the outline of his body in the snow, the black stains where his blood spotted the snow. Apathetic and drained, he turned and limped away, thinking of nothing but reaching Bearback.

And then he changed direction.

He was rested up now, but still very weak, still starving, needing food. And he was still lonely. The memory of Newmoon's voice in his head brought back thoughts of the pack. He needed to join a pack—he needed the companionship, as well as the food. As he walked, a large flap of skin dangled from his body, exposing a raw area on his stomach, a reminder of the attack. Various puncture wounds and bruises slowed him down and stiffened his body so that he walked like an old Hunter about to die. Not even Old Bull walked this bad, he thought.

By the time the moon was across the sky and the eastern horizon was turning gray, he was approaching the Starwatcher territory. This time he didn't even get a chance to cross the boundary; the Starwatcher Pack was there, marking their scent-posts with urine to leave a fresh marker at their border. They stopped as one and eyed Rabbitrunner, ready to defend their land. Rabbitrunner stopped, watched them and turned around, limping away with his tail hanging low.

He slept beneath a rock ledge, partially protected from the wind, until the next night, when he roused himself and continued on his way. The night passed, and the sun was rising as he crossed into the Tailless Territory. If the Tailless Pack did not allow him to join them, his chances of survival would be very small.

This time he did not hide from the sun. He limped on slowly, looking for some sign of the pack. He knew they were close; he could pick up their scents on the wind. He wandered deeper into their territory, aware of how far he was leaving his own boundary behind. He was coming over another hill when he spotted two Hunters from the Tailless Pack heading towards him through the trees.

He froze. As weary as he was, he knew he didn't have enough fight in him to defend himself from even one Hunter. He didn't have the energy to run. His only hope was that they would accept him into the pack. Seeing them coming closer, he knew he should have lowered himself to the ground as a sign of obeisance and a plea for pity, rolled onto his back, exposed his throat, but instead he stood straight, ears forward, and waited.

The Hunters were upwind, and didn't notice him until they'd practically run into him. They stopped when they saw him, their hackles up. Rabbitrunner's hackles went up, too. They still might accept him into the pack, but he was beginning to doubt it. More likely they'd attack, he thought, glancing from one to the other.

But they didn't attack. The two Hunters turned and ran off, glancing back over their shoulders before disappearing from sight. Rabbitrunner glanced over his own shoulder to see what they were running from.

What he could not see was his own appearance. His fur and face were stained and matted by his own blood. A huge flap of skin dangled from his belly, which looked like a cavity between his ribs and his pelvis. He was, in fact, little more than skeleton and skin. His hipbones protruded like rocks exposed through the snow by the wind; the same for his ribs, his shoulder blades, his backbone.

But his size was his most frightening feature. He stood a head taller than the other Hunters. That, combined with his tattered appearance, scared them off. Sighing, Rabbitrunner turned and limped towards his territory.

The sun was setting beyond the mountains two days later as he was climbing Bearback's snowy slope. He reached the clearing and crawled into his den. On the way back, he had stopped periodically to chew on snow and ice, but he actually didn't feel hungry any more. His tongue felt dry and bloated in his mouth. His paws were swollen and felt numb. His consciousness seemed to fade in and out, so that he felt like he had covered long stretches in his sleep. His vision was blurring and tunneling, but he was getting used to it. He was falling apart. When he crawled down the tunnel into the chamber, he curled up and fell asleep.

He remembered waking once after he urinated over himself, and he thought about hunting, but it didn't seem worth the effort, so he curled back up and again dozed off to sleep.

He dreamed of his pack—Treepisser, Bullmoosekiller,

Deerchaser, Newmoon, Sleepfarter and Ravenplay, and as he always did, he heard them, all of them, talking inside his head. This time he saw them, for awhile, until snow fell around them, and the White Death took them away, their shapes disappearing into the falling snow.

Lost, alone, Rabbitrunner found himself running up a mountainside, neither pain nor hunger in his body. The climb up the mountain through falling snowflakes seemed effortless. He felt a deep anxiety, barely able to see what was ahead of him through the blowing snow. As he approached the top, he saw a large, white-furred figure ahead of him, standing on the summit, looking away.

It's Cloudwalker, he thought, I found Cloudwalker! He saw the large, white-plumed tail half-raised, the muscular body tensed, the ears on the white head back flat against the skull, signs of being threatened, and he wondered what Cloudwalker was seeing through the falling snow. White neck and shoulder hairs were bristling, and his fur, blowing in the strong mountain wind, was flecked by blood.

Rabbitrunner crawled closer, his claws gripping icy rock. "Cloudwalker!" Rabbitrunner snarled. "We're alone! There are no others who will be with us. Who will run with us? We're alone, you and I, alone! What do we do now?"

Survive, Cloudwalker growled. *Survive. Nothing more.* And even as he growled, his deep throaty voice like the storm, the clouds around him thickened and swallowed him up, and Rabbitrunner could no longer see the living legend of his pack. He couldn't even see the rocks beneath his paws.

He sat up with a jerk and leaped up, trying to wander away, but instead walked into a wall of his chamber. He backed up a step and vigorously shook his head. His nose throbbed. It was as though he was blind, the darkness was that thick and eternal. The air was stale and smelled of sweat and ammonia. It was all his own smell, none of it was Cloudwalker or any other Hunter.

He settled down again, remembering the dream, and then thinking over the last few days, being driven away from one pack after another. Had he not been able to cross back over his scent-markers back into his own territory, he would have been killed. Since the first time he had crossed over a boundary, back just before he'd lost his pack, it had grown easier, and it had saved his life several times, because the Hunters of the other packs would not cross over the scent-markers he'd made, and...

"Wait a minute," Rabbitrunner snarled. "I haven't marked the scent-posts since..." Since when? It had been so long he couldn't remember. Or maybe he had marked them and forgotten.

He stood up in the chamber, bumping his head in the dark, wincing, feeling weak and dizzy. He was shivering from the cold, but he couldn't get the dream out of his head, or the question about the scent-posts. "Here I am starving to death," he muttered, "and all I can worry about is whether or not I remembered to piss on the stupid scent-post!"

Survive!

"What?" Rabbitrunner banged his head on rock again before realizing it was just another voice in his head. "Oh, shut up!"

Survive!

You can survive!

You can make it through the White Death!

Cloudwalker even told you that you could!

"Cloudwalker is a dream!" Rabbitrunner snarled in the darkness. "I dreamed him; he isn't real."

And I am?

"I dreamed Cloudwalker. I've never seen him but in my dreams. I've never touched him. I only heard stories—

dreams and stories!"
But you know he's real!
You've seen what he has done!
You've smelled his scent!
You've seen his paw print!
You know!

"Shut up!" Rabbitrunner puled, walking into the wall again. He knew they were all dead, but their voices remained, haunting him.

Deerchaser heard voices, he remembered. Did this mean he would end up as crazy as Deerchaser? Were the worms in his body, too? Would he be shitting worms someday?

He crawled through the tunnel and out of the den, trying to get away from the voices. Stumbling downhill through the snow, he felt comforted by the starlight. Then he noticed a gray line at the eastern horizon, where the sun would soon be rising.

He trembled, partly because the cold wind blew against his matted fur and partly because he feared daylight; it was the rising of the sun that brought Bigbird. His tattered left ear, a reminder of a punishment when he was a cub, throbbed as he thought about returning to the den, but he didn't want to be inside now.

Two of his wounds were open again. The flap of skin on his belly and the exposed flesh stung miserably. And his tattered ear throbbed—but that wasn't right. That wound, his ear, healed years ago. Pawsore took off half his ear when he was a cub to teach him there were some things a Hunter didn't do.

Rabbitrunner gazed down the slope of Bearback. A fresh snow covered everything. The landscape glowed with snow. "I've got to eat." Rabbitrunner sighed. "I've got to hunt." He raised his nose and sniffed the air. No smell of meat, no animal scent, nothing. Despite the rising sun he started down Bearback, a lumbering, weary skeleton covered by blood-stained fur.

He traveled for days and nights, stopping just long enough to rest and eat snow. He saw few signs of something to hunt, and when he did, it was either a moose or a deer. His strength was ebbing, and his poor vision was getting worse. The sunlight no longer bothered him—why worry about Bigbird when you're starving to death?

At one point he sat for a rest at the edge of his territory, scooping up a mouth of snow to ease his hunger when he picked up the scent of rabbit. His head shot up and he looked back and forth, drooling. Then he bent down, noticing a mound of snow just ahead of him. He began digging with his forepaw, his heart beating, until he uncovered the frozen half-carcass.

Some animal, a fox maybe, was probably scared off halfway through its meal and never came back. But none of that mattered to Rabbitrunner as he voraciously chewed the hard, frozen meat and swallowed it in chunks. It was gone in seconds, and Rabbitrunner sat, licked his chops and sniffed the hole where he found it, as though he might find more.

It was hardly anything, the half-rabbit he ate, but he settled down as though he'd just finished feasting on a deer. He finally got around to grooming himself, licking blood and dirt off his fur, then he curled up for a long nap.

When he woke, he smelled meat again, this time something further away, but meat nonetheless, fresh meat, not like the frozen rabbit. He gazed up at the stars, then sniffed the air again; meat, warm blood, meat, upwind, south, right across the border, coming from the Dirtscratcher Territory.

The little bit of rabbit he ate must have made him

brave. "So I can't join your pack, can I?" he growled softly. "So I have to survive on my own, do I? Well, let's see how well I do then, shall we?" With that, he rose and headed towards the Dirtscratcher Territory.

The cold wind smelled metallic, which meant a snowstorm was coming. There was also the scent of deer blood in the air, and the scent of Hunters, many Hunters. But Rabbitrunner was downwind, and he was determined to use that advantage for all it was worth.

Huddled down in the snow, he gazed from his perch on the hill to the carcass of the deer and the Hunters sleeping around it. Curled up with their bushy tails wrapped around their noses and paws, the Dirtscratcher Hunters slept heavily, dark shapes in the snow. The deer carcass had been chewed here and there, but not much else had been done to it. They must have caught a deer or two before this one, he thought. They looked well-fed.

"If they catch me, they kill me," Rabbitrunner muttered, drooling as he stared at the dead deer. "If I don't eat, I'll starve to death. Which is worse? I never could make up my mind on an empty stomach."

He slowly crept towards the carcass, his head held low as his gaze went from the deer to the Hunters. They almost killed him the last time, and he didn't particularly want to give them a second chance. He made very little noise, just his paws crunching through the snow, and that was drowned out by the wind.

When he reached the deer he was shivering, not from the cold but because he was surrounded on all sides by them. He lovingly sniffed the carcass, his head spinning from the powerful smell of blood. Saliva dripped from the corners of his mouth onto the trampled snow. The deer's intestines were long gone, all the viscera were gone, nothing left but a gaping cavity that led beneath the ribcage. But the legs and the rest of the body seemed virtually intact.

Rabbitrunner licked his lips, and the sound of it made him shudder, but he looked around at the sleeping Hunters, grateful they hadn't noticed. He couldn't eat right there, that was obvious, but neither could he drag the carcass away with him. Not only would it be too noisy but he was too weak to do so.

But maybe, he thought, maybe, he could just take one leg!

One of the deer's rear legs, thick with muscle, jutted out over the snow like a low-hanging limb from a tree. The muscle beneath the leg was mostly chewed away, probably by one of the Hunters trying to get at the guts. If he could chew apart the muscle over the hipbone, he would get the whole leg loose. He could take the leg away with him and eat it at his leisure. But he had to be quiet at his thievery.

He gently bit into the meat at the hip. The carcass was cold, but at least it wasn't frozen. Still, the skin and flesh were tough, and it was difficult to separate it without making some noise.

A Hunter stirred in his sleep. Rabbitrunner froze. The Hunter stretched his legs across the snow, rolled onto his other side and curled up again, never once opening his eyes. Rabbitrunner let out his breath and went back to nibbling on the hip. His lips were pulled away from his teeth, making him look like he was grimacing, as his teeth sheared through muscle a little bit at a time.

He kept one forepaw on the deer's back for stability. He was careful with every action now, despite the maddening taste of deer blood, and he worked as quickly as possible.

He glanced once at the sky, watching clouds roll slowly overhead, extinguishing the stars. His body trembled with anticipation and fear as he continued gnawing. His stomach growled with renewed hunger, growled so loud he stopped and looked around to see if the others might wake, but they didn't, and he continued with his task.

He bit through a tendon and the leg snapped free. The deer hoof plopped into the snow with a hard thud.

A Hunter raised his head and looked at Rabbitrunner, who, terrorized, picked up the leg in his jaws and took off running. The Hunter leaped up after him, snarling loud enough to wake the others.

Rabbitrunner dashed towards his territory, trying not to think about what happened last time and what could happen this time. He had a head start, but the weight of the leg slowed him down, and he could hear the sounds of the paws pounding the snow growing louder behind him.

It was all he could do to keep running. They were right behind him now. One snapped at his tail and came away with a mouthful of long hairs. Another tried to grab a hind leg in mid-stride to trip him up but missed. One Hunter now ran beside him, snarling and trying to find a good target for his teeth.

Rabbitrunner leaned one way, slamming his shoulder into the other Hunter, who managed to keep on running beside him. He drew closer again, baring his teeth, knowing that if he could bite onto Rabbitrunner's shoulder and hold on, he could drag him onto the snow where the others could finish him off. Rabbitrunner was thinking of the same thing. He jerked his head sideways, catching the Hunter in the eye with the deer hoof. The Hunter yelped and fell back.

Then they all stopped, and Rabbitrunner found himself running alone. He had reached his own territory. He slowed to a trot and glanced back at them over his shoulder, spotting the Hunter he'd just poked in the eye, and the other one, who lost an eye to him days before.

"Mess with me," Rabbitrunner mumbled, despite the leg in his mouth, "and I'll make you all half-blind!"

He put some distance between himself and the Dirtscratcher Pack before he crawled beneath the bough of a small spruce and fell asleep. The snowstorm hit while he was asleep, and was over before he woke. When he felt rested enough, he ate the deer meat, gnawing the bones clean. His belly was actually full for once, and he sat there beneath the spruce bough, astonished by the feeling.

He ate some snow to quench his thirst, then glanced in the direction of the Dirtscratcher Pack. "So I can't join your pack, can I?" he snarled, feeling amazingly confident with a full belly. "Well, I'm not dead yet, am I? Not yet!"

He rose, stepped out from beneath the bough into the sunlight, and headed for Bearback.

His strength returned slowly after that. His wounds healed, leaving small and large scars over his body, including a patch of bare skin across his belly. Sometimes he hunted, whenever he picked up the scent of a rabbit or other small animal, but more often than not he crossed over into other territories, approached the Hunters and their meat from downwind and stole off—usually without them knowing it—with part of their kill. He became adept at his thievery, and though he knew that stealing meat was not the Way of the Hunter, he was determined to do what he had to do to survive.

By spring, he was still skeletally thin; his ribs and hipbones seemed to jut out of his body. More often hungry than not, it didn't seem to bother him anymore; he somehow managed to keep on moving, and his vision even cleared up. He was ungroomed; his fur matted and filthy with blood and dirt, giving him a sickly appearance, but that didn't bother him, either. All that mattered to him was that he made it through the winter.

You survived this far.

"Yeah, now shut up," Rabbitrunner mumbled to the voices in his head as he wandered up Bearback one day.

But you survived. And you'll keep on surviving.

Rabbitrunner looked up at the full moon as he came to the den clearing. "I'm not dead yet," he snarled. "Not yet." They were once the words of Thickfur, the legendary Hunter, spoken when he was confronting Father Sky. He remembered that story, and he remembered that it brought an uneasy truce between enemies. What he needed, though, was a truce with hunger.

He stopped and looked around. The snow was melting, and buds were appearing on the tree branches, grass was pushing up, the air smelled of mud and dirt but more important than that, it smelled of animals, meat, food, which meant good hunting.

Look!

It was Newmoon's voice this time, followed by Pawsore's, as they seemed to take turns talking to him.

Do you see Father Sky's bad eye?

Do you suppose he sees?

Do you suppose he cares?

"Why should he?" Rabbitrunner growled, sitting down. "Why should I care about him? He's not in my pack!" A gentle breeze blew against his sticky pelage and sang into his tattered ear. He noticed a maple sapling nearby he hadn't noticed before.

See that tree?

Remember when it was a sprout?

Like you, it survived the winter.

And it will continue surviving...

...like you.

"Maybe," Rabbitrunner said, sniffing the air and thinking about hunting. But he was tired, and needed to rest

first. He took one last glance at the moon before mutter-
ing, "I'm not dead yet," then crawled into the den.

Chapter Eight

"Recruits"
(Summer, 1966)

Patty Tilton stubbed out the L & M cigarette, then retied her black ponytail, this time a little higher, on the back of her head. Zachary Flint came from the storage room carrying a full aluminum keg in his meaty arms as through it were nothing more than an oversized football. He grunted as he shoved it under the bar, and as he tapped the keg, his fat, arthritic fingers fumbling with hoses and connectors, he hummed to himself as he puffed the tail end of a Cuban cigar. His bald head reflected the light as he stood up, wiping his hands.

The Cuban cigars were another story. Before the Cuban missile crisis, as it was told, two men bought up every Cuban cigar they could get their hands on—John F. Kennedy in Washington, D.C., and Zachary Flint in Caleb, Minnesota. It was even rumored that Flint inherited the last of Kennedy's cigars when he was assassinated, and it was said that, on the day Flint smoked the last one, the Cold War would end so he could get some more.

Patty lit another cigarette, then checked her wristwatch. "Eleven o'clock, Zack," she said.

Flint reached into his apron pocket, pulled out a steel ring that jingled with keys and tossed it. Patty caught it and walked to the door, turning the "open" sign around as she unlocked it. As she walked back, she stopped by the wall, running a hand over a bearskin and noticing it was dusty. She made a mental note to clean the skins and stuffed heads—Flint would never think to do it—before going to the bar for her tray.

Timothy Cowan and Parker Roberts came in and took a table near the back. Patty felt their eyes on her, but she always made it a point to make them wait before serving them. When she finally walked over, she glanced first at one, then at the other, as though pointing a double-barreled shotgun as a warning. "What'll it be, boys?"

Tim quickly looked away, gazing at the animal heads he had seen so many times before, but Parker grinned, his own gaze like a laser beam. "Two bottles of St. Pauli Girl," he said. She wrote down the order and was about to walk away when Parker grabbed her free hand and stopped her. "And when do you get off work?" he said, knowing full well what the answer was.

"Long past your bedtime, kid," Patty said, her face stern. "Didn't your mother ever tell you that grabbing people's hands was rude?"

"Well," Parker said, grinning. "Like the song says, 'I wanna hold your hand!' That goes for the rest of you, too."

Tim laughed, still looking away. He was actually embarrassed by Parker's actions, but he had been Parker's laugh track for so long that the habit was hard to break.

Patty glanced from Tim to Parker, disgusted with them both. But instead, she grinned at Parker and said, "That's a lovely compliment!" She distracted him just enough so that she could move her hand, grip his fingers and squeeze tight.

"Hey!" Parker shouted, grimacing and pulling his hand back. Tim still laughed.

"It's a shame I didn't bring my chainsaw today," Patty said, smirking. "I could've fixed it so I could hold your hand all day, whether you were here or not." She walked off to get the beers.

"Stupid bitch!" Parker muttered, never noticing how carefully Flint was watching him from the bar. He didn't like the two young men. Cowan and Roberts always hung around together, and had been caught more than once trying to steal a car or break into a house. They rode around town in the red 1965 Plymouth Valiant Cowan's father bought him for his high school graduation. They were both nineteen, both wearing crew cuts as though belonging to a gang of only two members, and wherever Parker went, Timothy was tagging along. Sheriff Tanner had arrested them three times over the last couple years, but each time, to Tanner's dismay, Judge Birch had gone lenient and given them suspended sentences.

Flint could've thrown them out of the Crooked River at any time, but he preferred to do things his own way. Given their well-known weakness for temptation, it was only a matter of time before Parker and Tim decided to snatch a few dollars from his till, which suited him just fine. There were no technicalities, leniency, or probation in Flint's courtroom, where the bailiff was a Louisville Slugger under the counter named Macbeth. He was looking forward to the day he got to use it.

He went back to the storeroom with the empty keg in his arms and a minute later was returning with another full keg when a man pushed through the door, leaping to the floor as something flew in a blur over his head. An arrow passed clear through the tavern, hitting the bull's-eye of the dartboard in back and embedding itself into the woodwork behind it.

"Kee-rist!" Flint gasped, almost dropping the keg on his foot as he lowered it to the floor, then reached under the bar for his Louisville slugger. "Who the hell..." The words caught in his throat as a dozen men pushed through the door, laughing, and dragging in four dead wolves, dropping them onto the large, round oak table in the middle of the room.

"Hey! Hey! Hey!" Flint shouted, carrying Macbeth and pointing as he came around the bar. "Get those fucking things out of here! This ain't no meat market! Who the hell is behind all this?"

He turned just in time to see Jessie Armstrong step through the door. His sweat stained sleeveless t-shirt was splattered with blood. His gray-black hair was recently cut, a crew cut so neat it contrasted painfully with the gray beard stubble on his chin. His thick football player neck bore the trademark dirty red bandana, damp with sweat. "Goddam it, Cutter!" Flint yelled, shaking the baseball bat. "What was I thinking of? I shoulda known it was you, you sonovabitch! My chili ain't good enough for you; you wanna bring your own lunch now? Want some ketchup with your wolves?"

The men in the tavern were laughing uncontrollably, but Flint was only concerned with Cutter. Then he noticed the bow in Cutter's hands, and he glanced at the arrow with red-red-black fletching poking out of the dartboard. "You sonovabitch, Cutter," he growled, looking from arrow to archer. The men went silent; Flint just reached another plateau of anger. He calmly tapped Macbeth into his palm. "You wanna smash up my tavern, let's you and I smash it up together."

Cutter handed his bow and quiver to Ben Rose and stepped closer to Flint, his hands raised in surrender as he sported his most disarming smile. "Aw, c'mon, Flint, you misunderstand me! I apologize! No hard feelings, okay?" In his left hand, hidden from the view of the other men, was a fifty dollar bill, more than enough to make up for the dartboard and the wolves on the table. Flint glared at Cutter and snatched the bill, holding it up to the light, unconcerned that any of the men could see his mercenary side as he stuffed the bill into his apron pocket and held Macbeth up again.

The patrons of the Crooked River Tavern knew Macbeth well, some of them on a more personal level than others. The Louisville Slugger had brown stains on its wooden surface, highlighting the grain that they suspected was dried blood stains, and notches along the grip to mark every broken bone and cracked skull it left behind.

"I believe," Flint said, staring coldly into Cutter's eyes, "that the damage might be a little more extensive than that." In other words, the money was more than enough for damages, but Flint was pissed off, and Cutter would have to pay for that, too.

Cutter grinned, reached into his pocket and pulled out another fifty dollar bill. Macbeth lowered, certain now that its master was satisfied. Flint snatched the second bill and was about to leave when Cutter pulled out a third fifty. "Drinks for everyone," he said. "until this is gone." Flint snorted, took the bill and headed back behind the bar, returning Macbeth to its place.

When Patty returned from the storeroom, he handed her one of the bills and told her to keep track of the tab until the fifty was spent. As she picked up her tray and went to the big table to take orders, he quietly folded another fifty into a small cube so it couldn't be recognized right away and dropped it into Patty's tip jar behind the bar. A single woman with three boys needed all the help she could get, though Patty wasn't the kind of woman who would ask.

Cutter rolled a cigarette and lit it, looking at the men

gathered around the big table. They were talking and laughing about the four dead wolves, pointing at the jagged wounds made by arrows. He knew he had their full attention.

Five more men entered, and as Patty went around and took orders, Cutter pulled another arrow from the quiver held by the man next to him. "Listen up!" he shouted. Conversations tapered off as all eyes turned his way. "This is a hunting man's tavern!" Cutter said. "No faggots, Bambi lovers, teddy-bear huggers, nature-loving weenies or flower-picking pansies allowed!" As the men laughed, he took another drag and gazed at Tim and Parker in back, who seemed to melt under his gaze. Then he glanced at the men around the big table. "I need hunters!" he said. "Hunters to work with me! I'm looking for the Shadow Wolf!"

The laugher died down. "But nobody knows where to find the Shadow Wolf!" someone said.

"He's out in the woods chasing Bambi and flower-picking pansies!" someone else shouted, and the men laughed again.

Cutter didn't even crack a smile. "Now, nobody seems to have seen him, but we all know about him, don't we, fellas?" He used the arrow to point at the wall behind the bar.

Besides the black-and-white television on a stand just over Flint's head playing an "I Love Lucy" rerun with the sound off, besides the parade of eight-by-ten black-and-white autographed glossies of football and baseball players, including Joe DiMaggio, Honus Wagner, Sandy Koufax, Willie Mays, Jim Brown, and Joe Namath, besides the mirrors and shelves of bottles of domestic and foreign beers, a few skins, stuffed squirrels, bleached bear and cougar skulls, there was a line of a dozen plaster casts Flint had been hanging behind the bar for the last few years, each one having the form of the large wolf paw print in reverse, convex instead of concave. Nobody had really seen the wolf, except for very brief encounters, but many had seen that paw print.

Everybody in the tavern knew the paw prints were made by the Shadow Wolf. Each cast had a hand-printed label beneath it: "Danberry Farm, 1965"—"Double-J Ranch, 1962"—"Nolan's Woods, February 3, 1966"—"Hester Lake, 1964."

"I have a proposition," Cutter said, tapping his chest with the arrowhead. "I want that wolf. I'm offering five thousand dollars to the man who helps me bag him. Five thousand dollars! But there's just one stipulation." The arrow pointed from man to man. "I have to be the one who gets him. I have to be the one who kills him."

Clint Howell, a farmer from down the road, settled at a table by the window that was crowded by fly-specked dusty neon signs. He took the Hamm's offered by Patty and focused his eyes on Cutter. "I've been hearing about this Shadow Wolf for about a couple of years now, most of it coming from you. How do I know it isn't a hoax?"

"How do you know it is a hoax?" Cutter said.

"I dunno," Clint said, scratching his long, white hair with a calloused hand. "But I'll tell you this: I've heard talk about the Loch Ness monster for years, but no one's caught one yet. And who ever caught an Abominable Snowman, or a Bigfoot? Who here has seen a flying saucer? It's bullshit, I say."

"Bullshit yourself!" Jake Moss said, his fist pounding the table to quiet the other men. "I lost two cows to something that tore out their throats, and all I found was one big wolf paw print. I doubt anybody would do a thing like that as a joke!"

"Yeah," Clint said. "One paw print! What animal leaves just one paw print behind? I ask you? And, yeah, it does sound like someone's playing games!"

"What would you know?" Jake said. "You don't have to worry about a wolf attacking your corn. Hell, you don't even hunt!"

"Yer right," Clint said, sipping his beer. "I don't hunt. And this here's a hunting tavern. I guess I should go to a walleye fishing tavern next time." He smiled as several men laughed. "Someone's just playing a joke. There ain't no wolf that big goin' around and still no one sees it."

"Well, when I bring the wolf's body in here," Cutter said, "and show him to you, then you and I can laugh at the joke all over again."

Flint watched as he wiped a beer glass dry. He gazed at the four dead wolves dripping blood on the big table, knowing what Cutter was doing, playing the snake oil salesman. It wasn't the Cutter he knew. He was grand-standing, attracting attention to himself. Flint could tolerate a little blood on the big table as long as Cutter didn't try skinning the wolves on the pool table, and he had no complaints against the customers coming in to watch the show, but the way Cutter was acting seemed downright bizarre.

The men were now arguing over the chances of catching the Shadow Wolf when Jack Fipps asked Joe Rayford a question, raising his eyebrows. "Hold it, hold it!" Joe shouted, holding up his hands until he got everybody's attention. "I just want to know one thing." He pointed directly at Cutter. "Just where in the hell do you think you are going to get five thousand dollars? Ever since I've known you, you're complained about being broke. There's no longer a bounty on wolves, so you can't be making money that way. Ben Rose here..." He patted Ben on the shoulder. Ben adjusted his cap and looked up. "Ben has had to hire you on time and time again just so you could get grocery money..."

"Beer money," Cutter corrected.

"Beer money," Joe amended. "So how are you gonna come up with five grand?"

Ben grinned as he took off his New York Yankee cap and ran his fingers through his curly, red hair. He knew Cutter had enough cash hidden to finance a war against Cuba.

Cutter looked sheepishly at Joe. "I was shooting craps with the Ojibway at the lodge, and it was my lucky night." The men laughed. "I had that money saved, Joe, for years now. I'd been thinking about buying a new pickup, a few luxuries for the cabin, but decided on this instead. It's all there, five thousand, in a jar at my cabin."

At the back of the Crooked River, Timothy Cowan and Parker Roberts glanced at each other, thinking the same thought.

"The money's all counted out," Cutter went on, "ready to go, and it will go to whoever has done the most to help me catch the wolf. The Shadow Wolf is real, fellas, and as far as I'm concerned, he belongs to me!"

"And how do you know he's a he?" Joe asked.

Cutter shrugged. "Well, he's a he until I kill him and find out otherwise." The men around the table laughed.

"And you're gonna shoot it with a bow and arrow?" Glen Joslin asked, pointing at Cutter's archery equipment. "Are you crazy?"

"Sure he is," Joe said, pointing at the dart board with the arrow shaft protruding from its center.

"Hell, Glenn," Cutter said, leaning over the table. "I've hunted and killed bears with bow and arrow."

"That was twenty years ago, Cutter."

"I can get close enough to use this," he held up his bow and arrow. "Once I find him."

"So why not a good high-powered rifle with a scope?"

Cutter smiled, "Let's just say I'm giving the wolf a

fighting chance."

"Seems to me the wolf already got a chance," Glenn said. "Nobody's seen the damn thing. How you gonna find it?"

Cutter nodded at Ben, who cleared the table of beer bottles, wiped the wet rings with a handful of paper napkins, and unraveled a large, rolled-up map of Minnesota in front of him. Several men reached over to help hold the map open as others bent closer.

"Now," Cutter said, using the arrow to point at the red dots he'd make on the map. "Signs of the Shadow Wolf have been found in Lake, Roseau, Buford, Caleb and St. Louis counties, as well as a few spots on the Canadian side of the border. Obviously the Shadow Wolf likes to travel, and he doesn't want to be seen."

"So if this wolf really exists," Clint said from his seat by the window, "and he's doing all this running around, then what's his reason? What the hell is he doing?"

"Goddam, Clint, haven't you been paying attention?" Jake said. "The wolf is going around killing cows and tearing up leghold traps."

"I heard all that," Clint said. "What I want to know is why."

"Revenge," Cutter said, pausing long enough to let the words sink in.

"Doesn't sound right," Clint said.

"Yeah," Cutter said, glancing from man to man. "That's how I felt four years ago when someone told me this wolf was out for revenge. But we're talking about one large wolf who probably doesn't have a pack or a territory. This is no ordinary animal. The Shadow Wolf is smart, make no mistake about it, he's smart. This is a thinking, reasoning creature. He's cautious and watchful. And he knows how to get what he wants. Anybody who has lost animals to him—whether cows, sheep, pigs or dogs—

had been hunting wolves before it happened. The Shadow Wolf tracked them down and pulled off his act of revenge and gotten away before anybody could figure out what happened."

Cutter paused to roll another cigarette and light it. He had their undivided attention now.

"I'm not putting up a reward just to play a game," Cutter said. "I'm not hunting the Shadow Wolf just to bag a trophy. I'm out to stop a menace to our livelihood. Or, rather, your livelihood, because he ain't bothering mine. That money I'm putting up as a reward could go for a new Ford and leave enough change to install indoor plumbing and electricity at my cabin. But there's a monster in the woods, a giant wolf, and I want to stop him. He's dangerous and he's smart, and I can't get him by myself. That's why I'm putting out the word that I need help."

"So what can we do?" Clint asked.

Cutter pointed at George Smith and Ben Rose. "The three of us have been hunting since three this morning. This is the result of our trip." He pointed with the arrow at the four wolves on the table.

"Ben and George just herded them my way and I killed them, one by one, with this." Cutter held up his bow and arrow. The men mumbled among themselves as Cutter notched the arrow and took a stance as though striking a pose for publicity photos.

"But how do we find the Shadow Wolf?" Clint asked, as though he intended to leave his farm, put on his hunting cap and join them.

Cutter bent closer to the map, using his arrow again as a pointer. "Here's Caleb, our little town, just at the edge of the Shadow Wolf's circle of travel. There've been about three dozen sightings we know of since nineteen sixty."

"Nineteen sixty?" Jack laughed. "You'd better hurry and get your wolf, Cutter, before he dies of old age!"

Several men laughed. Cutter glanced angrily at Jack.
"Now hold on," Clint interrupted. "You can't cover all that
area with the few men you have here now!"

"I don't intend to," Cutter explained. "I've been talking to men in other towns, other counties, and they'll
be letting me know anything that happens up their way
concerning the Shadow Wolf."

"You still won't get him!" Flint shouted from behind
the bar.

Cutter turned around and glared at Flint. "Zack, old
friend, you remember that twenty dollar bet I lost to you
last year, when I said I'd have the wolf by New Year's Eve?
Well, why don't we make it again, only this time for fifty?"

"A fool and his money, Cutter," Flint said, smiling and
shaking his head. "A fool and his money! You got yourself
a bet."

"And what if someone else shoots the wolf first?" Jack
said, drawing Cutter's attention. "Say, me, for instance."
He pointed a thumb at himself. "Suppose I go out hunting, and I find the Shadow Wolf, and I kill it."

Cutter smiled, nocked the arrow and aimed at Jack's
forehead. "Now wait," Jack said, his grin gone as he
backed away from the table. "I was just kidding."

Cutter twisted around and let the arrow fly. It imbed-
ded itself through the dartboard into the wall next to
its twin. Cutter looked back at Jack. "If you get the wolf
yourself," he said, "then I guess I lose fifty to Flint here,
but I'll be spending my five grand on a new Ford and
indoor plumbing." The other men laughed as Jack's color
returned to his cheeks. "That's all I can tell you men,"
Cutter said, handing his bow to Ben and reaching for his
bottle of Hamm's.

Ben patted his shoulder, and Cutter gave him the
thumbs up for supporting him through his speech.
"Remember," Ben whispered. "I won't be here the next

two weeks. I gotta go back east to bury Aunt Margaret. I know how you are. No brawling, no fights, and stay the hell out of jail while I'm gone."

"You just take care of business," Cutter said. "Just get back when you can." He was glad Ben was there, thinking of the brief urge he had of killing Jack, an urge he turned into a joke with a swift sleight of hand. Cutter knew that Ben was the reason he hadn't killed anybody in years. Ben was his conscience, keeping him centered and sane.

He remembered the one time in Korea he had killed those commie soldiers from the other side who stole their jeep and morphine. He purposely sent Ben back to the MASH alone so he could go back into the jungle and find them. With Ben gone, he knew the killer instinct would come back, and it did, with a vengeance. He single hand-edly killed off all the men who stole their supplies. But that was it; he was done with killing, or at the least, kill-ing anything human.

As Patty worked her way around the men, her large tray balanced over her head, Cutter gestured her over. He pressed a fifty dollar bill into her free hand. "This is for Flint," he said, "for extra damages, so he won't try to bust my head with his baseball bat again. And this is for more drinks." He squeezed a second fifty into her hand. "I count about thirty in here. Might as well make it a festive afternoon, right?"

"It's not even noon," Patty whispered back. "Cutter, you sure attract the nuts."

"And see if you can get me a big bowl of Flint's beer chili, I'm feeling a little hungry." He pressed one more fifty into her hand. "And that one's for you."

The tray of bottles rattled precariously over her head as she glanced at the money and blushed; she'd never had such a large tip before. She smiled and nodded her thanks at Cutter, stashed the bills in her pocket and pulled out her pack of L&M's. She tapped one free and pulled it out with her lips, then lit it. "I'll have that chili in a minute," Patty said, pocketing her cigarettes. "It's a fresh batch. Zach made it last week."

Cutter nodded at her as she turned and headed back to the bar, unaware that Tim and Parker were watching him. "Think he'll get his wolf?" Tim asked.

"Fuck him and his wolf," Parker said. "All I'm thinking about is that jar of money."

"You fucking crazy?" Tim whispered. "You see the way he used that bow and arrow? He's not afraid of killing people, I can tell."

"Coward ass pussy," Parker moved closer, whispering intently. "Five grand is waiting for us at Cutter's cabin. Didn't you want to make a trip to California for the winter? Surf? Meet babes? Smoke dope and do acid and listen to the Beach Boys? Or you want to stay in Caleb, sip hot cocoa by the wood stove and listen to Perry Como on the jukebox while watching two old men playing checkers?"

"I don't want to mess with Cutter," Tim said.

"Cutter's older than your father," Parker whispered. "Hell, he's older than my father." He tapped a hand against Tim's cheek. "Think about it. Okay? Just think about it."

They both glanced at Cutter, who was telling another hunting story to three men in a booth as others gathered around the dead wolves and looked at the map. They were making plans.

Chapter Nine

"The Tower"
(Late Summer, 1966)

There was no lightning, no thunder, just the heavy, persistent rain. Dean Hoover stared out the window into the darkness, his chin in the palm of his hand, his elbow on the windowsill. The air blowing in was fresh and chilly, and the smell of pork and beans stirred his hunger.

"Close that fucken window, will ya?" LeRoy Arbuckle grumbled. "How can you let that cold air blow on you? You'll catch pneumonia. I tell ya, yer a nut, a real filbert, if ever I saw one."

Dean pulled the window shut, his mind someplace else. He picked up the ranger hat from the table and put it on his head. He wore the complete ranger outfit now, brown hat, light brown long sleeve shirt with the patch on the shoulder, brown pants, brown tie, and black boots and belt.

LeRoy's uniform hung from a nail at the other end of the room, next to Dean's cane. He tried not to use the cane so much these days, but sometimes it was painful just going ten feet. His wounds were finally healed, despite living on the streets for so many months, but there was still something there, some pain that would not leave.

LeRoy was busy working over a large portable stove, standing next to the portable toilet with the large horse blanket that could be pulled across the clothesline for a screen. He uses that tonight, Dean thought, and I'll open every damn window in this place. And then he remembered that tomorrow it would be his turn to empty the toilet's bucket, as well as cook the meals. What a job, he lamented; I gotta put it in, then take it out!

In just two months, he had already gained a reputation in the Forest Service for being a boozer and pothead, but this was going too far. It was a comical piece of irony that he was allowed to get a job as a forest ranger, albeit what he referred to as a "desk job" with minimal pay.

Wayne Connors of the Forest Service, who he met three years ago during a project on Isle Royale, contacted him after the Salvation Army reached him as a reference, trying to find a job for Dean. Wayne was now assistant manager of forest studies, and he managed to pull a few strings and bring Dean into the state forestry department, landing him a job in Rousseau County.

For two months of the summer, Dean worked at the main office near town, handing out pamphlets and road maps to tourists, hikers, and campers, and talking to kids about Smokey the Bear and the dangers of matches. He never thought he'd be transferred to the fire tower with LeRoy Arbuckle, tower resident for the last twelve years, on Horse Butte.

This was his first night. He gazed at the two army surplus cots with pillows and army surplus horse blankets. His back ached just looking at them, and he thought of his soft bed back at the ranger's office.

"Dinner's almost ready," LeRoy chanted in a singsong voice. The short thirty-year-old man stood at the portable stove in his red flannel underwear, his dirty, bare feet kicking up dust at every movement. Dean made a mental note to get a broom. Soon. "So what are you gonna make tomorrow night?"

"Curried pork over rice," Dean said, studying LeRoy's cherubic face and deep set brown eyes beneath the Neanderthal brow.

"Rice?" LeRoy shook his head. "Yuk! I don't think we have any rice, thank God."

"I got some in my backpack."

"Oh," LeRoy looked back into his pot, turning off the flame beneath it. "And what's that other stuff? Curry? Sounds French. Me, I'm all-American, even order a hamburger, Coke and fries at the pizza parlor."

"Oh, curry is American all right," Dean said with a straight face, watching LeRoy's hulking back. "I think you'll enjoy it." He made a mental note to add lots of curry powder when he cooked tomorrow.

Yawning and stretching, he looked around the room, fifty feet above the top of Horse Butte. The radio they used to keep in touch with the main office was army surplus, probably World War II, and the other instruments looked like brass medieval tools of torture on loan from the Spanish Inquisition.

Nonetheless, the Osborne Fire Spotter was particularly intriguing to Dean. Situated in the center of the room, it was on a raised platform so that it could be aimed at any of the windows. Once they spotted the smoke plume of a fire, they radioed in the coordinates to the main office. After several towers radioed in, the office could pinpoint the fire's location through cross referencing and send a fire crew to the area.

Other than his urge to try out the Fire Spotter at least once, he hated the job he was transferred to, hated LeRoy, and hated wearing his uniform in such a filthy room as this. What infuriated him most of all, though, was that he wasn't even needed.

Jobie Webb, his supervisor at the main office, didn't like anybody working under him being more educated than he was. Jobie had a Bachelor's from a small local community college, and was envious of Dean's Doctorate from Minnesota State. This made Jobie highly critical of Dean's work, and he somehow found fault where none existed.

At first Dean tried ignoring, then appeasing, his boss, but eventually he sought his revenge in talking to him in what Jobie called "twenty dollar college words."

"Do you prefer your reports terse or poignant?" Dean would ask.

"Well," Jobie answered, "I'd rather you decide."

"Would you rather have me deal with the tourists with lycanthropic zeal or digressive equanimity?"

"A little of each," Jobie would respond, wondering what he just said.

"Are you planning on hiring a personal catamite," Dean continued, "or would you rather continue practicing coprophagia by yourself?"

"Don't bug me now, Dean; I'll cross that bridge when I come to it."

Each time Jobie left the room after such an exchange, he always seemed to hear snickers coming from Dean and the other workers. Nobody ever figured out why it happened—perhaps Jobie cracked open a dictionary after one such exchange—but one day he came up to Dean, all smiles, to let him know that LeRoy Arbuckle needed help at the fire tower on Horse Butte. Before he left, Dean learned from a coworker that anybody who didn't get along with Jobie usually ended up in that tower. It wasn't what he wanted to hear. When he was first dropped off at the tower, he took the time before climbing the steps to smoke four joints in a row, just to relax and face the long climb with his sore foot and cane.

Even so, now that he was settled in, Dean was already beginning to take a liking to the tower, if only he could clean up the room soon. Once the Salvation Army took him in, they bathed him, shaved him, and dressed him up properly for his first job interview. Once they were done with him, he had a new addiction to dressing neat and staying clean, something he forgot during his long binge. The tower itself was okay. It was LeRoy who was getting on his nerves.

"So what do you do when you ain't working?" LeRoy asked, dishing up the pork and beans into two large bowls.

"Hiking," Dean said, taking off his hat and hanging it on the hook. That wasn't true. He had gone a half mile a few times the last couple months, and the pain turned him back. He wanted to go farther, but knew he would have to cross that threshold, not so much the pain but the fear that he couldn't handle the pain. He truly believed once he got into it, he would keep walking and eventually ignore whatever hurt, but he had to make that first long hike.

"I used to do that," LeRoy said, tearing open a bag of Wonder Bread. "But now I'm an adult. Now I go into town and play pinball." Without skipping a beat, LeRoy lifted a leg and farted to punctuate his remark.

Without skipping a beat, Dean threw open a window.

"Yeah," LeRoy went on, "I buy a pitcher of beer, grab me a machine, and off I go! Boy, and those points really rack up! Hey, close that window! What are you, a Brazil nut?"

"It's not too cold tonight," Dean said, staring into the rainy dark. "Only wet. Only wet." The sound of the rain on the tower roof was soothing to him, and he wondered if it might come down harder and drown out LeRoy's voice.

At that moment, the four bare light bulbs simultaneously blinked out, leaving the two men in darkness. Dean didn't budge. Resting his arms on the windowsill, he listened to the rain on the roof as he let his eyes adjust to the near total darkness. Already he could make out parts of the terrain through the murkiness.

"Damn," LeRoy grumbled. "I forgot to check the gas in the fucken generator again! Where are the oil lamps? Oh, hell, I burned myself!"

Dean inhaled the fresh night air, a slight smile shadowing his lips. He winced when he heard something crash behind him. "Damn!" LeRoy yelled. "I knocked the beans on the floor! Well, we still have one bowl left. We can share."

"I'm not really hungry," Dean lied.

"Where's the fucken matches?" The clatter of someone lost in the dark continued behind him.

"What the hell are you doing anyway?" Dean finally asked.

"Oh, hell," LeRoy said. "I just remembered, the oil lamps are locked in the foot locker, and it's a combination lock! And I can't find the damn matches!"

"You locked up the lamps?" Dean asked, turning from the window. "Who's going to steal anything out here, let alone oil lamps?"

"There's fucken bears in the woods!" LeRoy shouted, wondering why he had to explain something so obvious.

"So maybe they have their own lamps!" Dean shouted back. He felt in his pocket for his Zippo lighter. He had his stash in his duffel bag, but he realized from the beginning that he wouldn't be sharing any pot with LeRoy; the guy was perpetually stoned without it. "LeRoy, you're about the craziest person I ever met."

"And you're a nut," LeRoy huffed. "A real cashew. The least you can do is help me find the matches."

Dean lit the lighter. LeRoy turned and stared at the flame. "Will that help?"

"Why didn't you tell me you had that?" LeRoy held his hands together. "Here, toss it."

Dean shook his head, then walked it over to him. He returned to the window as LeRoy fumbled with the combination lock. "Damn, that ain't it."

Dean gazed out the window, almost hypnotized by the sound and smell of the rain. He noticed the absence of the heartbeat patter far below—the generator—and he was secretly glad it died.

"Damn, that ain't it, neither."

"Are you're looking for the piece of paper with the combination numbers on it," Dean taunted. "I think it's inside the locker."

"Oh, shut up," LeRoy mumbled.

Dean didn't respond. If only LeRoy could settle down and eat his beans in the dark instead of banging around the tower... If only he would just go to sleep on his cot... And once he was asleep, snoring—surely, LeRoy must snore! His voice was so adenoid!—Dean could open all the windows. LeRoy was the type of person who, if it got too cold while he slept, would only bury his head under the blankets and fart to stay warm. And Dean could sleep to the sound of the rain...

A noise outside caught his attention. Dean leaned forward, gripping the windowsill. He heard it again, a voice.

"Goddam, Dean, your lighter's too hot!" LeRoy grumbled. The flame was out, and LeRoy set it on the floor to cool. "What I need is..."

"Quiet," Dean said. "I heard something."

"All you hear is that fucken' rain," LeRoy said. "Nothing's out there."

"Somebody's out there," Dean said. "I know it. I heard it." He strained his ears, holding his breath for a moment as though that would help. LeRoy was listening now, too.

And then they both heard it, a human voice, shouting something. "Someone's out there!" Dean said. "You hear it?"

LeRoy was silent now, startled by what he'd heard. "What's he doing out there?" he asked. "What's going on?"

"A man's out there somewhere," Dean said. "I heard 'Help' and 'White head!' and 'Shot it!' He's out there, and he needs help. We'd better check this out."

"You fucken nuts?" LeRoy said. "Something might be out there with him!"

"Are you fucking nuts?" Dean shouted. "Someone, not something, is out there. A man's out there, and not only are we the only help around, but that's what we're paid for!"

Dean found his backpack and fumbled around inside it until he felt his flashlight, then grabbed his coat and yanked open the trap door over the steps. He rushed down the wooden steps, hearing the trap door slam shut behind him as he used his night vision and kept his hands on the railing. His left foot was sore already and he left his cane inside, but he refused to turn back, using the rail as his crutch.

When he reached ground level, he stood just out of the rain and listened. The voice seemed to have come from the south, but the rain may have distorted the sound enough so that choosing a direction would be impossible. The heavy rain and curtain of dark, such a comfort ten minutes ago, was now a burden, a roadblock between him and the man he heard.

"Hello!" Dean shouted, pulling on his raincoat. "Is anybody out there? Can you hear me? Do you need help?"

He listened, but all he could hear over the rain was the damp clomp-clomp of boots on the wooden steps as LeRoy came down behind him. All he could discern through the rain were the tops of trees in the distance. LeRoy came up beside him, carrying a rifle. Dean covered his flashlight with his hand and turned it on just long enough to get a good look at LeRoy, noticing that he wore his work boots, ranger's hat, and raincoat over his red flannel underwear. He turned the light off.

"Leave it on," LeRoy said, his voice shaky.

"We need our night vision," Dean said. "We'll use the flashlight if we absolutely have to."

"You're a fucken nut," LeRoy said, " a real pecan."

"If you mention one more nut," Dean grumbled, staring into the darkness, "I'm going to shove this flashlight up your nose and light up your brains."

"But there's bears out there!"

"Good," Dean said. "Why don't you pour some ketchup over yourself and lay yourself down on a loaf of bread?"

"You're a..."

"Don't say it!" Dean growled. "I meant what I said. Wait! Listen!"

Somebody was screaming in the dark. The rumble of the rain nearly drowned it out, but it was there, a hoarse, gravelly voice.

"Can you hear me?" Dean shouted, already figuring out the direction. The darkness seemed to increase as the rain pounded harder on the ground around the tower. "Do you need help? We can help you!" Dean listened for a moment, his heart pounding against his sternum like a hammer. The voice seemed to be coming closer, but the words were indecipherable, gibberish. Dean pointed into the darkness. "That way," he said.

"Good, now we can radio for...Hey!" LeRoy gasped as Dean turned his flashlight on and followed its beam, limping into the rain. "You can't do that!" LeRoy shouted. "It's not safe!" Nonetheless, LeRoy dashed after him, mumbling to himself just loud enough that only he could hear a few references to different nuts.

Horse Butte was flat and grassy on top, and there weren't any trees within a hundred feet of the tower, but there were rocks and stones in the grass. Dean had to limp on carefully as he searched for the source of the voice. His hair was soaked, and cold rain trickled into the collar of his coat and down his back. He had never been trained in search and rescue operations, and he hoped that he wouldn't have to use the first aid training he received in one of his college courses years ago.

As he neared the trees, he realized that he could no longer hear the voice. "Hey" he yelled. "Are you still there? Hello?" He picked up speed, nearly tripped on a stone, and stumbled downhill into the woods. He was gasping for breath as he stopped and aimed his light's beam back and forth, supporting himself against the tree he found closest, listening.

He held the flashlight towards the ground, feeling scared and frustrated, afraid the unknown person had died, and he was too late. LeRoy caught up to him, wheezing and sputtering and looking miserable. "No one here. Let's go back." He kept his hand on Dean's shoulder, more for emotional security than physical support.

"We heard someone out here," Dean said. "He didn't just turn around and go home." He held his breath, listening, then let it go with a sigh. "Maybe if we go that way."

Before either had a chance to move, cracking branches and loud panting brought their attention around. A large, dark form stumbled towards them through the bushes. LeRoy gasped as it collapsed against him, grabbing his coat, then letting go and sinking to the ground. LeRoy stepped back, slipped, landed on his rump and slid downhill in the mud, dropping his rifle as Dean brought the flashlight beam around. A bald-headed man with a muddy coat was on his hands and knees before them, choking and gagging. When he looked up into the light, Dean saw blood and phlegm running from his mouth and nostrils.

Something didn't feel right. Dean aimed the flashlight beam through the trees as he made a slow turn, looking for any movement or large shape.

As LeRoy recovered his rifle and pulled himself to a standing position, he felt it, too. Something was out there, but he didn't know what. The man, apparently in deep shock, not only felt it but had apparently seen it.

"Let's get him to the tower," Dean said, unable to keep the fear from his voice. He took one of the man's arms and LeRoy, too scared to make a reference to any kind of nut, took the other. His left foot throbbed miserably now, but he ignored the pain and took the first step. They headed clumsily up the hill.

The man's name was Rusty Bricker. They found his driver's license in his wallet when they helped him undress and get into dry clothes. By lamplight he drank some coffee, his prune skin hands shaking as he stared off into space. Dean radioed the main office to explain the situation and ask for advice while LeRoy cleaned the beans off the floor. As they worked, they both watched the man sitting on the cot. Though he seemed aware of them, he hadn't uttered a word, despite their questions, since he climbed the tower steps with them.

Dean was told by radio to keep the man warm, check his eyes for dilation, and watch him until help arrived, which wouldn't be until sometime in the morning. LeRoy offered him a plate of reheated pork and beans and a few slices of Wonder Bread, but the man only stared at the far wall.

"What do we do now?" LeRoy asked.

"I don't know," Dean said. "Let him sleep in my cot

tonight. You sleep on one side of him and I'll sleep on the other on the floor in my sleeping bag. If something happens, if he has convulsions or a heart attack, I hope you know what to do."

"Well, no," LeRoy said, his Neanderthal brows knitting together as he rubbed his chin, "But I have a book."

Following the plan, they helped Rusty Bricker lie down on the cot and covered him with blankets, then settled down on either side of him. He coughed up blood and mumbled unintelligible words as Dean cleaned his mouth with a wet washcloth, then laid still, his chest heaving noisily at each breath. Dean rested with his head propped against an equipment box, his long, blond hair stringy and damp. He read the first aid book, looking up every emergency he thought might occur during the night. The oil lamp burned on the box just behind his head as he read about tourniquets and arm slings. LeRoy's snoring and the constant drumming of rain on the roof were like Mozart to him as he turned another page.

"Run!" Rusty Bricker grunted.

"What?" Dean jerked awake, not realizing he had just dozed off. He put the book down and sat up, looking at the sleeping man on the cot. He thought he imagined the word, then Rusty said it again: "Run!" His voice was as rough as gravel, his eyes still closed. "Get away....Can't run fast enough..." He began shaking his head back and forth. "Run!"

LeRoy woke at the last word, raised up on an elbow and glanced at Rusty. "Dean, what the fucken hell's going on now?" he whispered. Dean silenced him with a gesture.

"Lungs....Lungs burning...." Rusty continued. LeRoy moved back in the cot. "Run, run, but my lungs hurt.... Where am I? Lungs hurt.... Chest hurts.... That was Kirkland's Gully.... Miles away now.... Keep running...." His head rocked back and forth. LeRoy's eyes widened. He slipped out of the cot and moved quietly around Rusty towards Dean. "Running.... Running...."

"Dean," LeRoy whispered near his ear. "Kirkland's Gully is over five miles away! He couldn't have run that far! Especially not in the dark!"

"Shhhh...." Dean held his finger to his lips. "He's big, and sure not young, but if he ran all that far, that explains why he was coughing up blood. He hurt his lungs somehow from running too fast for too long."

"But why was he running?"

"Maybe he was lost in the rain," Dean said.

Rusty suddenly turned his head towards the men and opened his eyes. "No!" he mumbled. LeRoy gasped, but Dean put his hand on his shoulder. Rusty seemed to gaze right through them. His forehead was wrinkled, his teeth gritting through parted lips. "It's right behind me! Can't kill it! Mother of Mercy, that monster is still coming! The skins! The skins! I dropped them, all right? Why won't you leave me alone?"

"He's a nut!" LeRoy whispered, his voice quivering. "A pistachio. What's he talking about?"

"I don't know," Dean said. "His eyes are open, but I think he's still dreaming. Maybe if he wakes up...."

"I'm awake," Rusty gagged, spittle on his lips. "I saw it. A monster." He glanced at Dean. "You gotta believe me."

"What was it?" Dean asked.

"A monster," Rusty said. "A monster with a big, white head."

"A bear?" LeRoy asked.

"No, I was hunting wolves, trappin...."

"A wolf," Dean said.

"Yeah!" Rusty's eyes lit up. He tried to rise, then slumped back down on the cot. "A wolf. It chased me. It killed my dog. The skins...."

"Bounty?" Dean asked.

Rusty shook his head, laughed with a voice like an old car with bearings wore out. "There hasn't been any bounty for a year or two. But I had four skins. I was going to have a rug made of them." He laughed again.

"I was heading back to my cabin," he continued, managing to sit up with LeRoy's help. His eyes were wild. Gazing at Dean, he reached out and put a hand on Dean's chest. Dean felt waves of fear pulse through his body, praying Rusty would say more to break the spell. For a moment, as he listened to the rain, he thought of the "Rime of the Ancient Mariner," the old sailor holding back the groom of the wedding and saying, "There was a ship...." He could almost see Rusty finishing with, "And only I am left to tell the tale!"

Rusty bent his head closer, his eyebrows rising. "It was dark. Rags, my dog, was running ahead of me. I had four skins, and it had just turned dark." The man paused, then broke into a fit of coughing.

Dean looked at LeRoy. "Heat up the coffee. I think we'll all be needing it."

"Now wait a minute," LeRoy said. "I'm not here to...."

"Just do it, okay?" Dean said, wiping Rusty's mouth with a handkerchief. LeRoy mumbled something about a peanut, then walked over to fire up the butane stove. Dean listened to the clatter of the rain on the roof as Rusty put his feet on the floor, took the handkerchief and finished wiping his mouth.

"It was horrible," he said. "I didn't expect anything to happen. We were following a path through the woods up a hill. My cabin was just beyond it. Rags was somewhere ahead. I heard him barking, but I thought it was some raccoon he treed. Then I heard a yelp, no, more like a screech, nothing I ever heard come out of a dog before. Then, silence.

"I thought he was hurt, maybe fell into an old pit or

gully, so I ran up the hill. It was getting dark, I could barely see, but I knew the path, I used it all the time.

"Then I saw something up ahead, right on the path. At first I imagined that some large boulder had dropped there out of the sky, it looked so big, but then it moved. I could make out legs, ears, shoulders, then teeth."

Rusty coughed into the handkerchief. Dean leaned forward. LeRoy stood by the stove, the blue flame beneath the coffeepot playing shadows over his features. "There were clouds overhead," Rusty went on. "Rain clouds. The moonlight couldn't get through. But I could still see a little, and as I watched, something small dropped from those teeth. It was Rags. He was worse than dead, he was shattered, crushed, and chewed.

"But I was only scared for myself by then. I shouldered my rifle and took aim. I figured it was a bear, and since there was only forty feet between us, I didn't want to have to chance running for it, not with that thing between me and my cabin. I fired a round, and I know I hit it, forty feet, you just don't miss. But it didn't move, didn't even roar with pain.

"I took my flashlight off my belt and turned it on. I had to see this thing. But...." Dean noticed a quiver in Rusty's cheek. "It wasn't a bear, it was a wolf. A big mother fucking wolf."

Dean glanced at LeRoy, who looked back, astounded. "That thing, big as a bear, I swear, was a wolf. Its jaws were bloody and its teeth were sharp, and its eyes were large and dark and half-human, like it was a thinking creature more than it was a wolf."

"What color was its head?" Dean asked. LeRoy looked at him curiously.

"Its head...." Rusty said, glancing from Dean to LeRoy. "Oh, yeah, its head. The wolf had a large, white head, white as snow, and its head looked deformed, like something happened to it. Its teeth were chipped, cracked, and broken. I could see it all from forty feet away, and its breath, even from that distance, was hot and horrible, like something rotten and being eaten by maggots.

"I should have run right then and there. I should have climbed a tree, something, but it held me, hypnotized me with those horrible eyes. That sonovabitch didn't stare into my light, like a regular animal would, but gazed right into my eyes. Nothing can see the eyes of a man holding a flashlight in the dark, nothing, it just isn't possible, but this sonovabitch did. And it didn't blink. It glanced at my eyes, then it glanced at my left side, where the four skins were tied to my belt.

"My body tingled. I knew right then and there why it found me, why it wanted to kill me. Trying to hold the rifle and flashlight both, I took aim again. I glanced one last time at its big paws where my dog lay mangled and bloody. And then I fired. One bullet, then another. And again. Until there were no more bullets.

"I even aimed for the head, I swear I did, between the eyes, and still I couldn't hit that big goddam white head. I saw fur fly off its back, I know I hit it, but it didn't budge or make any noise. Even a bear would leap and growl from the pain. Even a bear would do something. This thing took every hit and wanted more."

Rusty paused, gasping as he wiped the tears from his eyes. His voice, hoarse when he began, was barely audible now. LeRoy brought over cups of hot coffee, thick with sugar and cream, and sat next to Dean. Rusty steadied his trembling hands as he drank, then looked up, determined to finish his tale, despite what it was costing him.

"It began coming towards me," he said. "Not charging, just walking, like it had all the time in the world, its head low, its teeth bared, and I could see blood spots all over it where I'd hit its back.

"I threw down my gun and ran, and that's when it started coming at me faster, I could hear it running behind me, breaking through sticks and brush. My flashlight died, and I tossed it aside. I knew I was a goner.

"That's when the rain started. I was slipping and sliding on mud and leaves; couldn't see where I was going, but I kept moving. The last place I recognized was Kirkland's Gully. I kept running, dropping the skins because they weighed me down, and I could still hear that thing coming behind me, and I knew it could've killed me at any time, but it didn't, it wanted to run me to death instead."

The old man's hands shook as he took another sip of coffee. Dean, sitting at Rusty's feet, was quietly thinking.

"Well," LeRoy said nervously, "there'll be help here tomorrow."

"But he's still out there," Rusty said.

"The wolf?" LeRoy said.

"That monster," Rusty repeated. "he's out there, watching, waiting. He never went away. He wants me. I know it. I know it."

Dean rose and walked to a window, opening it and peering outside. The wolf doesn't want you, he thought, he wants me. It had to be a coincidence, albeit one hell of a coincidence, that Rusty was chased to this particular tower. Any yet, he thought, it wasn't so much a coincidence as two paths joining, coming together. A sudden need for change was coming over him.

Ethan Bell had been a ranger for over twenty years, but he had never seen anybody still alive who looked as bad as Rusty Bricker, stiff, terrorized, withdrawn. He'd seen men come out of forest fires looking better, or children who'd been lost in the woods several days. He guided Rusty to the dented pickup with the Forest Service emblem on the door.

LeRoy walked on the other side of him. "He was talking all night," LeRoy said. "He went off to sleep in the early morning. I don't know why he's so comatose now. A real filbert if you ask me."

"He's just tired," Ethan said. "All he needs is a few days rest at the hospital." All the while he was thinking that Rusty would need more than a few days. He opened the door to the passenger side and helped Rusty in.

The man's face was ash-gray; his eyes were sunken and dark-rimmed. He seemed more a refugee of Bedlam than the nervous coffee-drinker telling his story, as Dean and LeRoy described him. Perhaps the shock finally settled in, or perhaps it was something physical. Ethan hoped the doctor could puzzle it out.

Dean walked up to them, his backpack on. He was wearing his civilian clothes as he handed a string-wrapped package to Ethan. "Here," Dean said. "Give this to Jobie. And here's my letter of resignation." He pulled an envelope from his flannel shirt.

"I can't believe you're quitting," LeRoy said. "We were just settling in together, too." He turned to Ethan. "Make sure they send some replacement soon. I don't want to be up here alone when there's crazed wolves around." Glancing back at Dean, his brows furrowed, he grumbled, "A real...."

"Don't say it," Dean said, holding up an index finger. "Don't even think it." He glanced at Ethan. "The package is my uniform. It's a little muddy, but, hey, I'm sure they have a washing machine somewhere. I left the hat with LeRoy. He needed a new one, his was old and wilted."

Dean nodded at LeRoy, who shrugged and headed back to the tower. He glanced again at Ethan. "The letter of resignation has a post office box where I can pick up my last check."

Ethan smiled and nodded. He was tall and thin, and looked much younger than his forty-plus years. "Say, you only lasted one night with Arbuckle. Most guys usually manage to stick it out at least two weeks."

"It wasn't him, really," Dean admitted. "Though he could qualify as extenuating circumstances. I just got to thinking I'm not Mr. Ranger, I'm a biologist, and I don't need this job, stuck behind a desk or hanging from a tower." He shrugged. "So for now, I guess, it's time to move on."

Ethan nodded. "So where can I drop you off?"

"I'm hiking," Dean said smiling. "I didn't have time to hike while I was at the main office, all the paperwork they piled on me, and the public relations bunk to boot. So now I'm making up for lost time."

Ethan nodded. "Even so, it's as muddy as fresh moose shit. Let me at least drop you off at the highway."

"If I walk along the highway," Dean said, "it isn't hiking, is it?"

"No, I suppose not," Ethan said, glancing at his boots, still smiling. "But it's a little easier going, especially after last night's rain."

"I need to get some fresh air," Dean said. "Car fumes don't cut it for me."

"Bullshit," Ethan said. "Car fumes? You're lucky if you see a logging truck once an hour on that highway. And what if you run into that wolf the old man was talking about?" He pulled a toothpick from his shirt pocket, examined it and stuck it into the side of his mouth. "What if that wolf chases you?"

"Hell, Ethan," Dean said. "You've worked out here long enough to know animals and to know that wolf is long gone from here."

"I reckon you're right," Ethan said. "Well, good luck then." He got in the pickup and started the engine. Dean waved as the truck bounced down the rutted road. He then turned and glanced at the tower one last time. LeRoy was hanging out the window, waving Dean's hat. Dean smiled and waved back. LeRoy wasn't so bad, he thought, except for maybe farting and snoring in his sleep.

He walked off, heading down Horse Butte, heading south. The morning sky was cloudless and blue, the kind of sky that could almost blind a man in winter, the kind of sky Dean enjoyed while hiking. He adjusted his shoulder straps as he headed downhill over lichen-covered rocks and moss-covered trees. The sound of the truck was gone, and the sounds of the forest engulfed him, swallowed him.

He couldn't explain to LeRoy or Ethan why he was really hiking, that he believed the giant wolf had some-how tracked him all this way, and now he had to find out why. If he could. He picked up a large piece of dead fall, adopting it as a walking stick, as he continued his descent. His cane was still in the tower, his left foot was miserably sore, but he would ignore it, no matter how far he had to walk.

Chapter Ten

"Dogslayer"
(Summer, 1966)

The sound of barking didn't even affect Deerchaser as he stood and stared, his thin frame stoic against the screaming wind that pummeled his fur. *I gave birth many times myself,* he growled proudly, holding his ground against the wind, with the sheer drop of the cliff behind him. *I gave birth to white worms, rolling in my shit. A giant white worm mated with me one day. A giant.... A giant....*

He was still. Ice formed on his blowing pelage, ice formed over his eyebrows and eyes, over his nostrils and lips, and he stood there, frozen, the emptiness of the cliff behind him.

And there, coming up over the edge of the cliff, the massive, windy, noisy figure of Bigbird rose up behind him, hovering, rumbling, a large headless body with dozens of long, sharp, black talons, clenching and unclenching as dozens of wings beat in rapid succession on its back, just beyond the cliff edge, just beyond Deerchaser's frozen body. Bigbird opened its gaping maw, large Twolegs Jaws that were invisible only a moment before, and inside the mouth, two Twolegs waited to take his skin off his body. Then there was a crack, like the snap of a large tree branch in a storm, and Deerchaser's body shattered like a piece of ice on a stone.

Rabbitrunner woke in the darkness of the den to the sound of barking. He had been lying on his side with a dead rabbit he'd killed hours before laying near his head. Still shaken by the dream of Bigbird, he glanced unseeing around his chamber, puling, "Deerchaser! Deerchaser! Where are you?" The scent of the dead rabbit and the remains of other meals filled his nostrils, but nothing else.

No, Bigbird isn't here, he heard Deerchaser's voice say in his head. *Bigbird couldn't fit into the den. He tried and tried....*

"Deerchaser!" Rabbitrunner whined.

He was in your dream, Sleepfarter's voice said.

He's dead, Treepisser's voice said.

We're all dead, Newmoon's voice informed him. *There is nothing left of us but in your dreams.*

"But what was Deerchaser telling me?" Rabbitrunner asked.

Nothing, Ravenplay said through his thoughts.

You're going mad, Deerchaser's voice sighed.

"But what were you saying?" Rabbitrunner whined. "We all found you frozen dead, you and Bullmoosekiller. But what about the worms? Was that a warning?"

Listen, Deerchaser said.

"Listen?" Rabbitrunner growled. "Listen to what?" And then he noticed the barking for the first time. "A dog," he said, recalling his last trek across his territory several nights before when he passed by the lake at the border and saw the fire across the lake. He had never seen fire before, and the sight of the distant dancing light held him in awe until he made out the figures of several Twolegs sitting around it. He cautiously sniffed the air, picked up their scent, the scent of their fire, and relaxed, knowing they were upwind of him. Then he saw the dog.

It walked among them as he himself would walk among trees, its tail raised and wagging, its gait like that of a cub's. It began barking, and once started, it didn't seem to want to stop. Its barking was loud and obnoxious, a pain to the ear.

Much like the noise Rabbitrunner heard now. As he listened from inside his den, he recalled the stories he'd heard about dogs. They, too, were a breed of stupid people, like the cows and sheep and chickens, ruled over by Twolegs. But dogs helped Twolegs in their hunting, because Twolegs could not smell too well, and in return, Twolegs fed them as their reward.

And now a dog was outside his den!

Which meant, Rabbitrunner reasoned, that Twolegs was also out there.

They found you! Treepisser's voice warned.

"Oh shut up!" Rabbitrunner growled, trying to control his panic. "I don't even see why they'd trouble themselves for a single Hunter on a hillside. After all, what did I ever do to them?"

Yeah? Treepisser growled indignantly. *What did we ever do to them?*

"We ate their stupid cows!" Rabbitrunner growled. "And Twolegs are pretty sensitive about their cows. But I haven't had a cow since then!"

So what will you do now? Mousehunter asked.

"I don't know," Rabbitrunner grumbled. "If I crawl outside, maybe I can rush past them and get to the trees. They can't run fast, can they?"

But they can still kill you, Treepisser warned from the safety of Rabbitrunner's mind. *They have thunder sticks and Jaws and tainted meat....*

"Oh, yeah, tainted meat," Rabbitrunner said. "That

can only kill one who eats it, and I have no intention of eating it. What is Twolegs going to do with tainted meat? Drop it on my head?"

Stop joking! Scentcatcher whined. *You're in real danger.*

"Well, perhaps I can escape," Rabbitrunner said. "Perhaps."

He crawled up the slope of the tunnel, making the first bend, then the second, and passing through the old chamber on his way. He slowed as he approached the light, his head spinning as he readied himself to make a dash for the woods. Since the time of the slaughter of the pack, he was very aware of Twolegs' ability to kill, and he didn't particularly care to test them.

The light from the mouth of the tunnel hurt his eyes. He seldom left his den by day, knowing that Twolegs only hunted in the daylight. As he silently crawled out, he cautiously glanced around. He saw the dog, but no sign of Twolegs. He gazed uphill: nothing. Twolegs could be hiding behind trees, they did things like that, and they could kill from a distance.

But something told Rabbitrunner that this time they weren't around.

There was no scent on the wind, no Twolegs smell. The dog, too, indicated that they were nowhere near. It rambled about, sniffing around, not at all concerned with hunting for its master Twolegs.

Rabbitrunner rose from the den and snarled, catching the dog's attention. The dog turned and froze; it was the same one he'd seen before, white fur with black and gray spots, floppy ears, short hair, and wagging tail. Only this time thinner, hyperactive, and filthy. Obviously the dog and Twolegs had parted company some days ago. Rabbitrunner heard that dogs relied on Twolegs for food, and the ribsy condition of this one showed it probably hadn't eaten since he last saw it.

This particular dog also acted as though it relied on Twolegs for its grooming. The black thing around its neck with the dangly noisy pebble-like objects had Rabbitrunner confused, but the size and shape of the dog, if one ignored the strange shades and markings of its fur, made it appear almost like a Hunter, at least more so than a bear or squirrel would.

The dog, when he spotted Rabbitrunner, bounded playfully towards him. Well, I can't allow this, he thought as he charged downhill, snarling and bearing his teeth. The dog stopped and lowered its body in submission, then flopped onto its back, whining. Its tail wagged frantically in the dust as it urinated over its own belly.

Growling, Rabbitrunner stopped and bent over the dog, sniffing its head, its chest, its balls, its anus. He then raised his head, staring into the distance, a posture of dominance that said, "I have more important things to concern myself than with you." The dog, misunderstanding the message, tried to rise, but Rabbitrunner quickly snapped his teeth dangerously close to its face, and it settled down.

A vague odor of Twolegs still lingered on the dog, but it was just the phantom of an odor. Rabbitrunner maintained his stance of dominance. "Where are you from?" he asked. "Why are you here?"

"Lost! Lost! Lost!" the dog whined. "My Master is gone! No Master! No food! Hunger!"

"And where is this 'Master' of yours?" Rabbitrunner asked, his hackles rising. "Where is Twolegs?"

"I don't know!" the dog whined. "He took me from home—home and food and comfort! I ran off and played, and when I came back.... Gone! Gone! Gone! Gone! No food! Only hunger!"

"And do you not hunt with Twolegs?"

Still on its back, the dog cocked its head and looked

stupidly up at Rabbitrunner. "Hunt! What's that?"

"Hunt," Rabbitrunner said, "to get your meat."

"Meat?"

"Food. Food. Where do you get your food?"

"Food!" the dog yipped, his tail kicking up dust again. "Food! It came out of a hard egg!"

"What?" Rabbitrunner tilted his head.

"Food! A hard, round egg! Round on the sides, flat on the top and bottom! My Master puts the egg against a white rock that sings and growls and grinds and opens the egg, and he puts the food from the egg into my bowl!"

"Bowl?" Rabbitrunner was dumbfounded.

"Bowl! Bowl! I have a food bowl and a water bowl!" The dog seemed rather proud of this, and wagged his tail even faster. "A bowl can hold your food. It's like a hole you dig; only you can move it with your nose."

"You can move it with your nose," Rabbitrunner said. The idea was truly amazing to him, as was a singing rock and an egg full of food. He had eaten pheasant eggs he sometimes found in ground nests before, but he certainly didn't require a singing rock to do it. "But can you hunt?"

"Hunt?"

"Find food."

"Find food?" The dog rolled onto its belly and wagged its tail. "Sure I can find food! It's kept under the water that runs and stops, behind a wall that opens and closes."

"Under water?" Rabbitrunner wondered. "Behind a wall? Never mind all that. Can you hunt?"

"Hunt?"

"Chase a squirrel or rabbit. Catch it. Kill it. Eat it."

"Sure I can chase rabbits," the dog said, gazing at him. "But if I killed it, my Master would beat me. I am not allowed."

"Not allowed!" Rabbitrunner huffed. "Master!" There was that word again. He had discovered a word even more distasteful than Twolegs. He stepped back and allowed the dog to rise. It kept its head and tail low in submission, gently sniffing the corner of Rabbitrunner's mouth. It knew the signs of obeisance, but apparently knew nothing about how to hunt.

Perhaps it could be taught, Rabbitrunner thought. Perhaps it could become the pack he longed for. If he drove it off, it would most likely starve before it learned to hunt on its own. If it traveled into other territories, it would be driven off or killed. But here...

Perhaps it could be taught. But first it must be fed. Rabbitrunner gave a low snarl, indicating that the dog should stay put. He turned and trotted back to the den, and the dog leaped up and followed. Rabbitrunner quickly turned and nipped his cheek, an unwise move, because it began ki-yii-ing loud as a bird. "Stay here," Rabbitrunner growled. "And be quiet."

"Mercy!' the dog puled.

"Yeah, if you don't shut up, I'll give you a little mercy you won't forget," Rabbitrunner growled. "You want to be stupid all of your life?" He crawled into the tunnel and made his way through the dark to the chamber. When he reached it, he located the rabbit, picked it up and headed back. He could hear the dog yipping outside. In his mind, he could see it prancing about like a cub, making all kinds of racket, and as he clumsily pushed through the tunnel that always seemed to be shrinking and needing to be enlarged, he knew the first lesson he would have to teach it was how to be quiet.

Suddenly he heard a ghastly screech, followed by silence. He dropped the rabbit and pushed through the tunnel towards the surface, his heart beating like thunder as he squeezed out into the morning sunlight.

Down the hill from the entrance of the den where the clearing ended and the trees took over, the dog laid on its side, its neck ripped open and blood squirting shiny-black onto the grass. One hind leg still kicked, the jaw was open and trembling, and the eyes, already fogging over, seemed to stare at him with recognition. On a branch just beyond the dying creature, three black ravens, the largest one with a twisted beak and one empty eye socket, perched, impassionately watching everything. He saw them before he remembered.

"Look alive, Rabbit-Turd, look alive!" The voice, deep and raspy, thick and guttural, seemed to come from behind every tree that surrounded the clearing. Rabbit-runner glanced in one direction, then another, his neck snapping about like a beetle's carapace. "Look away from you I can NOT," the voice growled, "not for a moment, before you fraternize with Twolegs dogs! How dare you! How dare you!"

Rabbitrunner turned and took a fighting stance, his legs braced, his hackles up, and his teeth bared. "Show yourself, you cub of a dog!" he snarled. "Show yourself! I know you're out there somewhere defiling my territory! You're not a forgotten voice in my head! Not this time! You're real! There's spilled blood to prove it!"

He waited against the rock-hard silence for an answer, but the answer came in a change of the breeze, in the smell of something rancid, a smell of death, rotting, decaying, recalling to him a time when he was a cub and he passed downwind of the place Deerchaser used for defecation, only this smell was much worse.

Upwind behind his back he heard a low, rumbling snarl. He spun around on his paws and froze. Out from the shadows of the trees lumbered a humongous beast with the shoulders of a bear, the chest of a moose, and the thin, sinewy legs of a large, predatory bird that ended in the massive paws of a Hunter.

"By Father Sky's backside..." Rabbitrunner gasped,

watching the gargantuan thing move slowly downhill towards him. His gait was controlled and noiseless, as though he were stalking prey. His eyes were blazing with malicious rage, boring into Rabbitrunner like a hawk's talons into a squirrel's flesh. He was the offspring of many different creatures, but clearly he was a Hunter first, a head and a half taller than Rabbitrunner.

The sounds of crickets and bees and the summer winds suddenly stopped. The birds that flew high overhead or twittered on tree limbs were gone, as though they sensed the malevolence of the beast. The odors of flowers and grasses and small animals were consumed by the suffocating stench as he lumbered closer.

Rabbitrunner had not felt as cold in winter as he did now, terrorized, his legs like water. He lowered himself to the ground in obeisance, staring at the great white head, wrinkled nose, bared, chipped teeth, massive jaws. Rabbitrunner's ears were back, his tongue noisily licking his lips. The large Hunter's pelage was matted, dusty, and stained with the black blood of the dead dog. In spots his skin was bare and scaly and swarming with fleas, and there were open sores, tumorous lumps, cracks in the skin scabbed over or bleeding, so much sickness on his body he would've made Deerchaser look healthy.

But his head!

His head, as much bare white skin and flesh as it was short white fur, was as large as a boulder, supported by a neck thick as a tree trunk with muscles moving like powerful snakes beneath the skin. His head was scarred, melted skin with visible flaps and lumps; giant deformed ears that cocked back and forth; tattered eyelids over two massive, dark gray eyes; black, scarred lips drooling saliva and blood, pulled back and revealing tattered, bloody gums and large cracked teeth.

Rabbitrunner, too scared to run or fight, rolled on

his back and exposed his throat in a plea for mercy. His belly flashed with the large, white scar—a patch of fur-less skin—that marked the last time he took the posture and was attacked, but this time he felt he had no choice.

The large Hunter stepped up to him, walked around him, sniffing him. Rabbitrunner could feel the hostil-ity, radiating from the old beast's body like heat from a summer rock. He felt the breath on his face, felt the teeth brushing his throat. The old Hunter snapped his teeth, then turned, lifted his leg and urinated, hitting him with a thick, dark stream that almost burned, and stank as bad as he did. Rabbitrunner rolled away and leaped up, baring his own teeth as he growled and backed away. "I won't stand for that!" he snarled. "If you're going to kill me, then kill me, but I won't bow down to your indigni-ties again!"

The giant Hunter seemed to raise an eyebrow, and his lip curled into a strange grin Rabbitrunner had never seen before. "I wondered," he snorted, "if perhaps I would have to shit on your belly to make you stand up and act like a real Hunter."

"And what sort of Hunter are you?" Rabbitrunner asked. "Your stink would curl a tree. And your looks would make a moose puke."

"Such insults!" the large Hunter scoffed. "You would welcome a dog to your den, but tell me I defile your ter-ritory, do you? Can you not tell who I am, Rabbit-Turd?" He gazed at the dead dog, and Rabbitrunner followed his gaze.

"Dogslayer," Rabbitrunner snarled, glancing from the body to the Hunter. "Dogslayer? And Cloudwalker?" His eyes went wide, his body relaxed from the defensive pos-ture. "Snaretripper? Winddancer?" He felt lightheaded, as though Father Sky had just called his name. "Thun-dersnarl?" Rabbitrunner drew in his breath. "You?"

"Many names," Cloudwalker said. "But only one Hunter, my little dungworm."

"But you can't be," Rabbitrunner said, recalling dreams of a large, white Hunter, healthy and strong. He recalled the paw print he had once seen, but this Hunter was missing toes on all but one paw. With every new glance, Rabbitrunner saw more scars: deep pits in the skin, a large indentation in the right side of his chest that had to mean broken ribs that did not heal properly. And his head—"What happened to your head?"

Cloudwalker looked back at him, his ears twitching with amusement. "Stuck my head into Father Sky's good eye, one day," he said. "It burned like thunder, all that pain, and still I saw nothing inside."

Rabbitrunner gazed at Cloudwalker's eyes. Deep in those eyes was a hot flame that all but verified Cloudwalker's story, a flame that was a rage, a viciousness, a maniacal mischievous power, a sadness, a loneliness, and something big, something very, very....

"Cloudwalker," he said, then glanced at the dog. "Why?"

"Slay dogs, Dogslayer does. Why? Because."

"But a dog is almost a Hunter."

"A dog is no more a Hunter than you are a bird." Cloudwalker yawned. "You tried to fly, you tried to fly, and you fell, Rabbit-Bird-Turd. And such a fall!"

"You were there?" Rabbitrunner asked, recalling his leap off a cliff over a year ago.

"Yes, yes, saw you, I did," Cloudwalker growled. "I know all. I watch all the Hunters, I watch the Twolegs, and none see me unless I wish to be seen. Tell me, the wind does, when I cannot be there. I burrow through mountains, I walk on clouds, and more. And you.... And your pack.... The Stupid People you hunted? You were fools! Fools!"

Rabbitrunner felt cold, remembering the day all the members of his pack died, the day they killed and ate the cows on Twolegs territory. They had crossed one boundary after another to do it, and somehow Cloudwalker had seen it all. "We were desperate," Rabbitrunner said. "We were hungry."

"So you filled your bellies," Cloudwalker said. "You filled your bellies and died. You were all desperate to die. Fools! Fools! The Stupid People eaten by the Stupid People! I marked that territory with my own scent, I did, to warn you all away, and you ignored it. My markers, you smelled them, did you not?"

Cloudwalker's brows, still thick with white fur, knitted together. He bared his teeth and growled, furious at the memory of the loss of life, and the stupidity that caused it.

"Hungry," Cloudwalker said, wrinkling his nose as he paced away, then back. "Hungry you are, Rabbit-Turd, so I will leave you this meat." He glanced at the dog, flies already buzzing around the carcass.

"I would no more eat a dog than I would eat a Hunter," Rabbitrunner growled.

Cloudwalker gazed at him and snorted. "I have eaten the flesh of a Hunter, I have. You do not know what it's like. You have not been alone long enough, Rabbit-Turd. Such pickiness, such choosiness. Still a cub, still a cub." He sat down and scratched behind an ear with his good foot.

"Don't mock me!" Rabbitrunner growled. "I'm a Hunter! Im a Guardian!"

"And do you hear the voices, little Hunter?" Cloudwalker asked, tilting his head. "You talk to yourself, don't you, trying to answer those voices. I have heard you, I have, my insane cub. Such a Guardian!" Cloudwalker stood and shook out what there was of his fur. Dust rose off him like smoke from a grass fire. "You hear the voices, my Hunter, because you ate the unsacred meat."

Rabbitrunner knew only too well what Cloudwalker

was saying. The stories about going insane from eating the meat of cows were told to him since he was a cub. He didn't need to be told why he was hearing the voices, he knew the reason.

Cloudwalker turned and walked uphill towards the shadows of the trees. "Where are you going?" Rabbitrunner asked.

"Away," Cloudwalker answered, his massive bulk looking like an avalanche rolling against gravity, up a slope instead of down. "I am leaving you a meal, Rabbit-Turd, and you owe me a meal."

"Wait!" Rabbitrunner whined, trotting after him. "Stay. We need to stick together. We need to survive. We share the Blood of the Hunter between us."

"The Blood of the Hunter?" Cloudwalker scoffed, stopping and looking over his shoulder. Rabbitrunner froze, realizing the old Hunter would not let him follow. "The Blood of the Hunter—Do you not know what it is, Rabbit-Turd? Do you? Our kind is dying off! Twolegs are killing Hunters, and we are fewer and fewer. I see them killed, all my pretty ones, all, gone in one moment! Someday a pack, someday one, someday none."

He bared his teeth, not at Rabbitrunner but at some internal rage. "The Blood of the Hunter seeps into the ground, it does. Seeps into the ground, the bloody, bloody sand, where all the bodies lie." He turned and continued walking uphill, the tension now gone out of his body. He suddenly looked very tired. "A place there is, Rabbit-Turd, and walk there you can, going north, with sunrise at your right paw, sunset at your left, and a place there is, and snow is always there, and cold, and harsh living, but no Twolegs."

Rabbitrunner watched, and Cloudwalker disappeared beneath the shadows of the trees with the last of his words. He stared, but he could no longer see anything. A disturbance overhead caught his attention, and he looked up just in time to see the large raven leap off the tree branch, the other two following as they took to the air, flying with powerful wing beats, as they rose in the sky. Rabbitrunner glanced around for Zephyr. Like Hunters, ravens had their own territories, and Zephyr and his mate, Storm, were extremely possessive of theirs, but now they were nowhere to be seen.

He watched the birds disappear, thinking. He'd been aware of the scent of Cloudwalker over the last year, but it wasn't a passing scent, it was something he noticed daily, so he gradually got used to it in time, no longer giving it any thought, no longer recognizing the scent as anything uncommon. It was one of Cloudwalker's tricks, and it meant he'd passed through his territory off and on during that year, watching but never making contact. It angered and saddened him.

He turned and shuffled downhill, where he grabbed the dead dog's leg in his teeth and dragged it to the base of Bearback. Fly larvae were already crawling over it, and in a week it would be a pile of bones and hair.

He returned to the clearing and rested in the warmth of the sunlight, licking the dried urine off his fur. The smell was sickening and strong, and the taste was bitter. When he was clean, he rose and crawled into his den, wondering what Cloudwalker meant about the Blood of the Hunter.

You can do it, Deerchaser's voice told him as he crawled through the tunnel. *But I can't.*

"Do what?" Rabbitrunner asked, hardly paying the voice any mind.

Survive, Deerchaser said.

"Yeah, but for how long?" Rabbitrunner growled as he stretched out in his chamber and went to sleep.

Chapter Eleven

"Thieves"
(Early Autumn, 1966)

The red '64 Plymouth Valiant turned off the highway at the dirt road, driving along the ruts between the trees, the headlights cutting beams through the darkness. The engine rumbled angrily, the noise announcing the need for a tune-up, a valve replacement, and a new muffler. After a year of drag races, high-speed chases, and joy rides, the Valiant was pleading for retirement.

As Parker Roberts maneuvered the car over bumps and through deep ruts, Timothy Cowan checked his watch by the glow of the glove compartment lamp. The door to the glove compartment had been ripped off by Parker in one of his temper fits last month, and Tim was still pissed off about it. It was his Valiant, not Parker's and he was beginning to think this "What's yours is mine, etc." philosophy they shared was just another package of discontent he'd foolishly bought lock, stock and barrel from him. Even so, he still hadn't gotten around to talking to Parker about the problem, too worried about his temper.

The radio blared a Herman's Hermits song as they

heard something scrape the oil pan. The half-moon was visible to them through the bare branches as they rattled on, swallowed whole by the woods.

Tim pulled out the pint flask of whiskey and took a drink, then passed it to Parker. "Man, you sure this is the right road?"

"Christ, man, we saw him drive off this road just a little while ago." Parker took a drink and passed the flask back, then picked up the Winston smoldering in the ashtray and took a drag. "Hey, man, you see 'Star Trek' the other night?"

"Don't you ever miss that show?"

"Hell no, man, that Captain Kirk's a badass, whips those Klingons and the Romulans. And I bet he's making time in real life with the black bitch that plays Lieutenant Uhuru."

"Are you sure this is the right road?" Tim said. "It's half past midnight."

"What'sa matter, Tim, way past your bedtime?" Parker laughed.

"We been driving for five minutes."

"It's a long road. I told you that." Parker puffed on his cigarette. "Any how, Captain Kirk...."

"You watch too much TV."

"And you don't?" Parker laughed. "You watch Herman Munster, Lawrence Welk, and Ed Sullivan. Fuckin' square, man! Let's hear you speak like Ed. C'mon Tim."

"Shut up."

"'A really big shooo....'" Parker said and laughed. "'A really, really big shooo.....'"

Tim turned up the radio on a Dave Clark Five song, panicked by the sound of the oilpan bouncing off another rock between the ruts.

"Why don't you do Lawrence Welk?" Parker said, becoming vicious in his tone. "'Thank ya, boys, thank ya.

And now, let's have some Geritol.' Hell, Tim, you used to do it all the time." He laughed, mean-spirited and vindictive.

The Beatles were singing "Help!" on the radio as Tim looked out the passenger window. "And what about Cutter?"

Parker snapped the radio off. "So what about Cutter?" he asked, rage in his voice. They had waited since nine that evening, parked along the shoulder, for Cutter to leave his cabin and drive off the old dirt road onto the highway. He told Patty Tilton at the Crooked River he'd be right back, but whatever he did at the cabin took over three hours. Parker resented the waiting, but now they were finally on their way to his cabin—and the money.

"The hell with Cutter," Parker said, stubbing out his cigarette. "Fuck him. Fuck that old man. He's going to the Crooked River, and he ain't gonna make an early night of it. We'll be there and gone before he takes his first piss."

Branches scraped the side of the Valiant. Tim jumped. He felt like the trees were closing in.

"Don't forget, we got a deal to buy some good hashish from Turkey from that guy who comes from Duluth. And he's also gonna sell us some LSD. You ever try acid, Timmy, my boy?"

Tim shrugged, but his mind wandered to Jessie "Cutter" Armstrong. Cutter was nobody to mess with, and he felt uneasy about stealing a jar of cash from his cabin, especially nowadays, when Cutter brought his bow and arrows wherever he went, like a good-luck talisman. Even unstrung, the bow looked formidable, and the custom-made arrows, with black metal alloy four-sided razor-sharp barbed arrowheads, hurt just to look at them.

Engine fumes leaked into the Valiant through the firewall, but it was too cold to open a window, the heater didn't work, and they both left their coats back at the garage apartment they shared. The Valiant rocked like a rowboat in a storm, and the oil pan bumped against something else. Tim winced, then noticed the odometer. "Goddam, Parker, we've gone eight miles since the highway."

"Oh, whoop-de-doo!" Parker said, lighting another cigarette. "Why don't you give me a Goddam weather report while you're at it?"

"We're on the wrong road."

"C'mon, Tim, you know Cutter doesn't live by the highway."

"What if there's no money?" Tim asked. "And why would Cutter leave it out where anyone could steal it?"

"Because he's a country bumpkin," Parker said. "People who live out in the country or out in the woods don't think about getting robbed. I bet his front door isn't even locked."

"Maybe he hid bear traps around the house," Tim said. "Or maybe he rigged a shotgun with a string to the door."

"He's not that smart."

"Parker, I don't think this is the right road."

Parker laughed, fighting the steering wheel with one hand as he pointed. "Hey asshole—take a look." Through the dirty windshield they saw the tree-walled road open into a clearing. In the back of the clearing was a moss-covered cabin, dark and small against the trees behind it.

The Valiant stopped five feet from the wooden door as the engine died. Parker and Timothy gazed at the structure, looking at the two front windows. No light came from inside. They could hear the crickets over the ticking of the cooling engine valves, but nothing else.

"It really is a log cabin," Tim said, gazing at the horseshoe nailed to the old oak door. The log walls were bare of bark, weather-worn and worm holed, but they still looked sturdy and unbreachable.

They opened the car doors and stepped out, holding their flashlights. Parker reached in and turned off the headlights before he slammed the door shut. He could see his breath condensating into steam in the moonlight, and the cold soaked through his clothes and skin. A musty odor, seeming to radiate from the cabin, permeating the area. "Phew!" Parker said, turning towards Timothy. "Dirty socks!" They laughed together.

The yard was mostly dirt, with patches of frost-covered grass growing up around pieces of junk left where they had fallen, an old, cracked wood stove, an engine block, a stack of old tires. Downhill was an outhouse, complete with wooden moon door, and next to it was some sort of deep pit, looking almost like an empty grave. To one side of the cabin were two old rusted-out Ford pickup trucks with canvas tarps partially covering each. They were on blocks next to a third Ford pickup that at least looked drivable.

"Cool, man," Parker said, laughing.

Tim nudged Parker and pointed towards the roof. The chimney was smoking. "Relax, there's no one home," Parker said and headed for the front door.

One of the windows had a weatherworn window box with grass and a small, leafy bush growing from it, all covered with frost that sparkled in the moonlight. Parker gave it a passing glance before he pushed on the door. It squeaked open like a noisy cat. "Not even fucking locked," Parker said, opening it wide as he flicked on his flashlight. Tim followed him in, doing the same.

The wood stove, connected to the chimney of the unused fireplace by a rusty flue, had a smoldering fire crackling inside. As Tim closed the door behind him, he was grateful for the warm air. There were several wooden chairs around a heavy wooden kitchen table, a stuffed easy chair that looked out of place, wooden boxes, a couple stacks of newspapers, and skins and skulls on the walls. Iron skillets and steel restaurant pots hung behind the wood stove, and dirty dishes stuck up from a tub of dirty, sudsy water, by the fireplace.

"C'mon," Parker said, lifting a box lid. "We have some money to find."

"What's your hurry?" Tim asked noticing Parker's nervousness, glad it wasn't him for a change. "I thought you said the old man would be away for hours."

"Yeah, well, this place stinks," Parker said, tossing an empty beer bottle at Tim's feet. "It smells like an old clothes hamper, and I feel like I need a bath just being here and breathing the air." He began digging into another box, scattering its contents on the floor.

The cabin did stink, Tim noticed, pointing his flashlight beam around, but at least it was warm, and besides, their apartment wouldn't smell any better if they were not used to it. Tim decided to keep that insight to himself as he held open a bearskin curtain and stepped into the next room.

He saw more boxes, a chair, and a small table with an unlit oil lamp on it, an old, warped dresser, and a handmade wooden bed in the corner with a lumpy mattress and scattered blankets on it.

Tim made a slow circuit with the flashlight beam, noticing skins on the wall, two bookshelves, a gun rack with three well-oiled rifles, the only clean items in the cabin, Tim figured. There was a box of dirt-encrusted empty mason jars, and something gleaming under the bed.

Tim knelt on the dusty floor and held the flashlight ahead of him. The gallon pickle jar, nestled among dirty clothes that stank of sweat, was overflowing with paper currency. "Shit," Tim whispered.

He reached under the bed and pulled out the jar, holding it between his knees as he pulled out a handful of bills. A few ones, tens, twenties, fifties. The bills were old, and Tim held up the flashlight, checking the date on one, reading "1940." Old, but money was money.

He glanced around, having a sudden impression that Cutter was there in the room with him, watching him from the shadows. He picked up the jar and stepped through the curtain.

Parker was emptying the contents of another box with one hand while holding his flashlight with the other. The front window was just over his head. Tim watched as two bright lights crossed the window's surface, one following the other, lighting up dirt and cobwebs before they disappeared.

"Cutter's back," Tim said, kneeling and setting the jar on the floor before he dropped it.

"What?" Parker spun around. His flashlight beam caught the jar. "Kee-rist! Man, look at that! Cool! You found it, Tim!" He crawled over to the jar and grabbed a handful of bills. "Goddam, Tim, you hit the jackpot."

"Cutter's back," Tim said, feeling numb.

Parker looked up. "What do you mean Cutter's back?"

"Cutter's back. I just saw his headlights." He pointed at the window. "Parker, we gotta get outta here."

"Ain't nobody out there," Parker said, picking up the large jar and standing. "You've just imagining things. Nerves."

"Parker, listen to me...." His words were cut short by the sound of an engine outside. Even Parker heard it this time; Tim could see it in his face. He glanced at Tim, glanced at the door, then set the jar down.

Tim watched as Parker moved silently to the door, reaching behind him and pulling a revolver from the back of his pants, where it had been hidden only a moment before. Tim's eyes went wide. Parker owned two snub-nosed revolvers which he took into the woods for target practice, but this was the first time he'd brought one with him on a burglary.

"Turn off your flashlight," Parker whispered as he turned off his. Tim switched his flashlight off and watched. The room was all but black, except for the window letting in moonlight. He could just make out Parker's arm reaching for the wooden door handle. Something in the wood stove popped, and he shuddered.

Tim held his breath as Parker slowly pulled the door open. It squeaked angrily, spoiling any chance of surprise Parker had hoped for. Nonetheless, holding the gun in one hand, he slowly stuck his head out and looked around. Tim could see part of the landscape over Parker's head, bathed in moonlight and looking like a black-and-white photo. There was no sound of an engine, just the crickets.

"What do you see?" Tim whispered.

Parker gestured with the gun for quiet and stuck more of his body out the door. He's out there, Tim thought, he followed us and now he's out there.

Suddenly Parker made a gagging sound as the gun dropped from his hands. His body shook; one leg came off the floor and banged helplessly against the log wall. Tim leaped up, eyes wide, holding his flashlight like a weapon. Then Parker swung inside, closing the door. "Damn, those mosquitoes are strong," he gasped.

"Parker?"

"Boo!" Parker said, then laughed. "Scared the shit outta you, didn't I?"

"Sonovabitch, Parker!"

"C'mon, man," Parker said. "Fun is over. Let's take this jar and split."

"What about Cutter?"

"He's at the Crooked River," Parker said, holding the jar in one arm and the revolver and flashlight in the other. "But if you want to stand there and worry, I'm sure he'll be back in a couple hours."

Tim got to the door and glanced out before Parker stepped past him. "Man, I know I saw him out there! I saw his headlights in the window."

"You didn't see shit," Parker said, walking to the Valiant. "You have an overactive imagination."

"Yeah and what about that engine we heard? You heard it too, Parker."

"An echo from the highway."

"Ten miles away?"

They slid into the Valiant and Parker turned the key. "You had me going there for awhile," Parker said as the engine roared to life. "For a minute I believed he was out here too. But look around. He's not here. And you know he'd bust down his own cabin to get to us if he were here."

Tim situated the money jar between his feet. "I still think...."

"And that's what you get for thinking," Parker said, shifting into drive and bringing the Valiant around. Parker slipped his snubnose into his pants before they began bouncing along the rutted road.

Tim unscrewed the lid on the flask and took a drink, the flask neck rattling between his teeth. Parker put a cigarette between his lips, pressed the cigarette lighter in, and turned on the radio. A Grateful Dead tune came on as Tim passed the flask to Parker, who drank the last of it and dropped the empty flask to the floor. "Yeah, the Grateful Dead. I love 'em." He pulled out the lighter, lit his cigarette, and replaced it in its slot. "But their music is so weird they probably won't last another year. I wonder what they'd call themselves if Jerry Garcia died."

"I can't wait until we reach the highway," Tim said. "These woods give me the creeps."

"I wonder if there really is five grand in that jar," Parker said, puffing madly. "We'd better count it when we get back. The hell with that. Let's not count it. Let's just go to the Crooked River and buy a couple pitchers of beer."

"Christ, Parker," Tim said. "We can't do that. Cutter's there."

"Yeah, you're right," Parker said. "We're gonna have to buy Cutter a pitcher of beer too. After all, it is his money. Or was."

"Quit bullshitting."

"I'm serious," Parker went on. "I always wanted to do something like that. Buy Cutter a drink with his own cash."

"And when he finds his jar missing," Tim said, feeling the heft of it between his shoes, "and he puts two and two together, he'll hunt us down like a coupla raccoons."

"Holy shit!" Parker shouted, braking so quickly the engine almost died. Tim bumped his head on the dash board as Parker turned off the radio.

"What the fuck?" Tim howled.

"Look," Parker said, his voice shaky. Tim peered out the windshield. Thirty feet down the road, parked across the ruts, was a muddy army jeep.

"It's Cutter," Tim whispered. "I knew he was here. I knew I saw his headlights."

"Shut up," Parker said, shifting into neutral. He rolled down his window and looked out. In the glare of the headlights the jeep looked like a derelict. The engine was off and the lights were out. The door flaps were off so they could see that no one was inside.

"He's gotta be around here somewhere," Tim whispered. "But where is he? What's he doing?"

"Shut up," Parker whispered, panic claiming his voice. He pulled the revolver from his pants and checked the cylinder. Then, snapping it closed, he looked at Tim. "Watch the money," he said.

"Where are you going?" Tim said. "And how'm I gonna protect the money, Parker, you got the fucking gun?"

"Just stay here."

"Hell, no, I'm not going to stay here, I'm...."

Parker twisted and slapped him so hard that his head hit the passenger door window. The stinging in his cheek seemed to take a moment to catch up with the event.

"Look, pussy boy," Parker hissed. "Just shut up and stay put." He used the grip of the gun to break the glove compartment light. "Now just stay cool and everything'll be all right." He jammed the gun in his pants, opened the door and stepped out.

Tim reached over and slammed the door shut as Parker stepped away. He shivered, gripping the jar between his shaking legs. Parker stepped into the light of the headlamps, trying to walk casually towards the jeep. The revolver was hidden by his shirttail. Tim could hear the crickets and the sounds of Parker's footsteps over the rumble of the engine. He felt terribly cold.

"Cutter, is that you?" Parker said, his hands out to his sides as he stepped closer to the jeep. He stopped ten feet from the vehicle. "We were just looking for you. You're not going to believe this, but...."

Parker and Tim both heard a rustling and thud off to the right side of the road. Parker reached behind him, drawing the snub-nosed .38 while Tim watched and thought that the noise sounded like someone threw a large stone. He's not going to be fooled by that old trick, is he, Tim thought.

The air exploded as Parker fired three rounds into the trees. Tim winced at the noise, then held still, shivering, as Parker tried to see into the darkness. How could he be so stupid, Tim thought.

A hairy-knuckled hand reached into the open driver's side window, turned off the engine and pulled the key out. Tim snapped around, seeing a large form in the darkness. "Oh, shit."

Parker, still aiming his gun into the trees, looked back at the Valiant. "Tim, don't do that, the battery'll go dead. Goddam, I think I got him, I think I got him."

Tim glanced from Parker to the large figure, aware that Parker couldn't see him beyond the glare of the headlights. The large man raised something, a bow and a notched arrow and stepped in front of the Valiant.

"Holy shit," Parker said.

"Drop it," Cutter said.

Parker quickly spun around and fired one round. The air was split by the report of the bullet, and then a whitening hiss, followed by a grunt from Parker. Tim gazed over the hood, watching Parker fall to his knees. An arrow stuck through Parker's right arm. Cutter stepped off into the shadows, notching another arrow as Parker knelt between the ruts, hyperventilating, making sounds like a caged monkey.

"Christ," Tim whispered, shaking.

Parker's eyes gazed at the arrow, the red-red-black fletching, tagging him like a marked animal. His arm was speckled with blood. He grasped the arrow, then grunted and let go, howling with pain. The fingers of his left hand danced around the shaft, wanting to pull it out but afraid to touch it.

"So you needed a little extra cash," Cutter said from the darkness. A second arrow hissed through the air and hit the ground at Parker's feet. Parker staggered backward, propelled more by adrenaline than by muscle. "So you decided to come by tonight and ask me for a bank loan." Cutter's voice seemed unusually calm. "That was awfully thoughtful of you. I enjoyed the visit, didn't you?"

"Look, man, it was all a big mistake," Parker said, his useless right hand still gripping the revolver. "Just a big mistake."

Cutter stepped into the light, holding the bow and

arrow in one hand. Tim gazed at the back of the big man, at the thick arms, the thick neck, the red bandana. Cutter stepped closer to Parker and pulled the revolver out of his hand, then struck him with it.

"Fucking punk!" Cutter shouted. "Fucking, thieving punk!"

"Look, man, I'm sorry." Parker looked like he was about to cry.

Cutter raised the gun.

Tim, still inside the car, reached over and pressed hard on the horn. Both men looked his way. Cutter took aim, fired, blowing out one headlamp, fired again and blew out the other, then aimed through the windshield at Tim. He released the horn and fell back into the seat. Cutter pulled the trigger. The gun clicked. He laughed and tossed it into the trees.

"Man, just let us go," Parker pleaded. "We'll give the money back to you."

"I've met thieves before," Cutter said, standing over him. "I wanted to kill them. To me, if there's anything lower than a rat, it's a thief. But the ones I met—they, at least, were stealing because they were hungry. Because they had to feed their families. They had a reason to be thieves. You—stealing to get drunk, to put gas in your car, to have some fun. I can't see it. You know, I just can't see it."

"Man, c'mon," Parker pleaded, his hand on his wounded arm. "What else can I say?"

Cutter's booted foot was fast. The first kick caught Parker in the stomach, knocking the wind out of him. The second kick got his face as he doubled over. He collapsed backwards like a rag doll. Cutter placed a foot on his chest and notched an arrow.

"I guess I don't like you," he said. "'I'm sorry' just ain't gonna cut it this time."

"Please, please," Parker begged, both hands ineffectively gripping the boot on his chest. "Please, let's talk. C'mon, Cutter, please."

Cutter grinned and took aim. He drew back on the bow and looked at Parker's face, his tears glistening in the moonlight. Parker had just pissed himself.

He released the arrow.

Tim could hear the thunk from the Valiant. "God," he whispered. By the moonlight it looked like the arrow was embedded beside Parker's neck, the fletching beneath his chin. The blood squirted in the air as though the arrow was a tiny oil well. Parker's feet were kicking.

Cutter stepped back as Parker clawed at the fletching. Blood covered his chest, his face, his hands, but he didn't utter a sound, as though he were part of a silent black-and-white movie. Then Parker went still, his hands fluttering like butterflies, then landing on his chest, then sliding off.

Tim kept staring. He was hyperventilating by the time Cutter yanked open his door and dragged him out. He felt himself shoved against the trunk of a tree, then Cutter slapped him, again, and again.

"Calm down," Cutter said, shaking him. "Relax." Tim shook his head, his cheeks burning with tears. He tasted bile in his mouth. "Are you okay?"

Tim shook his head.

"Can you stand by yourself?" Cutter asked. "You're breathing a little better."

"Jesus Christ," Tim gasped.

"Yeah, I know," Cutter said, his thick, calloused fingers gently releasing him. Tim locked his knees to remain standing. "I know what you mean. Seeing a man die like that is horrible. I fought in two wars, and I saw men die by the hundreds."

The air had the metallic smell of blood. Tim didn't dare

look at the body. Cutter, still holding the bow in his left hand, rolled a cigarette with his right. He was about to take it himself, but instead offered it to Tim, who shook his head. "That's okay," Cutter said, striking a match and lighting his cigarette. "Can you stand on your own now?"

Tim nodded.

Cutter stepped away. Tim finally turned and looked at Parker's body. His cheeks were sore. The whole place seemed like a dream.

"Timothy Cowan," Cutter said.

Tim looked back.

Cutter was pulling another arrow from his quiver and notching it. The black leather wrist guard on Cutter's left arm looked like a giant wound. He took aim and drew back on the bowstring.

Tim shook his head.

"You have ten minutes head start," Cutter said. "Then I'm coming after you. There's nine miles from here to the highway. If you reach the highway, I don't touch you. Any place I find you between here and there, you're mine. Understand?"

Tim shook his head, more vigorously this time.

"Well, let me explain it again," Cutter said.

"No," Tim pleaded. "No."

"I'm giving you a chance," Cutter said. "Surely you'd jump at a chance. Surely you'd think you could outrun an old man."

"Please, please," Tim said. "I don't want to play this game." His voice trembled, his tears started again. He stared at the point of the arrow aimed at his chest.

"You can even take the money," Cutter said. "All of it. If you make it to the highway with the money, it's all yours. You can get drunk and forget tonight ever happened."

"No!" Tim begged.

"Yeah, you're right," Cutter said, grinning. "Carrying

a heavy jar like that would slow you down. I would've had a check for you had I planned this out better, but I'm ad-libbing now."

"Cutter," Tim said. "Cutter, let's talk." He was afraid his knees would unlock and he'd fall on his face. He already noticed Cutter's hands were shaking from holding the bow drawn back at the ready.

"How could you think you would rob me and get away with it?" Cutter said, almost whispering. "When I turned onto the highway, I recognized your car right off, just sitting there along the shoulder. I saw both of you when Parker lit his cigarette with a match. A soldier in a battle is very careful about lighting his cigarette. The enemy can draw a bead on him that way. I drove down the road...."

Cutter's voice was rising. His bow shook. It must have hurt to keep it drawn, but Cutter wouldn't relax. "I watched your taillights come on. I saw you pull onto my road. If there's one thing I hate more than a thief, it's a greedy thief, and if there's one thing I hate more than a greedy thief, it's a stupid greedy thief."

"Please," Tim begged.

"Damn, Cowan," Cutter said, tilting his head. "You act like you're the one who just killed him. Relax a little, will you? Now remember, you have ten minutes head start, beginning...." He looked at his wristwatch, his lips moving, "....now. Ten minutes, Cowan." He looked up and smiled.

Tim looked at Parker's body, expecting him to sit up and announce it was all a joke. He was shivering uncontrollably now, he could see his breath in the moonlight, and he wished he'd brought his coat. He glanced at his feet. "The money's all yours. Go ahead. The jar's in there, passenger side. You can keep the car, too." He looked up as Cutter turned and walked away. "Just let me go. Please."

Cutter stopped by the Valiant and turned around. "I'm so sorry," he said. "You have nine minutes left. No,

I reckon you are twenty years younger than me, so you can probably run faster. And with a nine minute head start you'll have me beat, I'm sure. But I wouldn't keep standing here, wasting time like this if I were you."

Tim felt like puking. Cutter again nocked the arrow and pulled it back, as though getting the feel of it. Tim turned and began running. "Cowan!" Cutter called without looking up. "Wait a minute." Tim stopped and looked back. "Highway's the other way. You're heading for my cabin."

Tim quickly changed direction, running past the vehicles, running past Cutter and Parker's body, then slowing to a fast walk, his eyes picking out details in the moonlight. He stuck to the road, jogging between the ruts, careful at every step. The trees passed him on either side like an army of tall soldiers. The road wasn't straight as he imagined, but meandered, making a long, slow arc around. By now he was thinking that he could have brought the jar of money after all. Then he thought about Parker, how he couldn't even defend himself with a gun, and now he was dead....

He saw Cutter standing a hundred feet down the road, alone in the moonlight, his quiver on his back, his bow and arrow in one hand.

Tim leaped off the road and shoved his back against a tree. He was gasping for breath, his vision was failing him, and his mind was spinning. It couldn't be Cutter. He left Cutter behind.

"Cowan, is that you?" Cutter shouted. "Your ten minutes were up four minutes ago. I'm sorry, I should have told you how this stupid road turns back upon itself and makes a horseshoe. Your best bet would be to run through the woods." Tim turned around. Was the voice getting closer? He didn't dare look. "Now if you leave the road from the right side, and if you can keep on heading

straight, you'll be going directly to the highway itself. The
night is late, and I'm a little tired, so I'll be walking the
first ten minutes, so if you want to continue running, go
ahead."

Tim reached behind him and gripped the tree. How
could Cutter figure out so much? How could he win in
this game? An arrow hissed past his head and embedded
itself in the tree across from him. Cutter knew exactly
where he was.

He leaped away and started running, praying that he
was keeping on a straight line to the highway, and not
making another roundabout turn. He tripped over something, pulled himself up and kept running. The image
of Parker's body kept appearing in his mind. He kept
replaying scenes, turning off the highway onto the dirt
road, driving to the cabin, stealing the jar of money. It
all seemed to have happened years ago. He tripped, hit
the ground, and picked himself up again. He stopped
and listened, but could hear nothing over the noise of
his own panting. He continued running, feeling the trees
close in on him.

He was now wheezing, tired, his head throbbing, his
legs like rubber. He stopped by a tree, holding himself
up with one hand on its trunk. He tried to hear some-
thing over his gasps, tried to hear if Cutter was coming.
If he kept going, he could make the highway by daylight.
How many miles had he covered? How many more to go?
Perhaps Cutter had lost his trail, but he didn't think so.
Cutter was one of the best hunters in Caleb County.

He had to go on, but he was so tired. If running took
that much energy out of him, he thought, then surely a
forty-year-old man like Cutter would be worn out somewhere in the woods. Cutter was probably propped up
against a tree, gasping for breath himself. Tim smiled
at the image in his mind. He probably gave up and went

back to the cabin.

But then, why was Cutter so confident when he gave him a ten minute head start?

It was almost like a dream when he heard the hiss and thunk of an arrow finding its mark on the tree beside him. The pain took two seconds to hit him, seeming to come from everywhere in his body. Tim jerked around, grunting, only to find himself stuck to the tree. The arrow was jammed through his left wrist and embedded in the trunk.

He didn't have the energy to scream. He made animal noises, whining, purring, whimpering as the pain took little bites out of his mind. His arm ached, but he didn't dare move—it would only cause more pain. His knees shook. His teeth chattered. He noticed that he could still move his fingers, but it hurt too much to do so. His wrist was swelling up, and blood was running from the wound, he could hear it dripping on the ground.

"I think you got four miles in."

Tim looked around. "Cutter?" he whimpered, still not believing.

"Too bad you were too slow," Cutter said, walking through the shadows towards him. "Too bad you were too slow."

"Goddam," Tim bellowed in despair. "Goddam." Tears flowed over his cheeks as he grabbed the aluminum shaft with his good hand and pulled. It wouldn't budge. He began blubbering as he grabbed his wrist and gave a yank. Searing hot pain exploded through his body as he screamed, but his wrist moved. Broken wrist bones crunched together as he jerked the wrist along the shaft, leaving blood along its length. When he reached the fletching, he leaned backward and pulled, and the feathers disappeared into his flesh and reappeared out the other side.

Sweat poured off him as he staggered backward, caught his balance, and held his wounded arm to his chest, feeling the warmth of his own blood leak through his shirt. He had to run away, but the pain in his wrist kept pulling at his thoughts like a magnet. He felt as though he were about to pass out.

The next arrow hit him in the knee, effectively crippling him. As Tim heard Cutter's voice talking about something, his mind twisted in upon itself, and he was unconscious before he hit the ground.

My God, my God, why have you forsaken me?

The words of the Twenty-Second Psalm, and the words of Jesus dying on the cross.

Tim recalled the words from his Sunday school class when he was seven years old, just now realizing that the lines from the Old Testament and the New Testament were one and the same. He never realized it before. They never discussed it. Why was he hurting so badly?

Pain drew him from the fog of unconsciousness as he realized he was in the back of Cutter's jeep, being bounced on an old mildewed tarp. Even unconscious, he managed to hold his wrist to his chest. His shirt was saturated with blood, and his wrist throbbed, as did his knee.

He reached down and touched the arrow still embedded in his knee. His pant leg was sticky with blood. Tears filled his eyes as he brought his bloody hand back and again gripped his wrist.

He couldn't see anything, but there was something large and lumpy next to him in the cramped space that had to be Parker's body. Besides that, an old tire iron and greasy rags surrounded him, and the rumble of the jeep's engine was all he could hear. Each bump in the road jarred his wounds and brought him back to reality.

He touched Parker with his good hand, managed to find his neck, and felt for a pulse, but there was none. His fingers moved and accidentally slipped into the gaping hole in Parker's throat. Tim tried to scream as he yanked his hand back but instead he again passed out.

The next thing he recalled was being dragged through the dirt, then dropped into a deep, black pit. He hit the bottom, knocking the wind out of him and jarring the arrow in his knee. He gagged until he was able to inhale again, then he moved from his knee to his wrist and back again, touching his wounds, fighting to hold to consciousness.

A twenty-five pound sack landed on top of him, and he screamed again. He screamed until he was gagging, and he coughed several times and looked up. Above him was the top of the pit. He couldn't see the moon, but he could see the stars shimmering like the reflective sparkles in a brook on a summer morning. The air smelled of fresh dirt and a strange chalky dust. He pushed the sack off with his good hand. He was cramped and miserable.

He reached back to adjust something behind his head only to find out it was Parker. He wanted to scream, but he was too tired and in too much pain. The sound of the jeep cranking to life somewhere above him caught his attention. Something was going on. He looked up as clods of dirt were dropping on him and a large, wooden platform slid over the pit, blocking out the stars. "Goddam you, Cutter!" Tim screamed. "Cutter! Cutter! What are you doing?"

The jeep's engine died. He could hear Cutter's boots on the ground outside, then tramping on wood above him. "Cutter!"

His answer was a stream of warm water splattering his head and chest. He sputtered and swatted ineffectively with his good hand. He could tell by the smell it was urine. "Goddam you, Cutter!" he yelled.

"Sorry about the inconvenience," Cutter shouted from above. "I had to take a piss, and you were in my way."

"Cutter," Tim cried. "Where did you put me?"

"Well," Cutter said, "my outhouse is on runners, so when I need to, I dig a new hole and drag my outhouse over it. So that's where I put you." He laughed.

"Cutter, please help me!"

"I'll probably take a shit tomorrow," Cutter said. "Of course, this new hole is already filled with shit."

"Cutter, I need help!"

"I gave you a fighting chance," Cutter said. "You just lost. But you shouldn't have robbed me, you and your buddy, Parker, down there. You shouldn't have robbed me."

"It was Parker's idea!" Tim cried. The pain was unbearable, the darkness claustrophobic.

"I'm sorry Parker mislead you," Cutter said through the wooden hole above. "I'm sorry I had to kill him the way I did. I didn't give him a sporting chance, did I? But I gave you a chance." He sighed. "I see everything as a game now, where both sides must have a chance. Hunter and hunted. Both must have an equal opportunity to win."

"Please, Cutter, help me!"

"Does the cougar help the deer?" he asked. "Does the lion help the antelope? The game is over, Cowan, you lose."

"Cutter," Tim was thinking fast. "What about your friend, Ben? Won't he be missing you at the Crooked River? Won't he be suspicious?"

"Ben's at a funeral in Minneapolis," Cutter said. "And even if he were here, I doubt he'd be suspicious of anything."

"God Almighty, Cutter!"

"Goodbye, Tim," Cutter said. "The sack I threw down there was lye. It should start dissolving you both when the water hits you."

"Cutter!" Tim screamed.

He heard Cutter step out and close the squeaky wooden door. "Cutter!" He heard footsteps, Cutter walking away.

He cried, he blubbered, not even caring about the pain of his wounds. He wondered how he would get out, then he wondered how long he'd live if he didn't get out. Would he starve to death? Would he eat Parker's flesh? And what about the sack of lye? What did Cutter mean it would start dissolving him when the water hit him?

He was still wondering about that when the door squeaked open and Cutter poured the large soup pot of boiling water into the hole.

Chapter Twelve

"Survival"
(A Year: 1966 - 1967)

The large Hunter trotted at a constant pace as he traveled though the trees in the darkness, ignoring the whistles and noises of birds in the bare branches overhead. The sound of the birds meant daylight was approaching, but he was only concerned with the deer he'd been tracking half the night.

He had yet to see her, but he could smell the infirmities of her old, weary body over the fertile odor of dead leaves and grass. He was worried that she was heading closer to the border of his territory. He didn't want to have to fight a pack for meat he'd brought down.

He knew she was wounded when he first picked up her scent. She should have collapsed from exhaustion by now, but instead she continued to maintain her distance, and he was only able to follow her by her scent.

The full moon was sinking beyond the distant mountains, and the sky opposite was turning from a star-speckled black to dark gray. He finally got a glimpse of the deer, a dark shape moving among the trees, the limp he'd detected by the sound of her movements obvious to him now as he watched her travel.

As the sun rose at their backs, Rabbitrunner picked up speed, going from a trot to a run. There wasn't much time before they'd reach the scent markers of his territory, but he worked too hard to let this meal escape.

He closed the distance by half before the deer realized that he was getting nearer. She began running, her breath steaming in the cold autumn air. Rabbitrunner had more stamina, and he was just a few yards behind her when she began dodging, left and right, trying to avoid his teeth.

Hooves and paws sounded in the crisp, cold air as they gasped for breath, running, Rabbitrunner baring his teeth, his muscles pumping as he lunged, chomping on air, missing, small clods of dirt being kicked up as he made a sharp turn with her. He watched the white tail, the muscular rump, just beyond the reach of his teeth. He closed the gap again, lunged and snapped his jaws. This time he grasped one leg just above the ankle.

The deer bucked and pulled, and Rabbitrunner braced his legs, his paws digging into the dirt as he jerked his head back and forth, his teeth going deeper into the flesh. He tasted fresh blood, and it spurred him on. He yanked sideways, and the deer lost her balance and toppled to the ground.

She tried to rise, but he kept dragging her backwards, keeping her from regaining her footing. He was about to release the leg and go for the throat when the deer's other hind hoof slammed into his head just above his left eye. The world went black, and all he could think about was holding on to the leg in his jaws.

When he finally came to, alone, he could still taste the deer's blood, but she was nowhere to be seen. The sun was still rising in the sky; he hadn't been unconscious for too long, at least. But the deer was gone! His meal!

She probably crossed over the border where the Tailless Pack most likely got her. He was furious. As he rose, his head throbbed.

You let her get away! Treepisser's voice said.

You would never have been able to kill her any way, Nighthowler's voice added.

"I almost got her," Rabbitrunner puled. "I almost had her. But by now she must be in the Tailless Territory, and his pack is probably feasting on the deer I almost brought down."

You would never get it by yourself, Bullmoosekiller's voice said.

"Maybe I didn't," Rabbitrunner growled. "But I could have." He licked his lips, tasting the last of the deer's blood and a little of his own. He felt weary, sore, and especially hungry. He hadn't eaten in a week, hadn't even found a field mouse, and it was his hunger and waning strength that compelled him to chase the deer, that and the realization the deer was wounded and old, which meant he had a chance to bring her down by himself.

Rabbitrunner stood and shook out his fur. He felt vulnerable in the sunlight, and he felt sore all over, but it didn't keep him from pausing to lick the dried blood off his muzzle. When he noticed the strong, familiar scent, his head snapped around. "Cloudwalker!" he yipped, but there was no one there.

Glancing in the other direction, he noticed the deer leg bone in the grass, one single bone, freshly gnawed clean of every scrap of meat, and smelling like the rugged old Hunter he'd seen only once that summer.

It didn't make sense.

Rabbitrunner cautiously sniffed the bone, wondering if Cloudwalker caught the old deer he'd chased and lost. Then he wondered why Cloudwalker would leave nothing but a bone. No meat, no carcass, just one well-gnawed bone. He bent and sniffed it one more time, then turned and started back towards his den on Bearback.

It turned out to be a lean autumn for Rabbitrunner, but at least he managed to catch a few rabbits and woodchucks after almost catching the deer, usually in other territories, and always staying downwind of the other packs. He usually traveled at night and slept lightly during the day under a log or rock ledge. He was always watchful, listening for the sounds or odor of Bigbird during the day and other packs during the night when he traveled through their territories to hunt.

The voices in his head no longer bothered him; he conversed with them sometimes, as though they were old friends, and in a way they were—the ghosts, from his past, though their images in his memory were slowly fading. He wondered if the voices themselves would go too, but that problem was overshadowed by his own need to survive.

One night as he crossed his territory he saw snowflakes falling. The moon was obscured by thick clouds, but some light was getting through. As the night wore on, his territory changed before his eyes: The ground was slowly covered in wet snow. The land seemed to glow from the snow's eerie reflective sheen. Winter, Rabbitrunner sadly realized, had arrived.

Food was scarce before, but it became even more so after the first snowfall. Rabbitrunner continued to make forays into the other territories, but now he traveled to places far beyond the territories that surrounded his, traveling, and hiding in the daylight, and hunting small animals, if there was anything to hunt.

He discovered other, more distant packs, and their Ones, Blackfang, One-eye, Bloodfur, and Largepaw, learning their scents and their habits, so he could pass through their territories with the least risk of discovery.

His travels only reached their range when he encountered the alien things of Twolegs —the long lines of wood pieces sticking up from the ground holding straight, horizontal thorny vines; the black rock rivers with the lines down the middles; the Twolegs' dens, some of them solid and some flimsy and portable—leaf dens—some of them wood, some of them stone, but all of them above ground, visible for miles. Whenever he confronted a Twoleg thing, he turned and rushed towards Bearback and safety.

Until the next time.

Though he often felt weary and lethargic, weak and hungry, he kept moving, hunting when there was something to hunt, or if finding nothing, eating snow and ice to temporarily fill his belly.

He grew thinner, just as he did the winter before. His ribs were prominent beneath his fur. His muscles became lean and hard, but they were losing mass, and he needed food to keep them working. Sometimes days and nights would run into each other, and sometimes he would stop in his tracks because he just noticed it was noon and not evening, and he wondered where the night went to as he grumpily stumbled to the nearest available log, pine bough or rock shelter to curl up and sleep.

Sometimes the snow was waist-deep, and sometimes it was fine and dry and dusty on frozen ground. When the moon was full on a cloudless evening, the snow was so reflective it was almost like day, trees and rocks and distant hills, all snow-covered and all clear and visible. The naked trees were sentinels across the frozen land. Paw prints were easy to spot, even to Rabbitrunner's half-snow-blind eyes, and odors were sharp, making hunting easy, when there was something to hunt.

One night as Rabbitrunner wandered over another hill

he saw Hunter facing away from him, and he stopped and crouched. The Hunter was only thirty feet from him, but hadn't yet noticed him. Rabbitrunner's senses became acute, as he looked about for others, but there was only the one Hunter, well-fed, unlike him, but hunched over, shivering and whining.

Rabbitrunner's ears were back, his hackles up. He was tensed to turn and run. Then the Hunter moved, and he heard the familiar rattle. The Hunter's left foreleg was held in Twolegs Jaws.

Rabbitrunner watched from his spot as the Hunter tugged at the Jaws, whining as the vine holding it to the ground rattled again. By the moonlight he could see drops of blood in the snow. He recalled Brookjumper, his dam, when she was held by the Jaws. He saw her die, and the memory never faded. He recalled how Twolegs came in the morning and killed her. With an overwhelming sadness, he realized there was nothing he could do for the Hunter. There was no way to set him free once he was caught.

He rose, turned and trotted away, but he didn't get far. He saw a second set of Jaws, partially hidden by snow, and then another. He hadn't seen them the first time he passed by, and it sent a chill down his spine to know that had he been walking too much to one side or the other, he would have been trapped too.

He went on, more cautiously now, until he came to a large, fallen tree by a creek that still gurgled noisily despite being half-covered with ice. The tree was half-rotted, and he climbed into a hollow in it and rested. Soon he was asleep.

He slept through the day and woke the next night, crawling from his warm hole inside the tree. A fresh snow covered the ground. It was time to move on, but before he did, he wanted to check on the trapped Hunter one last time.

He followed the same path he'd used the night before, more cautious now of the open Jaws. He came over the hill and stopped. The Hunter, his forepaw still in the Jaws, lay on his side, dead. His body was covered by a thin layer of snow.

Rabbitrunner tilted his head. It wasn't Twolegs that killed the Hunter, and it wasn't hunger. He stared at the frozen body, feeling his empty stomach clench. He knew what he had to do.

What do you think you're doing? Treepisser's voice asked from within his head as Rabbitrunner lifted his leg and urinated on an open set of Jaws.

"I'm marking them," Rabbitrunner said. "Maybe if I do this, another Hunter won't get trapped and die."

Don't you have something better to do? Treepisser snarled. *Like find some food? Look at you! You're starving to death, and all you can think about is pissing!*

Rabbitrunner went to the next set of Jaws, still nervous about what he was doing, wondering if the Jaws might leap up and bite him any way. He thought about the dead Hunter as he lifted his leg and urinated.

He was a stranger to you, Sleepfarter said. *What did he mean to you? He wasn't part of your pack.*

"Then who is my pack?" Rabbitrunner asked.

He was well-fed, Treepisser pointed out. *You aren't.*

Rabbitrunner found another set of Jaws. He lifted his leg. "He's dead now. I'm still alive. And what I do now is what Cloudwalker has done for many years."

So now you think you're Cloudwalker, Bullmoosekiller growled inside his head. *You want to look like him, too? You want to smell like him? He is an old, crazy Hunter who will get himself killed someday.*

"That's not how you used to talk about him," Rabbitrunner said, trotting through the snow towards a telltale lump. He was determined to mark all the Jaws. "You used to tell me stories about him. You used to call him the Guardian of Guardians. Enough from you. Enough from all of you. Leave me alone, okay?" He lifted his leg and urinated, melting the snow, revealing the deadly Jaws beneath.

As the days passed, he ate whatever he could find, rabbit, bird, old carcasses picked clean; he also searched out the Jaws. He developed a sense of finding them, and though most were so small even he could tell they were not put out for his kind but for the smaller animals, he marked them just the same, urinated on them to leave his scent.

It was about that time that he began finding bones; usually leg bones, along his trail. He found them one at a time, dropped on the snow with no scent or tracks leading up to it or away, but the bone itself stinking of Cloudwalker's scent.

Each bone was gnawed clean, left along his way as a taunt. Rabbitrunner had no idea how Cloudwalker could bring down something as large as a deer by himself, or how he could leave a bone along his trail with no tracks or scent in the snow. He broke the bones up with his teeth, eating the marrow and swallowing the bone chips with it, hoping Cloudwalker might leave a little meat on the next one.

He continued to steal meat from other packs when he could. He looked for carcasses left behind. He was always cold, often shivering, always weak and tired, but he knew he had to keep moving if he wanted to survive. As always, he wandered the snowy landscape by night and slept during the day, but he was growing weaker, and he knew he needed meat.

He was returning to Bearback one night, just crossing the scent markers into his own territory, when the wind changed direction and he smelled blood. His ears pricked up and he began salivating and breathing heavily. He arched his back and sniffed the air; it was a moose.

A moose!

He felt sick at the hopelessness of trying to bring down an animal so large. How could he? It was impossible. He couldn't even bring down a wounded deer in the autumn when he was stronger. Now he was weak, and cold, and hungry, and the animal was larger and more powerful than a deer. But the smell of blood kept pulling at him.

I brought one down myself, Bull said.

"That's different," Rabbitrunner growled. "You were stronger then. Look at me. We all called you Bull-moosekiller. You were a different kind of Hunter. Even in your old age, you still had fight. Even in your old age, you still wouldn't back down from Treepisser, who was half your age. I'm not like that."

So follow the trail, Bull said. *Maybe the moose will die of old age by the time you find it.*

"Maybe I'll die of starvation first."

Then forget it, Bull growled in his head. *Forget the moose. Go back to your den and starve.*

But Rabbitrunner couldn't forget it. His hunger wouldn't let him forget it. Maybe I can do it, he thought. Maybe I can bring down a moose by myself. He started following the scent trail.

The wind changed direction and he lost the scent, but he knew which way to go. He kept on a straight path through the dark night, plowing through the snowdrifts as heavy, wet snowflakes descended like pebbles from an avalanche.

The wind grew stronger and changed direction again. Rabbitrunner picked up the scent of blood, altered his line of travel, and continued on, moving at a hurried trot, already weary from traveling.

Eventually he saw it just ahead, a dark, tall silhouette,

a ghost of a large form in the distance. The moose was huge, muscular, his antlers rising like the thick limbs of an oak. He hadn't yet noticed the predator behind him. His gait was irregular with a distinct limp.

Rabbitrunner continued at the same speed, his head low, and his ears back. His hackles were raised as he kept his eyes on the dark, massive, limping beast. A blast of wind hit him from the side, and he stumbled, regained his balance, and gazed forward.

The moose was gone in a curtain of snow and wind. Icy snowflakes pelted the Hunter's eyes as he charged forward, panicked, glancing about, sniffing the air, his spirits sinking. Then he spotted the moose to his left and he changed direction again.

The moose began running, too, glancing just once over his shoulder before he galloped through the trees with Rabbitrunner running twenty feet behind him.

The snow was coming down harder and thicker now, and the wind was as strong as a bear. Sometimes everything would disappear from Rabbitrunner's vision until he passed and saw a tree trunk, the whiteness was so thick. The snow let up for a moment, and he saw he was still trailing the moose.

The land flattened out as Rabbitrunner was closing in, his chest hurting from running so long. Suddenly the moose slipped and fell. Rabbitrunner charged in after it to finish it off, but his paws hit ice, too, and he fell and slid through the thin blanket of snow. He stopped and carefully stood, feeling his body shaking.

The moose was also up, facing him with head lowered. Going against his better judgment, Rabbitrunner charged again. He bared his teeth for the kill, but it was as though a tree suddenly dove on him from the sky. The moose's antlers slammed into him and he was airborne, crashing down on the ice, spinning and sliding helplessly across it. When he stopped sliding, he found himself on his side, the breath knocked out of him. His tongue hung over the corner of his mouth, the moisture on it crystallizing to ice.

What happened to you? Bull asked.

Rabbitrunner finally managed to inhale, but his chest suddenly throbbed with pain. Two of his ribs were fractured. He stared ahead and saw the moose in the distance, not running away but charging this time, antlers lowered toward him. Rabbitrunner's eyes opened wide; he now knew what those antlers could do.

He pulled himself to a sitting position, his tongue snapping off the ice, his ribs aching. The moose rumbled closer, its massive hooves pounding the ice, its big, black eyes staring at him, its antlers rumbling towards him. He tried to struggle to his feet, but the wind was too strong and the ice too slippery. He fell to his side, and the pain from his ribs reverberated through his body. He tried to stand again, never taking his eyes off the large, charging beast intent on killing him.

Suddenly the air resounded with loud cracks, like giant limbs breaking off one by one. Rabbitrunner felt the ground shift beneath him. The moose was still charging towards him, but suddenly he was sinking, his body, and his rump disappearing into an ominous blackness as he struggled to break free of the icy mouth.

Rabbitrunner felt everything tilt, and he slid towards the moose, his claws uselessly scraping the ice for a foothold as he looked back. The moose sank from sight, antlers and all, and he slid into the water after it.

The cold shocked him, crippled him for a moment as he inhaled lake water, gagging, unable to breathe, unable to see. The cold shocked his mind to action as he tried to swim towards the surface, trying to hold his breath, feeling himself slide under the moose's body, almost getting kicked again as the moose struggled for its own survival.

A hoof kicked his leg, and he redoubled his efforts.

He struggled from the depths, kicking, swimming, keeping his nose above water, coughing up lake water and inhaling air. His nose was instantly coated with ice, and his eyelids froze closed. He got a forepaw out of the water and onto the ice, then another. He blindly tried to pull his body out, his ribs aching, but his paws slipped and he sank beneath the water again.

You need to get out of there! Bull snarled from deep within his brain. *You'll freeze to death! The moose is getting out – why can't you?*

Rabbitrunner sank deeper, his paws working hard in the icy blackness. Then his hind paw touched mud, and he pushed off, this time almost leaping out of the water. He got his forepaw up on ice again, then brought a hind paw up. After two failed attempts, he managed to get a hind leg onto ice, and by pulling and splashing, he managed to get himself out.

He managed to rise, shaking spastically, his fur heavy with ice when he spotted the large moose walking away. "Oh no you don't," he growled, half crazy with cold as he charged. He hit the moose's side with his shoulder, knocking him over, then leaped at him, biting the throat, tearing until hot blood splattered over his head.

The moose's chest continued to heave as its throat bubbled from the passage of air. He was not yet dead, but Rabbitrunner saw the thick casing of cracked ice all over his body, and he realized why he was growing colder. Lake water had frozen to him as soon as he climbed out. Rabbitrunner stood beside the dying moose, large chunks of ice in his fur, pulling heat from his body.

Shivering uncontrollably in the icy wind and falling snow, he realized he was dying, too. He frantically shook out his fur, but very little ice came off. He rolled on his back, twisting back and forth, breaking off pieces of ice, then he leaped up and bit at the ice between his toes. He turned and nipped at his tail, pulling ice off the long hairs. The shivering was worse, but he continued to search his body for ice, until he was sure he got it all.

Now find your way off the lake, Bull said. *Find shelter. You're still freezing to death.*

"I'm also starving to death," he snarled. "I'm going nowhere until I eat."

The moose was dead.

Rabbitrunner tore into the soft belly with urgency, his head and shoulders already splattered with blood as he pushed into the gaping hole in the abdomen and pulled the liver free. Holding on to the ice with one forepaw, he pulled large chunks off the liver and all but swallowed them whole. He then began pulling out the intestines.

As he ate, the wind blew hard across the frozen lake, but the moose's body partially sheltered him from its intensity. He had to keep prying his paws loose from the frozen blood, but he never let up from his feeding frenzy. He tore the kidneys out and quickly devoured them, eating until he was about to burst.

He stopped and looked up, feeling warmer but still worried about the wind and falling snow. He felt incredibly tired, but he still had something to do.

He quickly came around and began gnawing on a hip, biting through skin and flesh, determined to get one leg off so he could take it back with him. He had to squint to keep his eyes from becoming wind burned. When he chewed through to the joint, he grabbed the hoof and pulled. The hind leg snapped free and landed on the ice.

Rabbitrunner stopped. He needed to rest. He went around the moose's back, dug a pit in the snow and ice and curled up, covering his nose and feet with the plume of his tail.

It was the first time in awhile that he slept with a full

stomach, and in spite of the cold and wind and falling snow, he felt warm, huddled against the dead moose, his windbreak. His tattered ear throbbed and his ribs ached, but sleep soothed the pain.

He dreamed of eating, his head deep in the belly of the moose as he pulled a kidney loose, the smell of blood stimulating his appetite. When he pulled his head out, he saw Bullmoosekiller standing nearby. He felt overwhelming warmth at seeing a familiar Hunter in the falling snow. *Good meat*, Bull said, his cataract eye twinkling. *Good meat. Eat. You need to eat.*

Rabbitrunner stared at him, his jaws chewing until he swallowed the last morsel of kidney. "There's enough here for you," he said. "There's enough here for the whole pack."

We can't eat any of it, Bull said. *It is all yours. We ate the cows, the tainted meat. We ate, and went insane, and died.*

"I ate the meat, too," Rabbitrunner said, ignoring the strong wind and blinding snow. "Am I insane as well? Am I dead?"

There is no greater insanity than loneliness, Bull said, his pelage unruffled by the wind. *There is no worse death than loneliness.*

"But am I dead?" Rabbitrunner puled. "Am I dead? Answer me!"

The snow fell thicker, and Bull faded from view behind it, but his words were as clear as thunder from the sky. *No. No. Not yet.*

Rabbitrunner opened his eyes. The storm was over, and the snow around him was coated by a fine layer of ice, the kind that snapped and shattered beneath one's paw. The night was starless, which meant thick clouds overhead, but some light must have been coming from somewhere, because light reflected off the snow-dusted lake ice, and in the distance the trees on the shoreline. The cold was dry and static, the silence even more so.

Then he heard the rhythmic crunching of snow that indicated something was walking towards him. It stopped nearby. He raised his head and peered over the body of the moose. Cloudwalker stood twenty feet away, massive and dark, but for his large, white head. His hackles were up, his head lowered and his ears back. His eyes were like deep ponds, silent and mysterious. His legs were bent and misshapen, but this time there was no rancid odor surrounding him like an aura.

Rabbitrunner rose from the snow and gazed at the old Hunter, unsure if he should be elated or afraid. His breath steamed in the cold air. The silence was crystalline as the two Hunters stared at each other. "I've been looking for you," Rabbitrunner said at last. "It's hard for me to survive on my own."

"Don't watch for me," Cloudwalker snarled. "Don't just survive for yourself. There are more important things, Rabbit-Turd, than survival."

Rabbitrunner's hackles rose. He saw Cloudwalker look down on the ice and for the first time he saw shadows moving up behind the old Hunter. He glanced over his shoulder; shadows were coming up behind him. Many, many Twolegs were coming closer, surrounding both of them.

"Do you smell it?" one snarled. Everything became brighter, everything but the shadowy Twolegs.

"An intruder? Yes, I smell it, but what's that?" The voices were closer. Rabbitrunner opened his eyes. It was daytime.

"It looks like a moose. Something killed it, but I smell...." The noonday light was blinding as Rabbitrunner rose from the small snowdrift that covered him. He braced his legs and shook out his fur.

Snarls got his attention. He turned around and saw five Hunters charging across the ice towards him. They were apparently downwind of him, because he hadn't picked up their odors. His first impulse, looking over the moose carcass, was to run, but something kept him from doing so.

It's your moose! Pawsore's voice told him.

You can't fight that many Hunters, Treepisser argued.

You need to think about your survival, Newmoon pleaded.

And Bull's voice: *Wait.*

"Wait?" Rabbitrunner said to himself. "Wait for what? They're out to kill me! Are you crazy?" He glanced back at the attacking Hunters. "Am I crazy? I'm the one talking to voices in my head."

Hardly having any more time to think about it, he leaped up and planted his forepaws on the carcass's chest, bared his teeth and snarled. His nose wrinkled, his ears fell back against his head, and his hackles were up. The blood dried onto his face and shoulders made him look hideous. "Mine!" he growled.

Almost in unison the Hunters skidded to a stop, kicking up dusty snow from the slippery ice, surprised that a single trespassing Hunter would be so aggressive towards them. They continued forward, fanning out, and each one snarling. Rabbitrunner showed no fear as they slowly circled him. He glanced from one to the next as he growled, "Mine! I killed it!"

"Impossible!" the dominant Hunter snarled back. "A moose is too big for one Hunter to kill."

"I killed it!" Rabbitrunner said again, too weary and impatient to explain the details of how he killed it after it just about killed itself in the icy lake water. The hole where they both fell through was already frozen over, though noticeably different from the rest of the ice, almost one inch lower.

"Maybe he could have," another Hunter said. "Look how big he is."

It was only then that Rabbitrunner realized how much larger he was than the other Hunters. He used to be the largest Hunter of his pack, but now it seemed as though he'd grown more since then. And how much larger was Cloudwalker? He thought of how he had to keep digging out his den because it always seemed to be shrinking, when all along it was he who was growing. His thoughts were drawn quickly back to the present when he noticed the Hunters closing in. "This is my meat!" he repeated.

"And this is our territory!" another Hunter growled. "We don't care how many moose you killed, we don't care how big you are, you're a trespasser, and if we have to, we'll kill you."

"You just might at that," Rabbitrunner snarled. "But I'll be sure to kill a few of you in the process."

The Hunters didn't come any closer, but neither would they back down. Rabbitrunner didn't want to give up one nibble of his meat to them, but he doubted they'd wait a few days while he cleaned the bones of the carcass. He'd just have to compromise.

Looking down, he saw the moose leg he chewed free the night before. He could take that much with him and leave them the rest. He quickly moved around the body, grabbed the leg by the hoof and backed away, dragging it across the ice.

The others began to move in. Rabbitrunner stopped and dropped the hoof, putting a forepaw on the leg. He glanced from one to the next. "I'm leaving you plenty of meat. Now you can be satisfied with that or risk losing a few Hunters over this little piece of leg bone." None of them moved. Rabbitrunner had a feeling they were satisfied.

He picked up the hoof in his teeth, turned and trotted away, dragging the leg along the ice. He had to hold his head a certain way to do it, but it didn't bother him much. He didn't look back, but he listened for any attack, any sign that they had changed their mind.

Suddenly he heard a loud crack in the air. He dropped the hoof and crouched, his heart racing as he searched the sky for Bigbird. Then he glanced back. The moose carcass and the Hunters were in the lake water, the Hunters splashing to get out. "I knew I forgot to tell them something," he said. Content, he took his leg and went on his way.

It was tiring, traveling that long distance, dragging the leg through the snow beside him. He was especially uneasy about traveling during the day, but his mind was sharper since he ate, and he felt confident he would hear Bigbird a long way off, if it came to that.

The ribs on his left side ached with every step, and his chest was swollen and bruised over the fractures, but it didn't slow him down much. Bull once told him, if he had to break a bone, break a rib bone, not a leg bone, because the first was an inconvenience and the second was starvation and death.

When he crossed over one of the frozen black Twolegs rivers he realized he'd traveled a lot further than he originally thought. He must have crossed it before, while chasing the moose, only he wasn't aware of it, then. Now there were long lines that cut through the snow along its length and he wondered what sort of Twolegs creature left a paw print that stretched unbroken to the horizon, and why it left such a horrible odor behind. He felt uneasy about crossing it, but there was no other way if he wanted to return to Bearback.

When he was far beyond the Twolegs river, he stopped and ate, tearing the meat off the leg bone. It was beginning to hurt his neck, dragging the leg through the snow, and he decided to carry it the rest of the way internally. When there was nothing but bone left, he went on his way. Crossing through the Dirtscratcher Territory to get back to his own, he took the usual precautions, almost instinctually now, but there were no more confrontations on his journey.

After several hours, he reached his own territory. He was trudging through the snow when he saw something drop from the sky, hitting the ground ahead of him. He looked up just in time to see a large, black raven circle back and fly off.

When he arrived at the object, he discovered it was the leg bone of a deer, completely bare of meat and stinking of Cloudwalker's scent. Rabbitrunner glanced at the sky, but the raven was no longer visible. Now he understood how Cloudwalker could leave a bone along his trail without leaving a paw print or scent trail as well.

"Stupid games," Rabbitrunner muttered before continuing on his way. When he reached Bearback, he climbed into his den and slept for two days. Just that one good meal, and sleep, had changed everything.

Winter, the "White Death," fought hard, but could not hold on much longer. The weather warmed, and the snow on Bearback began to melt. The spring ran muddy, then trickled, then gushed like an animal ready to play games. Hibernating creatures rose from their burrows and birds migrated back from the south. The population of field mice, moles, and chipmunks seemed to double, then double again as grass and ferns grew and trees regained their leaves.

Rabbitrunner's rib healed, and he gained weight, mostly from field mice and rabbits. Finding plenty of game in his territory now, he had no need to travel beyond his boundaries. Worries about Twolegs and Jaws faded with his hunger, and after two White Deaths, surviving on his own, he was getting used to being alone.

He was also growing used to the daylight. He would sometimes sun himself on top of Bearback at the clearing, where he could see long distances in all directions, or near the dens, where he napped lightly, still listening for signs of danger from the sky.

Sometimes he would travel across the territory, awed that it all belonged to him and to no other Hunter. Neither Hunter nor Twolegs crossed through any part of his territory that spring, and the solitude was peaceful enough to silence, at least temporarily, the voices in his head.

The warmth of early summer brought an abundance of fleas, but it also brought changes that would turn Rabbitrunner's life around.

One afternoon he was relaxing under the warmth of the late afternoon sun. Nearby, the carcass of a rabbit gathered flies as he dozed. His stomach was already full from two groundhogs he caught in the morning. He no longer cached meat but brought it back to the den.

He was roused by a squawk and raised his head to see two ravens near the rabbit carcass. He recognized Zephyr and Storm as they both busily picked at the rabbit, tearing off tufts of gray fur and glancing up at him to gauge his reaction.

Rabbitrunner snarled, then leaped up and charged at them. They split up, one going left, the other going right, their large, black wings beating the hot ground dust into clouds as they took off. Rabbitrunner focused on one and charged after the low-flying bird, coming within a foot of its shiny black tail feathers when the other dived on him, nipping his rump and flying off, as low to the ground as the other.

Rabbitrunner u-turned and pursued that one, kicking clods of dirt into the air as he closed in again. The first raven, Zephyr, came around, nipping his rump and darting away, leading him on a new chase.

He hadn't played raven tag in a long time, but even after spending so much time alone, he still had the playfulness of a cub when the opportunity presented itself. And this was a game that bird and Hunter both enjoyed.

But just as quickly as the game began, it came to an abrupt end. Zephyr and Storm suddenly rose towards the sky, both squawking in panic, flying over the tops of the spruce trees and disappearing from sight. Rabbitrunner glanced around, his hackles bristling. Something didn't feel right. The bright sky, the sunlight, suddenly made him feel very vulnerable. Still panting from the short-lived game, he searched the sky and listened for signs of Bigbird.

"Tired, are we?" Cloudwalker's voice chanted. Rabbitrunner looked back but saw nothing. "Weary and scared, are you, my cub?"

Rabbitrunner lowered his tail and bared his teeth, searching the surrounding trees for the source of the voice; it seemed to come from everywhere. "Cannot catch a mangy raven; can you, Rabbit-Turd? Cannot catch a deer, a muskrat, or a gopher, only a rabbit, my Hunter? Only a rabbit to offer me for the kill I left you? A lot to learn, there is, Rabbit-Turd! A lot to learn, you have!"

The voice was behind him. Rabbitrunner quickly glanced over his shoulder. Cloudwalker stood ten feet behind him, his large, grinning half-bald head protruding from bony shoulders as sharp and angled as mountain rocks. He was a large mass of ancient muscle and tendons covered by tattered skin and fur, his bulk radiating tension like the air before a thunderstorm. The breeze smelled of decay, as if many animals were left beneath the sun after a slaughter.

The trees were twenty feet behind the old Hunter, and Rabbitrunner wondered how he was able to sneak that close while talking. It was another trick of his, like getting a raven to drop a meatless bone in his path.

The scaly-skinned, scarred white head blazed with dark eyes that radiated both death and life. He seemed to tower over the younger Hunter, like a mountain over a valley. How much bigger is he, Rabbitrunner thought, than I am? How much more does he dwarf other Hunters than I do?

Cloudwalker looked away, smacked his lips and raised his tail. "Survived the winter did you, Rabbit-Turd?"

"Survived?" Rabbitrunner growled. "Survived, yes, but with no help from you! All you left behind for me were chewed bones! Did you think I could survive eating snow? Did you think I could hibernate like the squirrels? Maybe I should store up some acorns for next winter! It would sure be more sustenance than you left me!"

Without answering, Cloudwalker lumbered up to him, sniffing his body as he tensed, not sure what to expect. Then Cloudwalker turned and trotted downhill, his tail raised and swinging back and forth. He stopped over the rabbit and picked it up in his jaws.

"Hey!" Rabbitrunner snarled, not moving from his spot. "That's my meat! Nobody invited you to share it!"

Cloudwalker ignored Rabbitrunner's angry outburst. His jaws were so large he didn't even bother tearing off a leg. He ate the rabbit whole, chewing up bones, fur, and organs, saliva dripping from his lips as he swallowed everything in one gulp. His half-hairless tail rose up and he let out a noisy fart. He turned and started back up the hill, smacking his lips. "Watched you I did," he said to Rabbitrunner. "Watched my little Rabbit-Turd, I did, through the winter."

"Hunters do not watch each other starve," Rabbitrunner said. "Hunters help each other survive, those that are alone, like you and me."

"Watched you, I did," Cloudwalker continued, "to see if you really could survive by yourself."

"And what if I didn't?" Rabbitrunner asked, almost as curious as he was angry.

Cloudwalker twisted around, nibbled a flea on his rump, then turned back and shook out his ragged, gray pelage. "It wouldn't matter to me if you didn't." He blinked and stared at Rabbitrunner. "But if you did survive, then maybe, maybe it would matter."

Anger and sadness mixed in the old Hunter's eyes. "Maybe the young Hunter might not survive, and maybe he would. And maybe the old Hunter might not survive, either. Who knows?" He gazed deep into Rabbitrunner's eyes. "And maybe the old Hunter would kill the younger Hunter, who knows? You and I, Rabbit-Turd, we are not a pack. We are not a pack! If you want to survive, you will survive, but not with my help, not with anybody's help."

Rabbitrunner suddenly felt cold despite the warm afternoon sun. "You wouldn't kill me," he said without conviction. "If you wanted to kill me, you would have done so a long time ago."

Cloudwalker licked his lips. "A lot to learn, there is, young Guardian. A lot to learn, there is." He turned and rambled away, but not before Rabbitrunner caught a whiff of deep anger radiating from his body. The old Hunter stopped at the den, sniffing the widened entrance, curious about the large flow of discarded dirt that went downhill from its mouth.

"I dreamed of you many times," Rabbitrunner said. "I dreamed you climbed mountains, and I dreamed you hunted great beasts, but now the beasts are gone...."

"Bison," Cloudwalker said.

"What?"

"Hunted the last bison, I did, in your dreams. But there are no more bison, no, maybe a few somewhere, but no more, I think." He looked at Rabbitrunner. "And the Hunter will be no more, either.... If!"

"If what?" Rabbitrunner asked.

Cloudwalker ignored the question. "And your ear.... I see one of your ears is tattered. Why is that?"

Rabbitrunner thought about his left ear. He couldn't see it himself, but when he belonged to a pack, the other Hunters sometimes mentioned it, and it throbbed when the weather was cold, reminding him it was not whole. "When I was a cub," he said, "my One bit it off to teach me a lesson about who eats first after a kill."

"A big lesson," Cloudwalker said. "Other cubs learn that lesson before their ears get eaten, but Rabbit-Turd-Cub had to learn the hard way. And winter, White Death, deadly cold, that's a hard lesson to learn, too, my young one. It is the hard way to learn, but effective, yes, effective." He stepped closer. "And did they teach you, Rabbit-Turd, did these last two winters teach you? Or must I bite off your other ear, your tail, your nose, your legs, must I? Have you learned anything? Have you?"

Rabbitrunner took a step back as the large Hunter's nose touched his. What was life or death to him was merely a lesson to Cloudwalker.

The old Hunter turned and walked around the grassy clearing, urinating as he went. The message was clear: he was claiming Rabbitrunner and his den as his own. Rabbitrunner bared his teeth at the insult, which implied he was as a dog was to Twolegs. "What have I to do with you?" he snarled, wanting him to go. "Why do you come back here when you refuse to help?"

Cloudwalker paused and gazed at him. "There is much to learn, Rabbit-Turd." He gazed towards the top of Bearback, but Rabbitrunner knew his gaze meant that direction and far beyond: north.

"That way, my Hunter," he snarled. "That way, you go if you want. And it gets very cold there, and colder still, and you see snow, you do, sometimes even during summer, and the cold you know here is nothing like the cold there, so much colder it is there.

"And if you look up at night, you see blood on the sky, the blood of Thickfur's feast when slaughtered the Nameless, he and his Hunters. The Blood in the sky, you can see it.

"And rivers of ice, not rivers of water, run down the sides of mountains, never melting, never melting, but moving slowly, so slowly that you have to watch them many days to see it. Plains of snow, and no trees, no trees, my Hunter. A harsh, bitter land there is up there.

"And yet.... And yet...." Cloudwalker's eyes glazed with the vision. Rabbitrunner cocked his head. "Hunters live there, yes, there in all that cold, where the air is so cold, and their pelage is white in that harsh land, and their life is hard. But great beasts roam those lands, great beasts as large as the bison, roaming the land under Father Sky's cold, cold gaze. And so many; their numbers spread across the land from one horizon to the other. But such a land there is, and room for more territories, room for more territories...."

"And you dreamed all this?" Rabbitrunner asked.

"Dreamed it?" Cloudwalker jerked his head around and stared into his eyes. "Been there I have! I have been there!" He shook himself, yawned, and walked uphill towards the trees.

"Wait!" Rabbitrunner puled, realizing he was leaving. "You can stay here with me! Make this your territory!"

"Hah!" Cloudwalker said, not looking back. "All territories are my territory!"

"Then let me come with you." Rabbitrunner pleaded.

"I don't want to be alone."

Cloudwalker's gait changed. He now scratched the ground with the claws of every paw as he lifted it to take another step. "Don't follow me, Rabbit-Turd, you must not," he snarled. He stopped a moment and glanced over his back. "And the Jaws, Rabbit-Turd, the Jaws! It is not enough just to piss on them. You must, close them...."

Rabbitrunner glanced at Cloudwalker, then glanced over his shoulder, gazing downhill, thinking of the Jaws he marked with his urine that one time, and wondering if Cloudwalker watched him doing that. He looked back; Cloudwalker was gone.

He followed the paw prints uphill, but they disappeared before coming near the trees, just as the scent disappeared, as though Mother Earth Herself swallowed him up. Paw prints were everywhere around the clearing as was Cloudwalker's rancid odor, but there was no trail leading away.

Rabbitrunner gave up and settled down to doze. When he woke, the sun was setting. He moved to his den, where he sat down and watched it sink over the mountains in the west. As the sky darkened, the stars claimed their places. A full moon rose before the sun was gone and now glowed overhead. He thought about Cloudwalker, wondering where he went to, and then he heard the distant howls.

"This, this is our Life!"

"This, this is our Play!"

"This, this is our Food!"

"This, this is our Sleep!"

Rabbitrunner yawned and set his head on his paws. His loneliness had returned. The Litany of a distant pack was like a fever, bringing back the memories of scents and faces of the Hunters of his pack, memories that were fading and would someday disappear. He closed his eyes and listened.

"This, this is our Hunt!" Windeater howled.

"This, this is our Song!" Grounddigger added.

"This, this is our Howl!" Blackpaw finished as the Litany died out. The harmony of their combined voices was like magic to them all. When the last howl had ended, Blackpaw watched her pack curl up in small groups, some going to sleep, some grooming each other, some playing. They were all shadows under the trees of Snow Hill.

Blackpaw watched them, thinking of the two recurring dreams she had been having lately. Spots of moonlight sprinkled the ground around them where light had squeaked through the leaves above. The smells of new ferns and last year's dry leaves on the ground was comforting, but her dreams threatened that comfort, like a rabid animal walking into their midst.

Her pack was once many. Now it was some. Even so, their numbers were increasing again, with two male and two female yearlings, as well as the cubs that played near their dam and sire. If the hunting went well for several more years, their numbers might be up to where they once were.

She rose and stretched her forelegs on the ground, her rump in the air as she noisily yawned. Arthritis was setting in. She could feel it. She stood, shook out her pelage and bit at a flea on her flank. She doubted she would be the One much longer. This last autumn she was challenged by Windeater, the Alpha-Male and sire of the yearlings, but she was the stronger fighter, and Windeater lost. He was shortly challenged himself by Grounddigger, sire of the cubs, who became the new Alpha-Male as well as her Second. It would only be a matter of time before he, too, challenged her authority.

But perhaps it would be good to have a new One, she thought. She had led her pack for too long already. Windeater, though, was too hardheaded to lead. He believed that force was the only requirement to being the One. Grounddigger, on the other hand, showed both wisdom and strength. It was nothing she could plan, though; the new One would be the Hunter who beat her in a challenge, nothing more.

Blackpaw gazed in the direction of Bearback, the territory of the Pawsore Pack (never mind that Treepisser took over the leadership—it was still the Pawsore Pack to her). She hadn't heard the Litany from their territory in over two winters. She thought perhaps they all died out—and yet, the boundaries were still being marked. They had to be still alive, but she couldn't imagine a life without the Litany. It was like a Hunter with three legs, still able to survive, but it wasn't a life worth surviving for.

Nonetheless, she often wondered: What happened in that territory? And what was still happening?

She yawned again and gazed up at Father Sky's bad eye. She remembered the dreams then: In the first, she was aimlessly wandering through her territory, looking for the other Hunters of her pack, but they were all gone. In the second dream, she was leading her pack. They were all there, and more, but they had no territory, and were traveling across ice. Every time she thought of the dreams, she felt like there was a choice to be made, and she didn't want to make it because she might choose wrong.

She set her head on her paws and closed her eyes, thinking of the Pawsore Pack Territory, and how strange the boundary markers smelled.

Chapter Thirteen

"A Sprout Takes Root"
(Summer, 1967)

"Hello. This is Mr. Grinner."

"Hey Fribitz, how're you doing!"

".................."

"Are you there? This is Dean."

"Dean?"

"Dean Hoover. Don't tell me you forgot me already!"

"Dean! Krazy Kat! Hell, no! I've been missing you ! It's been a year... "

"Yeah, I know. I meant to call you for the longest time, but it just didn't happen."

"I've been worried about you. Where are you?"

"Just on the road. I've been working here and there at different jobs, traveling around Minnesota, just walking about and biding my time. I have a backpack, sleeping bag and tent, and a pretty good little portable stove."

"Jobs? What sort of jobs, Krazy Kat?"

"Oh nothing really, dishwashing, a little garbage pickup, picking vegetables on farms, ditch digging, make a few bucks and move on. You know."

"Dishwashing? Ditch digging? Hell, you're a college professor! What are you doing all that for? Yeah, I know the university kicked you out, but you could go to another one!"

"I want the freedom I have right now. Make a few bucks and walk on."

"That's another thing. What do you mean walk on? What about your bum foot? Does it still hurt?"

"It hurts like hell. I use a walking stick, and it keeps me going. When I set up my sleeping bag I massage my bad foot before I go to bed and when I wake up the next day before I move on. If I'm working, I stand it as best as I can, then after work go back to my tent and massage my foot until I can at least get to sleep. It healed up really nice, by the way."

"When you come home, I'll make you some new toes for the ones you lost! Do you want them carved out of wood or ivory? But why are you wandering all over the place? And on a bad foot as well."

"You want to know why?"

"Yeah. Why?"

"I don't know."

Dean stumbled downhill through the woods, watching his step, using two walking sticks to help keep his balance as he maneuvered through the trees and boulders to the waters of Lake Superior. The harness he rigged to wrap across his chest like an "X", was already making him feel sore, but he dragged his canoe this far and didn't have much further to go.

When the ground leveled out and he stepped onto the sandy beach, he dropped the sticks and removed the harness. He stretched, looking up at the moon, then looked at his watch. It was almost one thirty in the morning.

Nobody would see him.

He had paid a man with a pickup twenty dollars to haul his canoe, which he recently bought for this trip, along Route 61 to the place near the Canadian border, just south of Pigeon River Provincial Park and across from Grand Portage State Park, where, he was pretty sure, he could reach the lake with the least effort. Once his canoe was set down on the highway's shoulder and the pickup was gone, Dean wrapped the large canvas sail he bought for five dollars on the bottom of the canoe to protect its hull as he pulled it through the woods, put on the harness, attached the ropes to the gunwale of the boat, and started down the slope to Wauswaugoning Bay.

Glancing at the water, he pulled out his flask and downed the last of the vodka before firing up a joint. It had been a long trip, all the while he was working as much as he needed to just to get by, occasionally renting a motel room but more often than not sleeping off the road in the woods just beyond anybody's view, and all this time walking—walking from place to place, mostly, sometimes hitching a ride, but more often wandering off into the forest, getting lost, sustaining himself on cans of pork and beans because he couldn't bring himself to hunt anything.

And still he couldn't stay dry for more than a few days.

Eventually he would have to find his way out of the woods, buy some beer or pot or rum or Night Train, and if he was broke, he would have to get a job and make enough for drugs, booze and more cans of pork and beans. Once he restocked, he went back into the woods, wandering, wandering.

He was looking for the Shadow Wolf. After his near encounter at the fire tower, he realized there was more he needed to find out—and he needed to know what connection he had with the wolf. He could have found his way

back to the cave, but something happened there, inside
that cave, something painful, something chilling, and he
couldn't bring himself to go back. He was scared, not of
the wolf, but of what that cave meant to him, what it did
to him, or maybe it was a month of illness, or just insanity, he wasn't sure. What's more, he couldn't remember
what he did at the cave, or what happened. Apparently he
had been very sick, and somehow had kept himself alive
until he was finally able to escape and find the campers
who pretty much saved him and took him to the hospital.

After he tossed the roach away, he pulled the canoe
into the waters of Superior. The canoe was aluminum,
painted yellow, and was full of supplies, including his
camping gear, soap and shampoo, toilet paper, matches, a
shovel and hatchet, warm clothes, cooking utensils, food,
and booze he stockpiled over the last week. After losing
toes to bad weather and poor planning, he was going to
make sure he had all the potential problems covered.

He tossed in his two walking sticks and climbed in
himself, pushing off from shore before sitting down and
paddling into the darkness. The air was chill and damp,
and he noticed a low fog over the water as he looked
towards the distant island. He could hear the water
slipping under his hull, hear the distant whoop of early
morning birds, and the whisper of a breeze that crossed
his bow. The water had a wonderful mineral-algae-fish
odor that he hadn't smelled in years, and it almost felt
like home.

He was heading back to Isle Royale, his third trip,
and looking forward to reaching the shore. The first time
he was there was a day trip, the second a month-long
study with Wayne Connors of the Forest Service, which
resulted in his doctoral dissertation. This time he was still
searching, not for the Shadow Wolf, but for the reason he
couldn't break free of him.

During the last year, he hiked to areas where he heard a wolf had attacked and killed livestock, or destroyed leghold traps, or killed dogs. He often arrived a week or two after the fact, but he wasn't in a hurry. He would eventually reach the location, talk to locals, and make notes, then, when he had enough, he caught the rumors of the next site and headed in that direction, stopping only to camp or work and replenish his funds.

As Isle Royale became more visible in the darkness and fog, he looked for a decent place to portage. He wasn't sure if the Forest Service was doing any studies on the island, but he knew how to disappear in the trees and avoid other people if he needed to.

When he reached the pebble-strewn shore, he pulled the canoe aground and surveyed the beach. The white spruce, black spruce and balsam fir trees were just twenty feet from the water, and he could easily find a place to hide his canoe in the brush. He could set up his tent there, then hike into the woods when he was rested and find a better place. Once that was done, he would hike the island for a feel of the place, and, most important, to see if he was alone. He glanced at the sky, noting the gray clouds. In a few minutes the sky would burst into reds and yellows, and in an hour or two he would be asleep in his tent. He smiled and lit another joint.

Isle Royale, Michigan, is on the American side of the border just a stone's throw from Canada. At 45 miles long and 9 miles wide, it is just big enough to sustain one eastern timber wolf pack and one herd of moose, making it the perfect habitat study location. When the moose population increases, the wolf population does likewise, and the same thing happens when the population decreases. The highest point on the island is Mount Desor at 1,394 feet, or about 800 feet above lake level. The largest lake on the island is Siskiwit Lake, which in turn contains several small islands, the largest of which is Ryan Island.

The permanent human population is 0.

Dean read many books about Isle Royale before and after his month-long study of the balance of predator-prey relationships when he stayed with Wayne Connors. He found the island to have a fascinating historical, geological and biological history, and had wanted to return since the day he left after his research.

He pulled his canoe deep into the woods, using the harness he made and the bull rope he bought days earlier at the hardware store. Once he hid the canoe with leaves, dead bushes and branches, he set up his tent and climbed in, rolling into his sleeping bag and curling up. He was snoring just as the sun was rising over the trees.

He was looking over a green field surrounded by trees, feeling nostalgic as he recognized the skyscrapers in the distance just beyond the hills. He knew his own house was just behind him, but he dared not look back. Once he did, it would all end.

"I'll come back for you," he told Sarah. She was ten years old, wearing her Howdy Doody t-shirt, blue jeans and tennis shoes with pink socks, and his brother Ben, playing in the distance on a grassy hill, was six. "I have to go away for four years, but when I come back, I'll have a good job and I'll take you with me. "

"And Ben too?" she asked, gripping her hands together against her chest.

"And Ben too," Dean said, smiling. "I'll take care of you. I'll take care of us all. I promise. "

"And Mommy too?"

Dean opened his mouth, but he had to think.

When he woke, it was night again, and a gentle rain pelted the canvas of his army surplus pup tent. It was the first time in a long while that he had such a vivid dream. He shook his head, feeling refreshed for once, and decided to get started.

Stepping outside, he held a canvas tarp over his head and smoked a joint. He was shivering, standing barefoot in his boxer shorts and t-shirt. The air was rich with the musk of deadfall and decaying leaves. He stomped his feet on the pine needle carpet, and when the joint was done he took a leak against the nearest tree, looking at the mound where the canoe was hidden.

He ate a can of pork and beans cold, then set the can aside to make sure he took it whenever he left the island. With the tarp over his head, he pulled on his blue jeans, socks, hiking boots, and other clothes, then grabbed one of his walking sticks and started hiking through the woods. In the dark his night vision was superb, but the woods seemed to have a dreamlike feeling about them.

He just wandered, getting a feel for the area. In the first hour, his left foot started aching, but he did as he always did, stuck with the pain as it got worse, kept walking despite the pain, despite the weakness in his body, despite stumbling sometimes and relying more on the stick for balance.

He walked through the night, and as the rain stopped and the day broke, he kept on walking until he felt weary. He headed back to his campsite, not following any paths but just sensing the direction. Ever since he found the cave during the blizzard, it seemed that his sense of direction was acute, as though he were attuned to the magnetic poles of the earth, or he was being guided by a new sort of celestial navigation. Without recognizing a thing, he effortlessly wandered back to his tent. He hadn't seen any sign of humans, so if someone was on the island, they at least weren't anywhere near him.

Once he was settled in, he made a campfire between his tent and a moss-covered log, set up a seven foot sapling tripod, and hung his Dutch oven from the top with the chain he brought. He threw in a couple cans of beans and chunks of bacon, added a little brown sugar, then went to the beach to bathe. When he got back, he cracked open another bottle of tequila, fired up a joint, and settled down, drinking and relaxing by the warmth of his fire.

The afternoon became a routine of drinking, eating and swimming in the lake. As the sun set, he let the fire die down, then settled down with the bottle, sipping and watching the embers, not thinking of anything. Tomorrow he would move his camp, leaving the canoe there until he needed to go back to land. He sang softly to himself until he realized he was dozing off, then crawled into his tent and rolled into his sleeping bag. As his consciousness waned, he heard the rain begin falling again.

"You have to go through the fire. "

"No you don't" Dean said.

"Gold is purified by going through the fire. " It was Fribitz; Dean recognized his voice.

"Yeah, yeah, yeah," Dean answered, "But I'm not gold. "

"Caterpillar," Fribitz answered. "You're a caterpillar. I'm mistaken. No, not the fire, you need to get inside the cocoon, come out a butterfly. "

"Yeah, and how does that work?"

"Once inside the cocoon," Fribitz said, "you liquefy."

The thunder woke him up, and he sat and looked around. Nothing was visible, it was pitch black, and he realized he was inside the cave. He could smell the stench—odors did not come into dreams. He glanced around, felt with his hands, but there was nothing to feel, just the sandy floor. There were wolf skulls and bones inside the cave, he remembered that, and bullet casings.

"You know what he did."

It was Sarah, his sister. "Yeah, I know what our father did, he killed you. He killed you all. He would have killed me too if he could, but he couldn't!" He was scared now, talking to ghosts, not sure who was alive any more. He was weeping, reaching into the darkness for her, wanting to help her, save her, pull her back into the world of the living, but it was too late.

His ten year old sister stood and faced him. "You know what he did."

"I told you not to be late from school," his father said. He unbuckled his belt. "Now you'll pay." Dean watched him slide his belt from the loops, his eyes on him. He felt the sickening feeling he got every time it happened. No, not this time, it's unfair. No!

"Take the position."

Looking down, Dean undid his own belt, then slowly slid his jeans and underpants down to his ankles. He turned around, bent over and grabbed his ankles. His body trembled. No! No! I'm eighteen years old! I'm bigger than him! He's small, he's a cop, he shouldn't be doing this!

He heard his father step closer, heard the belt, doubled up, take a few practice swings through the air. The pain was the punishment, but the waiting was just as torturous. Not again! He almost shouted it this time. His father began whistling.

Then the first blow struck. He winced, squeezed his buttocks together, and something changed. Not again.

He could stop it, he knew.

He didn't see, but he sensed his father drawing his arm back for the second blow. He quickly stood and turned, grabbing the arm on the second swing, stopping it.

His father looked at him, surprised. "You punk! You dare to stop me? You'll pay even more!"

"No!" Dean shouted. "No! Not this time!"

His father broke his wrist free, swung again, but Dean caught it again. This time he held on tight, and he could tell his father sensed his strength. I could take that belt out of your hand and beat you, he thought, but he held his father's gaze. "No," he said.

For once, he expected the full wrath of his father the cop, the enforcer, the executioner. For once, he expected to see his father drop the belt and start swinging his fists, pummeling him all over.

And for once, Dean was ready to take the full beating, because he knew it was worth it. He knew he was an adult now, and free of his father, thanks to scholarships and good grades. The only thing he did not know now was whether he would hit back, but either way he was now free, pain or no pain.

Instead, his father dropped the belt and smiled. "You've been a failure all your life, boy," he said. "Are you a man now?" Dean, thrown off balance by his father's reaction, nodded. "Then you can handle manly things. Watch." Dean dreaded what would happen next.

For a moment they held each other's gaze. His father relaxed, and Dean let go. "Okay, if that's what you want," he said. For a moment Dean thought he won. "Stay here, I have something to show you."

His father stepped from the bedroom, leaving the door open. Dean quickly hitched up his pants, refastened his belt, embarrassed to have been naked like that, but this would be the last time. One minute later his father returned with his sister, Sarah. She looked terrorized. "Your brother did something wrong," his father said. "Take the position."

She looked away, began unbuckling her belt and pulling down her pants. Dean turned around, he couldn't watch, realizing that it had happened to her too, and wondering, just for a moment, what else happened to her, what else did their father do. He blocked the thought as soon as it came...

"You know what he did," she said. "He raped me."

One week later he rested supine on the ledge, binoculars in hand, gazing down the hill at the wolves surrounding the dead moose, eating. He had followed them for days until this kill, and now he could see what they did. He took one last drag on the joint before stubbing it out, and took another hit from his flask. This time, he would not take notes, but he would watch, and try to understand them better.

They were not the same wolves he had studied before. The smaller male, the Alpha in the study group he saw years ago, was gone, and he didn't recognize any of the other wolves. Where once there was a pack of eight, there now was a pack of six. But how could all the wolves he saw only a few years ago already be gone, dead, replaced by their offspring?

And then he thought about the wolf he had been looking for over the last few years. That one came back year after year, almost immortal. The Shadow Wolf had, apparently, outlived them all.

Looking through his binoculars, he saw the wolves turn as one and look in his direction, then, as one, turn and walk away, ignoring the meat they just brought down. He gazed in shock, watching them leave, then noticed the breeze against his back. The wind shifted and the wolves could smell him. "Fuck!" he hissed. "Fuck-fuck-fuck!" They would return to their meal when he was gone, he knew that, but he had just lost an opportunity to watch them. Had he been paying attention, he would have realized the wind was changing and quietly found another spot. Frustrated, he stood, took one more swig, and shouldered his backpack, then stumbled back to his campsite.

He walked through the woods, and kept going over the piece of memory he had blocked for so long, that his little sister was being raped by his father.

The first day he remembered, he drank himself senseless, woke up and did it again. In his half stupor he cried, screamed, punched trees, blacked out, woke up and punched trees again, pissed and shit himself, vomited enough times he had to move his campsite. Now, the memory would not go away.

He promised to save her, he remembered that, but he never did.

He somehow had managed to block it for years, but now it was back. He was still chilled by it, still confused, more lost in his travels than before except for one detail.

Now he knew for sure, the reason he didn't want to find the cave was that he first remembered what happened to Sarah while sick and delirious in there. For all the trauma she must have gone through—he caught himself crying sometimes when he thought about it—he was also traumatized, mostly because he blocked the memory, how he left his sister to suffer alone while he went to school, and how wrong he felt by forgetting in order to protect himself. He didn't want to go back because it would bring up the memory one more time.

He tripped over a root, knocking the air out of his lungs when he hit the ground. When he got back to a sitting position, he looked around. "Goddam, I'm not drunk enough," he mumbled, looking into his empty flask. "Goddam memories, if I had it in me, I'd kill myself." But he no longer had it in him for another suicide attempt, and he didn't know if that was a good or bad thing.

When he got back to his campsite, he tossed his binoculars into the lake, then went to the canoe, removed the brush, and took out several milk crates full of bottles of vodka and gin.He set them up at his tent, then spent the next hours gathering deadfall for the fire. He got a pot of beans and bacon going, then started feeding the fire. When he was happy with the blaze, he pulled out a bottle, cracked it open, then took a swig.

As an afterthought, he told himself that the liquidation process had begun, and would have told Fribitz if he could.

He drank, ate beans and swam naked in the lake, sometimes singing, sometimes throwing up, then drinking again and continuing on. He kept the fire going, sometimes walking naked through the woods, thinking of his friend Fribitz Grinner and wondering if he should take up painting with his own genitals.

For hours, he lay in the fetal position, touching the place where his toes used to be. Then he got back up, refueled the fire and started another blaze from the last embers before he started drinking again.

Dawn came, and he put out the fire, got dressed, and grabbed one of his sticks. He loaded a backpack with three fresh bottles and started walking.

Isle Royale was formed by ridged layers of volcanic rock that were bowed upwards at two ends like a stack of magazines bent around so that the strata between issues were sticking up and visible. One end formed Isle Royale, and the other formed the Houghton Peninsula, both part of Michigan, Wisconsin and Minnesota, with Ontario to the north. Dean had studied the geology of the island for years, and by that afternoon, he was walking along one of those ridges, picturing how it was formed over the millennia as he stumbled along in the rain.

His left foot throbbed, so he settled down under a ledge, started a small fire with a metal match, and continued drinking. He picked up a piece of copper he found in the dust, squeezed it between thumb and forefinger, and licked it. He looked around, and found the telltale signs of ancient stone tools just a few feet away.

Around 1840, he remembered, a report by Michigan Geologist Douglass Houghton started the first copper boom on the island, and bands of miners began rowing across the water and tearing into the land. The veins were small, though, and transportation to and from the island was tedious, so most mines eventually closed down.

What the miners discovered, however, when they started digging, was that someone was there before them. The copper deposits had been mined long before Christopher Columbus crossed the ocean. Stone age tools and prehistoric copper objects were found around the copper deposits. Some of the ancient mining pits were 20 feet deep. A century or so later, carbon dating on ancient wooden tools indicated that people had possibly been digging on the island as long as six thousand years ago.

Despite the failure of the mines, Isle Royale still had possibilities. Years after the mines, loggers came and pretty much clear cut the island, exploiting as much of the wood as possible. And so it went, the island an apparent treasure trove of products, until around 1940, about a century after Douglass Houghton's geological report, when the island finally was designated as a national park.

Dean picked up the piece of copper and again touched it with his tongue, thinking of how blood and copper tasted the same.

"It was the taste all over the house when Daddy killed us all," Sarah said. "It was the taste of what he did to me. And you knew, you knew all along."

Dean bit the piece of copper, and began weeping. "What could I do? I didn't have any money. I couldn't take you with me." he glanced at the shadows under the ledge, thinking maybe she was there. Sometimes he saw her, sometimes he didn't.

"Do you remember the first time I told you? I was so scared you would hate me. I said he touched me, and you made a joke."

"It couldn't be that," Dean said. "I didn't think you knew what you were talking about."

"But you knew. You felt a chill down your spine. You made a joke to pretend it was not real, that what I said was a mistake."

"You were only ten. You said you wanted me to take you with me. I said I would come back."

"You came back too late. There was nobody left."

Then Dean thought of something. "The last time I Talked to you on the phone, you said I knew what he did. Why did you say that?" There was silence. He gazed into the shadows. "Did you tell him you were leaving? Did he know that he would lose you as well?"

"No," she said. "He knew you were graduating. He knew we were going to see you get your degree, and it would make us want one too. He knew even our mother thought it was possible to get away. He was losing control. He was scared."

"You have to go back to the cave," Fribitz said. Dean looked into the pouring rain, seeing him there, smiling, wearing his black suit. "You cannot be afraid any more."

"What about the wolf?" Dean asked. "The Spirit Wolf?"

"You have to save the wolf from that man Cutter," Fribitz said.

"You have to save the wolf from our Daddy," Sarah said. "You have to save Ben before he dies too."

"But Ben's also dead," Dean said. He was now crying, blubbering, so he could not speak any more. He held his face in his hands, his body trembling and heaving.

"You can't save him like that," Sarah said. "You can't save him by crying, by being weak. You've been weeping since we all died. You need to stop."

"You need to go through the fire," Fribitz said.

"If you were strong enough, you could admit what you knew when I was ten. You don't know how bad it was, being alone, and the one person you told didn't believe you."

"You need to liquefy," Fribitz said.

"I can't do it!" Dean screamed. "I can't do any of it! And what's the point? Everybody is dead."

"The Shadow Wolf is still alive," Sarah said.

Dean glanced into the shadows, but there was nobody there. He glanced into the rain, but Fribitz was gone. He collapsed on his side, reverting to the fetal position, one hand gripping the part of his foot where his toes used to be. He was weary but couldn't sleep. He listened and condered if the voices would come back, but they never did.

At some point, he wanted to move on, just go somewhere else. The rain was not letting up, so he rose on unsteady legs and staggered on, his walking stick almost leading the way. He was not following any animal trails this time but making a trail of his own, pushing through dead bushes, stepping over logs and deadfall, wading through streams and mud puddles. He carried one of the bottles in his free hand and took occasional sips, sometimes wondering where he left the cap.

As the sun rose, he had no idea where he was, just that he was far from the ridge. It was still raining, and he was drenched, but it didn't seem to matter. He sometimes glanced at his hand, noting his pruned fingers. The air smelled of rotting leaves and dead wood and fresh water.

Every now and then, he heard his sister whisper, "You know what he did." He didn't even look for her any more, he was ashamed that he never got back home to get her out of that house.

"Mama never believed me," she whispered. "She said I was trying to ruin her marriage. And he beat her, too."

"Let me show you something," his father said. No, Dean thought, please....

"Take the position..."

He almost did, but instead took another swig from the bottle, walking on, stumbling on without his walking stick and wondering where he left it, but by now, as Albert Einstein said, time was relative. His left foot throbbed terribly and he was afraid to stop and look at it, he was sure the holes where his toes used to be were seeping blood and pus, or maybe they did that in the hospital and he was just projecting.

He slept on the moss one time, he slept on a massive flat boulder, he slept on fir needles, remembering a dead spruce tree just outside the cave. How many hours had it been, how many days? His booze was running low, down to half a bottle. How many did he bring, three or five? How much time had passed? Hours? Days?

He woke up one sunny morning looking out from under a bush. Three men, Forest Service workers in uniform, were operating a drill grinding into the rock from a metal tripod. Core samples, Dean realized. He silently watched them, then tried to quietly crawl away. He pushed himself up to his knees against a large rock. The rock slipped, and Dean, the rock and his backpack tumbled down the hill.

When he sat up, the men next to the drill, ten feet away, were looking at him. Dean rubbed his head, then stood on unsteady legs."Nice morning, guys," he said, stretching his arms and ignoring his aching head.

"Your backpack's leaking," one of them said.

"Yeah," Dean replied. "I know. Can I have that long stick over there?" He pointed.

"It's not ours," another man said. Dean nodded and limped over to the stick. He bent over and with a great deal of pain, picked up the stick, and limped off, not looking back. He heard a few comments before he disappeared into the woods.

"You see how filthy that guy was?"

"And barefoot too,"

"What do you suppose happened to his toes?"

He walked a long time, then looked over his shoulder. He lost his watch, his boots, his socks and his other walking stick, though the stick he found worked much better.

When he found a mossy patch of ground surrounded by bushes, trees and ferns, he sat and yanked off his backpack. All his bottles were broken, all the whiskey gone, though he was pretty sure he didn't have much left in any case.

After sucking on a few wet parts of his backpack, he rolled it into a pillow, broken glass inside and all, and lay down. His bad foot throbbed and so did his head, but he felt a raw weariness dragging him deep into darkness. He closed his eyes and felt the mossy bed rocking him like a dory on the gentle ocean. In a little while, he heard himself snoring, wondered how that could be, and he heard the rain somewhere, though he didn't feel it.

He woke in the cave, looked at the candles against the wall, and saw prehistoric cave paintings he hadn't seen the day before. Sarah was there, ten years old again—she was killed when she was fourteen, he thought—in her yellow dress and black shoes.

"You know what he did," she said. He remembered when he heard her say that, on the phone, she was fourteen, very angry, very anxious, and it was days before she was murdered, along with his brother and mother, before his father finally killed himself.

"You know what he did," she said.

"I'm so very sorry," Dean said. It sounded lame, he didn't know anything else to say.

And he remembered the last time he talked to her before going off to school, what she said, not even looking at him. "Daddy touches me sometimes. I want to tell you something, but I can't, because he said something bad would happen." He knew back then, but did not ask, even though he knew he should ask.

But she told him when she was fourteen.

And something bad happened.

He heard a noise behind him and looked back. There, coming into the cave, was the massive silhouette of the Shadow Wolf, just as he remembered first seeing him. He leaned down to enter, pulled himself through the small mouth of the cave, and stood a few feet away By the candlelight Dean saw his massive gray eyes, whitish scarred head, exactly the way he remembered it from years ago.

But there was no hostility. The wolf was carrying the flank of a moose. He let it drop on the ground. Dean looked at the hunk of meat, then looked at the wolf. He glanced back at his sister, but she was gone. Instead there were only the cave paintings, lit by the candles, and among the paintings of stick men with spears hunting gazelles, he saw small hand prints, as though a baby or small child stuck its full hand in paint and left its own marks on the walls. The soft rain outside the cave sounded like a heartbeat.

He woke on the moss bed, drenched, soaked through by the warm summer rain. He was still tired, extremely weary, but he had to go, now, and figure out what had happened.

When he felt movement on both sides, he froze. He heard snorting, a soft whuff, and a curious growl. The smell of wet fur, damp dirt and old blood surrounded him, and he slowly moved two fingers, touching wet hair.

Slowly, cautiously, he eased up on his elbows, noticing the gray fur all the way around him. They were pressed against him, surrounding him, one of them actually snoring, one farting and readjusting his rump. Then a head rose and the wolf looked back at him, realizing he was awake. He didn't move as other heads popped up, and then the pack of wolves rose as one and trotted away. He glanced over his chest, watching their forms disappear into the falling rain.

He sipped hot tea from the white porcelain mug, burning his tongue. It was a good feeling. All that travelling, all that hitchhiking, all that walking, and returning to where he started. The walking stick was behind him against the cinderblock wall, and the smell of acrylics, oils and charcoal permeated the air. His coat and knit cap were wet, and the rain outside was like a mother's heartbeat.

"Here you go, Krazy Kat," Fribitz Grinner said, coming around several unused canvases on dirty easels. He was in a white bathrobe, his hands, his face, all of his body that could be seen, was stained by paints. His long hair,

beard and eyebrows were jet black, obviously dyed, but
that was his gimmick for his art admirers, who thought
it meant he was a Bohemian intellectual. He sat a large
bowl in front of Dean. "Shepherd's pie. I made it myself."

"Thank you, Fribitz," Dean said. "I was getting tired
of baked beans. I think I farted enough to send the next
rocket into space." He grinned, set his tea aside and pulled
the bowl closer. As he took the first bite, he gently removed
his cap and scratched his head.

"Wiiiiiiiild doggies!" Fribitz hooted, holding his nose.
"You can use my bathtub when you're done!"

"Yeah, I plan to," Dean said, subdued, taking another
spoonful. "It's been a journey and a half, and I really want
to soak myself into one giant prune."

"I saved this for you," Fribitz said, pulling a half-full
bottle of vodka from under the table. "I figured if you ever
made it back, you could use it."

"Thanks again," Dean said, taking the bottle. He
opened it, sniffed it, took a swig and poured a little into
his tea, then sealed it and slid it aside. He went back to
eating his meal, relishing every bite.

"I know you got a lot to talk about," Fribitz said. "It can
wait until tomorrow. I got you a bed in the studio so you
can crash all you want for as long as you want. You're a
guest here forever if you can stand the terrible artwork."

Dean set the spoon down and smiled. "Yeah, there's a
lot to talk about," he said. "This last year has been a sort
of walking, waking dream. But after all this, I'm ready
to start fresh and see what I can accomplish from here."

"Whatever you want," Fribitz said. "I really missed
you, Krazy Kat, I really did."

"I missed you too," Dean said.

"And I promise I'll never harass you to go back to the
cave again. As far as I'm concerned, it's a dead issue.
That cave, and that wolf, it has nothing to do with either

you or me."

"Nah, you're wrong," Dean said, "And I was wrong to say that to you. I think I'm ready to go back. I think the cave has lots to do with me." He rubbed his chin thoughtfully. "While I was away, I finally remembered why I didn't want to go back." He looked into his friend's eyes. "It took all this time to remember that, before my father killed my family, he raped my sister."

Fribitz covered his mouth with both hands. It was the first time Dean ever saw his friend's face reflect such profound shock and sadness. He felt it too, the overwhelming anxiety and shame he experienced when he remembered it on the island, the horror he felt remembering inside the cave that he didn't do anything to stop it, to protect her.

He could tell by Fribitz's eyes that he believed him, no proof or explanation was necessary.

"I remembered it in the cave during the blizzard," Dean explained. "I remembered it all, and that's why I couldn't go back, because there was so much horror inside me when it came back to me. And it came back to me again while I travelled. I went back to Isle Royale, and that's when I remembered it a second time, but this time I have to face it."

"And that was why you were so affected by the cave."

Dean nodded. "I was afraid. Maybe I was always afraid. But I'm going to try hard to change that. I don't know where this is all going, but I have to see it to the end."

Fribitz nodded and smiled, though his eyes seemed sad, perhaps because he could not forget what Dean just said about his sister. "I'm glad you figured that much out," he said. "But I still wonder how you survived so long in the cave when you were so sick."

"I already know. I was delirious, and I couldn't take care of myself. All that time, all that time while I was so helpless, the wolf fed me."

Fribitz shook his head, not understanding.

Dean pushed his bowl and cup back. He painfully lifted his left leg on the table. His shoe was already off, and he pulled back his pants cuff. "Look at this," he said. "This foot of mine—it was infected. The wolf licked it clean, kept the infection down. Somehow he pulled my boots off with his teeth. That's why I was barefoot when they found me. That's how I survived. And you see these scratches and piercings on my leg? They told me I got them running through the woods. He dragged me somewhere so I could drink. He brought me part of the meat he hunted. He did this. That wolf did this. That wolf saved my life."

Fribitz Grinner was a talker, a smiler, a joker, but now he stared in awe at his friend, and the wounds on his foot and calf. The foot still looked nasty, missing three toes, but now, it meant so much more. "Dean, your whole life is a miracle. How could I not see it? What the hell does all this mean?"

Dean put his foot down. "It's time for a change," he said. "I still don't know what to do next, but there is something I need to do, I know it now." He downed the tea, then opened the bottle, took one last swig, and held it up. "You got any more of this here?"

"That's it," Fribitz said. "I could buy you a few more bottles. I have money..."

"No," Dean said. "Dump it. Starting tomorrow, I get sober."

Fribitz tilted his head, not sure he heard right. Dean pointed over his shoulder with his thumb. "That stick--- that's the only crutch I'll need from here on out."

Fribitz grinned.

Chapter Fourteen

"Revenge"
(Summer, 1967)

Nightwind lowered his head and sniffed the ground by the maple tree. Moonhowler, his mate, stood near him, her ears bent forward. He glanced over his shoulder at her, his ears all the way back against his head, his hackles raised, the threat posture. "Something's not right," he growled. "I don't know what it is, but something's not right."

"I feel it too," Moonhowler whined. "The smell....it was there two days ago, and now it's back, stronger, like it's coming from everywhere." She glanced at the trees. "I was in the dens with the cubs, and I could smell it then. I was afraid to go out. It smelled like a Hunter, but it smelled so different, too. And I remember.... I smelled it once before, when I was a cub...."

"Me, too," Nightwind said. "I remember the scent from somewhere. A long time ago. It means something."

"Maybe we should leave," Moonhowler said. "Maybe we should go."

Nightwind looked at his mate. "Why? Whatever passed by is gone. It won't be back. If it caused us no harm before, it's not looking for anything here now. If it was a bear, and if it returns, I'm here, and so are Noonsleeper, Grassroller, and Hawkwatcher. No bear would come near us now."

"And what about Bonechewer and her two yearlings?" Moonhowler asked.

"Bonechewer and her yearlings can take care of themselves. She's travelling far from here, teaching them to hunt, and no bear is going to catch them unaware."

"I don't know," Moonhowler said. "If it was a bear, it would smell like a bear. But this is different—it smells like a Hunter, almost. I remember last autumn when I found old Rockhead dead among the bushes, and the worms and the birds all had their share of him, and I could see his bones, the smell of his remains disturbed me. Dead is like that. But this smell—this smell is like a Hunter who died and came back, only now with the soul of something else, something terrible and vicious. It smells like that now, and I'm scared. Maybe there's a Hunter who has come into our territory, and maybe he's diseased."

Nightwind glanced back at the den where Grassroller and Noonsleeper frolicked with the two cubs. He felt some sort of anxiety deep in his gut, and he, too, considered moving the pack somewhere else. But all of them had lived their lives around these dens, and as their One, he couldn't just lead them away just because of an imagined dread.

"I don't believe there are any diseased Hunters around," Nightwind said.

"Something's around," Moonhowler puled. "The cubs.... We should leave now...."

"Enough," Nightwind growled. "You're hurting my ears with your worries." He bared his teeth to emphasize his anger.

Moonhowler lowered her head. Her large, furless teats shook with her trembling as she pulled her tail up between

her legs and padded away. She knew better than to bela-
bor a point when Nightwind was like this.

Nightwind trotted off in the other direction, tired of
the whole business. He would look around for the source
of the scent, but he refused to get panicked and worked
up over it.

The afternoon was warm, though rain clouds were
gathering in the sky. Nightwind felt a strange chill deep
inside as he searched the area around the dens for that
scent. He wandered further away, leaving his scent on
trees and bushes as though trying to cover the trace odor
that had him so disturbed. It was also a warning to the
trespasser, if indeed there was a trespasser.

Nightwind had been the One since old Rockhead died,
and though there was plenty of meat to be hunted in the
territory, the burden of leadership weighed heavy on him.
It was not his place to control every aspect of the pack's
existence, but decisions had to be made, nonetheless, and
he decided that there was no reason for them to desert
the dens.

As he returned, he felt as though he were being
watched. His hackles rose on their own, and he felt a bit
of indigestion and gas inside, signs of nervousness over
something he could not identify. He stopped when he
saw his pack near the dens. Most of them were sunning
where the light broke through the leaves, making patches
on the ground.

Nightwind jerked around and nipped at a flea, then
glanced back at his pack. Moonhowler was reclining on
her side, the two cubs suckling at her teats. Suddenly
Moonhowler leaped up and bit at something on her rump.
A tremendous clap of thunder ripped the quiet of the afternoon. Nightwind glanced up at the gray clouds crowding
out the bright sky above the leaves, but already he sensed
it hadn't come from there.

His attention was drawn back to the den where he heard loud puling. Moonhowler was in pain. He felt a ripple of fear; something was very wrong. Moonhowler was hopping in circles, her right hind leg lifted off the ground. The cubs followed her, whining for attention. The other Hunters raised their heads and looked around.

Moonhowler jerked sideways. Nightwind saw black blood on her pelage as she staggered and fell on her side, her body jerking sporadically. The silence was shattered once, then again. Other Hunters rose, unsure whether to attack or run, and right then Nightwind knew the unwelcome scent was a warning.

He watched from his vantage point as Noonsleeper glanced south, glanced downwind as his body blossomed like a flower, a hole in his side sending black blood and viscera northward splattering the rocks. He collapsed to the ground, lifeless as blood pooled around him.

A chunk of Hawkseeker's head blew off, and she shook her head back and forth, running in circles. Nightwind could see she was missing an eye. Another bloody hole appeared in her side and she, too, fell to the ground. Grassroller collapsed beside her, legs shaking as the air thundered with explosions.

The stinging smell of burned minerals was in the air. The cubs were whining and climbing over Moonhowler's body. Nightwind stared, dumbfounded, and paralyzed at the carnage.

Something inside him told him to run away from everything, but instead he gazed downhill and saw two approaching upright creatures. He recognized them from the stories he'd heard—Twolegs!

Something told him to run away; he charged the Twolegs instead. They faced him as he ran. He could see more of them through the trees. He kept charging. He felt a burning pain in his shoulders. He staggered but still kept charging. He heard the explosions. He knew they killed his pack. He kept charging. He bared his teeth. Before he died, he realized that the bad stink was a warning after all. Before he died, he desperately hoped that at least Bonechewer and her yearlings might survive.

"Okay, am I doing this right?" George Smith asked. He gripped the wolf's chest skin and touched the tip of the knife to it.

"Jesus, George," Alex Martin said, squatting down beside him. "Start a little higher, up against the neck, then cut down."

George knelt forward and began again. The skin was much harder to cut than he thought, and his first try ended up with the knife buried to the hilt inside the wolf's chest and a cut on his thumb. He managed another try, and got the first cut from just below the neck to the penis and testicles. "Now what?" he asked. "Do I just cut them off? What about the asshole?"

"Didn't you ever skin a deer in the woods before?" Alex said.

"I never got a deer," George replied. "I got a lot of pheasants, but I'd take them home to the old lady, let her get it ready for dinner, let her pluck it. I don't see why I even have to fuck with this thing. You can't eat a wolf."

"You shot it," Alex said. "The skin is yours, your souvenir. Who knows, maybe you might get a few bucks for it."

"I wish I'd killed this thing back when there was a thirty-five dollar bounty. I could sure use the money. Here," He handed the knife to Alex. "You skin it. You keep the skin."

"Ah, get outta here!" Alex laughed. "I wanna see you do it! Now start here, use the blade, and begin separating the skin from the body." He pointed.

George sighed and grabbed a handful of skin. He glanced around the area. There were eight men altogether. They'd killed five wolves and two cubs. George glanced through the trees, where he saw Ben Rose and Jack Fipps standing and talking to Jessie Armstrong. The three men were the only ones who didn't actually kill any wolves this time.

Jessie had his bow, unstrung, in his left hand and his quiver of arrows on his back. He'd talked George into reluctantly coming along on this trip.

George looked back at the wolf he'd killed, running his fingers through the gray fur. It was the first time he'd ever killed a wolf, and he felt proud. He almost didn't get one, they were all dead as he approached, but then one charged out of the woods at him. Alex kept his rifle down, forcing George to shoot.

He lifted the skin up and began separating the skin from the meat, using his blade to slice away the connective tissue. Though he was getting blood on his hands, he was actually finding it pretty easy. Alex snickered. "Shut up, Alex."

"Jesus, George, you just fart?"

"It's this wolf," George said, noticing the smell of the wolf meat for the first time. "You gotta get used to odors like this when you skin animals."

"Listen to the Great White Hunter!" Alex laughed. "I've been skinning animals since I was ten, and you just started today, and you're gonna tell me how to do it? No George, that smell ain't the wolf. Your nose stuffed up or something?"

George stopped cutting. "Yeah, I smell it now. What the hell is it? A skunk? A garbage dump?"

"You can scratch the dump, George, this is the woods." Alex sighed. "Where did you hunt your pheasants any way? The city park? No, that stink is worse than a dump and a skunk combined."

"Yeah, you're right," George said. "Maybe we should just go now."

"Finish skinning the wolf first, George."

"This looks like a butcher shop."

"If a butcher can stand it," Alex said, "so can you."

"You haven't started skinning the wolf you shot yet, I've noticed."

"When you're done with this one."

"What if there's a skunk around?"

"Don't worry, you can defend yourself. Use your knife, and cut its throat if it attacks."

"But...."

Cloudwalker held still as one of the Twolegs stood and glanced back in his direction. He was uphill and in the shade of two thick wild apple trees, but not too far from them, and with no bushes nor trees between him and them. With no cover to hide behind, he tensed to run, but the Twolegs turned back around and again crouched over the body. He was not seen after all.

"Gas!" he snorted to himself. "Bad, bad gas! Bad, bad digestion!" He was uphill and also upwind of them, and he knew better than to tempt fate, but that last one just slipped out before he knew it.

He backed slowly away, watching all the Twolegs busy at their chores. Then he turned and trotted away, remembering what he'd seen them just do, and remembering, especially, their One, the Dark Twolegs, who had gray and black hair and carried long twigs in his paws. This was the one he had seen several times, the Twolegs with the feathered sticks. He carried this one's distinct odor in his memory.

As he trotted away, he continued in his usual gait,

lifting each paw in such a way as to drag his claws over his paw print, obscuring it from view. Unless the ground was muddy, this method of walking hid his paw prints, and Twolegs were incapable of picking up a scent trail on their own. He had used his unusual gait for so long that he instinctively knew not to scrape the ground when his paw landed on leaves or a flat rock, which would not leave a paw print. It was all automatic behavior now. As long as he wasn't running, he never left a trail for Twolegs.

Run....he thought. You could have run! You could have run!

The leaves of the trees created a dark canopy over him as he trotted away. His shoulder muscles were like twisted, intertwined roots moving beneath his mangy skin. He didn't glance around, but he was aware of every tree around him, aware of almost every bracket fungi, almost every mouse scampering beneath the leaves, almost every bug and bird. His arthritis hummed in his joints, but the pain meant nothing to him, because something in his gut burned like Father Sky's good eye.

And he knew about burning.

He knew!

We're all going to die! a voice whined inside his head. *We're all going to die!*

The voice was joined by others, many, many voices of Hunters he once knew and Hunters he didn't.

Twolegs is killing us all!

How will our kind survive?

We will be no more!

Twolegs can't be stopped!

"They will never kill us all, Twolegs will NOT!" Cloudwalker growled, his scaly, almost furless brows knitting together. He shut the voices from his thoughts, pushed them back, and concentrated on where he was. Sitting down, he closed his eyes and listened to the sounds around him.

He needed to calm down, catch his breath, center himself.

The wind rustled the tops of the trees. The warble of a distant mocking bird was drowned out by the heavy beats of the wings of a ring neck pheasant taking off in a meadow nearby. A feather drifted down and touched the ground. There was no danger near. He could begin.

He inhaled.

Then he exhaled.

He focused on the Blood of the Hunter.

He concentrated on the Tail.

The Tail and Anus.

Fear.Flight.Survival.Adrenalin.Hunger.Fight.Anger. And Mother Earth.

He inhaled and exhaled again.

The Blood of the Hunter.

The Testicles.

Mating.Pleasure.Play.Peace.Reproduction.

He inhaled and exhaled again.

The Blood of the Hunter.

The Intestines.

Digestion of food.Sustenance.Strength.Life.

And again....

The Heart.

Blood-mover.Life-muscle.Center.

And again....

The Throat.

Growl.Snarl.Howl.Pule.

And again....

The Eyes.

Sight.Senses.Thought.Wisdom.

And again....

The Top of the Head.

Strategy.Power.Cunning.

And Father Sky.

The connection was complete.

For a period of time he held his breath, sitting still, not moving, his eyes closed though he could still hear everything around him. Then he slowly inhaled, filling his lungs and emptying his mind. Part of his brain still paid attention to sounds, smells, and ground vibrations for signs of danger, and part of his mind reached for each voice in his head, touching nose-to-nose, warning each to be quiet for awhile.

The rest of his being descended into an inner darkness; caressing and nuzzling his fears, reliving memories and smelling dreams. Every part of him focused at the center of his being. He basked in a special silence, and the turmoil that fermented in him over many winters was put aside for awhile.

He could feel fleas biting him, but they weren't important. The only movement was his ears, twitching sometimes from side to front, still listening. Otherwise he was in his own silent world.

The Blood of the Hunter and his Heart make up his Soul....he thought. The Legs of the Hunter are his Spirit. The Hunter is the Guardian, the Guardian protects the Balance, and the Balance must be maintained. There is nothing to fear. Whatever happens is meant to happen. Whatever happens is meant to be.

First there was Winddancer, the Guardian of Guardians, who was swift and wary, marking her vast territory, including many territories within her own, after all the Hunters in her pack were killed by Twolegs. Winddancer was known by all, and all knew her by sight.

Then there was Thundersnarl, whose howl warned of the approach of Twolegs three territories away. He was alone after Twolegs destroyed his pack, but he nonetheless warned other packs if Twolegs were around. Sometimes he'd visit other packs, but not often. Thundersnarl and Winddancer became one.

Then there was Cloudwalker, who no other Hunter ever saw. Like the others, he was the last survivor after his pack was hunted down by Twolegs. Cloudwalker never left a paw print wherever he went. He was never seen, but he always warned others if Twolegs were coming.

Snaretripper arose when the Hunters of his pack were killed off, one by one by the Jaws, and by snares, those thin vines that could circle and tighten on a leg or throat. He was the first to discover that the snares and Jaws could be closed by a stick or a rock, and be safe, at least for awhile. He discovered the tainted meat that made Hunters sick and die, and he warned the others of his kind to stay away from them.

And then there was Dogslayer.

Dogslayer....

Cloudwalker, Winddancer, Thundersnarl, Snaretripper and Dogslayer, all were now one, but there was a name he had back then, a name he no longer remembered.

He was the Second in the Starwind Pack, he remembered that. And they all, the entire pack, lived in a single, large den created by Mother Earth just for them—Mother Earth's Womb, they called it. The territory was vast and bountiful, and the Starwind Pack thrived and grew in number.

Starwind, their One, himself had a different name at one time, but he one day climbed a mountain and touched the stars on Father Sky's backside, and some say he even flew in the wind of the stars.

It was one winter just after a kill when he and Starwind left their pack in the large den and went on a long journey, lasting days, marking the scent-posts of their boundary, and making sure the cold and the wind did not weaken the scent that bordered their pack's territory.

Starwind was determined to complete that task, then return and gather his pack for another hunt.

When they returned to Mother Earth's Womb, however, they found the entrance to the great den surrounded by many, many Twolegs and their dogs. There must have been more inside, because there were explosions, one after another and the sounds of Hunters growling and puling and keening from the darkness of the den as though coming from Mother Earth herself.

That day he could have run off, they both could have run off, and they would have survived, but instead they both attacked the Twolegs. And, that day, they both died.

Starwind charged towards Twolegs, knocking one down, biting into a leg, about to kill him when an explosion ripped through the air and Starwind fell on his side, trembling and trying to get up. Twolegs surrounded him, pointed sticks at him, and explosion after explosion echoed around the clearing.

Starwind's Second—the large Hunter who'd been at his side for a year—charged into the crowd, already dying from the sounds of suffering inside the great den. He ran fast, knocking a few of them over, then he knocked down a large, black dog, tore its throat out, left it twisting and bleeding to death, leaped on a second dog and did the same as other dogs surrounded and attacked, but they were all noise, their teeth like porcupine quills, only causing a little pain on his backside. He turned around, was about to kill a third when the air exploded.

His right hip burned with a pain he'd never experienced before. He yelped, twisted around and bit at the tiny wound. The dogs backed up, and Twolegs surrounded him.

He bared his teeth, looked from one to another, was about to charge when another explosion tore through the air. Half his left forepaw was gone. He whined, holding it up, and the air exploded again, and he felt pain in his right shoulder, and then in his side and his legs, and he collapsed onto the ground. He was trembling uncontrollably from all the pain, but it was only then he realized they, Twolegs, weren't trying to kill him.

The explosions had stopped. They stood around him like trees. Then cold liquid was poured on his head, bringing a new panic as he tried to rise and move away. His eyes burned. He shook his head.

Until the fire began.

The pain was incredible, so much pain, burning hair, blistering skin, and searing flesh. He leaped up, keeping his eyes closed and holding his breath. On wounded legs he charged away, running blindly, his head ablaze with fire as he bumped into a tree, then kept going.

The pain was unendurable, but it kept him moving until he went over the edge of a creek bed and fell into deep water, extinguishing the fire. He came up from the water, gasping, opening his eyes. His head still felt as though it were burning. He heard noise in the brush, Twolegs coming after him. He leaped out of the water and ran.

And there his memory ended, and did not return for two winters, except for vague memories of fevers, seeping sores, cracking, black skin, infections, odors, but somehow he survived, no memory of how.

Cloudwalker took a deep breath and opened his eyes. The loss of Nightwind's pack weighed heavily on him. "Run, you could have," he growled. "You could have run..." He left his scent behind two days ago as a warning after seeing Twolegs near them. He knew Twolegs would come back with more of their kind. When he saw them coming back, he left his scent again, stronger, in more places.

But Nightwind didn't understand the warning, and now most of his pack was dead.

As for the Dark Twolegs—Featherstick, Deathbringer, Blackhair—Cloudwalker seemed to recognize him more often now, not always in the lead, but always the One. Cloudwalker knew this Twolegs, by sight and smell he knew him. "Not dead yet, I am not, Dark Twolegs, I am not dead yet," he growled, thinking of the latest slaughter he had seen. "I have a message for you, Featherstick, a message for you. I watched you, that day, I did....Saw you, that day, and a message for you I have!" He rose and shook out his fur. Then he stretched once and set off in a new direction.

"Hey, Clyde, I'm thirsty!"

"Well, whatcha want me to do about it, Bo?" Clyde growled. "Piss a puddle for you? Thirsty-smirsty! I'm thirsty too, but you don't hear me whining about it, do you?"

The two dogs were resting side by side chained to one of the pickup trucks. Bo had the weaker chain because he was fat and slow. Clyde, who always bossed him around, usually tormented him into a cowering, whimpering mass whenever he was angry or whenever George Smith beat him. It was sort of a distribution of the suffering. Clyde sometimes wondered, though, who beat George so bad he had to come home like that every night and beat his dogs.

Poor Bo, however, was at the bottom of this hierarchy, and had no one to terrorize. He made up for it by eating twice as much food as Clyde. Otherwise, all he ever did was mope around the house and whine a lot. Nonetheless, he was the only company Clyde had most of the time.

Coming out to the woods was fun for both of them. They always rode in the back of the pickup, noses into the wind. Of course, all this waiting around being chained up to the truck got old fast; both dogs were already looking forward to the drive back.

"Hey, Clyde," Bo said. "George left his truck door open again."

"Well, whoop-de-do!" Clyde growled. "Why don't 'cha close it for him, Bo?"

"Well, maybe he wants it open."

"Well, maybe you ought to ask him when he gets back, Bo," Clyde said, not even bothering to open his eyes.

Both dogs were black-furred Rottweilers with brown eyebrows and muzzles. Bo was old enough to have sired Clyde. The years they spent with George softened their bodies, though, and they never became the hunting dogs George had once wanted them to be.

Sometimes when George was in a good mood, he'd pour each dog a large bowl of beer. His wife complained about it, and the beer tasted like urine, but, boy, one could sure sleep after a bowl of beer!

George didn't actually train Clyde or Bo; they all more or less trained each other. George was satisfied enough that he was able to get them to the point where they wouldn't piss in the house, and the dogs were glad they had George at the level where he would open the door for them when they needed to piss.

Bo usually whined, "Please, oh, please—oh, please, oh, please; let me out I gotta pee so bad please, oh, please, oh, please, oh, please!!!" While Clyde generally barked, "Look you, open this door or my guts'll bust and you'll have blood and guts and piss all over your ol' worn out rug!" Both responses got George to open the door in a heartbeat.

"Didja ever wonder," Clyde schemingly told Bo, "If we could ever figure out how to open the front door, we wouldn't have to ask George any more. And just think: if we could open the refrigerator door, we could take control of the house! Wow! All the food we'd ever want!"

"But doesn't George have to put food into the refrigerator," Bo asked, "before we can take it out?"

"Yeah, yeah, maybe you're right," Clyde grunted, a little jealous Bo finally thought of something he didn't. "I guess it wouldn't work after all." Neither of them stopped to consider that even if they could open the front door of the house, the refrigerator door, and even drive George's pickup, they still wouldn't be in control, because, whether they admitted it or not, George was still their Alpha-Male.

"My pretty ones resting, are they?"

Clyde and Bo looked up, alert, ears raised, heads snapping back and forth looking for the sources of the strange gravelly growl. The voice seemed to come from everywhere; they couldn't pinpoint a direction. It was a gritty, deep voice, powerful, deep, rough, like a wide, muddy river.

Then they saw it: the massive, dark figure moved out of the shadows of the trees and ferns. It looked like a giant dog with a deformed white head. And then they could smell it, too, an odor that burned their nostrils, a stench worse than all the dead things they ever rolled in, and they knew it came from the dog-thing.

"Clyde, what is it?" Bo asked.

"I don't know," Clyde snarled. "I don't know."

"Hungry, are we?" the big creature asked. "Thirsty, are we?" Its fur was mangy and matted, and bare, scaly skin showed through spots in its pelage, with deep scars over more deep scars. Muscles and tendons moved in its emaciated body like giant hungry maggots just under the skin. If it weren't walking towards them, they would've assumed it was dead. With each step, it dragged its long, black claws over the dirt, scratching the ground.

It kept its head low. Its ears were back threateningly against its skull. Its neck and shoulder hair was raised.

Its teeth were bared, yellow, cracked, and chipped, framed by black, tattered lips. It grinned and watched them, a walking, broken dead thing.

"Let's get the piss out of here!" Clyde whined. "It wants to kill us!" Both dogs turned and dashed away from it, only to be jerked short by their chains. Bo froze, watching the thing approach, but Clyde kept on tugging, his chain rattling as he pulled backwards.

"Scared are we, good doggies?" the thing said. "Scared are we?" It stepped closer. Then Clyde pulled free, the collar slipping painfully over his head and ears as he tumbled backwards in the grass. The thing stopped as Clyde recovered and dashed off into the trees, his tail between his legs.

"Clyde!" Bo puled. "Clyde! Don't leave me! Help me!" Bo trembled and dribbled in his panic. "Oh, Clyde! It's coming closer! Help me, Clyde!"

With just a few more steps, the thing stood over Bo. It bared its teeth in a grim smile, its lips black against a whitish face. It lunged forward and its jaws snapped shut, crunching down with hundreds of pounds of pressure on the chain that Bo pulled taut. A tooth chipped, a link broke, and Bo toppled over backwards.

Bo rolled over and got back up on his paws, staring numbingly at the chain attached to the pickup bumper. "I'm free!" he yipped. Then he glanced at the grinning thing rising over him, and he collapsed onto his side, completely passed out.

The hunters stepped out of the woods and into the grassy field, their rifles pointing towards the ground as they talked and laughed. Some of them carried wolf pelts on their shoulders, and the stories flowed back and forth like beer at a bar. Most wore caps and jackets, their hunting licenses on one or the other.

Storm clouds were gathering overhead, and clouds of gnats swarmed in spots above the ground. The air was heavy and ominous as the afternoon darkness spread across the sky like a tide.

"You should have brought the rain flaps for the jeep," Ben Rose said, his lower lip puffed out by a plug of tobacco. He carried his rifle and wore his dirty New York Yankees baseball cap over his curly red-orange hair. He nodded and gazed at the sky as he walked.

"A little weather never hurt anybody," Cutter said. "It's a warm day, and it'll be a warm night and all we'll probably get is a little sprinkle."

"Looks like a wildcat in the sky to me," Ben said, spitting tobacco juice. Cutter nodded, taking one last drag before tossing his cigarette butt. Ben grunted. "I thought you were gonna do some hunting yourself."

"Just felt like watching this time, Ben," Cutter said, rolling another cigarette. "Besides, it gives me a chance to see how well these guys shoot. And anyhow, I'm saving my arrows for bigger game."

"You just enjoy being the boss," Ben said, smirking. "Whenever I hire you out to take photos for the state, you're half the time telling me what to do. I don't see why you don't just charge these guys a fee and be their guide."

Cutter shrugged, but Ben knew his plan. The men he hunted with continued to spread the word that he was looking for the Shadow Wolf, and that he was offering five thousand dollars to the person who helped him the most in catching it. Surely, someone somewhere would be able to help him find it. Already there were regular reports of broken traps and large paw prints.

Ben gazed at Cutter as they walked back toward the vehicles. His hair had streaks of gray, and his wrinkles seemed deeper, like furrows in a field. But there was that side of Cutter that only Ben could see, when Cutter didn't think anybody was watching, and his disarming smile faded, and his eyes gazed at the world as though he were the hunted, and not the hunter. Then something else caught his eye.

"Cutter?"

"What?"

"Look up ahead. The men."

Cutter and Ben walked faster. Four men were squatting beside George's pickup. When one of them stepped back, Cutter and Ben saw the dead Rottweiler. Its throat was torn out, its belly torn open and its viscera spread around the ground, fanned out as though something were playing with it.

"He's been here," Cutter said, awe in his voice. "He's been here, Ben, and he's been watching us."

"Goddam! Who killed my dog?" George Smith shouted, dropping his rifle and wolf skin and running past Alex, Cutter, and Ben to his truck. The other men stepped away from the dog. "Goddam!" George screamed. "What the hell happened? It's Bo! Where's Clyde? Goddam! Goddam!"

The other men stood around uncomfortably as George knelt and cradled his dog's bloody head in his lap. Alex picked up the rifle and skin and walked towards them. The men looked at each other, then back at the dog as they formed a circle around George.

"Who did this?" George said, picking up his dog and placing him in the back of the pickup. His hands were shaking. "Who did this?" He pulled out his knife and cut the intestines that trailed onto the ground. "Who killed Bo? And where's Clyde? Where's my fucking dog?"

"It was that fucking wolf," Alex said, glancing accusingly at Cutter. "Look." He pointed. Paw prints were all over the ground. "The wolf got him."

"He was watching us," George said, glancing at the

other men. "Isn't that what they say he does?" He looked at Cutter. "You oughta know. You talk about him all the time."

Cutter stared grimly at George. "Yeah, the wolf watches. The wolf watches, and then he gets his revenge. I told you all that. That's why I want to kill him myself."

"You knew the wolf would do this," George said. He was in front of Cutter in six steps, his left hand gripping Cutter's shirt, his right holding the blade of his knife near Cutter's face. "You knew the wolf would do this, didn't you? You knew the wolf killed dogs!" Ben stepped closer, but Cutter waved him back as he nodded at George.

"So why didn't you fucking say something? Why didn't you tell me, 'George, lock your dogs in the cab of your truck? It's safer for them.' Why the fuck didn't you say that?"

At first Cutter said nothing as the other men glanced from him to George and back again, then raised a hand, slowly pushing the knife away from his face. "I didn't know the Shadow Wolf would be here," he said. "And I didn't know the wolf would begin killing dogs again."

"So what do you know?" George growled.

"I know the Shadow Wolf is nothing to play with," Cutter said. "He may be flesh and blood and bone, but he's a killer, and he's got his tricks. That's why I want him dead."

"It's just another fucking wolf," George said.

"Is it?" Cutter asked. "Just look what it did to your dog. Look how big the paw prints are around here. Even you can tell other wolves are dwarfed by this thing. Another fucking wolf, George?"

George released Cutter's shirt, spun around and sheathed his knife. "All right, Cutter, you made your point. So why didn't you kill it?"

"I can't find it, George," Cutter said, almost pleading.

"That wolf travels all over the state."

"Maybe you haven't tried."

"George, I've been trying for five years. Ask Ben." Cutter threw his hands up and glanced from man to man. "That wolf has tricks like you wouldn't believe."

"Hell, Cutter, look at all the paw prints," George said. "We could track him down easy."

"Go ahead," Cutter said. "The paw prints will disappear a hundred feet away. If you don't believe me, follow them and see how far you get."

"Then how about using hounds?" Alex said.

"Same thing happens," Cutter replied. "They lose the scent. Don't ask me how. I believe he has a way of changing his odor."

"You're full of shit," George grumbled. "It's just a fucking wolf."

"You think I'm making all this up?" Cutter asked.

"He's not." Ben said. "I was with him. We borrowed some hounds. They took us a mile following the wolf's trail, then stopped, as though it had flown off. We tried to coax the dogs to go further, but they got really agitated."

"How could he do that?" George asked, no longer sure it was all a story.

"This one doesn't act like a wolf," Cutter said. "He doesn't think like a wolf. He thinks like you and me. He hides and watches us—you can see for yourself. This is not a stupid animal, an instinct-driven beast, but a thinking, scheming killer. Just stop and think what it would do if it decided to go after us instead of our dogs."

The men silently looked at each other. Some of them had considered that possibility before, but carrying their rifles helped keep it in the back of their minds. The sight of the dead dog brought that fear to the forefront.

George stared down at his boots, "Look there. That bastard chewed clean through the chain. Now what kind of animal would do that?"

"Yeah," Alex said. The other men nodded their heads.

"What about your other dog?" Ben asked.

George looked at the other chain, still intact with the collar at the end. "He must've gotten away."

"You wanna search for him?" Ben asked.

George looked up at the sky. On the one hand, he was still bitter at the brutal killing of his dog. On the other hand, the clouds were minutes away from bursting. "I can look for him tomorrow. It'll be dark soon, and once it starts raining, we won't have a chance to find him."

"Why don't you call him?" Cutter asked. "Maybe he's within earshot, maybe he'll come. If he hears you, he'll know the wolf is gone and he can come back."

"I'll honk the horn," George said. "That usually brings him running."

As George gathered up the chains on his bumper, Cutter went to his jeep and put his bow and arrows in the back. Because Cutter left the door flaps back at his cabin, it would be a rainy ride back. Ben glanced at him through the other door and gave his best I-told-you-so smirk, then sat in the passenger seat.

"Goddam," George shouted. Ben gazed out his door as Cutter looked over the hood of his jeep. George was standing at the driver's side door of his pickup, looking in. "Goddam! That fucking wolf got into my truck! The upholstery's ripped up and he shit on what was left of my seat!"

Cutter and Ben got out of the jeep and joined the other men gathered around the truck. Sure enough, the pickup's seat was shredded, and a big pile of spoor sat on the driver's side. The dashboard was scratched up, and a pair of work boots sat on the floor of the cab, well-chewed.

"You shouldn't have left your goddam door open!" Alex said.

"This is a joke!" George said. "This is a sick joke. What sort of animal would play a joke like this?" He turned and looked at Cutter. "Has a good sense of humor, doesn't he? What else does your wolf do, Cutter? Fly like Superman? Tap dance? Play football?"

The other men laughed a nervous laugh, but George didn't, standing and staring wild-eyed at Cutter.

"You should've left the dogs at home, I guess," Cutter said. George turned away, reaching into the back of the pickup and pulling out a shovel. He scooped the pile of wolf shit from the seat and tossed it out, then slammed the shovel into the truck bed.

As the other men wandered back to their vehicles, George was tossing an old flannel shirt over the stain on what was left of his truck seat, climbing in and cranking the engine to life as the other trucks started. Cutter and Ben climbed into the jeep, and he started the engine. Neither one felt like speaking, and as the sky drew darker, he put his jeep in gear and took the rear of the caravan, driving along two old ruts that led through the trees.

Thunder rumbled overhead, and a strong wind blew the treetops as he followed the last pickup's taillights. His headlights made ominous shadows between the trees as he thought about the dead dog with mixed emotions.

On the one hand he was glad it had happened—it showed the men how truly dangerous the wolf could be, far better than anything he could tell them himself. The men would drink, and talk, and tell other men what they had seen. He would have more eyes working for him, more sources, more lookouts, and more support for him to get the Shadow Wolf.

On the other hand, the dead dog was a reminder that he was not in control, not yet at least, and that there were more variables to his pursuit of the wolf than he expected. The wolf had found them, struck and disappeared, and it irked Cutter to no end that an animal had outsmarted them, had the upper hand still, had gotten away unseen, though still leaving a message behind that he knew they would all understand.

And something else, something he hid very well from the others and tried not to admit to himself; he was beginning to feel afraid of the animal. He couldn't let that fear get to him. He had to fight it. And he would, he knew he would.

Ben closed his eyes and dozed, despite the rough ride. The jeep rocked like a small boat on a stormy sea, sliding and bumping in ruts that threatened to grab the vehicle. Wind blew through the open doors, and Cutter wished he'd brought the door flaps.

Suddenly the taillights ahead glowed brighter as the pickup came to a stop. Ben pushed his cap up and looked out the windshield. "Someone get a flat?"

"Hell if I know," Cutter said. "But everyone's stepping out and walking up front. C'mon, Ben, let's take a look."

With the jeep in neutral, Cutter and Ben stepped out and walked past the idling pickups to the one in front, George's. A radio was playing a Dolly Parton song, and a gentle drizzle was just starting to come down, making falling sparkles in the headlights.

George knelt in the light, his back hunched over, his hunting license on the back of his coat reflecting the light. Cutter could have sworn he heard whimpering. "Goddam stupid dog." George grumbled. "Goddam stupid wolf. Goddam stupid hunting trip and me too, I'm goddam stupid."

As Cutter and Ben stepped closer, they saw George lift his other Rottweiler from between the ruts, rise and turn around. Nobody joked this time. Cutter stared, eyes wide, his lips moving, but no words coming out. The dog was dead, limp as a rag, but there were no apparent wounds, and Cutter wondered how he'd done it this time, whether he'd broken the dog's neck or suffocated it somehow.

Men backed away as George carried the dog to the bed of his pickup and placed its body next to the other. He didn't seem angry or bitter, just quiet, empty, like something had been scooped out of his center. He walked around and was about to return to his cab, when he spotted Cutter and stopped. Cutter looked away.

"I guess Clyde didn't get away after all," George said fatalistically. "Just think, if they still had a bounty, I could get thirty-five bucks for this wolf skin I got. First wolf I ever killed. But instead of getting thirty-five bucks, I have to pay the price of two dogs. Isn't that funny?"

He spit on the ground, climbed back into his pickup and slammed the door. He revved the engine, put it in gear and jerked forward, as the other men walked back to their trucks.

Cutter looked up. He thought he heard something, the flapping of wings, and thought he saw something, three shapes flying off a branch and disappearing into the rain. The area stank, and he knew it was the smell of the wolf. He wondered if anybody else noticed, but nobody said a thing.

Ben was already sitting in the passenger seat when Cutter got back and sat in his. The drizzle was escalating into a full blown rainstorm, most of it blowing through Ben's door.

"Hey, Cutter, we got a problem here," Ben said.

"He knows," Cutter answered.

"Knows what?"

"It can't be a coincidence."

"Cutter, you all right?" Ben asked; concern in his voice as he tried to see something in Cutter's shadowy features. "You act like the wolf really surprised you this time. What's up? Who knows?"

"Nothing," Cutter said, turning the windshield wipers on and grinding the gears. "Just....Nothing."

Ben shrugged. "Okay, but about this rain...."

"Reach in back," Cutter said.

Ben twisted around, remembering the bearskin Cutter kept in back. He pulled it up front and covered himself, fur side in, then tipped his cap over his eyes and leaned his head back as Cutter released the clutch and drove on.

Cutter pulled a peach from the small sack on the floor, ate it and tossed out the seed, thinking about the small peach tree growing out of his cabin window box, surviving the winter, and still growing stronger. Nature has a way of surprising us, sometimes, he thought.

And then he thought of the real surprise, the Shadow Wolf not only killing both dogs but leaving their bodies that way. It reminded him of how he killed the two thieves, Parker and Timothy, that night, almost a year ago, one near the vehicle, one a mile farther on. It had to be a coincidence, how could the wolf know, how could the wolf think like that, it was impossible, but Cutter was having trouble believing it.

His palms were sweaty as he remembered that night, clearheaded when he killed them, but just drunk enough on whiskey and rage to not consider the consequences. Their bodies were out of sight, and their car was underwater in a deep pond, but why did he have to hide the corpses so close to his cabin?

He had nightmares off and on ever since, and though he, or anybody else in Caleb, didn't miss Parker Roberts and Timothy Cowan, he felt stupid for killing them over the money they'd stolen. He could have just taken the money back and administered a beating neither one would ever forget. Not even the guns posed a major problem— he knew how to disarm them.

Instead he killed them, brutally, sadistically, with a

thirst for vengeance that surprised even him.

He knew why. Had Ben Rose been there that day—had Ben even been in town or at the airport, some place nearby, he would never had done it. Ben was his pressure valve, his emotional barometer, his Jiminy Cricket. When he killed those men who stole the morphine, during the Korean War—more thieves!—He was only able to do so by getting away from Ben, and later, when he sensed Ben beginning to suspect what he did, feeling the disapproval, he felt ashamed of what he'd done. He needed Ben to keep him on the level, keep him from doing that again, and he knew that, had they not become friends in the States, he would now be in prison or on death row over something leading to a first degree murder charge.

He glanced over at Ben's sleeping form. Ben's cheeks were wet with rain, the skin slick but keeping him dry underneath. At least Ben supported him in his quest for the Shadow Wolf—maybe he understood his need to kill it—and he was grateful for that.

What he had seen today, however, shook him up, and he now wondered if the wolf had seen him kill the two men. Did the wolf now know where he lived? Did the wolf see into his soul? Cutter had a compulsive urge to wake Ben, tell him about the murders, seek absolution, but, no, he needed Ben on his side, he needed help to kill the Shadow Wolf, to seek a far greater absolution. He wiped his hands, one at a time, on his pants, following the distant taillights along the road, listening to the rain pound the jeep's roof as he tried to clear his mind.

Chapter Fifteen

"Over the Mountain"
(Summer, 1967)

The damp, musty smell of dark earth and mushrooms permeated the blackness as Rabbitrunner wandered through the tunnels of his den, stopping and standing erect in a passageway he never stopped enlarging. The labyrinth twisted around massive, buried boulders and solid rock walls that never saw the sunlight. Roots dangled from the tunnel ceiling, here and there, reminders of the trees far above through the thick soil. Somewhere in the darkness, several bats chirped and fluttered.

Rabbitrunner went on, blindly following a curve to where another tunnel formed a tributary, then wandered up that one. He knew the maze of tunnels by heart, and when the mood struck him, he began new tunnels. What was once a small den now had the room to shelter a pack, many packs, but there were no other Hunters, no cubs, only Rabbitrunner, only him, and the voices.

The roots dangled from the tunnel's ceiling like severed tails, and Rabbitrunner brushed against them as he continued on, headed for the dull throb of sunlight, picking up the pace until he leaped through the mouth of the tunnel, squinting against the burning brightness of Father Sky's good eye. "I'm not dead yet," Rabbitrunner growled. "I'm not dead yet!"

A cloud passed overhead as the wind picked up, moaning its dirge through the branches of the trees. Rabbitrunner noticed the storm clouds overhead, roiling across the sky with ominous rumbles. Beside the den was the tree he had seen as a seedling, slowly raising towards the sky, growing wider at the base, pushing up earth and rock as the sound of a fast-beating heart overpowered the puling of the wind. The maple tree beside the den was now a massive thing, its branches and leaves reaching out far above the ground.

The angry rumble of the heartbeat grew stronger as the wind whipped his pelage. Bigbird appeared over the leaves of the maple, its wingless, black body hovering as its talons opened and closed, and within the single, clear eye was the lone figure of Twolegs, the Alpha-Male of the Twolegs, the Twolegs One, the Dark Twolegs, peering down at him.

Rabbitrunner recognized him from the day all the Hunters of his pack were killed, and he shivered with terror and rage as Bigbird opened its talons and dived towards him, crashing through limbs and leaves, light bursting from its body as it pounced.

He jerked awake at the foot of a cliff. His eyes were sensitive to the brightness of the morning, though he was in shade, and he glanced around, still not certain yet that Bigbird was just a dream. The early morning fog was burning off, and the distant sounds of birds could be heard in the woods.

He knew this cliff well. He spent the night sleeping

here, at the foot of the cliff from which, two winters before, he leaped to what he thought would be his death. The deep snowdrift had saved his life back then, but there was no snow here now, just sharp rocks and boulders. He rose, yawning and stretching in a play-bow, then he shook out his fur and sniffed the air, picking up scents of grass, leaves, a dead raccoon somewhere and the nearby scent post of the Tailless Pack. One more shake and he walked out of the shade of the cliff.

The Tailless Hunters were spread out in their southern territory; he had seen a few of them from hiding places downwind, each one traveling nomadic until autumn brought them together again. The day before Rabbitrunner had passed their deserted dens, and later passed by two female yearlings playing near their sleeping dam. The yearlings were digging out an old gopher den between bouts of mock fighting, and he longed to join in their frolicking.

Now he headed southwest along the foot of the mountain. He hadn't gone far when he saw a pile of dried brown grass spread over the trail in front of him. He stopped; he knew what was underneath.

Glancing about, his ears cocked, he spotted a heavy stick nearby. He trotted over and picked it up in his teeth, returned to the grass pile and dropped the stick on it.

Like a striking snake, the Jaws leaped up, clamping onto the stick. Dust drifted up as Rabbitrunner leaped back, his hackles raised, his ears flat against his head. The Jaws made no other threatening move, and he sensed the danger was past. Crouching, he moved closer and sniffed; the smell was unrecognizable, but there was a stink of oldness about it. He sneezed twice and backed away. "This time, Jaws," he snarled, "this time I got you!"

"Talking to the Jaws, are we?" the raspy, deep voice asked. "Waiting for an answer, are we?"

Rabbitrunner twisted around and glanced uphill. Fifty feet up from where he stood, Cloudwalker stretched out on a large, flat boulder, his forepaws dangling over the edge as he gazed at him. His whitish, ragged face radiated curiosity and a mischievous playfulness. The ears bobbed back and forth, as they always did, picking out new sounds.

Rabbitrunner raised his tail. "I killed it!" he said. "You saw! I killed the Jaws!"

"It is not dead, my cub, not dead," Cloudwalker answered. He bounded off the rock, dropping effortlessly to the ground and walking downhill. "Twolegs can open the Jaws again, open them again, and again, to attack, again and again."

He stepped over the Jaws, sniffed them and looked at Rabbitrunner. "These Jaws are old, old since before the last snowfall. Twolegs forgot them, they did, leaving the Jaws behind. In the day, in the night, Twolegs comes, noisy, noisy Twolegs, but no noise has been here, no noise has been here in a long, long time."

"But the Jaws are dead!" Rabbitrunner protested. "I killed them!"

"See, Rabbit-Turd," Cloudwalker snarled, staring intently at the Jaws. "See what the Jaws does to a stick! And know, Rabbit-Turd, what Jaws will do to your leg! No, Rabbit-Turd, no, not dead, not dead at all, these Jaws are not! Twolegs can open the Jaws again! Rabbit-Turd can NOT, and Cloudwalker can NOT, but Twolegs, Twolegs can!"

A rumbling snarl rose in Cloudwalker's throat as he bared his teeth, his eyes riveted on the Jaws, and Rabbitrunner backed away, his tail curled between his legs, his ears back in submission as he wondered what provoked the sudden rage.

And then Cloudwalker struck, his teeth snapping on

the Jaws. He yanked it off the ground, pulling against the rattling vine that held it tight to the skin of Mother Earth. Cloudwalker jerked his head back and forth, snarling fiercely as slather and blood splattered from his lips. He pulled against the vine, his neck muscles taut, his paws pushing up dirt and pebbles, his body trembling, straining. He chewed, he bit, his teeth cracking and chipping, and he was panting now, his breath heavy and hot, his muscles and tendons pulling against the thing, blood and saliva dripping from his lips onto the ground. And then he stopped, letting the Jaws drop to the ground, bent, broken, like a forgotten corpse.

The strong stink of the old Hunter was enhanced by the smell of his blood. Rabbitrunner gazed at the Jaws, then looked at Cloudwalker.

"Look, Rabbit-Turd, Look!" Cloudwalker panted, licking his bloody muzzle, well-pleased with himself. His forelegs were shaking, his eyes blazed. "They do not know, Two-legs do not know, how much pain it causes me to do this, Rabbit-Turd, but they wonder, they do, who did it, and how. That, little Hunter, makes it all worthwhile, that, and knowing, knowing, these Jaws will never bite again!"

Cloudwalker yawned, then shook out his pelage. Rabbitrunner bent close, sniffing the broken, bloody Jaws. He was astounded that something so hard and unyielding could be bent and damaged after all, but it was. "When I was a cub," Rabbitrunner said, "I heard the stories of how you destroyed the Jaws. You were a wonder to all the Hunters of my pack."

Cloudwalker sat and scratched an ear. Only one of his paws, his right hind paw, still had all the toes on it. His left had two good toes, with a third dangling like a tumor. It flapped limp and useless as he scratched.

"Wonder," Cloudwalker said, lowering his leg. "Wonder, wonder, wonder. I walk far, and wonder, wonder, wonder.

I leave my paw print, I do, and wonder the Hunters do, and wonder the Twolegs do.

"And you, Rabbit-Turd...." Cloudwalker snarled. The younger Hunter took a step back, startled, as Cloudwalker's eyes burned into him. "Wonder about you now, they do! they saw you, they did, Twolegs and Hunter both, they saw you right here, flying, flying from that cliff. Flying Hunter, wingless Rabbit-Turd-Bird wonder!"

Rabbitrunner winced as Cloudwalker watched him. "You think I am mad, and of course, mad I am, my Hunter." He bared his teeth, snarling, "And you are mad too, Rabbit-Turd!"

"No!" Rabbitrunner growled. "You're wrong!"

"Wrong am I?" Cloudwalker asked, tilting his head, portraying a look of innocent bewilderment. "You ate the flesh of the cows, you did. You hear the voices, you do. You travel through other territories, you have. But a lot to learn there is — a lot to learn you have."

Rabbitrunner backed away as Cloudwalker raised his head and howled:

"There is nothing to fear!
Whatever happens
Is meant to happen!"

Rabbitrunner shook uncontrollably. He'd never heard a howl like that. Cloudwalker turned towards him, gazing into his eyes, then turned and started up a trail along the mountain. He paused to lift his leg and urinate on a stone, then looked back at him, just once, before continuing up the trail. This time he was meant to follow, he realized, and reluctantly he started uphill behind him.

The trees on this side of the mountain were thick and green, making a shadowy, cool journey for the two. Rabbitrunner recalled the last time he was here, the leafless trees, the wind, the snow so thick in some places they had to walk in a line to conserve energy.

It wasn't long before they came to a stop at a stagnant pond, no deeper than a foreleg and just a few body lengths across. Algae covered part of the surface, and mosquito larvae wiggled in the water like panicked worms.

There were tall strands of grass around the pond, and as Rabbitrunner drank from the water, he watched Cloudwalker methodically eat grass, drink again, repeating the ritual several times as he watched, wondering if the old Hunter was ill. The grass, he noticed, had a strange sweet-sour odor to it, like no plant around Bearback. Finally Cloudwalker was done, and he turned and continued up the trail, with Rabbitrunner following behind.

The journey took up most of the morning, but they soon reached the point where the path forked. Rabbitrunner knew where they were. One path ascended to the pass between the two mountains, the other led to the ridge trail that ended at the cliff, the cliff from which he leaped two winters ago, with Bigbird just behind him. His body trembled uncontrollably as he recalled that day, the killing, the escape, the sadness.

"Nervous?" Cloudwalker asked.

"Cold," Rabbitrunner lied, suspecting the old Hunter knew just why he was shaking.

They continued on, Rabbitrunner gazing over his shoulder at the vast landscape spread out behind them, the Tailless Territory. There were few trees this high up, and it almost seemed like they might soon walk onto the sky, onto Father Sky's bright pelage. Out there, across all that land, he knew, was Bearback, his home. He kept trying to see it, but he didn't know what it would look like from this far away.

Distance, and he remembered the bite of Twolegs, the bite from a distance, and he asked, "What about Twolegs teeth? How can they bite from so far away? and are their teeth sharp? Because they bit me, and I felt them. What about the teeth?"

"No teeth," Cloudwalker snorted. "Not sharp at all, Twolegs teeth are not. Throw pebbles from their thundering branches and sticks—Thundersticks!—Twolegs can do that, pebbles, to kill a Hunter."

"Pebbles?" Rabbitrunner asked, recalling something going through his leg that day—the day his pack was killed off—and remembering it was small as a pebble and left no teeth marks.

"Only pebbles, Rabbit-Turd, only pebbles. There are many pebbles in my body, many pebbles there are, pebbles in my rump, pebbles in my legs, and many, many pebbles bouncing around in my guts. Many, many pebbles; burning hot pebbles."

Rabbitrunner watched the backside of the old Hunter ahead of him, seeing the scars where splotches of psoriasis left bare, scaly patches, and those little scars that he could see, and thinking, so that is what made them.

The sun was at its highest point as the Hunters followed the path between the two mountains. A strong, cold wind blew dust at their faces. Rabbitrunner squinted. He could almost feel the mountain rumbling beneath him, angry that he had come back.

They wandered beyond the pass, and the valley came into view. Rabbitrunner's hackles rose as he searched the sky for signs of Bigbird, wondering if its nest was nearby. In the distance he could see the white masses of cows on the treeless plains, surrounded in square shapes made of the hard thorny vines he had only seen up close once. He could even see the cubic Twolegs dens down there.

He heard the barking of a dog, carried on the wind from so very far away. He remembered the sight of his pack at night, eating the flesh of a cow. It tasted pretty good, he recalled, bloody and warm, but in swallowing the meat, he imagined it becoming alive and devouring his insides, a little at a time. And then Bigbird came, and the explosions, and the Hunters of his pack dropping and dying....

He stopped walking.

Cloudwalker went a few steps farther before he realized he was by himself. He stopped and looked over his shoulder. "Rabbit-Turd...."

"I'm not going down there!" Rabbitrunner snarled. "I'm not going down there! I'll die!"

Cloudwalker stared at the clouds. "It matters not, it does not, whether we live or die, you and I."

"Well it matters to me!" Rabbitrunner growled, sensing a deeper meaning to Cloudwalker's words. "I'm not going down there!"

Cloudwalker raised his head in surprise, then turned around and walked back. He found a spot next to him, circled it twice, then sat down, closing his eyes. "Sit."

"I'm not going down there!" Rabbitrunner snarled. "We died because we went down there! We all died but me, and I'm not going down there now!"

"Sit!" Cloudwalker commanded, his eyes still closed. Rabbitrunner looked at him, then resignedly lowered his rump to the ground. "Now breathe," Cloudwalker said.

"I am breathing!" Rabbitrunner glared at him, baring his teeth.

"Not breathing!" Cloudwalker demanded. "Breathe!"

Not at all sure of what he had in mind; Rabbitrunner faced forward and stared straight ahead. "Okay, breathe. Now what?"

"Wait," Cloudwalker answered.

With that last word, he reminded Rabbitrunner of Bullmoosekiller, who was always telling cubs and yearlings to "Wait" during their training. He waited. The wind blew against him, but he held still.

Then Cloudwalker spoke: "A place there is, Rabbit-Turd,

a place there is, many, many days away, and walk there you can, when Father Sky's good eye gazes at your right paw in the morning and your left paw in the afternoon, and his bad eye sees your right shoulder at twilight and your left shoulder before sunrise. Pass through many territories, you must, to a land that goes on forever, a cold land, a white land, a brutal, brutal land, but there is Sacred Meat there, and very few Twolegs, if you go far enough. A land, it is, where the pelage of the Hunters grows thick and white, and Father Sky's pelage is still stained by blood from the time of Thickfur and Nightpaw, a land of cold and dying, but a land of survival, too. Go there you will someday, go there you will...."

"But...." Rabbitrunner began.

"Breathe."

"But if it's so far...."

"Wait."

Rabbitrunner reluctantly went silent, gazing into the valley. He had no idea what he was waiting for, but he trusted Cloudwalker. He felt closer to the old Hunter than he had before, closer than he ever felt to the Hunters of his pack. He closed his eyes, took a deep breath, slowly, picking up scents on the wind, then let it out slowly.

As a cub, he had played at hunting long before he had hunted, and he had imagined what it was like to hunt. Now he imagined himself inside Cloudwalker, feeling the heart of a fire that drove him from territory to territory breaking the Jaws and stalking Twolegs. He imagined himself as a connection between Mother Earth and Father Sky.

He inhaled, then exhaled, seeing all of himself within his own tail, all of him, the Blood of the Hunter, with his fears, his running, his fighting, and his survival. He inhaled and exhaled again, all of him deep within his testicles, with his pleasures and mating urge, his moments of playfulness and resting under the warm sun. He inhaled and exhaled again, and then he was in his intestines, where his sustenance was derived by the digestion of meat he ate. And then he took another breath and let it out, and he was in his heart, where his soul and inner feelings resided, where his blood was pumped.

He inhaled and exhaled. He was in his throat, the place where he felt his voice when he snarled or howled. He breathed, in and out, and he was in his head, feeling a third eye and a second sight among his thoughts, that thing which led him from danger when his senses were not enough. He inhaled and exhaled slowly, and he was at the top of his head, point of the Wisdom of the Blood of the Hunter, where he felt Father Sky, and he knew the connection was complete.

And he was panting, exerting himself, his heart beating fast, his lungs working as he looked down, wondering as he watched the passage of ground beneath him, his shadow on the ground, skimming along, but where were his paws, where were his legs, and why was the shadow so small?

He was gliding along the path of the ridge, knowing the cliff was at the end, as it always was in his dreams and memories, but this time he went over the edge and did not fall. The distant ground beneath him beckoned, but he glided through the air, feeling his chest muscles working, feeling his heart pounding as he moved his limbs and rose in the air, towards Father Sky's good eye.

He gasped at the scene! The trees were far below him, and he circled around and rose on an updraft, gliding back towards the mountains. He could see the pass, and beyond that he could see the small figures on the ground, side by side, and he thought, that's me, and that's Cloud-walker, look at us....

And he inhaled, long and slow, and opened his eyes.

The first thing he noticed was that the sun had moved considerably since he first shut his eyes, and he wondered how so much time had passed. He was shaking, recalling the vision of flying, or was it a dream, and he glanced beside him to tell Cloudwalker what he had seen.

But Cloudwalker wasn't there!

He rose from the ground, grunting from the pain in his joints—apparently he hadn't moved in awhile—and then he spotted Cloudwalker just downhill, resting in the afternoon sun.

"Ready?" Cloudwalker asked, opening his eyes at the sound of movement.

"Ready?" Rabbitrunner huffed. "Ready? Do you know where I've been?"

"Right here you've been. Now, ready?"

Rabbitrunner wanted to tell him about the strange experience he just had, but he didn't know how. The old Hunter was planning to lead him down into the valley one way or another, and for some reason it no longer seemed so frightening. He might as well get it over with. "Yes," he said. They started downhill together.

When they reached the foot of the mountain, Rabbit-runner's leg muscles were throbbing. It was late afternoon, and he walked behind the old Hunter. They crossed the grassy plain, passed through a shallow creek, and headed towards the cows. Rabbitrunner stopped when he saw the pile of grass Cloudwalker stepped over. The old Hunter stopped and looked back. "Close it, you can," he said.

Without any protest, Rabbitrunner picked up a rock in his teeth and dropped it. The Jaws snapped shut, and he jumped back. The air was full of the scent of newness— these Jaws weren't old and forgotten, like the other one he found.

"Twolegs," Cloudwalker said. "Set the Jaws wide, Two-legs did, yesterday. Many Jaws Twolegs opened here. Noisy

Twolegs, noisy, noisy Twolegs—hear them easily, Cloud-walker does."

A fury blazed in Cloudwalker's eyes, and as he did on the other side of the mountain, he bit and tore at the Jaws, pulling and snarling, dripping slather and blood, as Rabbitrunner watched, mesmerized. When Cloudwalker stopped, he was panting, and his lips were bleeding. He glanced at Rabbitrunner. "More," he said. "There." He gazed towards the cows. "Find them, you will. Close them, you will. Destroy them, I will."

"Over there?" Rabbitrunner asked, feeling a new wave of anxiety, knowing that he would have to lead this time, watch out for Jaws on his own, walk towards Twolegs cows near a Twolegs den. In daylight, no less!

"It isn't safe here," he said. "No Hunter would come around here. I smell your scent markers here. Every Hunter knows your scent. Every Hunter can see the danger. Hunters will stay away. Why do this?"

"You did not stay away, and your pack did not," Cloudwalker growled. "You know that. Fools, some Hunters are, fools and dead. And now you say they will stay away? No!'

"And you destroy the Jaws to protect the Hunters?"

"Yes, but more—there is more reason than that, there is! Destroy, I do, so Twolegs knows—so Twolegs knows!"

"Scare them, it will," Cloudwalker went on. "Scare them. But the Twolegs One, it does not scare him. It brings him back, I know not why."

Rabbitrunner wondered how Cloudwalker knew about the Twolegs One, but Cloudwalker wouldn't tell him. Reluctantly, he began his search for the Jaws, leading them towards the thorny Twolegs vines. He found more Jaws, closed them and moved on. The loud snap they made no longer frightened him, and he felt more relaxed in his task. They were safe, as long as you knew they were there.

But he was afraid, nonetheless, walking beside the Twolegs vines. He could hear Cloudwalker behind him, breaking the Jaws and making enough noise to cause the cows to move farther from the vines. It was still light, and the Twolegs dens were so close. They could be killed, and as he walked to the next Jaws, he recited in his mind: There is nothing to fear. Whatever happens is meant to happen. And still, he was afraid, very much afraid.

The cows on the other side of the thorny vines watched him impassively now, chewing and slobbering and staring with big, dumb eyes. They were so easy to kill, so easy. He closed two more Jaws when suddenly he got a strange feeling, and he looked back.

Cloudwalker had just squeezed through the strands of thorny vines and was walking slowly towards the cows. He held still and watched, panicked, as four cows rambled away, but the fifth held still, chewing and watching.

"What are you doing?" Rabbitrunner snarled, but not loud enough for Cloudwalker to hear. He watched the old Hunter approach the cow, staring straight into her eyes, rocking back and forth in a way Rabbitrunner had never seen before. Then Cloudwalker began bobbing his head up and down, rhythmically, moving closer, and then he stopped, no more than a couple feet from the cow. He slowly raised his head until his nose pointed at the sky.

To Rabbitrunner's amazement, the cow mimicked his movements, lifting her big muzzle as well. Cloudwalker lowered his nose and stepped closer, rocking back and forth, gazing steadily into the cow's eyes as she brought her head back down. And then he touched his nose to hers and held still.

The cow collapsed on her side, making a loud thunk as she hit the ground. Rabbitrunner's ears spun forward as the sound; he couldn't believe what he had just seen. Cloudwalker put her to sleep!

The old Hunter stepped forward, sniffed the sleeping cow, then turned and trotted back to the thorny vines, his head and tail held high. Once again, he was well-pleased with his performance.

He's showing me what he can do, Rabbitrunner thought. He's showing off for me.

After he crawled back through the vines, Cloudwalker stopped a few feet from him. "How did you do that?" Rabbitrunner asked.

"Patience," Cloudwalker said, before returning to his chores. Rabbitrunner watched him go, then returned to his own job.

By the time they found and destroyed the last of the Jaws, their shadows were stretched long across the grass. Before they left, Cloudwalker stopped and looked back. Rabbitrunner saw it, too. A small figure in the distance was moving from the house to the vines. He could see that Twolegs was walking slowly, which meant he didn't know they were out here watching him.

Rabbitrunner was nervous, but he also felt elated at how he and Cloudwalker outsmarted Twolegs on his own territory. That one would soon find the sleeping cow, and later, the broken Jaws. He would wonder how it happened. Rabbitrunner was tickled at that thought.

As they walked back towards the mountains, following a groundhog trail through the high grass, Rabbitrunner noticed Cloudwalker reverting back to that strange gait; with each step. Cloudwalker raked his claws across the ground, obliterating his paw prints. So they can't follow, Rabbitrunner realized.

To make it even more difficult to trail him, Cloudwalker stepped off the path and walked on grass so he wouldn't leave paw prints in the dirt. Rabbitrunner followed his example.

When Cloudwalker heard the scratching, he looked

back. "Have an itch, do we?" he snorted. "Digging a hole, are we?" And he stopped, squatted and urinated before going on. As Rabbitrunner passed the spot, he smelled a strange sweet-sour odor that didn't smell like Cloudwalker at all. Cloudwalker continued to leave his scent, and it was the same, a scent covering his own odor, and Rabbitrunner remembered the grass he ate when drinking water --- a way of changing his urine scent to confuse the dogs Twolegs used to track them.

As they approached a stand of trees, a screech above them stopped them in their tracks, and they looked up. Three ravens perched on a high limb, quietly looking down at them, their black feathers shiny and radiant. The one in the middle was larger than the other two, older, with gray at the tips of its feathers. It had only one eye, and its beak was twisted. He'd seen it before, seen them before.

The silence was murky, like a muddy creek. The large one watched them for a moment, then squawked and flew off, and the other two followed.

Cloudwalker glanced over his shoulder at Rabbitrunner. His eyes were dull and lethargic, no longer mischievous. "Many Hunters," he said. "Many Hunters of the Hillhowler Pack. All dead."

"The Hillhowler Pack?"

"Far away," Cloudwalker said. His large body sagged as though his muscles were dissolving. "Could not be there; I could not. Could not be there and here and everywhere."

Cloudwalker turned and wandered off. Rabbitrunner knew that   he was not to follow this time. He would head to Bearback, alone. He watched Cloudwalker lumber away, then he looked down at a bare spot, devoid of dry leaves and grass. Cloudwalker's paw print was in the dirt.

He placed his paw within the paw print, his paw now almost as large. He then pulled his paw back and looked at the mark he left, a paw print within a paw print.

"The whole pack dead," he heard, but how did Cloudwalker know?

Rabbitrunner looked up. Cloudwalker was gone, and night was falling. He snorted, turned and began his journey home.

Chapter Sixteen

"Kaddish"
(Late Summer, 1967)

"God, grant me the serenity to accept the things I cannot change, courage to change the things I can, and the wisdom to know the difference."

Dean stared at the floor, holding hands with the men on either side of him in the circle they formed. After chanting the serenity prayer, they were silent for a moment, then as one they all raised their clasped hands over their heads and shouted, "Keep coming back, it works!" As the men applauded, hugged and patted each other on the back, Dean shook his head, picked up his cane, and wandered over to the large urn on the table by the wall for one final cup of coffee. As he stood watching the other men and sipping from his Styrofoam cup, Bill, his new sponsor, came over.

"So are you doing okay, Dean?"

"You know, kind of trying to regain my balance and all." He smiled and took another sip.

Bill nodded. "You know you can talk to me about anything. I got five years of sobriety under my belt, and believe me, I've heard it all."

Dean glanced at him and tossed the empty cup in the waste basket as he sighed. "Okay, I've been a mess all my life, but I had a really bad thing happen just a few years back."

"Good," Bill said, smiling. "You're opening up. So what happened?"

"While I was going to college," Dean said, looking away, "my father killed my mother, my little brother and sister, and then killed himself. It has haunted me now for about seven years."

Bill crossed his arms over his chest. "You're not kidding, are you?" Dean just looked at him. No words were needed now. "Holy crap, Dean, I'm sorry, I didn't know."

"Nobody could. Nobody but me."

Bill forced a smile. "Dean, you have my number if you need to talk, or you feel the bottle drawing you closer. Just call."

"Thank you."

"Just so you know," he went on, "That five years I did so far, it wasn't easy either. How long you been dry?"

"Two weeks," Dean said, glancing away.

Bill nodded. "That's a good start."

"Something like that."

"So you finally up and went to Alcoholics Anonymous, huh?" Fribitz Grinner gasped, trying to keep up with Dean as they hiked through the woods.

Dean marched just ahead of him, his walking stick supporting him as he pushed through ferns and branches. "I gotta get clean, Fribitz. I was way too deep in booze and self-pity and sinking fast. I've been drunk before, but this time it was for a year."

"Slow down, Krazy Kat," Fribitz wheezed. "Maybe you need all this but I don't."

"You wanted to see the cave," Dean said. "I want to see

it again too, but hiking takes it outta you, and you need to get in shape, we need to get in shape. All you ever do is sit on your ass and paint, unless you want to paint with your prick, and then you just stand."

"My art is beyond reproach!" Fribitz whoofed, feeling winded already. "And I don't need all this walking around. And when do I see the cave?"

Dean stopped and turned around so fast Fribitz almost ran into him. "When we're in better shape. I plan to find the cave again, and once I do, I will do another trip and bring you along. But I need to go myself first to make sure I can do it without falling apart like the last time." He turned and started walking again. "At least this time I won't have a bottle or the flu to tear me down."

"You're taking this very seriously," Fribitz said. "Wait, Krazy Kat, let's stop here and rest, okay? C'mon, man, I'm outta my element here!"

Dean slowed down and found a log. He sat and propped his stick against a tree. As Fribitz joined him, he offered him his canteen. Fribitz drank, then coughed. "Goddamn, man, this is water!"

Dean laughed. "You still think I'll put booze in my canteen and then later go to AA?" He took the canteen back. "I'm serious, Bro, I need to clean up. I need to find the cave again, and I need to find the wolf."

Fribitz glanced at his friend. "I can't believe the wolf fed you. I can't believe it didn't just kill you or let you starve."

"I can't believe you believed me the very first time I told you that," Dean laughed. "And I can't believe I ate raw meat for a month." He glanced away, "More than anything else, I can't believe I've been a coward for so long, afraid of the wolf, afraid of the guy who's hunting him, afraid of pretty much everything and everybody. I have to change, if for no other reason than to go forward."

Fribitz nodded. "How can you walk so fast and so far

with a bum foot?"

"Easy," Dean said. "I've pretty much been walking for a year. I was looking for the wolf once I got the creepy idea he was following me."

"And was he?"

"Probably not, but whatever it was, it got me off my ass and got me back on track, sort of. I just have to make new plans."

"And what do you plan to do about that crazy guy who's hunting the same wolf?"

Dean shrugged. "I'm just going to go back to Caleb and talk to him. Maybe that will work."

"Maybe," Fribitz said, but he didn't believe it.

Dr. Wilson read through the file of papers again, then glanced over the top of his glasses at Dean on the other side of his desk. "Dr. Hoover, you were removed from this university because of drunkenness, fraternizing with students, and inability to perform your duties. Is that correct?"

Dean nodded. "Yes, sir."

"And now you want to reapply to work for this university again?"

"Yes, sir."

"And you claim to have overcome your former disabilities?"

"Yes, sir."

Dr Wilson, setting the folder down and removing his glasses, leaned forward. "Dr. Hoover, at this time we have no openings for professors. Furthermore, we already have applications from other candidates who have received their doctorates in the last year. I see you got yours several years ago."

"Just a couple years actually," Dean offered.

"Needless to say," Dr. Wilson went on, "at this time we have no need for your services."

Dean leaned forward. "You do know, Dr. Wilson, that while I was a student here, I wrote a number of articles with photographs in representation of this university. And I published a book through this university press about Isle Royale and the wolves in my study."

"I read it," Dr. Wilson said. "I found it pompous, self-absorbed and tedious." He sat back and laced his fingers together. "The photos were spectacular, your knowledge acute, but your ramblings regarding wolves and moose were absurd, as though you were talking about wizards and warlocks. Science is science, Dr. Hoover, it is exact and measured by whatever means we have developed over the centuries. You cannot speculate as though second guessing God."

Dean shrugged. "Maybe I did get carried away, but I wanted to express the facts in a way that the average person could understand. Statistics are boring."

Dr. Wilson held his gaze. "Before this meeting, I talked to Dr. Bowler and Dr. Coneurs, your former bosses. They noted you had great potential, but drank it all away in a bottle. It was their opinion that, after a number of years, you have reached your saturation point of embarrassing, shameful behavior. I was trying to be polite, but you cannot take a hint, so let me state emphatically, that you will not ever teach at this university again."

Dean gazed back, stroking his chin. "I'm just asking for a second chance."

"You used up all your second chances," Dr. Wilson went on. "This administration is tired of you, and I, meeting you for the first time, am already growing bored. In short, we will not hire you. Will there be anything else you need to know before you leave today?"

Dean shrugged. "I'll work as a janitor, I'll work in

maintenance, whatever you want. I don't have to be a teacher."

Dr. Wilson laced his fingers together again. "We didn't even have to have this interview, Dr. Hoover. The idea was to gently let you know you are not welcome here. But if gently does not work, I could call security and have them escort you out, with emphasis on pushing you out that door as roughly as legally possible." He grinned. "Good-bye, Dr. Hoover."

Dean stood and snatched his file, then turned and stormed out of the office, slamming the door behind him.

It was getting dark enough now that he had to reach up and grab the long light string, yanking it and collapsing back in his chair. A dozen neon factory lights dangling from the high ceiling came on at once, the smell of ozone and burned dust permeating the air. Dean slumped against the table, his chin on his arms, staring at the endless canvasses and sculptures in the studio. He felt alone and defeated. Fribitz was away setting up his paintings at another gallery for an opening night.

He wanted a beer, a scotch and soda, a rum and orange juice, a joint, anything, and he thought about Bill's phone number in his wallet. How many times, he wondered, had he wanted drugs or booze during a crisis or stressful situation? Probably once a day, he decided, and it didn't even have to be much of a crisis. Don't break weak, don't give up, he thought, and hoped Fribitz would be home soon. He didn't want to start another binge leading him into homelessness again, but he really wanted one good stiff drink to calm his nerves.

He sighed, glancing around the room, when his gaze targeted a painting he first saw years ago. It was a rough likeness of a wolf head, barely perceptible, almost splattered on the canvas a la Jackson Pollock. Except, as Fribitz told it, he painted it by slathering paint on his genitals and pressing against the canvas repeatedly for hours until he got the image he wanted.

Dean glanced at the painting, then at an empty four foot by four foot canvas on an ancient easel, and wondered if he could do it himself.

Ten minutes later he was squeezing three heavy dabs of oils onto a palate, red, blue and black. Then, eyeing the canvas, he stacked several wooden boxes at different levels. Once done with that, he stepped back and disrobed, undressing while eyeing the canvas, trying to figure out something to paint. Taking the palate in his left hand, he stepped up onto the highest box, then, not quite sure how to make the next move, he gently rubbed his penis and testicles in the red paint.

That done, he held the palate above his head and bent his hips towards the untouched canvas. He realized too late the boxes needed to be closer, and, risking his balance, he rubbed his genitals on the canvas. Easing his hips back, he admired his first strokes, then glanced at his friend's painting. Fribitz's work actually looked like genitals, his looked like a few sweeps with a bad brush.

Maybe he was doing it wrong. Maybe he had to hold his penis when he painted, like a brush, and then he thought of a teenager who, wanting to masturbate, used paint instead of Vaseline and had guilty red hands. He chuckled, studying the lone streak he made on the white canvas, when he heard a voice behind him.

"Whoa!"

He turned around and saw Fribitz, his arms full of long cardboard tubes, his mouth open in shock. Dean toppled backwards, and he, the canvas and easel crashed against the wall and onto the ground.

"I really did not need to see that," Fribitz said.

Dean sat in the tub sipping coffee, subdued by a warm bubble bath. The bathroom in the studio—sink, toilet and large white tub on four giant claw ball legs—was surrounded by an old purple velvet movie theater curtain that could either surround or withdraw from the bathroom area. Fribitz had explained to him that sometimes he liked looking at his studio while bathing.

Fribitz came around the curtain carrying a tube of ointment. "Here," he said. "This will take care of the pain. It soothes burning and heals rashes and excoriation."

Dean set his cup on the stool next to the tub, took the tube, and put ointment on his fingers, then reached under the water, ignoring his friend's chuckling.

"First off," Fribitz offered, "you never apply oil paint to your jewels, Krazy Kat. If you want to do that sort of thing, use acrylics. Next, I never, never did my paintings the way you thought I did. Up until now, I intended to keep that secret to myself, but now I need to explain, I never put paint on my goodies. It was just a story to add to my mystique. This is what I did."

He reached behind the curtain and brought a well-painted, large anatomically correct plastic erect penis and testicles. He held it so Dean could see the handle behind it. "I use it like a rubber stamp, and the rest is history."

Dean gazed at the device. "Fribitz, you're a real bastard. If you told me this earlier I wouldn't end up pouring turpentine on my cojones. Yeah, laugh now, but this is really not funny."

Fribitz shook his head. "So they won't let you back in school, so what. A dozen other schools will take you." Dean looked away, silent and fuming. "Yeah, it's just your ego. But just so you know, I ran into your old friend from Isle Royale, Wayne."

"Wayne Connors?"

Fribitz presented his large-teeth smile and nodded.

"He was in town but had to leave. He wandered into the gallery wearing a backpack. He was looking at a few of my renditions of wolves."

Dean put the coffee cup back down. "Holy shit. You think I can see him, talk to him?"

"No, he had to catch a bus, get back to his job. He said he and you talked about the Shadow Wolf some before you called him that. He said at the time you didn't really believe what you saw, but he did."

"Hand me that towel," he said rising.

Fribitz stood and gave him the towel. As Dean got out of the bath, he turned around, talking over his shoulder. "He gave me something to give you," he said. "He told me he just happened to be carrying it. He told me now he had contact with the wolf himself, and wanted you to know."

"Did he see it?" Dean asked. "Where was it?"

Fribitz shook his head, grinning again. "Never saw it, but he saw a pawprint." Dean now had his pants on and followed Fribitz to a work table, where he pointed at a cloth covering something. "Take a look, Krazy Kat."

He pulled the cloth away as Dean leaned closer. On the table, sitting on old drawings and brushes, was a plaster cast of a single paw print. Dean bent close enough that his nose almost touched. He ran his finger over the protrusions and bumps, the cast, a negative of a paw print Wayne must have found in the mud. Dean already knew the wolf had only one good paw—the other three were missing toes. The plaster cast was of the good paw.

To make sure he had the right wolf, Dean held both hands, palms flat, just over the print. He had done this before with paw prints he had seen. A normal wolf paw print was as wide as a human hand, palm flat. The Shadow Wolf had a paw print twice as wide. The plaster cast print was that wide.

"Whoa!" Dean whispered. "It's him!"

Fribitz nodded. "Wayne said you'd like it. He said the wolf is still out there."

"He's still alive," Dean said. "That's what counts." He looked back at Fribitz. "This came just in time. Fribitz, you remember you said you had inside information from the day you and I first met in the mental institution? Do you still have those connections?"

He sat at the table, facing Dr. Wilson, Dr. Bowler and Dr. Coneurs, the Deans of Biology, Education and Zoology respectively, unfazed by their angry countenances. The last time he came before Dr. Wilson, he wore a suit and tie. This time he wore blue jeans and a t-shirt with Mickey Mouse on his chest. He leaned back, his arms crossed, as he watched the Deans glare at him.

"Dr. Hoover, you said you wanted to discuss a proposition with us?" Wilson asked. Dean let the words hang in the air for a moment, then reached into the backpack next to his chair and withdrew a file folder. He dropped it on the desk and patted it like it was his pet. "Gentlemen, I need a job."

"I know," Wilson said. "But we don't need you."

"For years, your departments treated me like a freak, a good teacher who was off his rocker. Why was that, Dr. Bowler?"

Bowler looked at the folder. "Drunkenness, Dr. Hoover. Drug use. Various suicide attempts. Sexual misconduct with your students. General insanity."

"Just three suicide attempts," Dean said. "But I was just a blatant example of what goes on around here all the time. Just sex, drugs and rock and roll among the professors, except they are much more discreet than me, and they have tenure in any case. You have a school full of whoring, drunken teachers, present company excluded, as I know you three are too dusty for that much fun."

"State your case, Dr. Hoover," Coneurs said.

Dean patted the file folder again. "I have copies of memos and contracts of people who were assigned to spy on me and use me. Yeah I was a bad boy, but these papers have your signatures, and I know the witnesses to these signatures."

"We can smear your good name all over the state if you wish to threaten us," Wilson snarled.

"Smear me. I lived on the streets for a year. You think I couldn't take it?"

"You have nothing!" Wilson huffed. "You have useless files and papers that could not touch a hair on..."

Coneurs touched Wilson's shoulder, stopping his rant. "Dr. Hoover, am I to believe you plan to blackmail us for a job?"

Dean shoved the file towards Coneurs. "I have a little more class than that. But look it over, you'll see I was telling the truth. And if I could get this, you know I could get more." Coneurs opened the file. Dean went on. "I just wanted this interview. I wanted to tell you all that the wolf you thought I made up is real."

All three professors looked at him as one. "Here everybody thinks I'm a nut, and the wolf doesn't exist but in my head. Well, just head up to Caleb, Minnesota, to the Crooked River Tavern, and the wolf is common knowledge."

He leaned over his backpack and brought out the plaster cast. Setting it on the desk, he tapped the paw print. "This is my wolf," he said.

Coneurs glanced at it a minute, then back at Dean.

"It may be a bit bigger than a common wolf paw, but I don't see why..."

Dean set another plaster cast next to it, a regular sized paw print. Even the professors could see the first was twice its size. "Shit," Coneurs said.

"You give me my job back, I'll publish whatever I discover about the giant wolf."

Coneurs nodded. "And?"

"And it has a name. The Shadow Wolf. I want to be the only zoologist in this school that works this project. Do that and I'll behave."

The men were silent, but Dean knew they were waiting for Coneurs. "Do you have anything else to say, Dr. Hoover?"

Dean nodded. "God, grant me the serenity to accept the things I cannot change, the courage to change the things I can, and the wisdom to know the difference."

As he expected, he saw Coneurs mouthing the words as he spoke them. Fribitz was right, Coneurs was also a member of Alcoholics Anonymous. Coneurs nodded. Dean had his job back.

Chapter Seventeen

"Tricks and Pranks"
(Late Summer, 1967)

Rabbitrunner reclined at the clearing atop Bearback, sniffing the wind. He could smell four of them, Twolegs, in his territory. I know why you're here, he thought. I saw your leaf-dens by the lake. I saw the dog. I saw the Jaws. I saw the thundersticks you brought, and your fire. You're looking for my kind.

He yawned and glanced around. He'd first seen them walking through the Tailless Territory, so he made very clear paw prints in the dirt, pissing at intervals to make sure his scent was left behind, and he led them into his territory, where they set up their leaf-dens to stay the night, where they would not find any Hunters, because he was the only Hunter in his territory, he, and the voices.

When last he'd checked, they were wandering through the woods around the small lakes, south of Bearback. He suspected they were setting their Jaws around there, but he would take care of those later.

He glanced around in time to see a chipmunk peer out of its tiny den. It spotted him and disappeared into its hole. A few seconds later it dashed out of another hole further back and disappeared into the grass. Rabbitrunner's ears tilted forward; he was amused and fascinated. The chipmunk had a second way out of its den.

He thought about his own den, a labyrinth of tunnels, and he wondered if he could dig another way out. Even though the den descended deeper into Bearback, he could open another way by digging uphill. He had the time.

But that would be another day. A loud rumble drew his attention to the sky. Rain would begin falling before the day was over, and it would probably continue throughout the night. Twolegs didn't like the rain, but Rabbitrunner welcomed it. The rain's noise would cover the sounds of his movement and wash away his scent. Twolegs hid from the rain, but he didn't.

"Listen," Jerry Rideau said from his sleeping bag. "Just listen," It was black inside the pup tent, except when lightning flashed, the light illuminated through the canvas like neon.

"All I hear is the rain," Calvin Billings muttered from his sleeping bag. "Go to sleep."

The rain beat on the canvas tent like an enthusiastic drummer, which always caused Calvin to get drowsy, but it gave Jerry headaches. The air smelled like a mildew factory, and droplets were collecting via condensation on the inside walls of the tent.

"No, it's not the rain," Jerry finally said.

"Jerry, you're keeping me awake."

"But listen," Jerry said.

"To what?"

"It's Rusty. He was barking, then all of a sudden he went quiet."

"Maybe he got laryngitis," Calvin said. "Why don't you

go out there and check?"

No sooner had Calvin finished speaking than a bright flash of light glared through the gray-green canvas, followed a second later by a loud rumble. "You check on him," Jerry said. "He's your dog. I was only wondering."

"Well, if you don't want to wonder outside, don't do it here. Go to sleep."

"You think we'll trap any wolves?" Jerry asked. "We must have set out twenty traps."

"I think the wolves are smart enough to stay out of the rain and stay at home tonight," Calvin muttered. "You could learn a thing or two from them, Jerry. Shut up and go to sleep. If this rain ever lets up, we're gonna have some muddy traveling tomorrow."

Outside the two tents and beyond the swamped, lifeless fire pit, Rusty stood motionless in the rain. A thick-furred collie, he wasn't trained for hunting, but a minute ago, he thought he had seen something moving towards him through the trees. He was chained to a tree himself, unable to get to his master's tent, so he barked frantically to get his attention.

Then the moving shadow vanished. Rusty kept barking, glancing left and right until he simply stopped— not by choice. Something had clamped onto his muzzle, something flesh and bone with sharp, painful teeth digging into his nose. He whined once and it clamped tighter, then let up a little when he stopped. He got the message. It was a bad idea to make any noise. Just the simple gesture was enough to let him know that something could kill him but would let him live if he remained quiet, and Rusty was good at following orders.

Then lightning flashed, and he almost gasped. He got a glimpse of a large mouth, black lips, and humongous white teeth, before the darkness and thunder rolled over him. He saw an eye, a big eye, and a large, tattered ear.

Rabbitrunner released his grip on the dog's muzzle and stepped back. Rusty licked blood and saliva off his nose, facing the wolf. Canis Lupus Linnaeus and Canis Familiaris gazed at each other through the rain.

"I don't want to kill you, Dog," Rabbitrunner growled. "But I will if I have to. Stay there and be quiet and you will live. Ignore me, and tomorrow you go home with Twolegs. But yap once and I'll tear your throat out."

Rusty understood. He settled down, his head on his muddy paws, his eyes wide in the guilty expression he gave his Master sometimes. The large Hunter just stood there, massive and wet. Rusty could see, in the next flash of lightning, how very thin he was. He remained where he lay, the rain beating down on him like small insults.

Rabbitrunner moved away, stopping to gaze at the limbs of an oak. A flash of lightning showed him the Twolegs cache, dangling high above the ground by a vine that went over a limb and stretched to the roots of another tree. He wasn't surprised to find such a Twolegs trick. After seeing so many Jaws held to the ground by vines, he was sure Twolegs liked to tie things in place one way or another. As an afterthought, he glanced back at the dog tied to the tree.

Thunder rumbled from the dark sky. Rabbitrunner approached the spot where the vine was held to the ground between the roots. He sniffed the vine, then proceeded to chew on it. In less than a minute, the vine snapped apart, and the cache hit the ground with a loud crash.

Rabbitrunner jerked around, but before he could move further one of the leaf-dens flapped open. He froze. A Twolegs head came out, so near he could leap at it, then a long, straight thunderstick poked from the darkness. He held his breath and waited.

The Twolegs looked left, then right, making his verbal ululations, and similar sounds came from the dwelling next to his. Then he looked directly at Rabbitrunner.

More Twolegs noises passed back and forth. The thunderstick moved. Rabbitrunner fought the urge to run. The rain danced between them like a miserable creature rooting for food. And then the Twolegs and his thunderstick slipped from sight. He hadn't been seen—Twolegs looked right at him, and he hadn't been seen!

Slowly letting out his breath, Rabbitrunner approached the large, bulky cache and sniffed. The outer wrap was made of the same material as the leaf dens, but there were other smells, too. He grabbed the material with his teeth, placed a forepaw on the cache, and tugged. The material tore so loud he stopped and looked back to see if Twolegs heard. Once he figured it was safe, he probed the cache's contents.

Inside were foods and hard objects, but no thundersticks. He had to move things carefully, taking them out one at a time, because the Twolegs things tended to make a lot of noise if bumped against each other. He dropped them on the mud, not wanting any of it, only trying to make enough of a mess to let Twolegs know he was there.

You can't kill them, he thought. You can only scare them. And so I scare them. Again, and again, and again.

When he pulled out a large slab of raw, fatty, salty meat, the flavor both repelled and tempted him. He dropped it and stared at it. He remembered the taste of cow meat, but this was different.

He glanced at the dog. Then he picked up the meat, trotted over to him and set it at his paws. Rusty lifted his head, sniffed the meat, then glanced uneasily at the large Hunter to see if it was all right to eat it. Rabbitrunner turned and walked away.

"Go ahead and eat it," he growled over his shoulder. "You probably thrive on that kind of meat." And if it is tainted meat, he thought, it is better that you die than live with them.

But it wasn't poisonous meat, and Rusty was quite pleased by his reward. Resting a paw on it, he tore off some fat and began chewing, almost indifferent now to the Hunter's raid.

Rabbitrunner went back to pulling objects from the cache. He couldn't figure out what the hard, cylindrical things were, and he was likewise confused by the Twolegs coverings and the thick, rectangular batches of thin, white leaves with black freckles on them, but he tore each of these as he found them. Then his teeth clacked on something hard and black, and he knew what he had found.

His hackles were up as he pulled the Jaws from the cache by their vines, first two of them, then two more, and finally the last one. He was relieved that they were closed. Dragging them one at a time, he set them in front of the leaf dens. *To scare you, Twolegs,* he thought. *To let you know that I know about the Jaws.*

Yes! Yes! Pawsore snarled in the depth of his mind. *Let them know you aren't afraid! Let them know they can't beat you!*

Don't worry about Twolegs, Deerchaser said. *They're all crazy!*

Rabbitrunner raised his tail, satisfied with his labors, and wished he knew how to open the Jaws, let them catch their masters for a change. But, as Cloudwalker told him, only Twolegs could open the Jaws.

He turned and trotted past the dog, which looked up briefly before taking another bite of meat. Then Rabbitrunner stopped, feeling daring, and returned to a spot between the two leaf dens, where he howled:

"There is nothing to fear!
Whatever happens
Is meant to happen!"

He glanced at the leaf dens once more and trotted on, pleased at how well things went. The explosion was right behind him, loud and harsh, blowing a hole in the nearest leaf den with a flash as stunning as lightning.

Rabbitrunner dashed away with his tail between his legs, not daring to look back.

"Jee-zus, Calvin, why'd you do that?"

"To scare it away, Jerry."

"Are you guys okay over there?"

"No! Calvin decided to fire a warning shot through the tent!"

"Why'd you do that, Calvin?"

"It had to be a warning shot, Harry; it was standing between the tents. If I tried to shoot it and missed I coulda hit you."

"Well, you can sleep under the hole tonight, Calvin, and...."

Another howl in the distance put an end to the conversation. The only sounds were the rain and distant thunder, and the noise of a dog busily finishing off a slab of bacon.

Chapter Eighteen

"Signs"

(Early Autumn, 1967)

The rain was still falling, beating a droning tattoo on the ground throughout the woods of Lake County. The empty tent slouched like an old swaybacked mule—two of the stakes had come out, and the loose canvas, held up by the tent poles, rocked back and forth with each new gust of wind.

The fire in the fire pit burned low, protected by a ragged tarp roped taut to four trees. The tarp was slowly becoming a lake on top, sagging into the gray smoke. A frying pan was left in the mud, raindrops making craters in the coagulated bacon grease as a coffee pot next to the fire steamed. The campsite was muddy and trampled, well-used, with a stack of deadfall logs and limbs to one side of the tent and a tarp-covered pile of kindling to the other side.

Dean Hoover, pelted by the rain, sat on the log near the fire. He wore an army surplus hooded poncho, but with the hood down. His blond hair and beard were soaked, but he didn't seem to notice as he stared into the dying flames. His hands, pruned and slick, held a steaming cup of coffee, the black liquid bursting with tiny eruptions with every raindrop that fell into the cup.

He hadn't had a bath in a week. His eyes were dark-rimmed, bloodshot, and sunken, his cheeks were hollow and his nose runny—he was sniffing constantly. He'd just eaten the last of his bacon, and as he ran over the list of supplies in his mind, he realized that all he had left was coffee, rice, and curry powder. He was going to have to pack up and leave pretty soon.

He stared into his cup; the coffee was already growing cold, and he just poured it a few minutes ago. He sighed and gulped it down, then felt around inside his poncho until he pulled out a Tootsie Roll. He unwrapped it and bit off an end, savoring the last of his sweets.

The trip was a fiasco, he thought as he stood and urinated against a tree, then went to his tent, where he pulled out his knapsack and camera pack, strapped everything on, snatched his walking stick and took off down the trail. "Today's the last day," he muttered, wincing as a trickle of rainwater ran down the back of his neck. "Today's the last fucking day. And what've you got to show for it? Nothing."

He'd been camping in the same spot for a week, waiting and watching for the large wolf to return, but it was all in vain. His vigil was a waste, but then again, he knew, the whole thing had been quixotic from the beginning.

It all started when he first heard all that talk about Jessie Armstrong, the guy they called Cutter, who was making a legend of himself by saying he was going to kill the Shadow Wolf. Dean began wondering if he actually could. He only met the man once, but he had a feeling then that he was meeting a predator, a man with a black heart. It scared him. Because of that, he tried one more time to see the wolf, to try to get a better understanding of what he needed to do.

Now he'd reached the end of his efforts with no results. He was tired, worn out, and saturated from the three days of solid rain. After this last visit to the cave, he was heading back to the Corvair and returning to St. Paul. Or maybe to the first motel he saw. God knows he needed a shower and a comfortable bed! Besides, he needed to get back to the University. He had been reinstated, despite a few objections, and would soon be teaching classes again. He needed this job to keep things level, or his personal pursuit of the Shadow Wolf would wear him down.

He stopped and sneezed three times. A cold, like he didn't have enough problems! "Ah, shit," he grumbled, stopping to wipe his nose with a wet wrist. The cave entrance was just ahead, through the trees and across the clearing. As always, it looked like an old man's toothless smile, eight feet wide and two feet high, grinning from the foot of a hill. A fir tree grew from the side; a small one Dean suspected was the seedling he saw there years ago. Uphill was another fir tree, dead, just a husk, waiting to topple down someday.

That one still held his arrow, terribly weathered now, with the tattered fletching, green, blue, brown, faded but still visible.

Dean trudged to the cave entrance along a muddy path he'd made back and forth in the last few weeks from his daily visits. Maybe the wolf had seen the trail, smelled his scent, and decided to stay away. He didn't know. He stopped at the cave's mouth and pulled his flashlight from his backpack. "Be there today," he mumbled. "Be there so I can see you one more time." And do what, he wondered. Warn him?

Turning on his flashlight, he scanned the cave. Nothing had changed. The cave was still one large chamber. The whole thing could be seen from the entrance, there were no hidden tunnels.

He examined the mouth, from one side to the other, checking dozens of small black threads he'd strung from top to bottom. Every thread was there, intact, none of them broken. Nothing had passed through since yesterday.

"Hell's bells," Dean sighed and wiped his nose, getting a strong whiff of the cave. It hardly bothered him anymore, that stink, after a week of dealing with it. You could get used to anything, he thought, recalling the first time he smelled it.

He edged into the entrance, breaking the threads. He glanced down at one of his wrists, one of his scars from his suicide attempt, a white straight line that ran at a right angle to his arteries, like crossing highways on a road map. Tiny dots showed where stitches eventually sealed the wound. He closed his eyes, remembering the large wolf climbing through the cave entrance, so big he thought he would never squeeze through, but he did.

Dean thought the wolf had come to kill him, but he had already all but killed himself. No, it had come and saved his life, chased him from the cave, done something to him, though he didn't know what.

He opened his eyes, pointed the flashlight beam, and half-heartedly checked the cave one last time. The skeletons, skulls, and bones were still where he left them, and the bullet casings were there, too, undisturbed, just as he had seen them once before, several years ago.

The Shadow Wolf lived in this cave, among the remains of his pack, never disturbing the bones. What compelled him to sleep in such a mausoleum? What did it mean; this strange respect for the dead by an animal?

And what had it been trying to do since, breaking traps, killing dogs? Was he aware of the legend he was creating, the price he put on his own head, the enemy he made of Jessie Armstrong?

"Damn you," Dean mumbled. "You're going to get your-self killed, and there's no way I can warn you."

He sighed and swept his arm back and forth at the mouth of the cave, breaking the last threads, thinking that maybe they kept the wolf away, the wolf suspecting another trap, and not knowing the real trap was called Cutter.

He backed into the rain, picked up his walking stick and stood. Gazing at the sky, he saw three ravens in the distance, side by side on a branch high up an old oak. He shook his head and started to his tent. He was hungry, and he thought of stopping at a roadside greasy spoon once he drove out of the woods. OR maybe cook up a big pot of rice, before he left. A little salt in it, a little curry powder, that would work.

His tent was just ahead through the trees. Between the tent and the smoking remnants of the fire was a brownish object. He saw what it was just as he noticed the odor of the cave, and it took him a moment to put it all together in his feverish state.

"Oh, man," Dean gasped. "Oh man...." He stopped a few feet away, gazing at the dead rabbit in the mud just in front of his tent. He stepped closer, picking the rabbit up by the hind leg. Its neck was broken, and there were a few spots of blood on its fur.

He glanced around. The mud surrounding the fire pit and tent were covered by large, deep paw prints. The Shadow Wolf had just paid him a visit.

He suddenly felt icy cold.

Sneezing twice, he wiped his nose on his sleeve; between the rain and his cold, he just couldn't get himself to think well at all. He dropped the rabbit, adjusted his poncho and walked around the campsite, trying to see if anything had been damaged or moved. But nothing was.

The wolf had come to investigate him, drop the rabbit, leave his scent, and depart. He wondered how long the wolf had been watching him, and why he left the rabbit. Why he did not cover his paw prints like he always did. Because he wanted Dean to know. And the rabbit...

A gift, he thought. It was a gift from the wolf.

Dean glanced at the rabbit. He did have rice and curry powder. He never ate wild meat before.

He pulled out his pocket knife and checked the blade. He was hungry, after all.

Chapter Nineteen

"Triangles"
(Early Autumn, 1967)

The two light-gray wolves silently trotted through the trees, stopping to sniff a scent on the ground, or sometimes stopping to urinate. Their tails were up as they strolled beneath the canopy of leaves, sometimes playfully nipping at each other, not bothered at all by the early afternoon heat.

They stopped together when they heard the air hiss. The one in the lead raised his head and looked to the left. The arrow pierced his throat, the razor-sharp arrowhead slicing through an artery before embedding itself in a neck vertebra. He yelped and twisted around, trying to scratch at the pain with a hind paw, then collapsed on his side, kicking, blood squirting over the shaft and bubbling from his nostrils.

The other wolf crouched and looked around, then crawled closer to her mate, sniffing his twitching body, scared, but not sure of what, and not yet aware that he was dead. Another arrow whispered through the air and lodged in her right hind leg. She yelped, twisted around and bit the shaft, releasing it when it twisted inside her flesh, causing more pain. She rose with a moan, then a third arrow hit her chest, and she fell to the ground, dead.

The wolves lay side by side among the ferns in the shadows of the trees, and the air was buzzing with the droning call of cicadas. Cutter rose from his place behind a fallen tree downwind of the bodies, another arrow nocked and ready should he need it. He came around the log, replacing the arrow in the quiver and drawing his Bowie knife from its sheath.

Dried, caked mud streaked his cheeks and forehead, and a few dead leaves were caught in his long hair as he lit a hand-rolled cigarette. He blew a smoke ring as he knelt beside one of the wolves and set his bow aside. He put the knife down, gripped the first wolf's throat with one hand and with the other he worked the arrow from the neck. The blood felt warm and friendly on his fingers as he glanced at the red-red-black fletching, then set the arrow beside his bow.

Pulling the wolf onto its back, he stretched the skin and made the first incision, from the throat to the anus. The smell of wolf meat, fat, and blood filled his nostrils like a good meal as he speedily worked the skin loose with his blade and fingers, cutting the connective tissue and pulling the pelt free. He'd skinned both wolves in a matter of minutes, and when he was done, he wiped off the blade on his t-shirt and resheathed it. He checked his arrow shafts, holding them up to his eye as he turned them, looking for any warpage and finding none, then replacing them in the quiver. That done, he picked up his bow, unstrung it and gathered up the two skins under his arm.

As he started back, his hand went to the walkie-talkie hooked to his belt. Ben had told him to leave it on, but that would have broadcast his presence, all that squawking and bleating. The stupid things were from Jack Fipps, who lately was coming up with new ideas on how to catch the Shadow Wolf, like using the walkie-talkies. And the triangles.

The stupid triangles. Jack showed him on a map, but they didn't seem to work this time. It was because of the triangles they were now in Lake County --- and what good did that do? He tossed away the cigarette butt, lit another cigarette, and walked on, wondering how the others were faring.

"But Cutter, I tried to contact you," Ben said, holding his left wrist, wrapped in an ace bandage, with his right hand. "It's not my fault you had your Goddam radio off. It was a close call, but not as bad as you're making it out to be."

"Oh for Christ's sake," Cutter grumbled, pouring water on an old t-shirt and wiping the mud off his face. "Okay, Ben, just tell me what happened."

"I flew a little too low and picked up a tree limb, that's all. I wasn't watching. Hey, with a little practice, I could work as an airborne tree pruner." Ben smiled, trying to make light of the situation, but Cutter's look let him know he wasn't buying it. "Hell, Cutter, I'm all right. I just sprained my wrist, but the chopper's fine, I checked her over."

"Why fly so low?" Cutter asked.

Ben shrugged. "I spotted six wolves from the air. I was trying to drive them back to the other guys, but they wouldn't turn around. Jack advised me to fly lower, and I was almost on their backs, almost had them turned around, when the tree got in my way. I damn near almost didn't pull up in time, but luck was with me."

"We got six wolves, though," Troy Jenkins added, trying to smooth Cutter's anger. "I got two myself."

"And with your two," Jack said, "that makes eight for today."

"Eight," Cutter said, tossing the muddied t-shirt on the ground. He set his bow, quiver and skins on the hood of his jeep. "Eight. That's very good." He smiled at the other men, then looked at Jack, grabbed him by the shirt and slammed him against a white pickup. "You could've killed Ben for eight wolves."

"Cutter!" Ben shouted.

Cutter pulled Jack back and slammed him against the pickup again. Jack gasped from the impact, then struggled to break free, wide-eyed, pulling at Cutter's unmoving arms. "Goddam you, Jack, you don't kill a human being to get a couple of wolves. What the fuck's the matter with you?"

"It was a mistake...." Jack gasped.

"Cutter!" Ben yelled. "Stop it now!"

"Big fucking mistake," Cutter said his face close to Jack's. "You almost talked Ben down to his death."

"Dammit Cutter, let go of him now!" Ben ordered. "I was the one flying the chopper, not him! It was my mistake, my error!"

"Ben, you could've rolled your chopper, hooking a limb like that," Cutter said, not taking his eyes off Jack.

"Cutter, you and I had some close calls ourselves," Ben reminded him.

"Yeah, but we were in it together. I wasn't on the ground, safe, telling you to risk your life."

"That's enough," Ben said, putting his hand on Cutter's shoulder. "This is no time to scare everybody here."

Cutter released his grip.

Jack stared at Cutter as he turned away. "I would've been flying with Ben, but I had to coordinate things from the ground," he mumbled.

"You did a fucked-up job," Cutter said. "Don't you

remember me telling you how Ben crashed when we were in Korea? Don't you remember me telling you he pretty much burned half his body crashing his chopper flying too low?"

"Yeah, I remember," Jack muttered.

"What, you don't believe me? Show him, Ben."

"No, Cutter, we..."

"Fucking show him, Ben!"

Ben glanced at Cutter, sighed, and unbuttoned his shirt. The other men watched, wondering what Cutter was talking about. When Ben took off his shirt, most of them gasped. Ben's chest and back, up to his collar, were burned, the flesh red and twisted, his nipples missing, no hair on his upper body, and the burns stopping at his elbows, so that, wearing a long shirt, none of it was visible.

Several men glanced away, and Jack was covering his mouth, almost gagging. Ben quickly pulled on his shirt, buttoning it back up, glaring angrily at Cutter because Cutter knew it embarrassed him.

"Now you know," Cutter growled, turning and walking away.

"Remember," Jack said to Cutter's retreating back. "I was asked to join your little party!" He brushed out the wrinkles on his flannel shirt. "I was asked by you! I've hunted in Africa, Australia, South America, in Arctic Canada and Alaska. Maybe you know how to use a rifle and a bow and arrow, but while you were checking traps and drinking beer, I was trudging through the Amazon and dodging piranhas, snakes, and alligators."

"Shut up, Jack," Cutter said, his back still turned to him as he calmly restrung his bow.

"I know you can hunt wolves, but I've made a career of hunting. I know how to catch a temperamental animal. You need me, Cutter, you need me."

In one swift motion, Cutter notched an arrow and spun

around, pulled back and aimed at Jack.

"Cutter, no!" Ben said, surprised at how fast he had moved.

"You may know about hunting," Cutter said, his voice still calm, "but I sure don't need you. And you may know about wolves, but you don't know about this wolf." The arrow pointed at Jack's left eye. Cutter's arms quivered slightly, as though weariness were claiming him. Jack opened his mouth but nothing came out. The other men watched, mesmerized, not wanting to get involved but not wanting to see anybody get hurt, either. Ben was hesitant, realizing that this time Cutter was beyond his influence, wondering what unseen thing— it couldn't be just the wolf, could it?—was pushing him this far.

And then Cutter released the arrow.

It sailed just past Jack's head, over the top of the truck, and lodged in a tree twenty feet behind him. Jack turned around and looked back. Pinned to the tree by the arrow was the twitching body of a ground squirrel. Jack looked back at Cutter.

"I wasn't sure I could make that shot," Cutter muttered, then laughed. The other men laughed too, releasing the tension they felt the moment before. He tossed the cigarette butt on the ground, pulled up a straw of green grass, then put the end in his mouth. "Jack, why don't you wipe your cheek?" he said. "You're bleeding."

Jack wiped his palm against his left cheek, holding his hand out to look at the blood. "You son of a bitch," he said.

"I apologize," Cutter said, setting the bow on the hood of his jeep. "I didn't mean to do that." He reached behind his neck and undid the knot of his bandana. As Jack watched, Cutter removed the bandana and, leaning closer, dabbed at the cut on Jack's cheek.

Jack's eyes widened when he saw the gaping, crater-like scar on the left side of Cutter's neck, a mass of puckered, tattered red skin with streaks of white that looked like bloodless raw meat.

Cutter dabbed the cut clean, then just as casually retied the bandana around his neck. "That's better," he said. Jack couldn't help staring at his own blood on Cutter's bandana. All the men had seen the scar, and they were all silent. "Now, let's look at the map," Cutter said.

Jack stared at him, bewildered. "Sure," he said. "Sure. Let's go look at the map." He and Cutter walked away from the others, each one looking straight ahead as the men packed their trucks. In the distance, in a small clearing, was Ben's chopper, and next to it, Jack's camper.

Jack led the way to his pickup and camper, opened the cab and pulled a large cardboard tube out. "In back," he said. Cutter followed him into the camper, where they sat across from each other at a tight kitchenette table. Jack opened the tube and pulled out a large map of Minnesota. The map had overlapping triangles down over it, with dates printed in ink at each corner.

"Here," Jack said. "Here is where we are." His finger tapped a circle at the northernmost part of the state. "Here is where the Shadow Wolf should have shown up."

"Well, we've been here since five in the morning," Cutter said. "And we saw nothing."

"We'd have to be here a few days, maybe a week," Jack said. "The Shadow Wolf doesn't carry a calendar or a datebook, you know. Furthermore, all the noise we've been making might just scare him away. Also, this little dot on the map where he might show up represents as area of dozens of square miles. He might show up here or he might show up ten miles away in any direction. At best, we can only make an educated guess."

"Maybe, you're right," Cutter said. "What do you suggest?"

"Don't go hunting every wolf in the area," Jack said. "Don't go making it a party every time you look for the Shadow Wolf. Too many men, you'll scare him off. If you're shooting wolves, the Shadow Wolf won't come around."

"I think he might," Cutter said, studying the map, studying the triangles. "Though I do see your point about hunting wolves. But what if we get just one wolf—a decoy?"

A breeze blew in through the window. Cutter studied the map, holding down one end that threatened to roll up, eyeing the overlapping triangles. "So how does all this work?" He waved his free hand over the map. "How do you know where the Shadow Wolf might be going? All these lines you've drawn here...."

Jack smiled, pulling his glasses out of his shirt pocket and putting them on. "I managed to get the exact dates and locations of every occasion your little wolf showed up. Seems he shows up on an average of once every two weeks, though not everybody reports seeing him. He generally becomes active when there's a full moon or no moon whatsoever." He pointed at spots on the map. "He's making his rounds. He's made all of northern Minnesota his territory. He travels in apparent triangles, probably the best way to cover the most ground, the best way to hit the most spots in the widest distribution."

"So he decided to go around in triangles?" Cutter asked.

"He doesn't know he's doing it," Jack said. "At least I think he doesn't. His movements are probably subconscious, maybe instinct. And he doesn't travel in straight lines, the way these triangles show, but the straight lines are used to determine where he's been and where he will be, not what path he'll use to get there."

Cutter looked up at Jack, surprised. He had more brains than he previously suspected. "So you got every place the wolf has gone to?"

"No," Jack said. "When I didn't have the information, I took my best guess. But you did make contact with the wolf the last time you hunted, didn't you?" Jack looked up and smiled, knowingly. "I mean, I told you the wolf would be there, and he was, wasn't he?"

"Yeah," Cutter said, looking back at the map. He still had a feeling of uneasiness about the two dogs killed that day.

"The next time," Jack said, "he will be at this point, in Buford County." He circled a spot on the map, at the corner of another triangle. "And after that, he'll head south, straight to Caleb County, here."

"Hell," Cutter said. "I could just about walk there from my cabin. Are you sure about this? Are you absolutely sure? He's actually going to show up in my backyard?"

"He'll be there," Jack said. "And if you play your cards right, you'll get him here, where he'll show up next." He tapped his pen on the map.

Suddenly Jack's expression changed. He looked up. "Goddam, Cutter, you been eating sauerkraut? You're stinking up my camper."

Cutter looked up when he smelled it too. "Hell, Jack, even you never smelled that bad. It's coming from outside."

"A skunk?" Jack asked. "A skunk never smelled that bad!"

Cutter rose from the table, leaned over the map to look out the window. "It's him, Jack. It's him."

"What's him?" Jack asked, removing his glasses. "Him who?" But Cutter was already out the door, so he followed.

Cutter stood a few feet away, gazing through the trees, his hands at his side as he looked back and forth. Jack stepped up beside him. "Cutter?"

"He arrived, Jack, just like you said he would," Cutter whispered. "He's here."

"What?" Jack said. "That stink?"

"That's him, Jack."

"That odor? The Shadow Wolf?"

"That's the odor he left behind the last time he came near us. When he killed the dogs. He stinks awful, Jack, he has an odor to him I'll tell you that."

"No wolf smells like that," Jack said.

Cutter shook his head. "You're wrong. Every time we notice something new about this wolf, we say just that, no wolf does this, no wolf does that, but, Jack, this wolf does, believe me."

"So he's here?"

"He's not only here, Jack, he's watching us. He's watching me."

Jack felt the hair his neck prickle. He was beginning to believe Cutter. He put his hands in his pockets and gave a nervous laugh. "Well, he isn't a very good spy, if he's watching us from upwind—he's giving himself away."

"Don't you think he knows that, Jack?" Cutter stared off into the woods, almost hypnotized. "He wants us to know he's here. He wants me to know."

"Goddam, Cutter, you can't be serious," Jack said, but by now he believed every word. He stared too, thinking he might see something, something big and monstrous, charging at them.

"See you, I do," Cloudwalker growled, watching them from the darkness of the woods. He gazed at the Twolegs Alpha, the Dark Twolegs. "We meet again, and again, and again, do we?"

But why is he always there? a voice in his head asked him. *We came this way, and he was already here.*

He cannot be following your trail, another voice added, *if he's ahead of you.*

This one is not like the others, a third voice intoned.

This one is different. This one is looking for you. This one knows you leave no paw print, and yet he gets there ahead of you.

"But how," Cloudwalker asked. "How?"

This one is smarter than the others, the voice went on. *Maybe smarter than you.*

Cloudwalker weighted all the possibilities. The Twolegs One was looking for him, he knew that, but how could he figure out where he was heading? Of course, Twolegs were smarter than him in their own ways—they controlled cows and dogs, and fire, especially fire, he knew that better than most—but what was it that showed the Twolegs One where he would be next?

He is dangerous, the first voice said. *He wants to kill you. And if he succeeds, what will become of Rabbit-Turd? Will he be killed next?*

"Rabbit-Turd must survive on his own, he must," Cloudwalker growled, "if Twolegs kills me."

But still he felt no comfort.

Rabbit-Turd, the one he had been training, had to survive.

He had to.

He had to be kept safe from this one.

This one, this Dark Twolegs, is different, he thought.

But so was the other one, he remembered, the one who kept returning to the cave, looking for him, but with no intent to kill. What was he looking for? The Quiet Twolegs meant no harm, something unheard of and confusing, and Cloudwalker wondered—if there is one like that, could there be two? More?

The distant sound of Twolegs voices carried through the woods. Cloudwalker wished he could understand them; he didn't know what they were saying, but he could tell by their tones that they were cheerful about something, probably the Hunters he saw them kill. He was so enraged about it he left his scent in as many places upwind as he could, hoping they could smell it. But that was not enough. He sat and arched his back, drew a deep breath and howled!

"There is nothing to fear!
Whatever happens
Is meant to happen!"

Then he rose, turned and scratched the ground with his hind paws, releasing his bitter rage on the ground before he walked away. He hadn't gone far before he heard the first blast.

"Jesus!"

"What the hell was that?"

"Goddam! It's that wolf!"

Cutter glanced at the men, then stared off between the trees, seeing nothing out there. He'd heard wolf howls before, as did Ben and Jack and a few of the others, but no wolf ever sounded like that. A wolf's howl rose like a wave, then sloped down, descended from the skies like a fugue dedicated to the mountains. Even Cutter had to admit there was something graceful, yet unsettling, to hear a lone wolf at night, and when three or four harmonized in the stillness of the wood, it just about raised him from the ground, sent him soaring like no music ever could.

But the howl of the Shadow Wolf was different, unnerving in its dissonant, warbling call, brittle and raspy, a horrible tune torn from a despondent, vengeful throat. It rose and lowered three times, full of anger and hate, a boulder crashing down a rocky mountainside aiming itself at its victim.

"Where did it come from?" Ben asked.

"That way," Jack said, snatching a rifle from another man's hands, shouldering it and firing. Cutter jumped at the discharge.

"No, it's that way," Troy said, raising his rifle.

Cutter grabbed the barrel and pointed it at the ground. "All right, then. That's enough." He glanced at the men. "You're just wasting bullets. Even you know that. You don't shoot at a sound."

But he could see it in their eyes, a look of fear, all of that just for a single, chilling sound. The Shadow Wolf could do that, he knew—they'd named him right, a shadow, never seen, capable of scaring a man in broad daylight. There was something disturbing about an animal that continually outsmarted men, especially one that was never seen.

Again, the chilling lone howl came through the trees, defying a source like the horn of a ship on a foggy sea.

"That's him, isn't it?" Jack said.

"You know it as well as I do," Cutter said. "You were right when you said it would show up."

The howl rose in the air a third time, more distant, but no less disturbing.

"He's calling us," Cutter said. "He's telling us, 'Come get me, come catch me if you can.' He's daring us."

"If he's so close," Troy said, "then maybe we should track him down."

"And are you going to follow his voice?" Cutter asked, still looking off into the woods. "He already knows we're here, and he's leaving, you can tell that yourself. He doesn't leave tracks unless he wants to. So where do you go?"

"Christ, Cutter," Troy mumbled. "If he's that hard to catch, how are you gonna do it?"

Cutter glanced at him. Troy was in his twenties, black hair, and small black moustache. He'd killed his first wolf today, and had grown more talkative than he was before the trip. Cutter tapped his head. "We're going to use our brains, Troy, we're going to use our brains." He looked at Jack. "And we're going to think like a wolf."

Jack watched Cutter, then looked at the other men. They all looked shaken. What difference does it make, he thought, if we think like a wolf, when this wolf doesn't? And for once, he wasn't sure they would get the trophy this time.

Chapter Twenty

"The Crooked River"
(Early Autumn, 1967)

The blue and yellow Thunderbird pulled onto the gravel parking lot, sliding and spraying rocks as it braked. Except for the T-Bird, there were a few pickups and an old Buick near the brown wooden building. As the dust settled, the doors opened, and Fribitz Grinner stepped out of the driver side while Dean Hoover, using his cane, stepped out of the passenger side, both shaking the dust off their coats as they walked towards the entrance. The lone sign over the front door announced, "The Crooked River Tavern," and several windows had neon signs advertising Budweiser, Hamms, St. Pauli Girl, and Black Label.

"So is this the place?" Fribitz asked.

"This is it," Dean told him. "They have a big, round table in the center of the room, and other than that it is plain as hell, a few moose and deer heads, a few traps on the wall, a few ceiling fans, but not much else, and thin, wooden walls, pretty much like a bar you would find in Nome, Alaska, barely inhabitable, but once it's full, it's friendly."

Fribitz nodded. "Nice place, Krazy Kat. It reeks of you, man, and I'm glad we found it. I'm gonna order a beer or two, Is that going to do something to your alcoholism inclinations."

Dean shook his head. "I'm a big boy, Fribitz, I can handle it. And if not, I got a dime, and there's a pay phone inside. I can call Bill, my sponsor, and he can talk me down."

"Cool," Fribitz said. He was wearing his white suit, and this time his hair was black, his sunglasses dark and round. He headed for the entrance when he felt Dean grab his arm. Glancing back, he noticed Dean's eyes. "What's wrong, Krazy Kat?"

Dean shook his head. "I don't know. I guess I just remembered what a formidable guy Jesse Armstrong was. He's a hunter and trapper, and they call him Cutter because he can skin an animal faster than anybody else."

"So you're afraid he'll have his skinning knife on hand when you meet him?"

"No, not that," Dean sighed. He switched his cane to the other hand. "He doesn't need a knife or gun to be intimidating. He has an aura about him, a killer aura, like you know he would simply strangle you with his bare hands if he wanted. And it's not that either, but that he scares me, and he scares me enough so, just meeting him, I'm already afraid I'll fall off the wagon."

"You want to call Bill now"

"No, but I might later." He patted Fribitz's arm and led the way into the Crooked River. Once inside they bellied up to the bar. A Johnny Cash song was playing on the jukebox. As his eyes adjusted to the dark interior, Dean glanced around, noticing the other patrons, all of them staring at him. He realized it was Fribitz and his white outfit and black hair they were looking at, and he wished he had told him to tone his clothes down a little.

A large, bald man came out from the kitchen in back, wiping his hands with a cloth towel. "Can I help you folk?"

Dean looked up, tempted to put his fake eyeglasses on, but he had left them at home.

"Two Hamm's," Fribitz said, giving the thumbs up.

"One Hamms and one Dr. Nut," Dean amended. The bartender nodded, gave them both a long glance, then walked over to the taps, never taking his eyes off them. When he put the napkins down and the glasses on them, he nodded and headed back into the kitchen behind the bar.

Dean glanced at his friend. "Fribitz," he whispered. "Close your mouth and stop staring."

"Is that him? He's big and bald."

"No it's not him. That's the bartender, the proprietor, Zachary Flint. He's okay, sort of."

"So where's Cutter?"

"We'll have to ask later."

"Look behind the bar." Fribitz pointed. Two dozen plaster casts hung over the mirrors behind the bar. Dean could tell they were paw prints of the Shadow Wolf. Fribitz stared in awe. It was the first time he had proof of how big the wolf really was. "Like the one Wayne got you, aren't they?"

"Would you boys like to order chili for lunch?" the waitress asked, coming up from the other side of the bar.

"Two bowls," Fribitz said, holding up two fingers.

The woman wrote down the order, an L & M cigarette between two fingers as she scribbled in her pad. "And how about a salad to go with it? We got a good salad and..." she looked up, her eyes locking on Dean. Nervous, he glanced back at her.

"A salad is fine," he said.

"Dean?" she whispered. "Dean Hoover?"

"Yes?"

"You don't remember me?"

Dean squinted. He didn't know who she was at first, but the memory came back in a flash, a myriad of emotions with it. He felt his hands tremble briefly. "Patty Tilton?"

She grinned momentarily, but then frowned and looked at her pad. "Chili and salad. And you already have beer. Would you also like a glass of water? We have homemade apple pie for desert. You said you'd write!" She looked at Dean and slapped the pad on the bar. He jumped.

Fribitz glanced from one to the other, not sure what was happening. "Is everything okay? Do you know each other? 'Cause I'm a stranger in town and not sure of how things go around here."

"No," Patty said, her pony tail shaking. "We're just old friends, aren't we, Dean?"

Dean Nodded. "Yeah, it's been a while."

Patty crossed her arms. "So how have you been doing, Dean? Last I heard you were a college professor, unless that was just another story."

Dean shook his head. "No, it was real, but I'm not now, not exactly. Things have changed."

Patty stared at him silently. He glanced away as Fribitz glanced from one to the other. "I wrote you, you know," she said. "You told me you'd write back. You sent me one post card saying you owed me a letter and never wrote again. I wrote another letter and it came back, address unknown. You moved and left no forwarding address."

Dean looked away, embarrassed, and Fribitz, feeling it, patted his shoulder. "I think I'll go outside and have a cigarette." And, whispering near Dean's ear, "You okay, Krazy Kat?"

"Yeah," he answered. "And you don't smoke."

"Not normal cigarettes." He smiled and strolled out, ignoring the ashtray on the bar.

Dean sighed and looked at Patty. "I'm sorry," he said. "I had a lot of things I had to do, and a lot of things going on in my life."

"It doesn't take too long to find a pen and paper and a stamp and force yourself to drop a line. As I recall you took a lot of time to drink your booze and smoke your marijuana. Surely you could find the time to set one bottle aside to write a note."

"That's not fair," Dean said. "I gave up drinking a little while ago. I'm going to Alcoholics Anonymous now. I'm trying to get my life back in order. And what would it matter to you? As I recall, I didn't mean much to you any way. I was just another ship passing in the night."

"Yeah, right," Patty snapped.

"You okay out there?" Zack shouted from the kitchen.

"We're fine," she shouted over her shoulder. "We're just arguing about whose chili is the best. I said it was yours."

"That's my girl," Zach shouted back, before pots started clanging against each other behind the wall.

"This is the thing, Dean, I thought you were different. I thought you were more sensitive, and I thought you had a little heart. I thought you cared is what I thought. I got pregnant twice dating assholes, and I thought you weren't like that. I thought maybe you and I could connect, but I guess I just had stars in my eyes. I guess those high school crushes never really go away, huh?" She snatched Fribitz's beer and took a sip.

Dean stood up. "Okay, I should have written, but you don't know. It's been a rough time for me." He snatched his cane beside the bar and showed it to her.

"What's that?" Patty asked.

"I lost three toes to frostbite."

"Poor, poor you," Patty said. "I know a dozen men who come into this bar who lost whole hands and arms and legs in logging accidents. At least you can still walk. The whole world is hurting, Dean, get over it."

Dean braced himself with his cane. "So what do you want with me? Why are you being so hostile? This isn't about not writing."

Patty shook her head. "I had two boys when I met you. Now I have three."

Dean felt his cheeks flush. He already knew what she was saying. "Yeah, Dean, you got a three year old son, and for years I was unable to tell you."

"Oh fuck," Dean said. "Holy shit."

"Yeah, holy shit," Patty mimicked. She took a drag on her cigarette butt and stubbed it out, then downed the last of Fribitz's Hamm's. "Turns out my diaphragm had a hole in it. Holy shit. That's right, holy shit. And don't worry, I'm not asking for marriage, I'm not asking for child support, I'm not even asking you to change a diaper or tie a shoelace. The other two, they ran off when I got pregnant. Just once, I'd love it if one of my sons could meet his own father. Just once."

Dean sat on the barstool. The cane dropped from his hand and clattered on the wooden floor. "I'm sorry, Patty, I didn't know."

"And just why the hell are you here today any way?" Patty growled. "And who's your strange friend? He looks like a rich beatnik."

"I came here to..."

Patty held up her hand. "You came here to find Cutter, didn't you? You're still interested in that Shadow Wolf, aren't you?" Dean nodded. "So what do you think you can accomplish? What do you want any way?"

Dean shook his head. "I'm just trying to see if I can save the wolf, that's all."

Patty lit another cigarette. "Cutter's out there right now hunting that fucking thing, just so you know. Christ, Dean, you have a son, and all you can do is worry about

an animal." She tossed her cigarette on the floor and
slammed the bar with her fist. The other patrons glanced
at her, then looked away, feeling her anger. "Why should
you be different than anybody else?" she said, tears running down her cheeks. She snatched up her pad. "I'll take
your order in a minute. I gotta go to the bathroom." She
spun around, her ponytail whipping across her shoulders.

Dean watched her stomp away and disappear into the
ladies room. "Oh, fuck!" he whispered, glancing about, as
thought he expected someone to come out and tell him
it was a joke. But, it wasn't.

"Fuck, I can't be a father! Fuck! I don't have time! I
can't do this! I can't take care of a kid!" He stopped and
looked down at his hands. "I couldn't even take care of
Sarah." He felt cold terror run through his body. He felt
like he had just died. He was scared.

Fribitz was just coming into the Crooked River. Dean
saw him, tossed a twenty on the bar, bent down and
snatched his cane, and rushed towards the door. He
grabbed Fribitz by the arm and spun him around, dragging him out. "Wait, what about my beer?"

"She drank it," Dean said.

"What about Cutter?"

"Let's just go," he said. "I'll explain later. I just gotta get
out of here." Even as they marched to the car, he knew he
was dead wrong to leave Patty, now of all times, knowing
what she just told him.

Chapter Twenty One

"Mark Your Territory"
(Late Autumn, 1967)

Fribitz Grinner stepped into his studio through what once was the delivery door of the warehouse where he now lived and worked, throwing open the door and guiding the truck as it backed and stopped at the loading dock. The movers jumped out of the cab and opened the truck, unloading several dozen canvasses on frames of different sizes, from two feet square to ten on each side. They leaned them against the only empty wall, the west wall, and returned to the truck, one of them stopping to have Fribitz sign the invoice. Once they were gone, he closed the door and let his eyes adjust to the near dark.

After he poured himself a cup of coffee, he weaved among the half-finished stone sculptures to his sketch desk, covered with rolled up sheets of his uncompleted pencil and charcoal drawings, and took a sip. When he set the coffee cup down, he knocked three times on the table. "Are you back with the living yet?"

A mournful groan came from below, and Fribitz bent down, sat in the lotus position on the concrete floor, and

313

looked at the barely moving pile of blankets and coats under the table. "You can't stay here forever, Krazy Kat. You need to face the world again. They miss you at AA, you know."

"How will it look if I go to the meeting drunk?"

"You sound coherent right now, man, and besides which, they're so stuffy they could stand for you to shake them up a little."

"Just leave me alone. I thought I could handle things, but I'm wrong. Life is just too damn complicated."

Fribitz shook his head and reached up to snatch his coffee cup off the top of the table. "I don't know what the hell you're talking about, Krazy Kat, but it sure would be nice to see your face while holding a conversation." He took a sip. "So you got a girl pregnant. All the horndogging you did while being a professor and don't you think you had a baby or two along the way? What the fuck, she didn't ask you to marry her, to give her child support, or even to buy her milk for the baby and you fall clean apart. What gives?"

Dean shoved the blankets off and sat up, slamming his head on the bottom of the table. "Ouch! Fuck all this!" He crawled out from under the table and sat next to Fribitz. Reaching under the blankets, he brought out his bottle of rum and unscrewed the lid. He held it up to Fribitz, who shook his head, then took a sip himself. "What gives is I got her pregnant. That's Patty Tilton. I swear to god, I only met her once, but she's the nicest person I ever met. I spent a couple days with her, and probably could have settled down there just to live with her, but I couldn't do that. Now I found out she had a baby and I wish I had. I should have."

"Nobody's holding you back from moving back with her, Dean."

Dean glanced at him, the bottle halfway to his lips,

and stared for a moment before taking his next drink. He wiped his lips with his wrist when he was done and shook his head. "You just don't understand. I failed her, Fribitz."

"Then go back there and un-fail her. Marry her, or just move in with her, or just send her roses. Or don't. Whatever. But make a decision and live with it."

Dean stood, walking in circles, flailing his arms. "Jesus, Fribitz, I fell off the wagon!"

"So what?" Fribitz snarled, standing.

"Christ, don't you know? I've been trying so hard to stay clean, and now I've been drunk for three days and falling apart. I've been a failure most of my life, and I still can't find my footing."

Fribitz shook his head. "Goddammit Krazy Kat, get a grip. So what if you're drunk. So what if you fail every now and then. Christ, you were boring sober. Maybe you need to tie one on now and then. Relax, Krazy Kat, relax."

Dean stepped up to him and grabbed him by his shirt. "You don't fucking understand! You don't get it! I lost my family, everybody I loved, and I've been crashing and burning ever since! You don't know what it's like! You're a successful artist! You never lost anybody!"

Fribitz swung a fist, catching Dean on the jaw. Dean fell backwards against old framed canvases that were being painted over, breaking the frames. He gazed at Fribitz, shocked, then enraged. He stumbled to his feet, charged, and knocked him against the other wall with a hard right. Fribitz pushed off the wall and caught him with a left hook, then a right. Dean fell backwards, and Fribitz landed on top of him, landing one punch after another. Dean closed his eyes, feeling his consciousness fading.

And then it was over. He opened his eyes and looked

around. Fribitz was standing facing a bare wall, his arms folded, his shoulders hunched. Dean staggered to his feet and found his cane, then stepped closer. He reached out, laying a hand on his friend's shoulder. "I'm sorry."

Fribitz shrugged.

"I didn't mean to piss you off."

"Goddammit Krazy Kat, you gotta grow up. You're selfish, self-centered, self-pitying and just full of yourself. You're not an alcoholic, just chronically depressed. You don't care about anybody but yourself. It made you interesting for awhile, but now it's getting really old. You got so many fears, phobias and compulsions that you don't see anything in front of you."

Dean nodded, turning away. His drunk was wearing off too fast. He licked his lips, tasted blood. "Yeah, you're right, but like I said, my family is dead, all of them."

"Yeah, your situation is not quite Leave It To Beaver, but what makes you think you're any different from anybody else?" Fribitz turned around. "I lost my family too."

Dean shrugged. "I thought they were still alive."

"They are," Fribitz said. "But what makes you think any of them are any where near me? You see this studio? You think I can afford it, selling paintings and pieces of rock? All of this is just my fantasy. I put on a good show, but who rents the venue? Me! Who pays the advertising? Me!" He gestured and spun around the room. "I have a nice hefty trust fund, and it pays to keep me looking extravagant and crazy while I act like the wild artist. My father set it up, with the stipulation that I never come home. Otherwise he would have disinherited me and kept me in a sanitarium."

"I don't understand," Dean whispered.

Fribitz gazed at him. "My family is rich as shit. Not a child is born in my family who doesn't become a doctor or lawyer. Except me, the fifth child of nine brothers and sisters. I wanted to be an artist. And hell, I wasn't that good. My father sent me to Harvard, pre-med, and while he was footing the bill I switched majors. When he got word he dragged me back to Hyannisport and said he'd give me one more chance. I told him what to do with his one more chance."

As he talked, they sat on folding chairs around the drawing table. Dean put the bottle on the table, and they passed it back and forth.

"My father called a family meeting. Within a week, my mother, brothers and sisters were at the house, some of them showing up despite midterms. I figured my siblings would take my side, we were all best friends once, but they all sided with Dad, with the same feverish obsession about career he had. All of them—All of them!-—decided I should leave, and my father came up with the plan of a monthly stipend as long as I stayed away."

Dean took a long drink. "So what about that story that your father was drunk, and named you Fribitz instead of Fritz?"

"Yeah, that was a story," Fribitz said, laughing bitterly. "I made up this name so nobody would ever trace me back to my roots. My father paid to have my name legally changed. And though I miss them a lot, they no longer exist for me. I don't exist for them." He put his head in his hands. "Every year or two or three I call one of my siblings. As soon as they know it's me, they hang up. No goodbyes, no how are you's, just hang up. They are all successful doctors or lawyers, but you'd think one of them, one at least, would just for a minute disagree with my father and talk to me. Not even my mother..." He began weeping.

Dean set the bottle down and put his arm around him, the way he'd do at an AA meeting. "I'm really sorry," he whispered.

"Your family was killed. I know you'll hate me for saying this, but I sometimes wonder if it would at least be easier on me if my family was killed. Because, one way or the other they're all dead to me any way."

"If there's anything I can do..."

Fribitz held up his hand. "Yeah. Go and see that girl. It doesn't matter how it goes, but see her and settle things one way or the other." He turned and looked Dean in the eyes and put his hands on his shoulders. "Marry her or be her friend or say hello to your son, whatever, but you need to get this out of your system and act like a man. Be a man. Stop weeping that you lost something or you failed someone. Everybody loses someone or something, fails, dies. Just get over it. Get over it."

Dean gazed at him, then looked at the bottle. He pushed it away, wanting to break free. Fribitz reached over, took the bottle, took a drought, then slid it back to Dean. "Think like a Buddhist. The middle road, all things in moderation, that sort of stuff."

Dean glanced at him, smiled, took the bottle and gulped some down, then slammed the bottle back on the table. Fribitz pated his shoulder and smiled back. "No more whining, no more selfishness, no more worrying about failing. Okay?"

Dean shrugged. "Maybe."

At seven that morning, Patty unlocked the doors of the Crooked River and gazed out at the gravel parking lot, taking a long drag on her L & M. Flint was in the kitchen, banging pots around, and she could tell he would be in a mood all day. A blue and yellow thunderbird was at the far end but seemed to be empty, probably a patron too drunk to drive who walked home and left his car behind. She twisted the sign around to read "OPEN," turned and walked to the back, where she sat at a table, facing the door while she filled salt shakers and read Dear Abby in the newspaper beside the shakers. She heard the screen door screech open and slam shut. "Be with you in a minute. You want something to drink?"

"Now please don't get mad, and please hear me out."

She quickly looked up. "Dean?"

"Please don't throw me out until I at least have my say," Dean said, slowly limping closer without a cane. He was wearing a backpack, both his hands behind his back. "I would like for you to forgive me, but I'll understand if you don't."

Patty stood and stepped closer. "Dean, what are you doing here?" she snapped.

"I wanted to let you know how I feel."

"You let me know how you felt when you ran away again," Patty grumbled. "What more is there to say?" She charged up to him and slapped his face. "How do you feel now, Dean?"

Dean shook his head. "Hurt," he said. "Hurt and scared. And sorry I hurt you." He brought his right hand from behind his back and presented the dozen roses he was carrying. "These are for you."

Patty glanced at the roses, then back at Dean, then at the roses again. She opened her mouth but could not make the words. Dean brought his other hand from behind his back and presented the box of candy. Patty raised her hands as though halfway to a gesture, then dropped them at her sides. She huffed and stomped her feet, then snatched the candy and roses and gestured to the back. "Go sit down, and I'll put these in water."

She charged off around the bar. Dean unshouldered his backpack, went to the table. He sat and watched her as she tossed the candies on the bar and fished out a beer pitcher, filling it at the tap. She tossed the roses in and set it on the bar, filled two coffee mugs, then stomped back to the table where Dean sat. Taking the chair across from him, she pushed a mug at him.

"Thanks for the roses and candies. If any patrons come in, don't tell them they're for me. Okay, so let me ask again: why did you come back?"

"Because," Dean said, "I should never have run out like that on such an important moment in your life, in our lives."

"No you shouldn't have."

"And I should've kept in touch, had my mail forwarded, found some way to write back to you. There's a lot of should's I should have done, but I didn't, and I can't change any of it. All I can do is apologize to you now."

"Oh, is that all?" Patty said. "Well, go ahead, give me the apology and go ahead and leave. I'll mark this day on the calendar, when I got a box of chocolates, roses and an apology."

Dean shook his head. "Apologize, and figure out how I can make it up to you. Figure out how I can start talking to you again, and figure out where we're going."

"There is no we, Dean, there never was a we. Something happened between us and then it was over. I didn't confront you the other day to make you marry me or anything else. I just wanted your son to get to know you. That's all."

Dean held up his hands to get her attention, then pulled his backpack closer, opening it. He pulled out two leather baseball gloves and two baseballs, setting them between them on the table. "Someday, maybe he and I can play catch together."

Patty stared at the gloves, then reached out, a finger gently sliding over the oiled leather. She sighed, then she smiled for the first time. "Thanks, he'll like that. Now I think I'll have to buy gloves for my other boys so they don't feel left out."

"Not a problem," Dean said, reaching in his backpack and pulling out two more gloves and two more balls. "I also got a couple bats. Maybe we could start a team."

Patty frowned and nodded at him. "Okay, Dean, you're forgiven. What else do you want?"

He stared at her, then looked away. A smile slowly came to his lips, and he shook his head. "What else do I want? To do what you said, meet my son." Dean wiped his eyes with the back of his wrist. "What's his name, any way?"

"Adam," Patty said. "His name is Adam."

"Oh, fuck!"

"What?"

"I really should have been there. I wanted to name him Wade Giles Goat Boy Hoover!"

"Fuck you Dean!" Patty shouted, throwing a glove at him and laughing. She sobered up and looked at her hands. "If you're not serious, then say so now. I had the rug pulled out from beneath me so many times I got calluses all over my body. I'm getting too old to do this any more."

"I'm serious," Dean said.

"Then tell me why you came looking for Cutter. I knew you for just a few days, but in a few days I really got to know you."

"I was going to see if I could talk him into stopping the hunt."

Patty smiled and shook her head. "Now I know you're insane. Cutter never gives up the hunt, and this wolf means all that more to him. When he was just a kid he went after another big wolf, a local called the Caleb County Mangler. The wolf killed cows and sheep, but more often left them alive and terribly chewed up. Even did the same with a few mules and horses. Cutter took his best friend, actually trapped the wolf, almost killed it, but when it was over, the friend was dead and Cutter was almost dead himself."

Dean shook his head. "Hell."

"The thing was," Patty went on, "Cutter wasn't attacked by the wolf but by his best friend, who wanted credit for the wolf. Turns out the wolf was really scared of people, but Cutter's friend was about to change that story and say Cutter was killed by it. Somehow Cutter got the upper hand, and killed his friend instead. That's the scar on his neck, if you've ever seen it."

Dean shook his head.

"Cutter was never the same, or so I heard. He's friendly with the townsfolk here, wants to be buddy-buddy with everybody, but everybody knows he's got a real bad temper, a real dangerous side. And despite what his friend did to him, he blames the wolf, all wolves, and this big one of yours, the Shadow Wolf, is the one he blames the most. Don't ask me why, it isn't logical, but Cutter wants the wolf real bad, and there's no logic in the world that's going to stop him."

Dean leaned back, glanced at the front door as two patrons stepped in and took a table. Patty waved at them, let them know she'd be a minute.

Patty reached over and touched his hand. "Dean, I don't want you getting killed. Cutter could do that, I know it, Flint knows it, the whole town knows it. Let the wolf go, and get back to your life. I know what happened to your family, I know that, but it's time to move on."

Dean absentmindedly bit a fingernail and glanced away.

"I have someone I want you to meet," Patty said. "Okay, you can come in now." Dean stepped through the door, walking with his cane, which he got from his car after their talk, carrying his backpack in the other hand. He gazed at the three boys, dressed in blue jeans, t-shirts and tennis shoes, standing straight. Patty stepped behind them, adjusting their stance as though posing them for a portrait. As one, they stared at him, frowning, and he nodded at each, then looked at the three year old, still sucking his thumb, shy and wide eyed.

"Dean," Patty said, "these are my sons, Jason, Aaron and Adam. Boys, this is someone I want you to meet."

"Hello," he said. "My name is Dean. I'm an old friend of your mother. I just wanted to say hello to you guys."

"Why?" the oldest asked.

Dean glanced at Patty, who smiled, not offering an answer, allowing Dean to make his own impressions and mistakes. "Well..." he knelt and opened his backpack. "To give you these." Even he could hear the wavering of his own voice. He opened the backpack and began pulling out the gloves, handing one to each boy, starting with the oldest. When he got to the youngest, he held out the glove. This one is named Adam, he thought.

The three year old stared at the glove, then stared at Dean. Without a word, Adam rushed at him and threw his arms around his neck.

Dean froze, his arm still held out, his hand still clutching the glove. He looked at Patty for help, what would he do now, but Patty did not answer, just smiled at him. He dropped the glove and slowly, slowly wrapped his arms around the boy, his son. The other two stepped closer, as though Adam were setting the example, and they joined in the hug, and just for the moment, Dean felt whole and complete.

Chapter Twenty Two

"Caught"
(Late Autumn, 1967)

Something was different.

The sun faded into grayness behind the mountains, leaving just enough light to silhouette trees and hills and emphasize the twittering birds hidden in the branches. The air was brisk, and smells became more apparent as Rabbitrunner paused and lifted his leg at one of his scent markers. His urine hit, not in a strong stream, but in an unselfconscious squirt, like an afterthought, a token scent that let others know he had returned to his territory. As he did so, he realized that he hadn't marked his boundary in a long time, and decided he would do that after he rested a few days.

For now, he was exhausted and bone weary. After many days of long-distance journeying from one territory to the next, he finally traveled two days and nights without stopping to eat or sleep to get back to Bearback, not out of any urgency but out of a need to be back in his own territory.

As he wandered along the shore of the lake that bordered his territory, he felt his body sag. His legs moved wearily, and his head hung low. Sleepiness, hunger, and thirst weighed heavily on him. He stopped by the lake to lap up water, his paws sinking into the mud, and he almost fell asleep standing there. When he opened his eyes, he looked at a mark that resembled a Twolegs paw print. Next to it, a small almost white leafy thing they used to make smoke. He took one last drink and moved on. He was absorbing the feelings of his home, his place, relishing the familiarity.

But something was different.

There was a vague sense of danger, a very vague feeling, and though he half-heartedly sniffed the air, stepped carefully among the trees while hiding his paw prints, the way he'd seen Cloudwalker do, and watched all around him in the waning light, there was no sign of anything amiss. There was still the feeling, but that was all.

With sore muscles and swollen paws, Rabbitrunner no longer cared if he reached Bearback. The urgency that pushed him to travel for two days was gone now that he was back in his own territory. Without another thought, he crawled under the low boughs of a young pine and scratched a shallow sleeping hole in the needles, collapsing on his side and dozing off instantly.

He slept without dreaming. He slept without moving, without rising and circling around his resting spot to settle into a more comfortable position. He slept as though dead, not even stretching his legs. Only his chest moved to indicate any sign of life.

He slept heavily, through most of the night, into the morning, unmoving, until he heard a shuddering howl of pain.

Rabbitrunner jerked awake, glancing back and forth, his ears swiveling, searching for the sound. It was daytime; he hadn't meant to sleep that long. He rose quickly, stumbling through the pine boughs and collapsing on his side in the dirt. His legs were numb from lack of circulation from not moving as he slept.

Confused and perplexed, he carefully stood up again, noticing the stiffness and soreness throughout his body, as well as the complete lack of feeling in his right foreleg and hind leg.

The painful tingling in his right side meant his feeling was slowly coming back. He yawned and tried to stretch without falling over, and then he straightened up, ears cocked—he heard it again, the weak howls. The sound was coming from across the lake. He trotted in that direction, his legs unsteady and tingling, his hackles up.

Something's wrong, he thought, something's really wrong.

He drew closer to the lake shore, and he saw a single figure across the water, lying in the grass at the lake's edge. *What's that?* Deerchaser whispered inside his head. *A Hunter, but what is that thing stuck into his side?*

Look Pawsore said from within his skull. Rabbitrunner squinted his eyes. A stick protruded from the Hunter's body, a stick with feathers on its end. He was breathing heavily, his rib cage moving up and down with the quickness of the beats of a sparrow's wings. He looked like he was very ill.

Then he raised his head, opened his mouth, and puled, the sound barely reaching across the lake.

"He needs help," Rabbitrunner snarled.

No! Pawsore whined. *Don't go!*

"I lost all of you," Rabbitrunner growled. "I won't lose another Hunter."

Don't Treepisser said.

It's dangerous! Newmoon puled.

Rabbitrunner turned and followed the path he used the day before, running along the lake's edge as the feeling started coming back into his legs. Something was different. Something was wrong. Didn't he see the Twolegs paw prints in the mud near where he stopped for a drink last night? It was Twolegs who wounded the Hunter across the lake, he could tell by the feathered stick. But why were they, the Twolegs, on this side of the lake in the first place? And where were they now? He couldn't think of that, the Hunter needed help.

He ran quickly, noticing a smell he couldn't quite recognize, but he couldn't think of that now. He had to reach the Hunter, still worried and still confused. What was the Hunter doing there? Was he one of the Tailless pack members? That side of the lake was in their territory, so it had to be.

Suddenly he tripped and collapsed.

His head was sore, and everything hurt, but he rose again and stepped forward. He heard something rattle before he was jerked back by an unmoving force.

A wave of panic hit him as he pulled himself against the thing behind him holding him tight. He looked back; his right hind leg was already swelling. His skin was torn where his paw was gripped by the black, hard thing: Jaws. Shock and pain hit him at the same time.

"No!" he growled, tugging at the thing that wouldn't let go. "Not me! It can't be! Not me!" He tugged harder, feeling the throbbing pain shoot up his leg bones. Even his hip ached now, and he pulled with a wrenching desperation, wincing at every yank.

The Jaws held tight. "No! No! No!" Rabbitrunner whined, twisting his body back and forth to get away. His body grew feverishly hot with a new rush of pain as three paws dug and shuffled uselessly in the dirt, and despite his efforts, despite his determination, he knew he was going to stay there, and he was going to die there.

Cloudwalker's head snapped around. The gentle wind played with his mangy coat, but there was no sound.

It's that Hunter, one of the voices in his head said. Cloudwalker blinked and bared his teeth at the uneasy feeling he had. *It's that Hunter!*

Yes, another voice said. *That Hunter!*

That Rabbit-Turd!

That Rabbit-Turd is dying!

"*No!*" Cloudwalker snarled. "He is not dying, Rabbit-Turd is *NOT!*"

Dying!

"Enough!" Cloudwalker growled. He closed his eyes, blocking the voices. When his head was clear, he opened his eyes and started walking again. He had changed direction and was heading towards Bearback. He hadn't intended to go that way this time, but something strong was pulling him. He only hoped his instincts were wrong.

The vine rattled sluggishly, no feeling, no urgency. Rabbitrunner stood still for a moment, panting, his eyes dull, and slather around his lips. His right hind leg was swollen and stiff. He'd been pulling on the vine from late morning to early afternoon. Twice during that time he'd heard the Hunter across the lake whining, the voice growing weaker. There were blackberry bushes between him and the lake along this stretch of the path, so he could see parts of the lake through breaks in the bushes, but not the Hunter.

He swallowed what little saliva there was in his mouth and glanced back. The bone wasn't broken but the skin was torn, and now the wound was gaping wide, exposing dried muscle and tendons. A small puddle of dried blood was on the ground.

He turned, took a deep breath and pulled again, his

claws digging into the dirt, his neck muscles bulging, his breathing constricted by pain and panic, thinking to himself, maybe, maybe this time I might pull free.... The dull throb of pain reached through his body, and his paws kept sliding in the dirt.

Then he stopped, again, wheezing, drops of foamy saliva dripping from his chin. Blackness shimmered at the edge of his vision as he turned and gazed at his leg. And then, just as he knew they would, the Jaws began singing to him.

The massive old Hunter had just lowered his gaze from the bright afternoon sky when something large, dark, and fast passed just over his head, painfully wrapping his skull with a loud "Thok!" before beating its wings and gaining altitude. Cloudwalker jerked around and looked up, snarling just in time to see the old, tattered raven with the wide wingspan settle on a limb near the top of a spruce. This was the one he called "Flame," old enough, he knew, to have outlived many Cloudwalkers.

With one eye missing and a twisted, black beak that looked like arthritic talons, Flame stared down at him from his perch. Scaly, thick black talons gripped the branch, and the one eye held Cloudwalker's gaze. And Cloudwalker knew.

"Rabbit-Turd!" the old Hunter hissed. "Rabbit-Turd! No!" He glanced at the mound in the distance, rising above the trees, that he knew to be Bareback. "No! By Father Sky's shriveled balls, no! By Mother Earth's wilted pudenda and teats, no! No, Rabbit-Turd, No!"

He glanced at Flame one more time. The massive bird that had seen Rabbit-Turd leaped, spread its tattered, black wings and dived, banked left, and flew away. Cloudwalker glanced at Bearback, now more worried than ever, and continued towards it. He trotted faster, then, despite the pain in his joints, he began running, the first time he ran in many, many seasons.

Something was different. Something was wrong. It was the smell of Twolegs, and the smell of the oily Jaws, and it was everywhere. He could smell it now, he'd smelled it last night in his dreamless sleep, but then he wasn't really aware.

Rabbitrunner stopped pulling, feeling hot, then cold as the pain throbbed through him. His muscles had reached the point of nearly complete weakness; he'd been pulling for so long. He hadn't eaten in days, during his long journey back, and now hunger gnawed at his insides, but it was the thirst that bothered him the most. He was becoming dehydrated, and though he kept pulling towards the lake, the rattling vine was ungiving. He could see the water though patches in the bushes, but he couldn't reach it.

He remembered what it was like watching his dam die, Brookjumper, her leg held fast in the grip of the Jaws. It was a death of slow waiting, not knowing when Twolegs would return to kill what the Jaws caught. The waiting would go on, and he would still try to pull free, even knowing he couldn't, until Twolegs came, and the waiting was over.

But something else was going on; he couldn't hear the voices any more. The voices in his head were now silent. He was alone except for the Jaws, singing pain to him through his leg, singing that he was going to die. There is nothing to fear, he thought, even as he was shivering from terror. Whatever happens is meant to happen. We will all die someday. Our kind will die out, none will be left, and life will go on, life out of balance, until it is gone.

There is nothing to fear....

He closed his eyes. Froth dried on his lips, and he breathed the labored breathing of the dying. He knew there was no way to break free of the Jaws, but he kept on thinking, kept on grasping for possibilities that weren't there.

Twolegs were hairless, and would freeze to death when the first winter came, but they killed Hunters and deer and elk to remove their skin and fur to cover their own bodies. Twolegs adapted. Twolegs used reason to survive. Why couldn't he?

Then something occurred to him, something insignificant but different. Something not quite right. Rabbitrunner opened his eyes and glanced down the path.

They were there, covered, poorly hidden, but there nonetheless. Jaws. And when the breeze changed, he smelled more Jaws. Oiled. And more Twolegs odors. And there was the Hunter wounded across the lake. There must be more Jaws there, too.

But why so many? he wondered. All around the lake? Just for the moment, his mind was off the pain and fear as he looked around. There were too many Jaws—but why so many? What was Twolegs up to?

Cloudwalker was just approaching the lake when he felt the ground beneath one of his forepaws give in an unfamiliar way. He leaped back just as the Jaws snapped shut where his paw had been, only a moment before. Not cautious enough, he thought, realizing how nervous he was now. His hackles rose as he looked around, seeing other Jaws buried beneath grass and leaves. Twolegs must have dug shallow holes to make the grass seem level with the ground, and the Jaws waited underneath, waited patiently. He went on, stepping cautiously, the smell of Twolegs potent and oppressive. There was also the scent of a yearling, and another scent.

"Rabbit-Turd!" he growled.

He stepped along the trail, trying to control his feelings, avoiding the Jaws. The presence of so many deadly Twolegs things made him uneasy. It wasn't normal Twolegs behavior. He passed Jaws that had closed on a squirrel, snapping its spine, not what Twolegs had intended, he knew. He kept glancing through the trees, listening, wondering if they were around.

Then he saw the yearling. The stick protruded from his side, and blood covered the ground, a black stain of brutality and lust for death, the sign of Twolegs. The yearling was still breathing. Every breath rattled like pebbles bouncing down a talus slope. The feathered stick wasn't too deep in him, just enough to bring a slow death, but even without the stick, Cloudwalker could tell, the young Hunter wasn't going far; all four legs of the yearling were broken.

The dying Hunter opened one eye and looked at him. "Cloudwalker," he whined. "You came, you really came...." He coughed. "The stories told me you would.... And your fur, so thick, so white...."

The old Hunter stood near the yearling, bending to lick his ear. The yearling closed his eye. Cloudwalker's insides knotted as he sat by the dying Hunter. "You did this to catch me, you did," he growled, the image of the Twolegs One, the Dark Twolegs, vivid in his mind. "You knew I would come here, you did. You did all this to catch me.... Kill me.... But how did you know? How did you know I would come this way? How did you know?"

The yearling coughed; blood and snot splattered the grass. Cloudwalker glanced at him as he took a deep breath, let it out, and lay still.

Dead.

"Sleep well, you will, my Pretty One. Sleep well, you will." He gently touched his nose to the yearling's muzzle. "They killed you to kill me, young Hunter. But by Father Sky's good eye, I will, hurt them for you, I will...." His chest constricted, his resolve waned. "He will kill and kill, he will kill all my Pretty Ones just to get to me, but maybe I can get him first!"

Cloudwalker wearily rose and moved on, his great bulk like a boulder on a pinnacle, about to topple in any direction, and as he walked, he wondered why so many dying Hunters had seen him as white-furred, and so much larger than he ever was.

Rabbitrunner remained still, his eyes closed, his ribs heaving at every breath. He moved his swollen leg, and pain leaped through him again. He winced. Don't move, he thought, don't move. Wait, just wait. And don't move.

"Rabbit-Turd, Rabbit-Turd, standing in the grass, he is, my Rabbit-Turd!" The voice was deep and dusty and raspy as talus. Rabbitrunner opened his eyes. "Caught your paw, the Jaws did, my Pretty?"

Cloudwalker stepped towards him, his hackles up, his scarred, white head low. His large shoulder blades moved beneath the skin like creatures beneath flattened grass. His tail swung low behind him, and his odor preceded him like a rolling fog. He stepped over open Jaws without looking down, guided by some unseen sense.

Rabbitrunner lowered his head in submission, his ears back as he humbly licked his lips with a dry, sticky tongue. "Cloudwalker," he puled, "I need your help!"

"Hurt our little paw, have we?" Cloudwalker snarled, baring his teeth. He walked around the other Hunter, leering with cruel maliciousness. "Disappointed, I am, my Pretty, disappointed, I am. Expected better of you, I did, Rabbit-Turd. Much, much, better."

Rabbitrunner glanced at him, his eyes wide. Cloud-walker brought his bared teeth close to his tattered ear. "Clumsy you are, my Pretty. Rushed to see the dying Hunter, you did, and look at you now, my lonely, lonely Hunter of Jaws and pain." Cloudwalker snorted. He turned and began walking away.

"Wait!' Rabbitrunner whined. He pulled until the Jaws pulled back, gnawing his leg, jolting his mind like lightning. "Don't go! I need your help!"

"Help?" Cloudwalker stopped and looked over his shoulder. "Help? How?"

"If you can open the Jaws, I can pull my leg free!" Rabbitrunner's eyes were pleading. "I need to be free, Cloudwalker, I need your help!"

Cloudwalker looked back sadly. "I have passed through many territories, I have," he said. "I have closed many Jaws. I have broken many Jaws. But open those Jaws, my precious, precious Hunter....Open them I can NOT!"

"But...."

"I cannot, Rabbit-Turd, I cannot!" Cloudwalker turned around, faced him, but he wouldn't get any closer, and he wouldn't look directly into his eyes. He had witnessed dying many times, but this was one death he couldn't bear to witness. "Such pain I have felt, so many times.... The Thundersticks and their pebbles.... All the pebbles rolling around in my muscles and guts.... All the winters, all the travels, all the deaths have seen, I have.... But your death, my whelp...."

A glint of compassion showed in Cloudwalker's eye as he forced himself to look. "Your death, Rabbit-Turd, is the worst pain I have ever felt."

Rabbitrunner shivered uncontrollably. He had hoped that Cloudwalker would show up and free him of the Jaws, but Cloudwalker was here now, telling him it was hopeless, talking about him as though he were already dead.

The old Hunter looked away from him. "How hard it is, Rabbit-Turd, how hard it is to survive, survive from one winter to the next, from one day to the next. Hard enough, my Pretty One, without being clumsy."

Cloudwalker turned and looked at Rabbitrunner again, rage and compassion changing the features of his face. "Do you not know, my precious, precious Hunter, why no other Hunter stepped into your territory—no other Hunter! Do you not know why? Because I have been marking your boundary posts long after you have forgotten! I have been marking your boundary posts, marking them, and watching!"

Rabbitrunner gazed at the old Hunter.

It was all becoming clear, the scent he always smelled when he left or returned to his territory. He had grown so used to it that he never associated it with Cloudwalker, not any more.

The old Hunter turned around and walked away again. "Clumsy, clumsy Rabbit-Turd!"

"No!" Rabbitrunner growled. "I was not clumsy! The Jaws were not here yesterday!"

"They were put here in the early morning," Cloudwalker said without stopping. "You should have heard Twolegs putting the Jaws down! You should have! Noisy, noisy Twolegs. Clickety-clack, rickety-rack Twolegs. And for you, Rabbit-Turd, I had many plans, I had. Me, the old Hunter, the old Guardian of Guardians. But a young one.... Maybe.... But now.... Rabbit-Turd, Rabbit-Turd, so much potential, but now, now, watch you die, I can NOT!"

Rabbitrunner could barely hear him now, he'd walked so far away, but the fear and anger at being deserted made everything else seem meaningless. He watched the old Hunter lumber through the trees, and his ears pointed back, so far back they could have been matted against his head by rain, not out of obeisance but out of rage, ragged, torn, and raw rage.

His nose rippled and wrinkled, his lips pulled back, exposing white, sharp teeth as a snarl rose from his depths, something deep from where no strength could be left, something vicious. "Go!' he growled. "Leave me alone! Let me die! I don't need you! Go!"

Cloudwalker stopped and looked back through the trees. The sun, low in the sky, made shadows across the ground between them. Rabbitrunner strained against the Jaws, snarling, the pain blazing through his leg, through his body. Cloudwalker watched in awe. "There's life in you yet, there is, little Hunter. Life is in you yet."

"Go away!" Rabbitrunner demanded. "Take your life and choke on it! You're a Guardian of shit! A Hunter of dead bones and maggots! Leave me alone! What did you say? There is nothing to fear? Whatever happens is meant to happen?" His hackles were up, his muscles were tense. He was lightning and thunder bundled in a dying body, wanting to fight, wanting to kill. "I think there is everything to fear, but now, now I don't care, I've got nothing left to fear because I'm dying! Dying! So go away!" He yanked again, straining, his blood splattering the ground. One more pull, he thought, and my leg comes off, my body will tear in half...

"A little life there is in you yet," Cloudwalker puled. "But, oh, too late, too late."

"By Father Sky's fat rump, go away!" Rabbitrunner howled. "Crawl away into your worm-den! Drag your lousy flea-bitten carcass out of my sight!"

"Dying you are, my Pretty One," Cloudwalker said. "But you will not die easy, you will not."

"Yeah I'm dying!" Rabbitrunner snarled. "I'm dying, and I don't care!" He yanked on his trapped leg, biting his tongue and convulsing with the pain. The agony sang in his head, up and down his spine, dug its claws into his stomach from the inside and raked deep, bloody wounds trying to get out, and Rabbitrunner snarled its song: "I'm dying, and I have nothing left to lose! The Jaws are chewing me to the bone, Cloudwalker, do you hear me? I have nothing left to lose!" He yanked his leg again. "Nothing!"

He twisted around and bit at the Jaws. Cloudwalker curious and amazed, turned around and raised his head to see better.

Now in a frenzy, Rabbitrunner snapped at the Jaws time and again, twisting and kicking up dirt and dust, snarling and gagging, sometimes biting his own leg, froth and blood splattering the ground around him. He bit his tongue again and swallowed his blood, his throat raw with snarls and dust.

He twisted back and forth, yanking at the chain, face contorted, joints popping as his claws furrowed the dirt. The air stank of madness around him as he pulled and tugged and jerked back and forth like a snake. Every tendon stretched, every muscle strained, and the Jaws sang to him, "You have nothing left to lose, nothing left to lose...."

Blood streamed from his wounded leg, the wound opening wider like a hungry mouth, showing the fragile bone inside. Skin ripped and pulled away from the muscle it covered. Then the leg pulled free in a sudden jerk, and Rabbitrunner stumbled and collapsed on his side.

He was free. He just pulled his paw out of the trap, something he thought he would never be able to do. He was free.

He wasn't aware that he had passed out until his sight returned, along with the throbbing pain, and he saw Cloudwalker through the dark fog. The old Hunter was doubled in his vision. Rabbitrunner stumbled off the ground, stood, shook his head, and looked again. There was only one Cloudwalker now.

Then he remembered.

He turned and dashed away, leaping over Jaws, more aware now than ever before to their presence, as though he could see through the grass and leaves that hid them. He ran on three legs, staying close to the lake as he hurried, his pain forgotten, his hunger and thirst left behind, until he reached the place that was a hive of Jaws, where he found the body of the yearling.

The young Hunter was dead.

Cloudwalker later found Rabbitrunner standing over the body, nuzzling the head. Rabbitrunner, despondent, knowing he was being watched, stepped back and glanced at the old Hunter, his eyes full of weariness, then he limped to the lake, steadied himself by the shore, and lapped up water. When his thirst was quenched, he turned and started for Bearback, not even acknowledging Cloudwalker as he passed, walking slow and awkward as he limped over the hidden Jaws.

Cloudwalker followed. They traveled in silence until Cloudwalker was abreast of him. "And tell me, Rabbit-Turd, tell me," he said. "Worth it, was it, to find a dead yearling? Worth it, was it?"

Rabbitrunner made no answer. They traveled on, neither one looking at the other. It was dark, and rain clouds were gathering over the treetops thick as mud, when Cloudwalker spoke again. "Tell me, Rabbit-Turd, tell me: How will the Lone Hunter hunt with a gimpy leg? How will the Lone Hunter survive?"

Rabbitrunner stopped and looked back at his injured leg. Strips of skin, muscle, coagulated blood, running black as night, all mottling on his leg around the wound. His pads were still intact, but two toes were missing from his paw. The leg was a dull throb that he could ignore as long as he kept moving, but he couldn't guess how well it would heal, or if it would heal at all.

He turned and glared at Cloudwalker. The old Hunter's eyes sparkled with a warm mischievousness, but there was a driving rage behind them, too, and Rabbitrunner's eyes blazed back just as strong. He looked away and limped on, his legs tired, his mind clouded.

"When Twolegs sees your toes dangling in the Jaws, Twolegs will ask themselves, they will, 'What kind of Hunter can pull his leg out of the grip of my Jaws? What kind of Hunter?'" Cloudwalker snorted—he found his comment humorous. "What kind of Hunter? And answer, the wind will, 'The very same Lone Hunter who can hunt and survive with a gimpy leg, that kind of Hunter!'"

A drizzle began, but Rabbitrunner was impervious to it. He wanted to get back to the den. At some point in his walk, he looked around and Cloudwalker was gone, no longer following.

He had reached Bearback by the time the rain was pouring down. He dragged himself into the tunnel, and when he reached the main chamber, he flopped on his side and slept, still hearing the rain.

A light morning mist was already breaking up as the seven men gathered at the grassy area near the water's edge. Five carried rifles; one, Cutter, carried a bow and quiver of arrows. During the hike to the lake, the talk had been lively and noisy. Now the voices were low and solemn.

"How could he have pulled his foot out of the trap?" Jack Fipps asked. "I got my fingers caught in one, once, and I couldn't get them out until a friend pushed the spring down."

"Maybe the trap just caught his toes," Cutter said, rolling a cigarette one-handed. "That's all we found."

"But there's pieces of skin in the trap," Jack said. "And blood everywhere. His leg was caught, Cutter. It was stuck in there."

Cutter lit a cigarette, took a drag, and opened his hand and looked at the two giant wolf toes he found in the trap. The toe claws were black, worn, and bloody. "Was that before or after he found the wolf we left behind?" He glanced around, noticing the anxiety they were all feeling. "I mean, if I lost two toes, I'd be pretty pissed off myself." Cutter looked at Jack. He was angry, goading the others, daring them to say something.

Ben took off his baseball cap and ran his hand through his red hair. "Christ, Cutter, that wasn't pissed off, that was madness, brutal, savage madness. And throw those toes away. What're you gonna do, bronze them?"

"I seem to be catching the Shadow Wolf one piece at a time," Cutter said. "I need to save these so I can put him back together when I'm done." Nobody laughed at his joke, but he didn't care. "Maybe I'll fry them up with some onions, have them with beans."

Jack lit another Chesterfield cigarette. He absentmindedly felt for the walkie-talkie hooked to his belt. "We lost four hundred traps here, you know." He blew smoke in the air. "All broken, except the one with the toes?"

"They were my traps, Jack, my loss," Cutter said, taking another drag. The set-up had been Jack's idea. They thought the Shadow Wolf would come to see the wounded wolf, and they were apparently right. "Nobody said it was going to be easy. If you want to pull out, fine. But this time we almost got him. This time he made a mistake."

"I'm not pulling out, Cutter," Jack said. "You didn't see me puking my guts out, did you?"

"Shut the fuck up," Troy said. "Just shut the fuck up." He walked away from the others, still looking pale.

He hadn't expected to find what they had found. None of them did.

"All I'm saying is look at the way this thing thinks." Jack said. "He gets trapped and barely gets free. A normal wolf would run for its life. This one sticks around to find and break all the traps. Wounded, no less. And then look at what he left behind...."

Nobody wanted to comment about that. Jack flicked his cigarette onto the mud. Everything was muddy. The lake was calm. The men were uneasy. "Let's pack it up," Jack said, lighting another cigarette.

"What about the traps?" Ben asked.

"What about them?" Jack said, "We can't fix 'em. Leave 'em here." He kicked a trap with his feet.

"We'll get him next time," Cutter said. "He's heading for Caleb County next."

"He got away this time," Jack said, gesturing with his arms. "He'll get away next time. Who're you kidding?"

"Yeah, but don't you see?" Cutter's face was animated. "He showed up here twenty-four hours after we did. You were right, Jack. You do know where he's going. We can get there before he does. He'll be back. We'll get him."

"After what's happened," Jack said, "he might be changing his plans. What with a torn-up foot and leg, he might not be in any mood to travel. And if his leg gets infected...."

"That wolf's too lucky to get an infection," Cutter said. "He'll be there. He's obsessed. He's a terrorist in the body of a wolf."

Jack tossed his half-finished cigarette on the ground. "All right, all right, let's get back and pack our tents. It's a long drive home."

"You go ahead," Cutter said. "I'll be back in a little while."

"You're not going to look at it again, are you?" Ben

asked. He glanced at Cutter and saw that he was right. "All right, okay, but don't be long. Remember, he might still be out there."

"Don't worry," Cutter said, holding up his bow. "I'm hunting him, not the other way around."

"He's a wounded animal now," Ben reminded him, and then added as an afterthought, "But then again, you're a stubborn animal, Cutter, I forgot."

Cutter laughed, and watched as they walked away, then turned and headed in the other direction.

Fifteen minutes later, when he reached the wolf carcass, he squatted down in the mud. Nobody wanted to get close to it. Nobody trampled on the paw prints around the carcass, big paw prints, impressed deep in the mud. Nobody wanted to get that close.

Cutter carefully reached over, gripping his arrow and putting his other hand on the bloody thing. It wasn't easy, but twisting it back and forth, he got the arrow out. He didn't want anybody finding the arrow there, if anybody ever came that way. He wiped it off on his shirt and put it in his quiver, then stood, looking for what he saw the first time.

There were no paw prints around the broken traps— the Shadow Wolf would have taken care of those during the rainstorm, when his tracks would have been washed away. He came back when the rain stopped, leaving fresh paw prints around the dead wolf, but there were no signs of his arrival or departure.

Cutter's eyes were unmoving as he looked at the flattened grass, the rain-washed flat rock with a dab of mud on it, the spot where something large scratched the ground to hide its mark. Without moving, he could see the paw prints lead to the lake—he wanted me to see them!—and disappeared into the water, where the wolf could swim away.

But where had he come out? Cutter felt a chill, imagining him under the water, holding his breath, watching, laughing.... In his imagination, there was nothing the wolf couldn't do.

He spit out his cigarette butt and put a stalk of grass in his mouth, then looked at the dead wolf. When they first saw it, Troy had to walk away and puke. The other men were close to doing the same. Cutter had never seen anything like it, and he knew he would carry that memory to his grave.

Except for where the arrow had pierced it, the wolf was mostly bone and tendon, its body mostly gone, its viscera eaten, its rib cage empty, devoured by a hunger that provoked cannibalism. The Shadow Wolf had eaten one of its own kind. Drying strips of meat stuck to bone. Leg bones still connected to each other. The wolf ate carefully, not in a feeding frenzy, but as though it had all the time in the world.

The triangles on Jack's maps did not reveal everything—even when the wolf was predictable, he was unpredictable. Wounded, missing two toes, he still took the time to break the traps and then eat before he left. Not even the lungs and heart remained, Cutter had checked, and only the head, tail, and paws still had all the skin and fur on.

But why had he done this thing?

Cutter pulled the grass from his lips and dropped it. He turned and headed back the way he came to join the others, astounded by what the wolf had done, and more determined now to kill it.

Chapter Twenty Three

"North"

(Late Autumn, 1967)

Travel in the direction that will allow Father Sky's good eye to peer at your right paw in the morning and your left paw in the late afternoon.

Travel in the direction that will permit Father Sky's bad eye to gaze at your right shoulder at twilight and your left shoulder just before the coming of the day.

Travel that way.

In that direction.

I'm hot. My body trembles. But I'm hot. And everything around me is so strange, so different....

Dizzy and feverish, Rabbitrunner crawled down another tunnel. He'd dug out so many tributaries from the main tunnel that his labyrinth was even confusing to him. His joints ached, and he couldn't remember when he started moving, only that it began a long time ago, and he was tired, and weak, and needed fresh air.

Then he saw a glimmer of light, paleness at the end of a long tunnel of black. He kept pulling himself along, feeling his right hind leg throb like something almost separate of him, and he heard rumbling as he approached the tunnel entrance. He saw light spread around him as though the tunnel was splitting horizontally on either side of him.

Terrorized, he realized that he was surrounded by giant teeth, and the tunnel roof became the ribbed arch of a palate as the earth beneath him undulated, becoming a massive, wet tongue. He was inside a giant beast's mouth, and when it swallowed, he was pummeled backwards into the churning depths of darkness and rancid odors, roiling backwards down its throat.

He woke up, hot, congested, in the main chamber of his den. He pushed his thoughts up through the dried leaves of his mind and tried to reorient himself. He could hear mice scurrying about in the darkness, and crickets up the tunnel at the den's entrance. Night smells reached him through the bends in the tunnel, but the moonlight never made it past the first turn.

He lowered his head, feeling dizzy and thirsty. How long had he been sleeping? A day? Two? He wanted to go out and drink at the spring, but he felt so tired, so heavy. He yawned, feeling his lips unstick. Dried mucous and saliva coated his mouth and nostrils, and his throat was parched. He almost raised his body, then collapsed onto the other side. He could smell the heat radiating from him, a feverish stench like a stagnant pond. His right hind leg throbbed, reminding him of the Jaws that bit him, wounded him, and nearly kept him. He rested, panting heavily, feeling curiously relaxed, hot, misty, until he was asleep.

And again, he dreamed.

He dreamed of the howls and pulings of Hunters being

killed by the thundersticks and the pebbles they spit, devoured by the Jaws, and he saw a large pack of Twolegs being led by the Twolegs One, a big creature with many limbs and many claws.

When he woke again, he was gasping for breath and burning up. His fever was worse. He heard thunder and rain outside his den, and he wanted to crawl out and drink, too far to go, and he felt so tired. He could smell ammonia in the air, urine and feces, and he realized that he had fouled himself in his sleep. He'd have to clean himself up, he realized, with a feeling of disgust for the chore. After he got a drink outside.

But it was the smell of rot that worried him. He knew what it was; his wounded leg was infected and needed cleaning. It was only a matter of time before it would begin rotting, if it hadn't started already. He raised his head to lick the wound, but dizziness hit him and his thoughts floundered. He felt lost on the windy waves of grassy plains. He flopped back down, deciding to clean the wound later. The pain wasn't much now, just a dull throb.

He listened to the flies buzzing in the den, settling on his wound, and he felt his flesh tingle as they fed. He was too tired to shake his leg to get them off, and his leg was so stiff it probably wouldn't move any way. They crawled all over him, the flies did, and the sounds of their buzzing were becoming more annoying as they took off and landed. He could see them on the walls of the chamber, a shiny black mass that undulated sickeningly like the movement of black flesh, and he felt hot and digested. Then he remembered it was autumn, and in the next moment the buzzing and the moving mass of flies was gone, they were only in his head, but the itching remained.

He saw a large, white shape move in the chamber, he knew it was Cloudwalker, standing over him in the darkness, doing something, licking him, sniffing him, but he couldn't feel anything. He tasted meat and chewed on muscle and bone, and saliva filled his mouth, it seemed so real, and as thoughts and images coagulated in his tattered mind, he saw Deerchaser standing over him, large as Bearback, puling, *One male will be like two, like many, a Guardian of Guardians. He is the one. We all died. All except one....* And Deerchaser bulged all over, full of maggots devouring his flesh, his skin rippling with their feeding frenzy. *He's the one....*

Rabbitrunner found himself walking on an icy plain, snow and whiteness everywhere. Ahead of him was Cloudwalker, leading the way, with the rising sun blazing on his right side and the setting sun on his left, and he did not seem to wonder at the oddity of seeing two suns in the sky. And the sky itself, bright, but just ahead, stained with black blotches, blood in the sky from the time the great pack walked on Father Sky's vast pelage, killing the Nameless Ones.

But something else was different. Cloudwalker's fur was glistening white, clean and unbroken by mange or scars. And where they walked there were no trees, no mountains, just the white plains and the large white Hunter walking in front of him. Suddenly Cloudwalker stopped and looked back. "Don't follow me!" he snarled. "You need to go this way, but don't follow me! If you do, you'll die!"

Rabbitrunner shuddered awake.

Death was white, he remembered.

He glanced around; he could almost see the outline of his den. It had to be noon, perhaps a cloudless day. How much time had passed since the Jaws held his leg? He wanted to go outside, see the trees and sky, with an urgency that burned hotter than his fever. Weariness pressed him to the floor of his den, but he struggled to overcome it. Anxiety and fear raked his cloudy thoughts; he knew if he kept sleeping he would starve to death.

He raised himself on his forelegs, feeling his head spin and his body throb. He tried to raise his rump, but his legs weren't working. Frustrated and scared, he pulled himself towards the light with his forepaws.

Along the tunnel he stopped to rest several times, his breathing heavy, his heart pounding. Then he went on, his claws digging in the dirt, and after he strained to move further, he noticed that he was down; he had passed out. Still uneasy about his weakness, he rose and pulled himself further, until he managed to get outside.

He squinted his eyes at the blinding sunlight, then twisted around to look at his wounded leg. It was swollen, but the wound was clean, and everything was healing.

He took a deep breath.

There is nothing to fear.

Whatever happens

Is meant to happen.

Dragging himself, stopping to rest, dragging again, licking his lips, his mouth and tongue dry and sticky, he managed to pull himself from the clearing into the woods, the cool, dark shadows of the trees, the air icy and smelling of dead leaves and dried ferns. He continued on until he reached the spring, a trickle now, almost dry, but he drank water and mud, lapping voraciously until his stomach was full to bursting. Dead leaves floated down at each new breath of wind, and he rested where he was, a few near-bare branches allowing the light to warm him.

He dozed, contented, and when he woke, the full moon was high in the sky. He managed to stand erect this time, and he squatted to urinate before going to the spring to drink again. He licked the dried feces and urine off his hind legs and rump, then tended to the rest of his fur.

"This, this is our life!"

His head snapped up at the distant howl, a tidbit of a voice that tasted of sweet, fresh meat, a rising note coming from the Blackpaw Territory. Even as he listened, he heard other harmonious voices join in:

"This, this is our Food!"

"This, this is our Play!"

"This, this is our Sleep!"

"This, this is our Hunt!"

He felt a deep longing inside to add his own voice to the Litany, but somehow it wasn't right. Instead, he turned and limped back to the den, his right hind leg held off the ground. When he crawled back into the chamber, he could tell by smell and touch that it was filthy with his wastes, but he also discovered scraps of meat, a deer's leg bone gnawed clean, the small, caliginous hoof still attached, half a rabbit, and the remains of a regurgitated meal.

Cloudwalker had been there, feeding him during his sickness. He had no memory of it, but the old Hunter's scent was everywhere. He must have come into the den, fed him, and he must have licked the infected wound clean.

For once, Rabbitrunner did not feel alone.

During the next week, he grew stronger, hunting mice and exercising his bad leg. The fever was gone, and his pelage glistened with proper grooming. To his heavy disappointment, Cloudwalker never returned, but he knew it was only a matter of time before he did.

The last leaves were dropping from the oaks and maples, and he felt something prodding him to move on. He killed a few muskrats, then a deer and though he was full, he felt a deeper hunger inside, a yearning to travel. His leg was completely healed but for the missing toes, and contrary to Cloudwalker's prediction, there was no gimpiness to his gait whatsoever.

One day he climbed to the clearing on Bareback. He watched the sun set, then stood so the last rays of light played on his left shoulder. The air was cold, but he felt some warmth, a drowsy distraction to the scenery below. As the sun glided behind the mountains and the stars came out, he listened to the whispering wind. After awhile, he looked to his right. The moon, less than half full, was ascending from the horizon, clean and rugged, Father Sky's cranky bad eye. He looked straight ahead. He knew which way he had to go.

Cloudwalker had told him.

Cloudwalker, who had marked his boundaries when he forgot. Cloudwalker, who taught him how to survive on his own, not by showing him but by watching him from a distance. Cloudwalker's territory was everywhere, and it was bountiful with sacred meat, rabbits and squirrels and deer, and in his hunting he maintained the Balance.

Cloudwalker, Snaretripper, Winddancer, Thundersnarl, Dogslayer—the old Hunter had many names, and all he knew was part of the Blood of the Hunter. His spirit was in his paws and legs, his soul was in his heart, and his Litany was a guide for Rabbitrunner's travel: There is nothing to fear—whatever happens is meant to happen.

The wind was growing stronger. Keep the rising sun and the rising moon to the right shoulder, Rabbitrunner thought, and keep the setting sun and the setting moon to the left shoulder. He knew which way to go, so he started downhill. He never looked back.

Chapter Twenty Four

"A Blossom Like Thunder"
(Late Autumn, 1967)

Dean stumbled along the trail, trying not to grab a tree or bush for support. He was determined to hike without a walking stick this time, though his foot ached with every step. The trees were bare along the trail, and the air was chilly. He could hear the wind in the branches, but no bird sounds, no animal sounds except for the clomping of Fribitz Grinner trying to keep up behind him. They had been talkative for the first hour of walking, but now they were both silent, weary and focusing on keeping the pace.

"How much farther?" Fribitz groaned. He was not used to walking, and was just realizing how sedentary his life was.

"Almost there," Dean said, limping but not slowing. He stepped through a wall of dead, leafless bushes, and in the next moment he was back at the cave. Fribitz stopped beside him, at first gazing at his face, then glancing at the round clearing.

Fribitz was an artist, a showman, a performer. He was an introvert but acted marvelously like an extrovert, pulling whole crowds into his circle and wowing them with his constant chatter. He had a stunning wardrobe that ranged from Salvation Army rejects to costumes suitable for The Beatles to coats that might have come from a Gilbert and Sullivan operetta to black clothes, black socks and turtlenecks and Nehru shirts and black coats and ties. He changed his hair color week from week, shaved it all off, painted naked, sculpted and hurled stone, welded metal, mixed oils and acrylics, carved wood, all for show.

There was no show now.

The clearing didn't look like much, but he saw everything he'd heard in Dean's stories. This was the clearing, surrounded by a circle of trees, looking like a dried up shallow pond, a few rib bones jutting up through the dead grass, and across from where they stood was the grim, toothless smile that was the cave entrance. He saw the arrow Dean shot into the dead spruce seven years ago, still stuck there, the fletching, one hen feather blue, one hen feather brown, the cockfeather green, the colors all but faded and bleached by the sun but still visible even this far away. On the other side of the dead tree was a new, young spruce, several feet tall.

The place had that stench of death, the smell Dean knew so well, but Fribitz got a whiff of it for the first time. At first he was about to throw up and had to control his gag reflex. But the stories he remembered Dean telling him came back to him, and now it was a different odor, the scent of the creature he had waited years to see. Now he was steps away from its lair, and he approached with anticipation.

As Dean limped towards the cave, Fribitz reached up, gripping his shoulder and followed like a child walking into a toy store for the first time. The smell grew worse, but neither of them recoiled or reacted.

At the entrance, Dean gently pushed Fribitz's hand off and gestured for him to watch. He knelt, pushed his head in, and disappeared into the darkness. Fribitz glanced away, glanced back at the cave, then knelt. He could see the flashlight beam in the dark, the stench so strong now he almost threw up.

"Okay," Dean said. "Come in."

Fribitz crawled in, sliding on sand and pine cones, pulling himself around and sitting upright. Dean slid over to him and pointed with his flashlight beam. "Over here, you can see it looks like a perfect dome, a half bubble almost. The walls and ceiling are black. Somehow they set fire inside here, though I don't see how, the oxygen would have been used up in seconds and the fire would have gone out. So things happened that I cannot fully explain. I just know they happened."

Fribitz reached up and ran his fingers against the stone ceiling. He lowered his hand and glanced at it, looking at the soot on his fingertips. "Shit."

"This is where the Shadow Wolf came from," Dean went on. "This is where he was born. You see that raised floor to the right? He sleeps there. It's coated with hair from all the years he was shedding. It's thick with hair. I touched it the last time. And the pack. A normal pack of wolves is about two to ten wolves. This pack was once fifteen to twenty. I counted a dozen skulls in here, including three cubs whose heads were wired together before they were burned alive."

"Shit," Fribitz whispered.

"Someone knew about them, this pack, and someone was determined to get rid of them all. I checked the maps, checked the records, there are no ranches or farms or cows or sheep any where near here, so I don't know why anybody would care, or why they'd need to do this. But someone came, and someone brought lots of friends and guns and gasoline. There's this stuff they use in Viet Nam , called Napalm, it sets fire to buildings and people and sticks to them and burns them to death, like mixing gasoline and glue. I can't help thinking they did this to the wolves."

"Yeah, Krazy Kat, but why would they do that?" Fribitz whispered.

Dean shook his head. "These wolves, this pack, they weren't a threat to anybody. By being so large a pack, it meant the hunting was good, because the wolf population adjusts to the game population. I learned that on Isle Royale. No, this was just some meanness and cruelty some men had in them, the same thing that inspired men to wipe out the wolves in the Dakotas, the same thing that brought our cavalry after the civil war to wipe out the Indians in the early west. Conquer, take, destroy. That's what it was, nothing else."

Fribitz patted his shoulder. Dean wiped his cheeks with a dirty palm. He turned his flashlight off. In a few minutes, they both could make out things in the cave without it.

"When I first found this cave, I planned to die here. I swear, I could not look at this place, once inside, without thinking that there were once cavemen who lived here. I still don't know how it formed, but wolves lived inside here and men could have, too. But I was so self-absorbed in killing myself that I crawled across this floor to the other side and never thought once about all the bones and skulls I crawled past. I set up an altar against that wall, lit candles, and slit my wrists. Those wolves were killed outside and inside this cave, and I didn't even think about it."

Fribitz was silent. He was looking at wolf skulls, complete skeletons, scattered bones, a couple wolf bodies dried and mummified. He shook his head. "The wolf is not here. Yeah, Krazy Kat, he just isn't here. But I swear, I feel him, I feel him through you and through these bones.

That stink, that odor in here, it's him, you told me so, all those stories of yours, oh Dean, you have no idea. If I never see him, I swear, I already met him."

Dean sat silently for a long time, just staring at the cave wall. Then he nodded. "Come on, Fribitz. You need to see something." He crawled across the sandy floor to the back of the cave. "Don't disturb the bones. I don't know what the wolf wants with them, but maybe they mean something to him." Fribitz crawled after him, glancing back and forth, not bothered at all by the stench.

"Right here," Dean said, sitting next to the wall and turning his flashlight back on. "Here is where I had the stuff. Here is where I set up my altar."

Dean handed Fribitz the flashlight, then brought out a book of matches. He lit the eight red candles, then adjusted them in the sand so they were in a line. When Fribitz turned off the light, Dean pointed to the things he left behind, propped against the cave wall, his books, the family photograph, his mother's Bible, his sister's Elvis records, his brother's tin airplane, old cameras, and the razor he used to slit his wrists.

"I brought them to take something of my family with me when I died. Turns out I didn't die. And in seven years, the wolf never touched the things I left behind."

Fribitz reached out to touch the airplane, then withdrew his hand, as though he were afraid of damaging a holy relic.

"There was soot on the walls," Dean went on. "Soot all over. I didn't see it the first time, but the second time I was here, I wiped the soot off the walls and discovered something. After I saw it, I forgot about it because I was so sick. I forgot about it until I went to Isle Royale. Then everything came back to me in a dream, and I remembered." He turned and pointed the light beam.

Fribitz stared, his mouth open, no words, but Dean

knew what he was thinking. Fribitz crawled closer, careful not to disturb any bones. He reached out and touched the cave paintings that had been hidden for years behind a curtain of soot until Dean found them. There were pictures of stick figure men with spears, chasing a mammoth, others of women, men and children around a fire, and farther along the wall, hand prints, small hands, a child's hands. Fribitz touched one of the handprints, understanding what provoked Dean's memoires about his sister. The little hands.

"The only other cave paintings I saw like these were in France, in a few caves being excavated while I was there. There are no such paintings in Minnesota. What are these pictures doing here?"

Dean shook his head. "I don't know, but here they are. The ones who killed the wolves, they covered those paintings up with soot and dirt and blood, and I think they never saw them, they were so set on killing. And look at this one." He pointed. The small animal in the corner was poorly drawn, but there was enough detail that they both could tell it was a wolf. "This place, this cave, this is where it all began for me. All of it." Dean sat on the ground, touched the wall again, and Fribitz, awed by the paintings, did the same.

"What about the wolf?" he finally asked. "Where is he right now."

"He's either travelling or off at a distance watching us. He won't attack me, I'm sure of it, I have faith in that. But he's probably scared of you."

"Yeah but..." Fribitz put his hands together, palm to palm, in the Buddhist Gassho bowing position. "Yeah, but, what are you going to do now? You know that guy, Cutter is hunting him. How are you going to stop him from killing the Shadow Wolf?"

"That's just it," Dean said. "I really don't think I can. I

really don't think I can stop anything. All I can do now is be a witness to what comes next, to the end of something big, something wonderful and horrible."

They heard the rain start outside the cave. Fribitz remembered Dean talking about that, the rain, and being inside the cave and listening to the sound coming in through the entrance and echoing in the large chamber. It did have a distinctive sound. "So you think the Shadow wolf is going to die? You think Cutter will kill it?"

Dean stared at his friend. "For some time, I had this feeling, now that I feel the closest to him, he is on the very edge of dying, whether I try to stop it or not. He's not dead yet, but I know it will be soon. All this time I've been worrying about it, I couldn't do anything about it any way. Like I came this close only to watch him die. What was the point?"

"So what will happen to you?"

"I don't know. I got my old job back teaching, and I promised a book about the wolf. Now the book will be a retrospective. There's Patty and the boys. I don't know what to do about that. I never wanted to be a dad." He touched the cave painting. "I guess if you live long enough, you get to see how everything connects, but I haven't lived that long yet."

Fribitz nodded. "Okay, Krazy Kat." He drew a deep sigh. "Thanks for showing me the cave. I wanted to see the wolf too, but maybe that won't happen. Whatever comes next, I'll be there with you. Deal?"

Dean turned and looked at him. "I like that," he said. "But the truth is, Fribitz, I'm scared."

"Me too," Fribitz said, sighing. "Me, too."

The rain came down harder, and Fribitz gazed at the paintings, his flashlight beam playing along the wall.

Chapter Twenty Five

"The Fall"
(Early Winter, 1967)

Jack Fipps and George Smith waited supine in the shadow of the fir trees, adjusting their binoculars. A rifle with scope lay beside each man, and Jack carried his ever-present walkie-talkie, attached to his belt, the earpiece faithfully in his ear.

"Nothing," George said. "All I see are a few ravens perched in a tree."

"Maybe we're wrong this time," Jack said.

"You said this was the place. I didn't."

"This is the general area," Jack said, frustrated. "But you can't just pick the exact spot. It doesn't work like that." Jack lowered his binoculars. "We might be wrong this time. And even if we were right, he might not come, not after we almost got him in Buford County up north. God, it's cold. Look at that sky, blue, but it still feels like it's going to snow. I don't think he's coming."

"But then again, he might come."

"I remember hunting rhinos in Africa," Jack said. "One was nicknamed 'Plowman' by our guides. He'd spot hunters from a good distance, then run off in the other direction. Rhinos have bad vision, you know, so it was a mystery how this one could see so far."

"I didn't know," George said.

"The hunters would take off after him, lose him, and no sooner would they head back than he'd come plowing through a bush. He'd learned from being shot and wounded. One time he killed three men, so I was called in to dispatch him."

George didn't comment. Jack took a deep breath and went on, "I found him and chased him for awhile, and when I lost him, I knew he was doubling back. I had the guides scrape the ground with branches, make noise, you understand, but when he came charging through the bushes, I was ready. I knew just which way he would come."

"So what's your point?" George asked. He was bored with Jack's stories, and didn't believe most of them. Jack seemed more like a small-time gambler than a great white hunter.

"Animals learn," Jack said. "They learn from their wounds."

"So what if he shows up?" George said.

"If we see him, we alert Cutter, then Ben, who'll be in the air in five minutes."

"Yeah," George said. "If."

"You gotta learn to trust your instincts, George," Jack said. "Take a few chances."

"Well, how about some hooch while we trust our instincts, and take our chances?"

Jack looked at him. "It's not even noon."

George looked back. "Close enough for me. And didn't you say you brought chicken salad sandwiches and potato chips?"

Jack sighed, glancing up at the spruce boughs. "Well...."

At one time, loggers had cut down the trees in the area, leaving a copse of trees covering a few square acres in the center. What resulted, when seen from an airplane, was a bull's-eye of trees surrounded by a circle of grass, stumps, scrub brushes and weeds, and that surrounded by a larger circle of trees.

No normal wolf—it was pointed out time and time again—would walk through the grass to get to the island of trees, especially in broad daylight. But Cutter insisted the Shadow Wolf would, and in the end it was there that the trap was set. And what with all the bottled wolf scent they used, Jack thought, radiating in every direction from the trap site like spokes from a hub, well, they ought to end up catching something.

"I'm going to get the hooch," George said.

"C'mon, George...."

"And the lunch," George went on. "Why wait 'till noon."

"Hell, George," Jack said, and gave up. George was in one of his moods.

George crawled out from beneath the branches and walked through the bare trees to the knapsack at the base of a pine. Jack continued to gaze through his binoculars, wondering what he would be missing on Ed Sullivan tonight. "Get a couple Hershey bars for me," he shouted. "They're under the t-shirt."

"Jack...."

"And the coffee thermos. If you're gonna drink, so am I."

"Jack...."

Something about George's voice sounded different. Jack looked back. George was braced against the tree with one hand; looking over the ground as though he had dropped a pocketful of change everywhere. Jack stood and got closer, and that's when he saw the large paw prints.

"Oh, Christ!" Jack said. "He's here!" The wolf had come within ten feet of them, behind them, watching them, and they hadn't heard. Jack's flesh crawled like ants under his clothes. George backed away as Jack glanced through the trees. "He knew we're here! He's seen us!" They'd never trap him now, Jack knew. He'd leave, discovering the trap, but Jack didn't care. If the wolf got this close to him, it was good he did leave. Let him go away.

And then he thought of Cutter, of how angry Cutter would be, and how much he wanted Cutter to trap the wolf, and how much he wanted to get the reward money. He was barely aware of George returning to his side as he thought of calling Cutter on the walkie-talkie, telling him about the paw prints. And then he turned and saw George raise the rifle, look through the scope. He felt sick.

"George! No!" he shouted.

George pulled the trigger.

Cutter's body jerked when he heard the distant rifle report. He almost knocked over the large jug he'd been pissing into for the last two days. He clicked on his walkie-talkie, put the earpiece in his ear, pressed the button and spoke into the mouthpiece. "All right, who fucked up? Who fired that shot?"

He let go of the button. All he heard was the hissing static. He was about to speak again when he heard Jack's voice. "Sorry, Cutter."

"Jack? What the fuck you think you're doing?" Instinctively, Cutter's left had reached for his bow. A gunshot might mean something. "What were you shooting at? Did you pull the trigger by accident?"

"It was George." Jack said. Of course he'd want to pass blame to someone else, Cutter thought. "He found some tracks!"

Cutter was charged with electricity. "Paw prints? The wolf? And what did George do? Shoot at the ground? I hope he blew his toes off!"

"He came within ten feet of us, Cutter," Jack said. "Come up right behind us. Pissed on our knapsacks. George just panicked, he imagined it was still there."

"He might have scared it away!" Cutter yelled. But he didn't believe that, and he was barely able to control his excitement.

"Let's wait and see," Jack said. "If he came this close, he doesn't scare easy."

You're not so stupid after all, Cutter thought, you and your triangles. "Okay, I'll...."

"Is he here?" someone said.

"Did you shoot him?"

"Off the air!" Cutter shouted. The other men were trying to put their two cents in. "Don't call unless you see him! Jack, I'm leaving my radio on; tell me if you see anything. And that goes for all of you. And Jack, get that fucking gun out of George's hands!" George might still be thinking about his dogs, Cutter suspected, and couldn't be trusted.

"We might have scared 'im off, Cutter."

"I doubt it," Cutter said. "I think he'll come my way. So hold your posts. Everybody. Over and out!" He put the walkie-talkie on his belt, kept the earplug in his ear, listening to static as he crouched against the tree, fondling his bow.

It was another boundary marker to cross over, another territory to enter, and he had entered so many territories and crossed so many boundaries that he couldn't go back. But this was different. This would be the furthest he would have ever gone.

The air was rich with the smell of autumn grasses and the scent of four deer, a mile upwind, the odor of a groundhog nearby and of a rabbit that had crossed the trail just an hour before. But what he noticed more than the rest was the scent of a Hunter, which had to be part of the trap, like last time. He expected it.

But it was the other odor, the odor of a female Hunter in heat, which had him so confused. It was not the time for that odor, and he felt disoriented and wary over it. Nonetheless, his plans were just as disturbing to him, and he continued walking slowly through a haze, knowing what he had to do.

The female mating scent radiated out from the copse of trees surrounded by a large field of grass, dead brush and stumps. The scent went off in all directions from that point; an intentional trail leading to what Cloudwalker knew was a trap. He was sure he would find the Dark Twolegs there.

He'd spent the morning wandering around the area, watching the Twolegs with their things of death, and he got a pretty good feel of what they had planned. If he walked into those trees across the field, he would most likely be killed, but if he didn't....

Taking one last deep breath, he opened his eyes, stood erect and shook out his pelage. He stepped cautiously from the shadows of the trees into the sunlight of the grassy plains. He had never done this before, stepping into the open when he was sure Twolegs would be watching him, seeing him, pointing their thundersticks at him. His stomach twisted with a fear he dared not show, but there was no other way to reach the trees. The scent led that way, the smell of a female, and the smell of blood. It was where the Twolegs One most likely was, it was the trap, and it was where he was headed.

He wanted to break into a run, turn and escape. The Twolegs thundersticks hadn't started sounding yet, but for the one he heard some time ago, and he suspected they were holding off, allowing him to reach the trees. As he walked among the stumps and grasses, he watched for the Jaws, though he was pretty sure Twolegs wouldn't try using them against him now, after the last time. He could feel the Twolegs, hiding behind the trees with their thundersticks, holding back because they knew the Twolegs One would be waiting to kill him. But Cloudwalker had other plans.

It was another boundary marker to cross over. It was a new type of killing he would do. He had never killed a Twolegs before, never thought he would, but if this one lived, more Hunters would die. He had to try to kill the Twolegs One. There was no other way. It would end here. It had to.

Turn back!

Cloudwalker kept walking. It was just a voice in his head.

Turn back! This is a trap! He'll kill you! You can't beat him!

"Must try, I must," Cloudwalker snarled.

You're going to die!

"If I die, and if the Dark Twolegs dies, then it is the right thing to do," he snarled. He reached the copse of trees, surprised that most of them still held their dry leaves, and as he stepped into the shade, he sniffed the air. He felt his body tingle with sensitivity and fear, as though the trees were a giant Twolegs Jaws.

"He's heading your way."

"I'm ready."

"Ben's starting up his chopper now. He'll be in the air in a minute, but he'll stay away until you give the order."

"Good," Cutter said, squatting, holding the walkie-talkie in both hands. "Remember nobody gives the order but me."

"Cutter, you should have seen him. He's bigger than we thought. And his head!"

"Calm down, Jack, I'll be introducing myself to him in a few more minutes. In the meantime, I can't talk now. He'll hear. Just hang tight; I'll let you know when I get 'im.'"

With that, he pulled the earplug from his ear and set the radio to his left. His eyes were wide, his reflexes primed. He grinned with expectation despite himself. As he picked up his bow and nocked an arrow, he noticed his hands were shaking. He needed a cigarette, but even here, the Shadow Wolf could smell it.

Cloudwalker stepped cautiously through the trees, his hackles up. His head pivoted back and forth, watching, always watching. His ears twitched. He spied every dried fern, every bush. The scent was strongest here; it was everywhere.

Then he stopped.

Just ahead he saw her, a Hunter with her right forepaw in the Jaws. She stood motionless, her eyes closed, her body thin with malnourishment and dehydration.

Though she was standing, she looked dead. Cloudwalker stopped ten feet from her when her eyes opened. "Go away!" she snarled. "Get away from here! Death! Twolegs! Get away!"

Cloudwalker glanced around. Twolegs was nearby, he could smell him, but where? There was no movement, no sound. He couldn't fight what he couldn't see.

Then he heard the air hiss.

It was a long shot, Cutter knew, but it paid off. Days of waiting, cramped, tired and frustrated. Days of eating cold army surplus C-rations. Days of trying to stay awake, of pissing into a jug and capping it, drinking out of water bottles, of climbing down once a day and walking a mile away to shit, hoping the wolf didn't show up then. Days of waiting.

When Jack called in about finding the paw prints, when he heard the rifle fire across the field, he nearly collapsed with despair that the trap had been discovered, and the Shadow Wolf was now ten miles away. But he kept the nervousness out of his voice, told the men that the wolf would soon be seen, and sure enough he was.

The waiting paid off.

Perched on a five-foot-square plywood platform on a two-by-four frame ten feet up the trunk of a tall spruce, Cutter almost knocked over his piss jug when he saw the giant walking below him. The Shadow Wolf was over twice the size of the other wolf, the one held by the trap. Their sizes were so different Cutter thought something was wrong with his eyes.

Days of huddling on the platform, wrapped in old bear hides covered liberally in wolf scent and smelling like the bottom floor of an outhouse, his boots wrapped in wolf scent-covered skins when he made his daily walk, the empty cans kept in a large plastic bag, cold C-rations, Spam, crackers, days of wearing the walkie-talkie like it was a growth on his side, and now the Shadow Wolf was below him.

He knelt at the edge of the platform, his bow in his hands, an arrow notched, his leather wrist guard and finger guards strapped on. The gaunt, giant wolf stepped closer, watching the trapped wolf.

Cutter licked his lips, and pulled back on the bow-string. The large wolf was still, glancing around, sensing the danger, but not looking up. His pelt was ragged, mangy, old gray fur with patches of bare skin, scaly from psoriasis, and scars he could see from his perch, they were so deep. The wolf's head, though, held Cutter's attention most of all. It was a large, misshapen white head, virtually bare of hair except for patches of white fur on different spots. The mottled flesh indicated the wolf had been injured in a fire. Such an ugly thing, Cutter thought, taking aim.

He released the string, and the arrow shushed through the air, hitting the wolf's left flank. The Shadow Wolf collapsed on the ground, yipped in pain and twisted around to bite at the shaft, yipping again when he tried to pull it out, kicking up dust as the small wolf tried to back away from him, tugging at the trap and chain that held her.

Cutter notched a second arrow, cursing his bad aim, but before he drew his bow he looked down in time to see the wolf regain his footing, stand and look up at him. The arrow shaft protruded like a part of his body, but he paid it no mind. He looked directly at Cutter, looked right into his eyes, knowing, and feeling.

Cutter froze. Ten feet off the ground, he suddenly felt afraid of the beast below him, so large, so enraged, and so single-minded. He drew his bow, aimed, and as he let the arrow fly, black feathers pelted his face, claws raked his cheek, and he heard something squawk very close to his ear. He fell on his back, swatting at air, still gripping his bow, and then he rolled off the platform, gripped a branch before falling, but he dropped his bow.

He grasped the branch with both hands, trying to climb back up, his skin-covered boots scraping the tree bark as he thought of the giant wolf just below him. He glanced down, expecting to see teeth, but instead saw the she wolf standing next to his bow, looking south. He looked the same way and saw the Shadow Wolf limping through dried ferns, making his escape.

He leaped six feet to the ground, swooping up his bow

and startling the wolf as he dashed after his prey. His quiver was on his back and his walkie-talkie was already out as he ran, hyper-ventilating. "Ben! Ben! Do you read me? This is Cutter! Over!"

"I read you, Cutter!" Static blurred Ben's voice.

"Sonovabitch got away!" Talking was slowing Cutter down, but there was urgency in his voice. "He's heading south." South. Cutter stationed men all around the clear-cut except south because there weren't enough men. The Shadow Wolf knew it. The paw prints Jack mentioned, the wolf had scouted out all their locations, and knew there were no men south.

"I'm on my way, Cutter!"

"He's wounded, Ben, he's mean. Drive him back my way, Ben. If he gets away this time, I won't get another chance no matter how many triangles Jack draws on a Goddam map."

"Gotcha," Ben said. Static was worse.

"Over and out, Ben." He hooked the radio to his belt and stopped long enough to untie the strings and get the skins off his boots. Then he continued south, panting, the arrows rattling in his quiver, his heart pounding.

Cloudwalker limped quickly through the trees, still watching out for Jaws. The stick in his side seemed to bite into him again and again, at every movement, like a living, hungry thing, gnawing him in tiny bites down to the bone.

He never thought he'd find Twolegs up a tree; he didn't know they could climb. Up a tree, among the branches. There was no way he would get the Twolegs One. Not that high.

The only thing left to do was to make his escape, get away, go back to the cave and rest up. Twolegs were out there with their thundersticks, and they would use them when they realized their One hadn't killed him. For the second time in many seasons he ran, but this time slower, his wound eating into him at every movement. He had to get the stick out, but first he had to escape.

If he could reach the tree line in the distance he would be okay, even if they didn't have many leaves. He hurt—even the pebbles never hurt as much as the feathered stick.

He finally broke free of the cluster of trees, running towards the next line of trees beyond the clearing, no longer watching for Jaws, he was so panicked. He was listening for the thundersticks, but he heard something different, the angry roar of Bigbird.

He leaped over a small brook, panicked, trying to move faster, but his wound was getting worse. He thought of running back to the trees behind him, but then he would never get away. He had to reach the other side, beyond the stump-laden field if he wanted to escape.

Bigbird rumbled louder, drawing closer, and he could feel the wind beating on his back, and for the first time in many seasons, he began to doubt he would survive.

"My God!" Ben gasped, flying over the wolf. They all knew the Shadow Wolf was big, but none of them thought it would be this big. It was as though the world shrank around it.

He held the controls steady, flying just behind it, watching. The paws were massive, the body long and thin, more like a gray-furred tiger than a wolf. The tail and fur had thinning hair and bald spots, as though the wolf were sick and the head was white, mostly hairless, and showing scars. Ben could tell that it meant it had once been badly burned. But why would the head turn white like that, except for the nose and lips?

Ben checked his instruments, then glanced through the Plexiglas bubble. He had to turn the wolf around before it reached the trees. The wolf was barely running, hindered by the arrow shaft bouncing from its hip.

Ben dipped, flew lower and hovered over the wolf's head. This close to the ground, he felt a wave of vertigo. It was one thing to land or take off, but he'd never felt right about flying low since his accident in Korea. The wolf's burn scars reminded him of his own. Holding the control stick with one hand, he talked into the headset mike—his radio was adjusted to the frequency of the walkie-talkie—while holding the earpiece tight against his ear. "He's not turning!" Ben shouted over the noise of his rotors. "He's making a beeline for the woods!"

He could hardly hear Jack's voice over the noise and static. "Fly lower!" Jack shouted. "Get right in front of his face! He'll turn around!"

"Don't fly lower!" It was Cutter. "I just got out of the woods! I can see you and the wolf, Ben, take your time!"

"Cutter, stay out of this!" It was Jack.

"Fuck off, Jack, you don't know...."

"You just stand ready with your bow and arrows and we'll...."

"Ben, don't fly lower...."

"Ben, turn the wolf around...."

"Who's in charge here, anyhow? I'm...."

"Goddammit, Cutter!" Ben shouted. "The trees are coming up! I gotta turn him around now, there's not much time!" Ben felt his palms sweating.

"Christ, Ben, if you flew any lower, you'd be pulled by reindeer! Listen, Ben...."

"Over and out!" Ben shouted, pulling his headset off and tossing it between the seats. "I listen to you two argue any more, I'll crash for sure." He pushed the chopper forward, hovering over the wolf, just in front of him, going lower, biting his lip and fighting the vertigo.

The explosions and burning pebbles never came, but Cloudwalker felt too exhausted and in too much pain to wonder why. He was gasping for breath, feeling the stick cut deeper into him.

Bigbird flew just above him and to the right, screaming and rumbling, whipping wind on him, and he knew any time now he would feel the talons dig into his back. He kept on, knowing he might not reach the trees.

One talon was just above him. He tried changing directions a little, but it followed. Suddenly it came down hard, hitting the top of his head. It hit him again, harder, dazing him, but he kept moving. One more time and he might be knocked out. In a fit of panic, he reached up and snapped, locking his jaws on something thick and hard. Without warning, he was yanked off his feet and was airborne, still holding on, and ground and sky rolled in his vision.

"What the hell!" Ben shouted, battling the controls, overcompensating and trying to readjust as the helicopter rolled. He looked out his door; saw the wolf gripping the runner in his jaws, dangling in the air.

"Jesus," Ben gasped, gazing into the hideous white face, the angry, gray eyes, and then he realized he was looking at the ground like a wall beside his door. The chopper shuddered as rotor blades furrowed the earth and snapped into pieces, and Ben's mouth opened as he thought about his machine breaking apart, and how he might never afford another one. He felt an overwhelming sadness.

Cutter's legs pumped faster as he watched the helicopter crash. He ran shouting and screaming over the explosion. His head hummed with fear and panic as he saw the fireball rise towards the cobalt sky. "Ben!" he screamed. "Ben!"

Sweat saturated his clothes, and he could feel the heat as he closed the gap between himself and the burning wreck. "Oh, sweet Jesus, Ben! Oh, God, Ben! Don't let this be real!"

What was left of the helicopter looked like a crushed, blackened insect caught dying in its own flames. Black smoke rose into the cold, cloudless sky, a funeral pyre, a black grave marker, black memory, but Cutter never stopped running, never took his eyes off the wreckage. He'd dropped his bow and quiver behind him somewhere, he'd lost his radio, but all he could think of as he pumped his legs was that Ben might have been thrown clear, might still be all right. His chest was ripping with massive pain, radiating from his heart, and he prayed that it wasn't a heart attack, not now.

Then he saw movement, and he stopped running. It rose from the flames, a fallen bird of prey, twisting in pain, then turning and running, a blazing creature putting off smoke, setting the dry grass on fire as it ran.

"Jesus," Cutter gasped, feeling cold, slowing to a stop. It was the Shadow Wolf, covered in chopper fuel and burning to death, but still running towards the woods.

The pain was worse than it ever was before, worse than the stick in his thigh could ever be. The fire on his body was eating him alive, a living thing with a terrific appetite, consuming him, the pain sucking him dry, but he kept running.

He reached the woods, dodging the trees; he could

smell his own flesh burning, his fur blazing, but all he could do was run. Can't die, he thought, can't die, not yet....

He leaped, fell into a creek, dousing the flames, but the shock of cold water threw him into near unconsciousness. He crawled from the creek, shivering, his bare, blackened body smoking, his skin cracked and bleeding. He limped on, gazed ahead, aware that only one of his eyes was working now. He was scared, in terrible pain, feeling his mind fading, knowing that somehow he had to get back.

When the others got there, they found Cutter kneeling on the ground between two weathered stumps, holding Ben's blackened body. Ten men stood around him as others approached. One bent down and reached out a hand.

"Don't you fucking touch him!" Cutter screamed, enough murder and hatred in his voice to push the hand back. And then he looked up, blackened face, eyebrows and lashes and half his hair and most of his beard burned off, his clothes smoldering.

"It's okay," someone said, though he knew it wasn't. They all knew. "It's okay, Cutter. Help is coming. Bill is driving his jeep out; we'll cushion the back with our coats. Hell, Cutter, we'll have you and Ben at the hospital in a few hours."

"Ben don't need a hospital," Cutter said, his voice raspy from smoke inhalation, and they knew he was right. Cutter held Ben's body with charcoaled hands that were blistered and seeping blood. Behind him, the fire still rose among the wreckage, and they could sense what Cutter had gone through to retrieve Ben's body, climbing into the flames, grasping red hot metal, unlatching Ben's seatbelt with burning fingers and dragging him out. Dragging out a body. He even held what was left of

Ben's New York Yankees cap.

"What happened?" Jack asked. Cutter looked wordlessly at him, a look of sadness, but something vicious, too, like an animal that was wounded and dying, but coming back one last time to kill the beast that wounded it. Jack could see Cutter blamed Ben's death on him.

"The Shadow Wolf got away, Jack," Cutter said. He looked back at Ben. "I saw him, Jack, that wolf, leaped up and grabbed a rung. A wolf that big, almost three hundred pounds, he caused the helicopter to roll. And when I saw the chopper crash, I saw the wolf run away, in flames, but he ran off, he got away. He got away. But Ben didn't."

Cutter went silent, looking down, rocking Ben. The men stood around him until the jeep arrived, then they began placing their coats in the back, making a bed, knowing it would be a long, rough ride.

Epilogue

"After The Fall"
(Early Winter, 1967)

He could not tell if he was walking or dreaming.

He could not see where he was going.

He could still see with his good eye for awhile, at least until he knew he was travelling the right way, heading back to the cave, but during his journey, his vision blurred, and then it was gone altogether.

And still he limped on.

Snow was beginning to fall, he knew it, he could hear it, but he couldn't see or feel it. He was cold, but he couldn't feel much else. He could hear the wind but couldn't feel that either. He had no idea what he looked like, but by now he believed he had no fur left, not after all the burning, not after all that pain. He walked straight, kept steady, though he kept tripping and sometimes walked into trees.

He had to get back. If he could.

He knew he was heading the right way back to the cave. Maybe it was the smells, maybe it was his powerful sense of direction, as if the turning of Mother Earth guided him, or the breeze, or just the warmth of the sun as it began setting, or the air growing colder for the same reason.

The feather stick was still in him, hobbling him, about to force him to drop and never get back up, but he kept moving. He felt his body lean, forced himself to straighten, but he was not sure how many more times he could do that.

And the pain.

The pain was so horrible at first, but now things were different. He felt nothing, nothing but the ground beneath his paw pads, and the occasional wind, and the warmth of the setting sun, but even that might be in his head. He could not feel anything much anymore, and he could not see. He was dying, and he wondered why he was even trying to find the cave. It was maybe a day or two travel, and he was growing weaker by the minute.

He stopped, gasping, wondering if he was dreaming or still conscious. The voices in his head—they had tormented him for many winters—they were now silent, and he felt intensely lonely, lost in the darkness of his mind.

And he thought of the other one, Rabbit-Turd, the one who showed so much potential. Rabbit-Turd, he was either dead or heading north to the cold lands, the white lands where the white Hunters lived, because he himself told him to go. He believed it would change him, make him stronger, make him the one to continue watching the other Hunters, to be the Guardian of Guardians, but now he was not so sure. Maybe he was dead, maybe they would all be dead soon.

The despair crippled him, made him want to die standing right there.

There was nothing left to hope for.

There was nothing left to wait for.

Just the dying.

Just the dying.

Suddenly he heaved and vomited the meal he ate yesterday. He felt himself piddling, no longer able to control his bladder.

He could not even bring himself to howl; his throat was scorched.

Nothing left...

Then he heard the beating of wings...

And, blind, dying, he knew where to go.

He took another step.

Author Bio

David Wood was born in Manassas, Virginia. He grew up in Pittsburgh, Pennsylvania, graduating from Baldwin High School and later got a Bachelors of Arts from the University of South Florida. Later he studied comparative literature and comparative religion at the University of Oregon in Eugene, Oregon.

He began writing at the age of twelve, but never published anything until he got to college. He joined "The Seminar," a writing group in Eugene run by R. Gaines Smith, and had two stories published in the anthology, Popular Fiction by Oregon Authors. He has been editor or associate editor of a half dozen small press publications and newsletters. He continued writing and publishing stories, poems and short pieces about his life. His first book, Inside, Outside, was a collection of anecdotes and vignettes of his life experiences.

He now lives in St. Petersburg, Florida, where he still writes and works. He has a dog named Rex.

Legend, the first in a trilogy, was his first full novel.